CRADLE OF DESTRUCTION

BOOK TWO

ANGER OF THE GODS

Copyright © Gareth L Williams, 2024

The moral right of the author has been asserted

This is a work of fiction. Names, character, places and incidents are either the product of the author's imagination or are used fictitiously, and any resemblance to actual persons, living or dead, businesses, companies, governmental bodies, events, or locales is entirely coincidental.

Dedicated to my late parents, Jane and Leslie Williams

To whom I owe so much.

May their names live forever.

Gentle Reader:

IF YOU HAVE NOT READ 'HIDDEN WORLDS' (BOOK ONE OF 'CRADLE OF DESTRUCTION') THIS RÉSUMÉ WILL GIVE YOU THE BACKSTORY AND HELP YOU UNDERSTAND THE EVENTS IN 'ANGER OF THE GODS'.

THOSE WHO HAVE READ 'HIDDEN WORLDS' DO NOT NEED TO READ THIS INTRODUCTION BUT IT MAY SERVE AS A USEFUL REMINDER

THE STORY SO FAR:

It is the 25th century and humanity has reached the stars, but only after emerging from a second 'dark age' brought on by a massive super-volcano explosion and the worldwide winter which followed, and which wiped out two thirds of the Earth's population. However, a regeneration of human civilisation followed, which included the rediscovery of science and technology, but only after a century long interruption. But then more and more rapid advances were made, including the rediscovery and renewal of space travel.

Within a hundred years came an epochal discovery which made travel to other star systems possible!

Soon afterward came the discovery of **Oceanus** – sometimes called, 'Earth's Twin': the only other world, of the thousands found, easily habitable by humans, but incredibly distant. Orbiting a star similar to the Sun, this world was a mostly benign, but spectacular planet:

Oceanus: a world with an even larger proportion of ocean than the Earth and only one, very large, continent, named by the earliest human explorers, Bhumi-Devi, a Sanskrit word, meaning the personification of 'Mother Earth'.

Oceanus: a planet of vast, wild, rugged, wildernesses, unusual plant life, no sentient species and a strangely limited array of complex animal life. With more reptile-like species and fewer mammal-like species, most of the flora and fauna seemed to have evolved along similar lines to those on the Earth; sometimes said to be an example of the theory of convergent evolution.

Oceanus: A 'colonised' world, where over 95% of the continent was still unsettled by humans, by intention.

Oceanus: Orbiting an orange-red dwarf star, called Ra, the new world was a mind numbing 123 light years from the Solar System.

BUT ...

Oceanus: *Doomed planet!*

THE SHOCK

Within a century of the first explorers Oceanus was colonised by a small number of people, who survived against the odds, growing into a vibrant society, but one determined to learn the lessons of the past, so to limit their growth, and their impact on the planet. But a century after its founding the human society on Oceanus was under extreme threat. Solar System scientists claimed that within 10 Earth years, the outermost layers of Ra would explode in nova-like super- prominences. Although falling far short of a supernova, the eruption would still be utterly devastating to life on

Oceanus. The nova was expected to kill every human on Oceanus, and much of the other life on the planet – a 'super extinction' event.

The human population needed to be evacuated as soon as possible but it was not going to be easy. Oceanus was isolated and distant. Despite the awesomely powerful nuclear fusion drives now used by humanity's spacecraft, many weeks or even months, could be spent in travelling from the Solar System to star systems like Ra's.

An unfortunate feature of interstellar travel was that most of the travel time was taken up by ships having to reach the outermost regions of the Solar System, and other star systems, where the openings of the mysterious 'conduits' were located (thought by scientists to be negative energy filaments or interdimensional tubes – no-one knew), phenomena which linked or bound the Sun's planetary system with some other stars. Transit through the conduits themselves varied from just a few minutes to around thirty minutes, a mostly safe but uncomfortable journey for most humans. The consequence was that, despite the incredibly fast speeds of the nuclear fusion powered spacecraft, journeys to other star systems were, in many ways, more like the journeys of ancient sailing vessels from Earth's past.

Human expansion, travelling to other stars through the (poorly understood) networks of conduits, was also limited by an effective 'cage' effect, because beyond a certain distance the disassociation of molecules would mean the disintegration of ships and their crews. And for reasons not yet understood, only stars linked directly to the Sun by conduit filaments could be traversed. Yet more restrictive was the fact that no electromagnetic communication through a conduit was possible. Once a ship left the Solar System, for another star, the only way to communicate with 'home' was by direct travel back through a conduit, by either a crewed vessel or an automated message probe.

For Earth's so called, 'twin world', this meant that any attempt at evacuation was likely to take a very long time! It happened to be longer than Oceanus had.

THE HISTORICAL BACKGROUND:

The extreme isolation of Oceanus resulted in a degree of divergence of its human culture from most of the societies living in our own Solar System, including an unusual dialect of 'Anglo-Span', the lingua-franca of most of the Solar System.

In the Solar System, popularly now called the 'Home System', humans had spread out to form colonies or autonomous societies on other worlds, such as on Earth's Moon, on Mars and several artificial habitats orbiting the Sun. But the earth was still very much the nucleus of human civilisation, The democratically elected 'Allied Home System Government', based on Earth itself, governed most of the societies of the Solar System but disputes meant that an increasing number were ceding from its control. It was also under existential threat, mainly from 'Ultima', an extremist, militant, rebel organisation, that waged a vicious, open war, in the recent past. Attacking from a base outside the solar system it was only narrowly defeated. The aftermath saw many changes, including the creation of a space-based 'Navy' for the Home System, and the restriction of interstellar travel to Navy ships and interstellar research vessels. But Ultima appeared to have 'gone quiet' and memories of their horror had begun to fade.

Then, Oceanus itself was granted political independence from the Solar System. Also a democracy, the people of Oceanus were not only fiercely committed to independence but also to preserve and conserve as much of Oceanus as possible. As well as restricting the expansion of their society, to encroach on as little of the wilderness as possible, they were also concerned about maintaining limited levels of 'advanced' technology, to keep their lives relatively simple. Their technology was sufficient to make life comfortable but not to let in some of the excesses and rapid cultural changes they believed they saw in the Home System. Second generation pioneers wanted to bypass what they saw as some of the more pernicious effects of the mass communications and public media seen in the Home System, and the placing of 'all the eggs' in the high technology 'basket'. Over the 132 years, since the beginning of settlement by humans, successive generations tenaciously stuck to that philosophy. But there were factions of dissent within Oceanus society itself, but mainly by those wishing to increase isolationism yet further.

So it was, that for the most part, Oceanus society held their technology at a level no greater than that which existed in Europe and North America between the 1930s and 1960s, and being a small and cohesive society, theirs was one without advanced weaponry. And, part of their philosophy was a wish not to embrace more than a very limited degree of (now, very old-fashioned) computer tech.' What they had was being used mainly for some administration and for communicating with the Home System (particularly the H S Navy, who, by Interstellar Treaty, were allowed to visit the planet and who could be invited to assist Oceanus with security, but only if the whole of the planet was under threat), and to maintain some degree of interstellar political relations.

Despite appearances the Oceanus people were very far from being backward or regressive, but again, mainly due to the isolationism brought about by the staggering distances between them, the intentions of the 'Home System' were not generally trusted by most people. The enormous gap between the levels of technology on

Earth and those on Oceanus, had deepened the cultural disengagement between them.

After Home System scientists had made the startling prediction of the destruction of most life on the surface of Oceanus, attempts were made to alert the former colony. But the time delays involved in direct communication, political infighting between various factions on Oceanus, plus suspicion and distrust of the Home System, confused the issue. Most Oceanus people were unheeding or were simply unaware of the claim of impending doom.

ENTER - THE HOME SYSTEM NAVY:

The prestigious flagship of the fleet, the enormous 'space carrier' vessel, The Monsoon, was sent to Oceanus. The fastest, largest, vessel in the Navy, with the vitally important ability to carry several hundred evacuees, was tasked with a mission to begin the large-scale evacuation of the planet. But the Home System government misunderstood the nature and extent of the suspicion and resentment in which they were held by the people of Oceanus.

The main players from 'The Monsoon':

For historical reasons, each ship, in addition to its crew, carried one 'Secretary', a non-military person, versed in space law and Navy protocols, employed by the government to be a civilian presence aboard the ship. This was ostensibly to advise the senior officers on those very protocols and interstellar laws but, given the remove of Navy ships at any one time, was really meant to reassure the peoples of the Solar System that the force was complying with all the directives of the elected government. The Secretary of The Monsoon was Michaelson Delenius Tanniss,

('Mike'), through whose eyes we mainly see the world. An emotionally shallow young man of 23, generally liked aboard ship but resented by some, who despise his womanizing activity, Mike's real wish was to be an astrophysicist. Mike also had, to his great disadvantage, on the world of epic Oceanus landscapes, a deep-seated fear of large, open spaces. The spectacular vistas of Oceanus worried him but not as much as those of the only other world, in another star system, partly settled by humans: the mostly toxic, planet of Prithvi, larger than the Earth, with little animal life, but a failing human colony. Most people on Prthvi had already been repatriated to Earth.

As for Oceanus, Mike seriously doubted whether it would ever be possible, in a social sense, to relocate to the Home System, the society which had grown up on this planet.

On this mission The Monsoon was commanded by the inspirational veteran, Admiral Arkas Aurelius Tenak, and efficiently Captained by Ssanyu Ank Ebazza, ever loyal to Tenak. Tenak and Mike were tasked with assisting the Oceanus government to begin the process of evacuation and reassure them about concerns they had about it. But, like their political masters, they too misunderstood the social issues and were not aware that those concerns ran far deeper than anyone 'back home' imagined. In particular, they were not aware of the rise of a new, local, political force, the powerful 'Metateleo' party, a quasi-religious sect opposed to close ties with the Home System. They belief was that the HS wanted to evacuate Oceanus so they could exploit it for their own purposes.

Mike and Tenak landed, by shuttle, or 'landing boat,' at Janitra, the capital of Bhumi-Devi, and were granted an audience with the planet's president, Arbella

Nefer-Masterton. The President was a capable woman, but she was in a weak political position due to her party's declining popularity since the early days of independence, and the increasing prominence of the Metateleos. Partly due to this, and because of her own suspicions, she refused the attempts by Mike, Tenak and their team to persuade her to begin evacuation. This placed the Admiral and Secretary in a difficult situation, but, at the Admiral's instigation, they set out to convince the people of Oceanus that all their lives are in danger.

Mike considered Tenak an avuncular figure, perhaps even a fatherly one, his own father having died some years ago, but at this stage he was not convinced of the wisdom or practicality of their goal; a seemingly thankless task which he felt doomed to failure. He resented Tenak's apparent reliance on him for support for a task he felt should be left to ambassadors or professional negotiators. Tenak berated him for his naivety, lack of commitment and apparent lack of understanding of the urgency of the task. But Mike's heart was not in it – yet.

Mike and Tenak also encountered some resentment on the part of the ordinary citizens of Oceanus, who were mainly peaceable, but firm. They also drew no support when they met other political parties on Oceanus and a meeting with the Metateleos themselves proved useless and – in this case, dangerous. The Meta' leader, Remiro, and his wife, Pendocris, behaved like the high priests of a new religion. But, unknown to everyone, including her husband, Pendocris turned out to be a local contact, albeit reluctant, for agents of Ultima in the Home System, who wished to stoke up dissent on Oceanus.

Meanwhile, the problems with Ra revealed themselves in several severe electrical and plasma storms, caused by massive solar prominences, which were a hazard to health and wreaked havoc with the old electrical infrastructure on Oceanus. One such storm hit Bhumi-Devi while Mike and Tenak were returning to Janitra. In the ensuing fires and destruction, and while trying to save someone Tenak was seriously injured, almost killed. Mike was shocked by this and gradually began to feel more motivated to the cause Tenak had set for the two of them. Before being taken back up to the ship for life-saving treatment, a seriously ill Tenak entrusted Mike with continuing the search for an answer.

Later, Mike met with the brilliant professor Muggredge, a leading biologist at Janitra University and known sceptic of the Metateleo's stance. It was now that Mike met Eleri Nefer Ambrell, a clever young research biologist, a specialist in sea life, and a teacher at the University. She also happened to be Muggredge's niece, and the niece of President Masterton; the Professor and President being completely estranged siblings. Mike became attracted to her physically, but also intellectually. For her part she also appeared attracted to him and the two began a serious relationship – which this, ultimately, had widespread implications for Oceanus.

Meanwhile, outside the Ra system, a small but bright burst of gamma wave radiation was detected by The Monsoon's science team. They believed they had observed signs of a strange object the size of a dwarf planet, swinging into a far distant orbit around Ra. The scientists and ship's AI system considered the phenomenon to be a natural event of a type never seen before. Mike, however, speculated that the mysterious object might be artificial, but it was simply too distant to be investigated directly. And Mike's ideas were dismissed, partly because in all the years of astronomical observation and travel through interstellar space, no hint of another self-aware species or civilization had ever been found.

But Mike's guess was eventually proved right.

THE ALIEN PRESENCE:

Unknown to any human, at this stage, the appearance of the object really marked the arrival of a massive vessel from a world the other side of the galaxy. It was on a journey, eons long, and it carried many members of a super-intelligent species of sentient, non-humanoid, semi-amorphous beings, partly organic, partly cybernetic; beings with several brains and multiple, tentacular, arms. These were, however, beings, to whom Oceanus was somehow familiar; a planet which in some way held a very deep meaning for them. And they had arrived to do something fundamental and irreversible to its sun – Ra.

A WAY FORWARD?

Back on Oceanus, 'Professier' Muggredge advised Mike that a scientific solution of a type which could convince the majority of the people on Oceanus, was the only way forward, and Mike learned of the theory (with only very limited supporting evidence) that similar eruptions of Ra's surface may have happened in the very distant past, perhaps often. Muggredge believed they may have caused a similar extinction event some millions of years ago, on Oceanus. Mike and his colleagues needed to find conclusive evidence of one of these events to try to convince the government that they could not stand by idly and refuse to order evacuation. Evidence would have to be found in the geology of Oceanus, to support this theory, probably in the form of rock strata bearing the unmistakable signs of a conflagration, buried somewhere in the strata on Oceanus, caused by a nova. Unfortunately, most of the geology of Oceanus was not well surveyed and almost all known rock strata on the continent were not the right age. And permits for surveying were difficult to obtain with first having evidence. The task still seemed impossible.

Mike, still distraught by Tenak's accident, but trying not to show it, was teamed up with Eleri, who became determined to help him and his colleagues make a difference. Mike, through his own past infidelity, had a checkered history with women so far in his young life, but he now found he had different, very unfamiliar feelings about Eleri and, for the first time, he gradually fell hopelessly in love with her. She appeared to reciprocate, though she demonstrated that she was nobody's fool.

In search of evidence for the location of the crucial geological strata Mike and Eleri tried to locate papers written by a former geologist at the University (whose ideas first led Professor Muggredge to initiate the quest), but which had long since disappeared. The search proves fruitless. During this effort Mike met Danile Senusret Hermington, a young geologist, who was a good friend of Eleri's. At first Mike saw him very much as a rival for her affections until he learned that Hermington was gay. Mike eventually became a genuine friend and Hermington became another guide in Mike's long process of learning about Oceanus.

Tenak, with the help of 25th century (Home System) medicine, had, meanwhile, recovered and, covertly, in breach of Oceanus rules, he ordered probes launched from the ship, carrying long range sensors, to try to pick up evidence of the vital rock strata from orbit. These attempts are partially foiled by a very small group of traitorous, fifth columnists or 'quislings', planted amongst the crew by 'Ultima', the modern reincarnation of the extremist Rebels in the Home System. They aimed to sabotage efforts to find any evidence supporting Tenak's mission. They hoped that when human life on Oceanus was destroyed it would bring about political destabilization in the Home System which they could then take advantage of. They had also forged links with the Metateleos on the Oceanus, by pretending to have the same spiritual aims as them and to be helping them maintain Oceanus independence. Knowing life on Oceanus would be destroyed their real aims were to, eventually, use the planet as a base for their operations.

Meanwhile, more solar storms hit Oceanus, causing widespread electrical and comms disruption and despite previous local resentment the Navy assist in repairs. A riot resulted in serious injury to a crewmember of The Monsoon.

Tenak also sent an automated message probe back to the Solar System, advising the political situation and requesting that a senior ambassador be sent out 'immediately' (a journey of many weeks of course).

THE ALLIED HOME SYSTEM GOVERNMENT DELIBERATION:

In the Solar System, the government had, meanwhile, discovered that their plan for the evacuation of everyone from Oceanus was likely to fail, with a significant number of people being left behind. Further delays were making this worse. Greater urgency was given to the building of a new fleet of vessels for evacuation, to supplement existing Navy ships, but there would soon be further complications.

Eventually, Tenak's message was received and in response, the Secretary-General of the Allied Home System government, Yorvelt, and his Deputy, Brocke (also Chief of Home System security), reluctantly sent the only ambassador who was available, Yardis Octavian Sliverlight, considered by some a second-rate ambassador, perhaps even a dubious character. Unknown to Yorvelt, this had been engineered by an aide of Brocke's, and a security officer, called Dervello, who happened to also work for Ultima. Dervello, an aggressive and ambitious man, conspired with his colleagues, Proctinian and Despinall, to subvert the attempts to rescue Oceanus by blackmailing Sliverlight into working for them, in conjunction with the aims of Ultima, and the unwitting connivance of the Metateleos, on Oceanus.

The Ambassador traveled as a passenger aboard the major science research vessel, Antarctica, newly assigned to Oceanus, Captained by Jennifer Livia Amily Providius, once a confidante and, possibly, an 'old flame' of Tenak's. Whilst aboard the vessel Sliverlight was contacted surreptitiously by a rebel operative amongst the crew of the Antarctica itself; a female agent who is later killed, at Oceanus, after hijacking a shuttle from The Monsoon, which burned up in the atmosphere.

There being little serious progress toward evacuation (despite a small number of willing citizens, alarmed by the solar storms, and the warnings) Tenak decided to remain in orbit around Oceanus in the hope of encouraging more evacuees aboard The Monsoon. He encouraged Mike to take extended shore leave and spend it with Eleri, ostensibly to 'assist' her in her university research on Fire Island, in the 'Great Eastern Ocean'. Mike suspected (correctly), that it was actually to encourage him to develop a deeper, meaningful, relationship. Muggredge also appeared behind this.

LOVE STORY:

Eleri, an experienced amateur pilot, flew herself and Mike to a small island, 'Fire Island', where they linked up with two other isolated researchers. On this island Mike and Eleri' relationship deepened, becoming romantic, and Mike found, for the first time, that he was now emotionally committed to another person. The two of them visited a remote part of the island and Mike was reluctantly talked into swimming in a mysterious, mostly enclosed, bay formed by a meteor crater impact.

Eleri, not having reason to believe any of the dangerous sea creatures of Oceanus would be present at that time, encouraged Mike to boost his confidence by swimming far out. Using a breathing device, he swam deeper than he'd ever done before, and was suddenly attacked, and nearly eaten, by a huge squid-like sea creature, called a 'grotachalik'. Realizing her mistake, Eleri jumped in, used an electrical gun to ward off the creature and rescued Mike, but the poisonous stings Mike received made him seriously ill. Eventually, Eleri and her colleagues managed to get him repatriated up to The Monsoon, where he was only saved by their advanced medical technology. Nevertheless, he was told he had been infected by a previously unknown form of blood plasmids which were likely to affect him seriously, periodically, for the rest of his life.

On recovering from the attack, Mike found he could not remember Eleri or the attack of the creature. He took extended sick leave but when his memory returned tried to contact Eleri, to no avail. As there had been little progress in persuading more people to evacuate, Tenak sent a willing Mike back to the surface to assist (at Muggredge's request) an Oceanus led expedition, to strike into the 'Great Purple Forest' which clothed the northern regions of Bhumi-Devi. This was in furtherance of the professor's new plan, to collect gametes, or sex cells, from as many different species of plant and animal and to freeze them, so they might be used to 'seed' another, suitable world, after much of the life had been destroyed on Oceanus.

THE EXPEDITIONS:

The small Oceanus team, mainly local scientists, joined by Mike and Erbbius, an engineer from the ship, turned out to be ill prepared and disorganized. To Mike's horror Eleri had split up with him because she had been told about his philandering behaviour on board ship. Although this was before she'd met him it abrogated her deeply held, Oceanus bred, convictions about relationships. He tried to explain he had changed – mainly because of her, but she still rejected him. In the Purple Forest, Erbbius was nearly eaten by a large, flesh-eating, plant but was saved by Mike, who was also injured, and later, the rest of the team. Eleri later forgave Mike, for what she saw as his past indiscretions, when he was able to demonstrate his loyalty to her, and their relationship was renewed, and later intensified.

However, the expedition ground to a halt after a message from Tenak, who had finally discovered some evidence for the location of the much-sought rock strata. These were rocks showing deep carbonization (evidence of widespread burning in the deep past) and Tenak's covert activities (from orbit) showed them, as originally expected, to be found on a massive wild, island, called Simurgh, some thousands of kilometres from the mainland. They obtained permits from a reluctant President Masterton, forced by gratitude for the Navy's assistance following the ion storms, and rioting (initiated by the Metateleos) causing injury to some Navy personnel. Tenak and Muggredge organized a better prepared, joint Oceanus and Navy team, to go to Simurgh – but this time to be flown to the island by a Navy landing boat, piloted by Lieutenant Lew Pingwei, a great pilot, natural leader, and good friend of Mike's.

Landing near the relevant rock layers the team confirmed heavy carbonization, the result of fierce burning of organic matter when the deposits were laid down, a likely ecological disaster, possibly planet-wide, which occurred some eight million years ago. Astonishingly, below the layers, predating the disaster, they also found the fossilized remains of bipedal beings, exhibiting a mixture of vaguely humanoid but also reptilian features. Preliminary investigation revealed they were probably a highly intelligent, but technologically primitive, species which had since disappeared. The team realized that this was an epoch-making discovery for all humanity, since no sign of any such 'advanced' species had ever previously been found.

None of the team were unaware, however, that Erbbius, was another quisling rebel. He sabotaged the site of the strata and killed a much-loved member of the Oceanus team when she stumbled across his treachery and could have revealed his true identity. Erbbius started a landslide, made to look natural, which covered the relevant strata with millions of tons of rubble, thereby destroying the carbonizing evidence. But the island was home to a species of gigantic, flightless birds, which killed Erbbius, and prevented the team from discovering the sabotage and his part in it. The team realized that their written and photographic evidence was not likely to be enough proof to foil the Metateleos, or to convince the government. Though demoralized and grief-stricken Lew rallied the team. Tenak and Muggredge recalled them from Simurgh while Oceanus inquests, and an Inquiry, took place in Janitra.

Yet more damaging solar ion storms hit Oceanus.

While waiting for the Inquiry findings Eleri took Mike to meet her parents, on their farm. Her mother, Elene-Nefer, another sister of Muggredge, was warm and welcoming. Her father, Marcus, was rather cool toward him, mainly because of concerns about what would happen to them and the rest of the Oceanus people if they were uprooted to Earth. However, to Eleri's great chagrin, there was barely disguised anger and bitterness, toward Mike, from Eleri's younger sister, Meriataten, who, with her two young children, lived with her parents. Meriataten clearly resented the Home System, but Mike felt her resentment was for reasons similar to those of Marcus. At least they were among the few who were beginning to understand their predicament and the need to relocate. Like Marcus, they desperately did not wish to leave their homes, their beloved planet, and become dispossessed people in a strange, incredibly faraway world. Their desire *not to have to emigrate* was an almost palpable pain.

Tenak was drawn into intrigue when contacted, covertly, via Muggredge, by a member of the Oceanus government, inviting him to meet, alone, at a remote, decaying town, far from Janitra. At this strange meeting the Admiral learned that the body of the Oceanus team member, killed on Simurgh, was found to have with it physical evidence of the ancient humanoid / reptiloid culture uncovered by the team before the landslide. This evidence was starting to convince some members of the government that the Navy's arguments may be more reliable than thought. But there was still a long way to go a long way to go. The 'agent' also revealed that the college academic, whose papers Mike and Eleri had been searching for, had been found and although exiled in person, his papers had been confiscated. His claim was to have found more solid evidence of the sought rock strata, on an island in the middle of the ocean, the other side of the planet from the continent. The agent also furnished Tenak with details of the island's location but made it clear his own position was not secure enough for him to help further. It was now down to Tenak and Muggredge.

THE GREATEST DISCOVERY OF ALL:

A new mission was planned, to a distant location called 'New Cambria', a relatively small island, more than 16,000 kilometres from the mainland. Arbella Masterton (unaware of the information imparted by the 'agent') allowed the Navy to fly the joint team there, an expedition organized by Tenak and Muggredge, with a mostly reconstituted group. This time the Navy was in charge, with Lt Pingwei in overall command. Mike had been assigned again, as he was now accepted as an important scientific advisor, and Eleri was placed in charge of the expedition's specific science objectives and procedures.

It took only a few hours for the new team to fly from the continent to New Cambria, in a Navy landing boat, piloted by Lew. Rocks, like the carbonized material on Simurgh, were found, but when overflying the chain of mountains running along the length of the island, the shuttle's new suite of sensors picked up a strange anomaly: evidence of a massive, perfectly shaped, dome, over 300 metres across, with six wall-like structures radiating from its circumference. Although mostly obscured by soil and debris, the huge artefact could not be anything other than artificial and yet the team estimated it to be millions of years old. After landing nearby, the team made their way to the nearest 'wall', more a type of causeway. The team included professor Akrommo, a member of the Antarctica's science team, and his invention, and 'protégé', the huge 'Strider', a massive, wheeled, robotic machine. Strider confirmed that the material of the dome was harder than anything humans had ever created.

A small doorway shaped slab of the material appeared to offer entryway into the dome and after Strider, with some difficulty, managed to cut around its outer edges, the removed slab revealing a tall but narrow, deep, tunnel into the dome. The team, kitted out with protective gear and suits, entered. The dome material prevented easy EM communications, but after Lew set up a relay system, progress could be made and monitored by Tenak and the science teams aboard The Monsoon and Antarctica. Upon reaching a deep, vertical pit, most of the team turned out to be claustrophobic and so, a reluctant Mike was 'elected' to go down the shaft. A long descent by winch caused him to emerge into a gigantic chamber far below the dome. Appearing to be undisturbed for millions of years the chamber was discovered to be full of strange, non-human, artefacts, including what appeared to be exotic machinery. And astoundingly, in the middle of the chamber was a large cabinet containing a statue of an impressive bipedal being! And it was certainly not human.

In its cabinet the being stood erect, at around three metres tall, appearing to have a strange mixture of reptilian and anthropoid characteristics. The being's head in particular had distinctly reptilian features. Most of the team agreed it represented a species of sentient being, as it appeared to have a brain cavity with signs of a capacity larger than that of a human's and, given the existence and nature of the dome, with possibly even greater intelligence. The team began to refer to the creature as the, 'Reptiloid'.

The team realized that this discovery would change human history and their own lives, forever. Mike was lauded as being the first human being to have set foot in the chamber and the first to see the Reptiloid. They dubbed the chamber, 'the Hall of the Native', for there seemed little doubt that the creature in it represented an advanced civilization native to Oceanus, millions of years ago – but which then vanished.

THE ALIENS ACT

In the same time frame as the discoveries on New Cambria, and completely unknown to any human on the planet, or in orbit around it, a gigantic alien ship orbited the Ra system, far beyond its outermost edge. The massive ship disgorged streams of micro-machines; many millions of miniature robots, or 'robotinoids', which traveled toward the innermost part of the system – toward Ra itself.

Back on Oceanus, within weeks of the New Cambria discoveries, the government allowed teams of scientists from The Monsoon and Antarctica to collect at the Hall of the Native, under the general oversight of a small team of Oceanus scientists and government officials. At last, the Oceanus government began to accept that 'the lid' could no longer be kept on recent developments, and, as news began to filter out, the numbers of people wanting to evacuate increased. But there was still no solid, unequivocal, evidence that upwellings of Ra's surface caused the disappearance of the original, non-human, inhabitants, nor that it would happen again. But things were changing fast.

While investigations proceeded on New Cambria Mike and Eleri decided to get married but Tenak relayed an invitation to Mike, from Jennifer Providius, to join her and her science team aboard the research ship, about to be flown on a close-up survey of the inner system of Ra. The aim: to firm up data about the changes observed to be happening to Ra, as the data obtained on swinging past the star, when they first entered the system, had been deleted by the actions of the quislings. This was a prestigious invitation and Tenak convinced Mike it could pave the way for him to return to a career in science. Though excited he was reluctant to leave Eleri, despite the separation being only for a couple of months. Eleri, though very reluctant for him to leave at this point, convinced Mike it would help him. With a heavy heart, he accepted, and he took his fateful leave of her. Mike knew that Eleri (not invited by Providius anyway) would not be comfortable on an extended journey on a spacecraft, at this point, and that, in any event, she had her own, important, work to do on Oceanus. So, with sadness, Mike took his leave of her. She remained on New Cambria, temporarily, to assist with investigations, the two of them consoled partly by being able to keep in regular contact by means of radio, laser, and holographic communications. But as the ship moved further away the signal delays made this increasingly difficult.

Mike was ferried to the research ship by Sanders Utopius Dagghampton II, a relatively new Navy recruit, but a good pilot. During the voyage Dagghampton told Mike that, having researched the matter, he had reason to doubt that the landslide at Simurgh was an accident. Mike was suspicious of him but soon, other matters occupied him, the science team and crew of the ship, as they encountered the streams of robotinoids released by the alien ship. The researchers thought this a large, strange, cloud was comprised of interstellar soot particles and that they were all going to die, as the ship could not avoid flying through the huge cloud, which at the speeds involved would likely destroy the vessel. But their belief in the natural origin of the cloud particles began to evaporate when the cloud split in two, just as the ship was about to fly through it, and then joined up again afterward!

Also, during the voyage, Eleri updated Mike with news from New Cambria, reporting that the 'Native' was, in fact, an embalmed body, not a statue. And a new chamber had been found, full of the desiccated, naturally mummified, bodies of natives, who were theorized to have died when Ra's surface last erupted. The reality of the danger from Ra was confirmed by investigations of the many, strange, polyhedral, artefacts found in the Hall. When stimulated by various forms of radiation, the artefacts had generated an advanced and mysterious from of hologram, showing vivid scenes of the native beings, and their civilization, when Ra last went nova. These images were somehow, disturbingly, projected into the minds of many of the investigators, including Akrommo and Hermington, actually making them think they were part of the scenes of panic and civil strife amongst the native reptiloids, as they tried to deal with the coming apocalypse from Ra. It was later found that the natives, or most of them, had left the Ra system altogether, in many, large, advanced, spacecraft.

Complex, unexpected, psychological effects from the holograms were found to affect most of those researchers affected by the holograms. Also clear was the fact that many of the beings decided to stay or were unable to leave, causing Hermington and the others to be slightly traumatized, but they recovered quickly. However, they were warned to expect recurring 'visions' of the events in the holograms, or other unwanted reminiscences, perhaps even from their own pasts, but these would eventually fade. Eleri was more distant than the others but felt some effects during the experiments. She saw no visions and examination of the results of assessments suggested she was not affected.

END OF THE LINE:

Her later reports to Mike said that artefacts were now being investigated by remote, automated procedures and the holograms captured on 2D media, avoiding any more risk of unwanted psychological effects. Hundreds of artefacts then (safely) showed that the native reptiloids had carried out extensive investigations of Ra, but then began a large-scale evacuation of their civilization from the planet. The technological advancement of the natives was self- evident, as was the present, renewed, danger posed by Ra.

The government officials at New Cambria advised the government that it was no longer tenable to object to evacuation as they felt it likely (finally) that there would soon be another nova, as originally predicted. As news began to leak out the steady trickle of emigrants quickened to a steady flow and Tenak began to plan departure, as soon as possible, with a ship full of evacuees, once they have been 'processed'.

Shortly after hearing Eleri's news Mike fell seriously ill with a recurrence of the plasmid infection, as warned. He never managed to speak to Eleri again.

In view of the urgency of the situation Eleri had decided to return to the project originally started by Muggredge, involving the collection of the sex cells and other samples of Oceanus animal and plant life. Stores of the samples needed to be transported to Janitra from an island called, 'Jungle Island,' a few hundred kilometres from the mainland. She had kept in regular contact with Tenak, whom she now regarded as more of an uncle figure, but, due perhaps to overconfidence and deeply held reliance on herself, she refused his offer for transport back and fore, by shuttle. With full confidence in her flying ability, even when advised of the presence of large cyclonic storms pressing into the mainland off the ocean, Eleri took off for Janitra. But she never arrived. Storms blocked her route, and her detour took her over a ridge of mountains near the coast, far south of Janitra.

And, as she flew along her detour she suffered from unbidden, vivid, reminiscences, more like visions, of a time when she was a small child; when she first witnessed the presence of a fierce 'metamorph', a small but extremely fierce, though rarely seen, Oceanus animal. She started to recover from the strange effects her memory had generated. Then. she was shocked to find that, somehow, a metamorph had managed to get into the rear hold of her aircraft, perhaps while cargo packages had been left unattended on the ground. The door to the hold was open and before she could close it the animal got into the cockpit and attacked her, but she succeeded in fending it off, and it bounced back into the hold. After locking it inside she recovered herself, only to find that her aircraft had lost height and was approaching the side of a mountain. Too late to do anything about it, she was killed instantly in the subsequent crash!

****

Will the Home System be able to evacuate the population of Oceanus in time? If so, how? What awaits those who are unable to escape?

Just who are the aliens and how will they continue to respond to the presence of humans? What are they trying to do to Ra? Will they increase its instability and eradicate the human population on Oceanus?

What will happen to Mike when he finds out what happened to Eleri? What will the fallout mean for the mission of The Monsoon and Oceanus?

THE STORY CONTINUES – WITH THE SHOCKING CONCLUSION TO

'CRADLE OF DESTRUCTION'

PART ONE:

AFTERMATH AND THE FLIGHT FROM OCEANUS

CHAPTER ONE

FALLOUT

Arkas Tenak paced around his private quarters aboard The Monsoon, periodically glancing at the com unit built into his desktop. No sign of life. He continued to pace. A couple of minutes later the desk unit bleeped and he told it to open the secured link. Arbella Nefer-Masterton's grave looking face flashed onto a large screen that had, within an instant, unfolded from the top of the desk unit.

'I am yet truly sorry for keeping you waiting, Admiral,' she said, 'but I am glad to be speaking to you once again.'

'And I with you, Madama,' said Tenak, 'so how can I help you?'

'Double-fold, Admiral,' she said, 'and the first thing is to ask how that young manry Tanniss is nowday?'

'Mike? Well, he's starting to make a recovery, I'm glad to say. He's aboard the Antarctica. Still out of it most of the time but his episodes of waking consciousness are getting longer each day. Thank you for asking but, I'm sorry … I am a little surprised.'

'Yet I am surprised too, at your implied question, Admiral. I have such grown to like what I have heard of that young manry, since … since my loverly nieceling took up with him. If she found reason to love him then least I can do is inquire if he is well. And she did love him, Admiral, so believe me.' As she spoke her eyes welled with tears. Tenak felt his own eyes start to moisten and he nodded. 'I know, Madama

President. I know. I haven't really worked out how we're going to tell him what happened.'

'I am supposing he has been too unwell up to now-time? Yes, of course. 'Tis strange to think her wake was yet two weeks ago, already.'

Tenak nodded silently.

'I am wanting to thank you, Admiral,' she continued, 'for the words you spoke then. I am sure our family and friends didst appreciate.'

'Maybe not her father,' said Tenak. 'I'm sorry to have to say it but I can't help feeling he resented my being there. I can understand that, but I was invited by Eleri's mother, and I felt it was important for there to be a Navy presence.'

'Absolutso, Admiral, and I for one was very grateful for your presence. I know Marcus is having problems adjusting.'

'As are we all, Madama. As are we all.'

'Deedly. I cannot stop wondering – what in the oceans went wrong on that flight – all of six weeks ago, now? You have yet read the Inquestor's report?'

'Yes, Madama. I also got to see the full Investigator's Technical report. It's still a mystery. Sadly, many air crashes are. I've had several sleepless nights trying to work it out. Been going over things and over. I've had my engineers look at all the reports but they can't give me any clear answers either. It certainly wasn't mechanical failure. The only thing we're left with – I'm sorry to say, is pilot error – but how that happened will probably stay a mystery. It's a shame my own team weren't allowed to visit the crash site itself. We might have uncovered more evidence but it's too late now.'

'Yes, deedly, Admiral. I do agree totally with you. T'was the local governor, for the Swamplands District, who didst make that order. In excess of his jurisdiction. I was not aware of it till too late and much of the wreckage yet been moved. That official has lost his job. I wouldst yet have him more punish-ed, if could but I am told I carnt do that, Admiral. And the damage is yet done. I am so, so sorry.' Arbella practically snarled those last sentences.

'Don't be sorry. I didn't think you were responsible for his negligence, Madama. My crew are good at piecing together puzzles, even when a lot of the primary evidence is missing. But this one still comes up blank, I'm afraid.'

'I thank you most kindly for your efforts, Admiral. As you will know, the Inquestor's finding was also of accidental death through pilot error. They could not yet determine any reason for her to lose so much height. Or, that she should be where she was. Records show she was advised to make for South Tanglemoss but still, she knew the terrain she had to overfly before reaching such an place. And so, it seems she was travelling there … from the wrong direction. What was she doing on the wrong heading, Admiral? I cannot sleep at night, thinking about it.'

'It appears she originally tried to head for New Tenby but changed her mind. She might have been making for Teminisirios. Even so, the Pentorian mountains are relatively low. They shouldn't have proved a problem for her because she had enough fuel to get over them. But you know the weather conditions were foul at the time. Weather has been the nemesis of many an aviator, Madama President. Even good ones … like her ….'

'I can see you do start to choke up too, Admiral. I am finding your affection for my nieceling to be touching, and I will always remember you were her friend.'

Tenak looked at the floor and held his hand to his face for a brief moment. Then, clearly and genuinely making a great effort to recover his composure he looked up again, 'Was there something else you wanted to speak about, Madama President?'

'Please, let us stop this formalising, Admiral. Please call me Arbella and – may I call you, now, Arkas?'

Tenak nodded, as Arbella continued, 'I just wanted to tell you that I have resigned.'

'What? I mean, … why?'

'Tis hardly so surprising, ist yet, Arkas? I am sure you saw the media storm a few days ago. I should not have sanctioned the delay in releasing news about the findings on New Cambria. T'was foolish of me. I now pay the price.'

'I really didn't know.'

'No, I am yet sure you have been such busy of recent times but still, I am surprised. I did think that your ship monitors *everything* that is broadcast on the planet. Please know then that things have become very difficult for me - politically. And ... otherways. Certain voices on the Inner Policy Committee persuaded me to hold onto the news contained in the alien or ---should I be saying, "Native" cavern. Artefacts, holograms and such. I was foolish enough to listen to them. That was three weeks past. Then the news was leaked out – somehow. Maker knows, I do not have any idea who keeps doing such an thing, but I am supposing t'was inevitable. This news is far too important to hold onto. I know that now. I just ... I just wanted us to ... have some time to plan how we would deal with it. That time was taken away from my hands. I also wanted to avoid public panic, Arkas.'

'I'm sure you ... had your reasons, Arbella.'

'I am sure also you are aware that there have been many protests and suchly demonstrations against me and my government. They have been happening all across the continent, special-so in the cities and towns ...'

'That I did know, Arbella.'

'Some of them have been quite ... ugly, Arkas. There is a big hatefulness campaign against me. That is why I have to step down. To save the government. Now is not the time for full elections. Unity is needed now-times, more than ever.'

'I'm sure most people do not *hate* you, personally, Arbella, but I understand your decision. I don't wish to seem impolite, but may I ask who will take over from you?'

'That has still to be decided. There will yet be an election inside the party. A quickly one. In the middling time the Minister for Security, Crassostria Hebway is to be government Praetor. That is yet the name we give a, how you say, care-taker President? Hebway has the full confidence of the IPC.'

'So, what will you do now?'

'I have said I want more time with my family, but tis not just empty words in this case. If Eleri's terrible premature death proves anything tis that your family must come first. I have two daughters who need my support in the coming months and years. The whole society on this world will have to undergo rapid change, Arkas. And yet, speaking of such, I just want to say … I am sorry. Truest sorry, I did not listen to you in first such time. I was wrong there also. Very wrong.'

'It's done with now, Arbella. No point in dwelling on it. I know you had your reasons. A leader, of any sort, always must deal with constant trials and tribulations. Balancing many different things at once. It's always been like that.'

'Thankso you, Arkas. You could have been smug, you know. Self-righteous. But you have not been. No wonder our loverly Eleri didst think so highly of you. And I fear now for her poor young manry. I know how much she loved him Arkas, and he her. T'will not be easy for him. Mayst I ask when is he due to return to your ship?'

'The Antarctica is catching up with Oceanus as we speak, but the ship will continue to a rendezvous with the third planet in the system. I have asked my pilot to bring Mike back as the ship crosses behind the orbit of Oceanus. He should be here in about three weeks. And you're right to be concerned. It's not easy for any of us who knew her. I can only imagine what it'll be like for him. The question is, when do I tell him? I don't want to make him ill again.'

****

Arva Pendocris and Patchalk Remiro struggled along a narrow path lined with giant angara- thorn bushes. The two wore capacious cloaks to conceal their identities but the thorns kept snagging on them, almost as if deliberately trying to haul the two of them back, away from their intended escape route. Thick cloud that evening had caused darkness to come early. It also helped to conceal them but made it tricky to navigate through the dangerous vegetation. They had checked out this path once before, to make sure where it led, but never in the darkness.

Behind them the sky along the horizon glowed, flickering orange and red, the only light to be seen, and a grim one. It was surprisingly cold for the time of year, and they drew their robes around them as they hurried along, trying to make their way toward Amnisos.

'I carnt believe things would come to this,' said Remiro. 'My own people turning against us … against *me*.'

'You had better believe it, dearest,' said Pendocris, 'because "your people" have just burned down the Meta-teleo' temple. I know you don't really believe in the "Great One", not really, but we were smiled on today – despite what you mayst think.'

'How in the Oceans do you work that one out, Arva? As you just said, they have burned down our temple. T'was our great beacon of reason in an unreasoning world. And you are correct when you say I do not believe in any Great One. And neither should you.'

'Oh, stuff it, Patchalk. You are missing the point. We are alive and not injured. We got away. Should we not give thanks?'

'Yes, got away, but by slimmest chance. That mob came out from nowhere yet and t'was set to destroy the temple. If our brothers and sisters had not surrendered and yet pleaded for forgiveness, their lives might not have been spared.'

'They only lit those fire brands and started throwing them over the walls when some of our own people started throwing rocks at them, loved one.'

'The mob yet threw rocks firsting. They came out here looking for trouble, Arva, Make such no mistake. And they did not "throw" those fire brands. They used some sort of catapultie thing. My worlds, t'was like something out of a medieval siege on old Earth.'

'I know dear, but at least they did eventual-like agree to let our acolytes leaving by the main entrance. They promised not to harm them if they left in peace. And didst keep true.'

'I am not having much confidence in their promises, Arva. Besides, they were baying for *our* blood. Thine and mine. Tis fortunate we had access to the ancient tunnel below-ground. I do not yet think they would have spared us.'

'You like so to exaggerate Patchalk. They were not "baying for our blood". Well, maybe *yours*. Not mine.'

'And why should I trust them? You have no idea of the hate campaign that has been launched against me of late-times. And wherever were the Securi-pol? I know the mob didst cut the telephonic lines, but the Securi-pol must have seen the flames all way from their station away in Amnisos.'

'Listen, *dearest one*, you could not expect them to tackle something so serious as this without garnering greater resources? More officers? Vehicles? And the road yet from the town is not good, is it?'

As they wandered through the murk, they heard sirens, distant at first but rising in pitch as they drew closer to their position.

'Teenywise bit late,' said Remiro, his mouth twisting in bitter irony.

****

In the Number One Observation lounge aboard The Monsoon, Captain Ssanyu Ebazza greeted Tenak with smiles as he strode in.

'You look like someone who's expecting an extra special present,' he said when he saw her beaming face. 'What're you so happy about?'

'The rate of migrant applications has gone hyper, sir. Ground stations report a six-fold increase over the last twenty-two hours, and people are starting to queue at every processing station. Can you believe it?'

'Yes, I know. It seems unreal but it's what we wanted. Guess it's come at a heavy enough cost, Ssanyu.'

'I know, sir, but it means the sacrifices haven't been in vain, have they? I've ordered three new processing stations to be set up on the surface and assigned as many staff as I can afford. I've left the rest to finish off the refit to accommodate the migrants.'

'Excellent Ssanyu. Excellent. Good that we started the refit when we did. Carry on Captain. By the way, I think I prefer the term *"evacuees",* rather than migrants, in this case. Migrants make it sound as if they have a desire to leave, and we know they don't have much choice, don't we?'

'Evacuees, it is sir.'

****

The Antarctica slid silently through space, enveloped by the 'backdrop' of hundreds of thousands of pin sharp stars and the broad hazy band of nebulosity of the Milky Way. But the brightest object visible was the blazing orb of Ra, way out to the ship's starboard and slightly astern of it. The planet Oceanus was an increasingly bright blue marble on its starboard bow.

The spacecraft's true destination was far to its port bow, being Kumuda, the next furthest planet out from Ra, after Oceanus. A rocky, terrestrial world, approximately two thirds the size of Oceanus, Kumuda was around 60 million kilometres further out from Ra. Named after the night lotus held in the right hand of the Indian Goddess Bhu Devi, Kumuda shone a startling ivory colour, the tone of its barren surface. It was a rocky, freezing, world with a very thin atmosphere and no standing bodies of water.

The Antarctica's immensely powerful long-range sensors had, some time ago, detected a strange light signature coming from Kumuda's surface; a glint of something metallic, but indicative of an alloy, not a native ore. The reflected light was very weak, as if coming from something buried in dust or sand but, if not spurious, it had to signify something *artificial.* At the time of the original detection the ship had been nearly 200 million klicks distant, so the possibility of a spurious signal was high, and naturally, for something fixed in position on its surface, the mysterious source had moved in and out of view as Kumuda rotated on its axis.

Aboard the Antarctica, a weary Mike Tanniss floated toward the tube connecting the hub of the ship with its rotating torus. He had been in the Antarctica's observatory, watching Kumuda on its giant screens. The microgravity environment was a relief because, following his illness, he had developed a nasty problem with his left leg. That had been the leg stung by the grotachaik, long ago, or seemingly so. The sick bay's auto-med-bed had provided therapy for all parts of his body, as needed, but the leg problem persisted and seemed to be due to whatever the grotachalik's plasmids were doing to him. He was in a bad mood too. He was in a bad mood most days, and it wasn't simply because of his relapse. He had been warned he could have relapses, of course, though he hadn't expected one so soon. No, his ill temper was mostly due to his isolation from Eleri. Worryingly, no further messages had been received from her.

He'd been assured there was nothing wrong with the ship's long-range EM transceivers. And yet, Mike had received no replies at all to the messages he'd left for her. Just as mysteriously, Eleri had not left any more H-lets for him: the holographic recordings. Not since the one when she reported the discovery of the 'hall of bodies', on New Cambria. Even more mysterious was the difficulty he seemed to be having in establishing communications with either Tenak or Professor Muggredge. His messages to the Admiral had met with autoreplies explaining that he was busy with ship's business. Understandable, he'd thought. His calls to the Professor had just met with silence, but then, he knew Draco went on frequent research trips around Bhumi-Devi. So, then he had tried to get through to Arbella's government but there seemed to be utter chaos in that direction. He'd never taken a 'telephone number' for Eleri's parents, an oversight he'd never forgive himself for, especially as the Oceanus authorities kept no private citizen directories. But on the other hand, he realised he might be worrying unnecessarily. He never used to worry so much about things, he mused. *Did he?*

Now, he saw Sanders Dagghampton, as he emerged from the cubicle entryway at the top of the tube's elevator. The gradual restoration of gravity as he neared the top of the tube had started off the pain in his leg, coursing through it like acid and when Dagghampton greeted him with his characteristic bonhomie, he just said, 'Not now Sanders.' He began to hobble away as fast has his one good leg would carry him, almost dragging the other behind him.

'Okay, buddy,' said Sanders, 'just wanted to know how're you doing?'

He can see how I'm doing, thought Mike, and just threw him an offhand gesture of acknowledgement. The pilot shrugged as he disappeared along the up-curving corridor of the torus. Mike reached his small cabin and sank onto his bed, but his leg didn't stop aching. Pressing an auto-pain-adjustor gun to his hip, for a second's burst, would give him pain relief for a few more hours. Afterward he checked his wristcom but there were no messages on it, or on his linked hypercomp desk-unit. Having given up on Tenak for the moment he tapped his wristcom again and asked it to link with Professor Muggredge. He was surprised when, after some minutes, the unit chimed in reply and told him it had established communication with the professor. Maker, he thought. At last. The wristcom patched through to his desk unit and a large screen unfolded before him. Given the ship's speed and distance from Oceanus live holo-vision was out of the question.

The Professor's benign face appeared on the screen. But he was definitely not smiling.

He looks like he's been flattened by a fusion engine coupling, thought Mike.

'Greetings Professier,' he said, making an effort to look upbeat. Muggredge seemed to attempt a vague reciprocation but it was even bleaker than Mike's own, which he could see as a thumbnail inset on one side of the screen. But it was worse than that. Unlike his own image, Muggredge's eyes and face seemed almost *dead,* somehow; his visage a grey mask.

'Mike, my dearing boy. Yes, my greetings too. How are you now, my friend? I hear … Um, I hear you have been unwell again. I was yet so sorry to hear that.' Muggredge coughed and put his hand to his mouth. He brought a paper tissue up to his mouth and dabbed it.

'Thank you. I'm okay now Professier, or so I'm told. What's been happening Professier? I can't get hold of Eleri. Haven't been able to get hold of you, either. Not for ages.'

'I am yet sorry young manry. Um, I have been away on a lecture tour – though I would rather not have done so. It was rather difficult to do. In facto, I cut it short on the grounds of my health.'

'I'm sorry to hear that Professier. No wonder I couldn't reach you. Please forgive me.'

'Coursry,' said Muggredge, his voice sounding weak, and cracking with emotion. A ragged cough burst from his lips. Mike felt desperately sorry to see him like that.

****

Tenak and Ebazza sat in the Admiral's quarters aboard The Monsoon and watched the first public address of the Praetor: Acting President, Hebway, speaking on all those strange things called TV channels, being broadcast across Oceanus. The Praetor sat at an ordinary desk in an ordinary, unimpressive room, presumably somewhere in the Janitran government buildings. He wore sombre clothes in the same style as did most officials on Oceanus. He also wore a sombre expression on his elliptical, cleanly shaven face, as he gazed forlornly at the camera lens. He looked to be about 50 Oceanus years old, by facial features, but had prematurely grey, wispy, hair.

'My friends, people of Oceanus,' he began, 'I speak to you today as the Praetor. Reluctantly, but purposefully yet, standing in as leader of the government, by way of the resignation of my colleagry, Madama Arbella Nefer-Masterton. Despite all that has happened, I hope you will yet join me to be thanking Madama Nefer-Masterton for all her hard work over the last few years. We are wishing her a happy retirement. I was asked by my colleagry, to stand in until such time as a new President may be elected by the whole Party. There will then be a vote of confidence in the Curia, and if there is a call for a general election at that time, we will so abide by it. I will be saying more of that momentarily.'

The Admiral and Ebazza watched, thoroughly intrigued, as Hebway went on to apologise for any distress caused to the public by what he called the government's 'lack of faith' and secretiveness. He said that the hugely important archaeological and scientific discoveries of recent months should not have been withheld and he promised this would not happen again.

'A politician's promise?' said Ebazza, with an undisguised look of cynicism on her face.

Tenak slightly wryly and said, 'You know, most of the time, I think we tend to get the politicians we deserve.'

But Hebway shocked them when he went on to say that the Home System Navy, and the people of the research ship Antarctica, should have been listened to in the first place. And he hoped the people would now come to understand that it was necessary to work with them, not against them, in planning a safe future for all on Oceanus.

Ebazza sneered audibly. Tenak just rolled his eyes. Hebway referred to very short extracts of the holo-vids from the Hall of the Native, which had already been shown, in 2D format, and somewhat edited, immediately prior to his address. He mentioned the hard work and sacrifice of all those who had brought them to light. He said drily that parts of the press had already thrown doubt on the videos, but he strongly urged all viewers to take them seriously. Sounding suddenly stern, he went on to say that things had now changed, and that the government was committed to begin the process of evacuation of the planet, *without delay*.

At this point Tenak sighed and said, 'Finally.'

'You know that's due to you – and to Mike, don't you?' said Ebazza. Tenak looked slightly embarrassed.

Then, the Admiral's wristcom buzzed. It was Lieutenant Statton, the First Officer, from the bridge. His visage popped up in 3D in front of Tenak.

'We've just received a comm from President Hebway's "Private Office", sir,' said Statton. 'They don't need to speak to you right now. They've just said you have permission to send an automated message buoy back to the Home System, to advise them, formally, of the change of policy. If you wish, of course.'

'Just that?' asked Tenak and when Statton nodded, he turned to Ebazza and said, acidly, 'That's so nice of them, don't you think?'

'Their generosity overwhelms me,' said the Captain.

Tenak ordered Statton to compile a suitable message to be sent back home on a data-pod, which happened to be the ship's last available one, to be launched asap.

Meanwhile, Hebway was saying, '… such necessary arrangements are being made so, for full evacuation, while we work with the HS Navy. There are to be many more application and interview centres set up to achieve this. May I be saying, now, that the purpose of the centres is to take all necessary detail yet, so we can help you to achieve a safe journey to the Earth and any onward destination. I am very aware that this is going to be a difficult transition *for all of us*, but this government is determined to do our best to make the processing smooth-most. Further information will be given out by this government at all necessary juncturies and times, in the form of TV and radio broadcast and leaflet deliveries, and yet by way of news-sheets. Please so be keeping well updated. Tis essential-most.

'This is a time for all of us to pull together. Now is the moment for unity, a time to support your fellow popularia, through the difficult months and years ahead. We will do as much as can do to ensure that the Home System Government shall live up to its promises. And yes – its responsibilities – to help us all yet adjust and lead productive and fulfilled lives, in our new homes in the Solar System. We say they must, and will, provide safe haven for us and opportunities to find suitable occupationry for all.'

'I just hope he's right,' said Tenak, 'but I guess we'll find out soon enough.'

The Acting President's face then took on an even more serious look, as he called for general calm. He said he had been assured, by Oceanus naturalists and HS scientists, that there were at least 9 more years before Ra's surface became too unsafe for humans to remain on the planet. He called in earnest for civilised behaviour during the difficult process of evacuation.

Tenak and Ebazza listened with special interest as he gave the first details of the process of selection for evacuation. This was of vital importance, even though very late in the day.

'Written invitations so to attend at the evac' centres, will be sent to all homes, in batches, picked at random by our one, large mainframe, computer. The HS Navy will not be in charge of this or have any such say. Plenty of notice will be given. You should know that a twelve personry committee is formed, made up from local populari who are elected to serve or have been elected to office in past-times and remain in honour. They it is who will decide on various issues which will yet arise. They will, if so necessary, refer to Arbitration Centres, led by experienced judges and magistrates. We are determined *there shall be order* in all this.'

He continued, '*And please make no mistake in my next words.* We will not tolerate any violent protests or wanton destruction, or yet life threatening behaviour in the matter of evacuation. Some of such behaviour has been seen in recent days and I can assure you the perpetrators will be caught by the Securi-Pol and Intelligentia Agenci. And they will be punished. The law is being changed to enable the courts to pass longer sentences for this type of behaviour – and the worst perpetrators yet run the risk that they might have to serve the remainder of their sentences in Home System prisons. Those prisons may yet include the penal colony on Mars, in that system. Be so advised.

'So, I make the plea for peace amongst us all, as well as patience and faith. Together, we can, and we will, make this the painless and easy transition to safe haven such that we all want.'

His image disappeared from the screen, as Tenak stood and offered Ebazza a cup of kaffee laced with "sweet synth-alc".

'Straight talking,' he said, 'that's not bad for a politician, as they go,' he said.

'I suppose,' said Ebazza, 'but I wonder how he got the Home System's agreement to that last bit about the prison sentences, especially when we've only now able to send his news, by dataprobe. By the way, who in the galaxy is that guy? I don't recall seeing him, or his name before, but he seems to have been a member of the IPC.'

'Well, he's been a relatively small fish in a large pond till now. Even so ... there's something familiar about his voice. I've heard it before,' said Tenak, swirling the warm beverage in his cup.

After mulling this over for some seconds Ebazza stared at Tenak, as realisation seemed to dawn on her.

'He's the one,' she said. 'You're thinking he's the one you met in Ramnissos, aren't you?'

'Maybe. I'm not sure, Ssanyu. The voice is similar to that of the mystery man I met, yes, but – yet not the same, somehow. He was using a voice synthesiser, remember? But it wasn't a very good one.'

'You didn't see his face at all, did you? A voice disguiser sounds a bit high tek for these people.'

'You're right. I didn't see his face. I wasn't meant to. I had no choice but to respect that. Don't let appearances, down on that planet, deceive you, Captain. There is still some high tek, maybe not much, but some. Most of it is left over from the colony's founders. The "mainframe" he referred to is probably one the founders brought with them. I suspect it's the only one they've got and probably not used very often. After all, there's not usually any need for one down there.'

'I know. They seem to have let most of their tek go to ruin-rack. Just chosen not to pursue that kind of lifestyle, I guess.'

'Exactly Ssanyu, and that's why these people are unique and, dare I say it, precious. They'll find it hard to adjust to life back home.'

'I applaud his call for unity, though. I also applaud the plan he has for organising the evacuation.'

'Yeah, and I hope his optimism is justified - about *full* evacuation – especially given the time frame. I'm not sure about *that* bit at all. There's been well over a year's delay, so we can only try and make up for the time lost.'

'I'll drink to that, Admiral.' said Ebazza.

There was a thoughtful silence and finally, having not actually drunk anything, Tenak excused himself and walked through to the kitchenette part of his quarters. He poured his drink down the waste recycling unit. Ebazza joined him as he said, 'Sorry Ssanyu. I don't feel in celebratory mood tonight.'

She regarded him for a while, as he looked into empty space, then said quietly, 'It's that young woman, isn't it? Eleri.'

Tenak glanced at her and gave away his feelings by the merest flick of his eyebrows, for he said nothing.

'You know, you need to stop punishing yourself. There was nothing you – or any of us could have done.'

'Maybe, maybe,' he said, almost mumbling.

'No. Definitely not, Arkas. How many times did you offer her transport between that island and the mainland? And how many times did she refuse? I know you spoke to her at least four times.'

'Maybe I should have tried harder. The weather on that day of …. Well, it was foul over those coastal areas, Ssanyu.'

'Then she shouldn't have been flying, Arkas. You know that. And don't forget, we were just a bit busy right then – ferrying evacuees and whatever, from the planet. That's why we came here, isn't it?'

'I know. I know. I just can't help feeling responsible.'

'So, I suppose there's nothing I can say that'll really stop that? You know, you're just grieving. We've lost a lot of people on this mission. Too many. But she was extra special to you. It's that boy I'm concerned about now.'

'That sounds like a change of tack, Ssanyu. I thought you didn't like him.'

'Well now, I still don't *really* like him but – I must admit – but I have misjudged him. His conduct has been exemplary in recent months, as far as I can tell. Specially all that trail-blazing stuff he did out on New Cambria. And I really do believe he loved that girl. He doesn't deserve what's happened now.'

'That's why I keep wondering how I'm going to tell him.'

'He's young, Arkas. It's going to be hard, but he'll get over it. Just takes time.' She paused, looked into thin air and said, 'At his age I was in Navy Training School. I didn't fraternise with any of the boys – or girls, for that matter.'

'Really? Oh, yeah, I suppose …'

'Yep. My religious upbringing, you were going to say – again. Maybe I missed out, but I don't regret those things, you know.' She moved close to Tenak and looked up into his eyes. 'What was training school like in your day, Arkas?'

'You mean, during the age of the dinosaurs?'

'You're very far from being one of those,' she laughed.

'Oh, I think it was a bit different from the way it is now. We had to do it all in four years, not five. Not much time for "fraternising" but it didn't stop me trying. Didn't find anyone special at that point, though.'

Tenak became wistful.

Ebazza sidled up closer and closer to him until she was standing tight against him and then said, in pure liquid tones, 'Course, if *I'd* been there at the same time as you, both of us might have had a very different story to tell.'

He looked down at her shining eyes and blushed. He made a point of glancing up at the antique, ornate clock that hung on his wall and smiling broadly, said, light heartedly, 'By the way, it's 02.30 ship's time, Ssanyu. Don't you think you ought to skedaddle back to your own quarters?'

He laughed and added, 'After all, flattery is not really your thing.'

'I know,' she said, sighing as she turned to leave, 'but it got you smiling, didn't it?'

CHAPTER TWO

THE SPLIT

'Anyway, I'm real glad to get hold of you, finally,' said Mike, gazing at the image of Draco Muggredge, on his screen aboard the Antarctica. As he regarded the Professor's characterful visage Mike felt that something in the older man's face spelled trouble of some sort. I wonder what's happened now, he mused.

'There's something wrong, Professier, isn't there? Can you tell me what it is?'

When Muggredge didn't answer Mike became more concerned. There were a lot of non-verbal communications occurring but Mike wasn't sure how to read it all. Something dark and foreboding began to creep into the back of his mind.

Muggredge seemed to be constantly looking down at his lap but then raised his face to look at Mike. His eyes were starting to spill over with tears. 'Oh, dearly boy,' he said, with a rasping voice, 'so no-one has told you, this far?'

The hellish thing niggling at the back of Mike's consciousness started to thrust itself, snarling, into the slightly sunnier parts of his mind, clouding them over completely.

'No-one has told me what, exactly, Professier? What haven't I been told?' He couldn't keep the tremble out of his voice.

Mike could see Muggredge swallowing hard, and the man's voice seemed to fail.

'Professor? What is it? Tell me, please,' Mike pleaded.

By now he virtually *knew* what Muggredge was going to say. Maybe it was instinct. Maybe it was the effect of accumulated anxiety over the long gap in communications; cold analysis mixed with primal instinct. And yet the raw, emotional part of his mind clung to the hope that Muggredge wouldn't say what he feared most.

But he did.

'I am so sorry young manry,' said the professor, with voice as thick as crude oil, 'but tis ... Eleri. Tis my loverly niece.'

There. He knew it. Mike's skin started to crawl.

Muggredge straightened in his seat, coughed slightly and then just came out with it, in a voice barely audible, so faint that Mike could hardly hear him, 'Dear boy. Dearly boy. She ... is .... gone ... dead. I cannot tell you otherwise. I am so sorry.' The reservoir in his eyes seemed to burst its dam and rivulets of tears ran freely.

So, he had said it after all. The words seemed to sit in the air like noxious fumes. Mike had known, from the start of the conversation, in his heart of hearts, that something was dreadfully wrong – and this was just about as bad as it could get. He simply sat there, staring at the screen, a feeling of physical numbness spreading throughout his entire body. The hairs stood proud on his neck and back and his scalp crawled as though overrun by a million tiny insects. His thoughts became a jumble, and he couldn't bring himself to say anything; the inside of his throat seeming to swell to painful proportions. Muggredge just sat staring back at him, the tears running down his wizened face, dripping off his chin.

'Say ... say something, dear boy,' said the Professier, as he dabbed at himself with a kerchief, 'please so, my boy.'

Mike's thoughts were still in scramble mode. He felt physically sick, but he tried to stop himself from vomiting. After a few moments, which seemed to last an eon, he somehow found his voice again, though it sounded weak and reedy, even to himself, as if he was hearing it through a head full of cotton wool.

'How?' he managed to croak.

That one word seemed to hang in the air like a solid object. The silence that followed it seemed to roar like a wild beast. Finally, Muggredge spoke again.

'She ... yet crashed ... Michaelson. Crashed ... in that damnatious airplane, Arcingbird. She was flying ... back home.'

Mike could only separate single words out of his jumbled, spinning thought patterns, A long silence was followed by another word, creeping from his dry lips, 'When?'

'Five ... I do think, nearly ... six weeks ago.'

'Six weeks? Six?' said Mike, struggling to make his voice audible. It felt as though he'd had a glove shoved in his throat. Muggredge's words still slammed through him like blows from some mythical demon. His stomach lurched and he suddenly realised he couldn't take it anymore. Racing through the door at the back of his cabin, he barely made it to the fresher unit, before throwing up. Grimacing, Mike flushed the unit, then, when he felt able, he staggered back to the desk screen. Muggredge didn't ask where he'd gone. There was no need.

'I am ... even sorrier to be so saying this, Mike, but I yet have to tell you ... she ... has already been cremated.'

This was too much. Now the anger came. He felt cheated. Destroyed.

'Why Professor? Why? wasn't I ...,' he tried to shout, his voice coming through louder and more clearly now, 'and I ... missed it? You're telling me I missed it? I can't even pay my respects in the ... the decent way. Why? Why did you let that happen, Professor?' Tears finally started to stream down Mike's face. He had never had a problem with being able to cry. He just didn't let it happen often. That was something many back home seemed to find irritating, but then people back home seemed to cry at the drop of a power wrench. But this – this – was worth crying about. He couldn't have stopped himself even had he wanted to. He'd have cried about this in front of anyone, anyone at all.

Muggredge stared at Mike with seemingly huge eyes. 'I am so sorry, dearly boy. Please.... I could not prevent it. The law here does say that a persona's ... remains ... must be buried, in a natural way, or cremated, within four weeks of any Inquest. And there was an Inquest, Mike. An Inquesta ... which found, ... no suspicious circumstances. And Mike, her parentia .... Her parentia would not wait for you to return. They insisted on crem-burning. And I am sorry, but tis their right, young manry. We asked them not to do so. We asked them to wait. Wait for you. But, in the end, we just had to accept such was their judgement. I am sorry.'

'Please don't keep saying you're sorry, Professor,' said Mike, with his eyes tightly closed, his mind turning ever angrier, but trying, somehow, to keep it capped.

What do I do now? What now?' he blurted, more to himself than Muggredge.

'I am sorr... No. List now, you will have to learn to bear this, my boy. Like me. Like her parentia. Like Admiral Tenak. Leastways, he was able to be at the wakerie. I am glad too. He said very nice things about Eleri. You would have been proud-such.'

'Oh, *he* was there, was he? Him? Who else was there? The rest of the ship's crew?'

'Yet I hear dark thought-tones in your voice, Michaelson. Please do not allow this. Admiral Tenak did the Navy proud-such. You just could not be there. Sorry for you, but list to me, boy,' said Muggredge, his voice returning now to its usual strength and becoming surprisingly stern, 'Eleri loved you and, in different way loved me too – and loved Arkas Tenak, different again-like. Be glad for that. Be glad of her love for you.' His voice softened a little but remained loud, as he continued, 'I do not how what you will do next, but Eleri would want you to find the strength to carry on, would she not? Yes, you must find such an way. For *her* sake.' He was now almost shouting.

Mike's confusion continued. He looked down at the floor and, straining to gather the energy needed he lifted his head once more and said, 'Yes, well, I have to go now, Professor but first ... just ... one more thing. Tell me ... if she suffered. And, Professor, please be honest. Don't spin me falsity.'

'I would not do such. The answer is, certainly no. She would not ... have ... known anything about it. If you want to know about the exact circumstances, ... not now, ... praps when you feel up to such, you can look at the preliminary emergency services report. I shall send it to you in an electro-comm, if I can remember how to make it work. No, I *will* make it work. But please do not look at it until you are ready.'

'Yes, Professier. Thank you for being the one to have the courage to tell me. Tenak seems to be avoiding me.'

'I will not have that thought-tone, Michaelson.' That stern manner was back. It made Mike take notice in a way that surprised even him. 'He has yet been ver-a-worried about you. I know this truest. And he has been vera busy recent-times. You will find out why when you return to your ship. I also know he wanted to tell you himself, being face to face. Not over the space-net or whatever it is. You have been out of touch, yoursen', for very long times.'

'I am not to blame for that,' said Mike. He felt the opposite though. He should never have gone on this mission. Mission? What nonsense? A pointless trip which had generated more questions than answers.

'Neither am I to blame. Nor still your Admiral,' said Muggredge. 'What happened cannot un-happen. You will not have peace in your mind til you understand that - but I know you are in the firsting throws of grief. You will come to understand – eventual-like.'

'I suppose, Professor,' said Mike. 'but I have to get some rest now or do ... something.'

He told the wristcom, curtly, to end the transmission and Muggredge's visage disappeared. How rude of me, he thought, but it couldn't be helped. He didn't really care anymore.

**

Half an hour after speaking to Muggredge, a half hour of complete mental numbness, Mike hobbled to the scientist's mess room. His mind was whirling. He felt it always would. Perhaps he dreamed it all. Maybe she was okay after all? No, he knew he was being silly. He didn't know what to think. He believed he must try to get caught up in some of the deep scientific discussions which regularly took place on the ship; lose himself in high level physics until he could process what Muggredge had been saying. He got as far as the corridor and changed his mind. He would go to the gymnasium and do some exercise. It might help to drain some of his frustrations. His anger.

He got to the gym and – bumped straight into Sanders Dagghampton II. Him, of all people, he thought. But he should have known. Dagghampton was always in there. Mike sat at the rowing machine, an exercise device seemingly as eternal as barbells and weights. Sanders nodded at him and said, 'Ho there, buddy.'

Mike gave him an unfriendly, perfunctory nod, and started to row. His left leg hurt but he stuck at it. Sanders frowned momentarily and said, 'You okay, buddy? You don't look so good.'

'Not now, Sanders,' said Mike, starting to breath heavily as he pulled the artificial oars with vigour, but he was still inhibited by the pain in his leg, which worsened quickly. He continued to row, faster and faster, his face starting to turn red with engorged blood.

'Whoa,' said Sanders, 'slow down matey man. You're goin' at it som'at' hard.'

'I told you ...' said Mike and then stopped rowing immediately. He had begun to feel weird. His head started aching and his chest felt like it was bursting. Not the exercise, surely? He wasn't that unfit, was he? Suddenly he felt himself starting to pass out. Not again, he thought, just before he blacked out.

***

Strange impressions. Something sharp being stuck into his right wrist. A feeling of being strapped down and a vision of a metal panelled ceiling passing above him. He awoke more fully to find himself being carried on an automated bed-trolley. Two med bay staff, one male, the other female, walked on one side and on the other, strode Sanders.

'You did well, Mer Dagghampton,' said the female med tek. 'If you hadn't carried him to the med gurney he might not have survived. The gurney transfused adrenalin and theta invigorators straight away.'

Mike tried to say something, to tell them he was awake, but his voice failed him. Then his trolley was pushed through some sort of screen. Sanders did not go through with him.

'Thank you, Mer Dagghampton,' said the male med tek, 'we'll look after him now.'

Almost the last thing Mike remembered before passing out again was Sanders saying, in his deep, booming voice, 'Okay. Take extra care of this one. He's one of the good guys.'

'Sure, sir. Don't worry,' said a med tek, and Mike heard no more.

****

Mike's gone aboard the corvette, 'Oberon', said Ebazza, as Tenak joined her on the number two bridge of The Monsoon. 'Seems he got taken ill again a couple of days ago. They almost stopped him from coming back to us, but Sanders asked if he could transport him on a medi- autobed, aboard the corvette and they let him come. It should take care of most of his physical needs. Can handle any med emergencies én-route. Seems they've given Sanders a crash course in how to read the bed's instruments. Good of them, on all counts. And I think Lieutenant Daghampton can be quite … persuasive, too.'

'Yes,' said Tenak, 'I think he's in good hands on that corvette. What's the latest ETA?'

'Should get here in about four and a half days, Admiral. Bit longer than expected but that's due to getting the medi-bed programmed for Mike's physiology. I wonder what caused this relapse.'

'I think I know,' said Tenak with a stony face. 'Draco Muggredge just contacted me. Seems he told Mike about Eleri, around six days ago. Said he felt he had no choice, even though we all knew Mike wasn't strong enough yet.'

'Why, in the planets did he do that?'

'It gets worse. Seems that several newspapers published her name and described her as, "the previously unnamed victim of the mysterious plane crash on the Pentorian mountains," Or something like that. We've been monitoring the radio and vid from the planet, but we haven't been monitoring the papers. Seems we forgot about those. Not good.'

'And Muggredge was afraid Mike would learn about it from them before he got back to The Monsoon?' Ebazza said, frowning.

'Mike's a resourceful guy. He was trying all sorts of ways to find out why she wasn't responding to calls. He might just have picked up on it. The Professor didn't want to take the risk. Thought it better coming from him. Good decision. And if Mike was going to have a relapse, he was in the best place to do it. I should have anticipated this, myself.'

'Very well, Admiral,' said Ebazza, looking disapprovingly at Tenak's and his apparent insistence on blaming himself. There were other officers present, so she said nothing.

'Excuse me, Admiral, Captain,' said the XO, Gallius Statton, striding along to join them, 'I understand that Ambassador Sliverlight has now boarded. We've put him in the A Wing "Brechfa" suite.'

'As befits his standing, I suppose,' huffed Tenak.

Ebazza rolled her eyes. 'I sense a "but" coming, Commander Statton?'

'Yes Ma'am. He wants to know how soon we can get underway. Says he needs to get back home to report, as soon as …'

'As do we all, Commander. As do we all,' said Tenak. 'Tell him we have capacity for another 50 evacuees, but we can't take them aboard till we've completed refurbishment of the hangar vacated by the Agamemnon. When we've done that the AI will have to make last minute calculations and we'll be under way. He'll have to wait.'

Statton started to use his wristcom but Tenak winked at him and said, 'Go tell him in person, XO – but only when you're ready. He can stew.'

Ebazza gave Tenak a sly smile.

*****

Over the few days Mike was aboard the Oberon, on his long journey to join The Monsoon, he was surprised to learn he was becoming more tolerant of the pilot. Mike had managed to get out of bed on the second day after undocking from the Antarctica and had hobbled around the corvette on a stick. He knew the med teks on The Monsoon might be able to insert a tiny cybernetic "energiser" in his leg, if needed, making it unnecessary for him to use an old-fashioned stick. It wasn't that they couldn't have done it on the Antarctica. Mike knew that these days there were strict rules to be followed in the fitting of cybernetic enhancements; protocols which involved obtaining legal authorisations from the Home System government, and that just couldn't be done in the Oceanus system.

Sanders insisted Mike return to the medi-bed to sleep, rather than in one of the corvette's own cabins, in case he had an emergency. Mike was not entirely happy, but he complied. The medi-bed was a huge affair and its profusion of tubes, cables, and festoons of wicked looking instruments, not currently in use of course, gave him the creeps. But he realised that it had saved his life and Sanders was right. When they reached the mother ship Sanders *told him*, rather than advised him, that he would need to report to the med bay straight-away. So much for the 'authority' of being a ship's Secretary, he thought but he knew that Dagghampton only meant well.

During the trip Sanders and Mike had all their meals together in the ship's refectory. The corvettes were wider but shorter, stubbier, than a standard landing boat. They were not capable of landing on planets, only being designed for interplanetary, or orbital work. Bulky vehicles, their shape reminded Mike of the head of a very wide gauge bullet or artillery shell. So, there was way more than enough room for only two people; the corvettes could hold more than thirty.

En route. the pilot revealed more about himself and Mike found his light and easy-going manner surprisingly pleasant. Sanders seemed happy to talk for ages, and the probing behaviour Mike had earlier found to be slightly disturbing, had vanished. Mike tried to take as much interest in what he was saying as possible, but it was extremely difficult to keep his mind off what had happened to Eleri. But burying himself in Dagghampton's chatter was a way of trying to force out more unpleasant thoughts about what had happened to her, but he though he knew he'd have to face them eventually. Just not right now. The thought that kept occurring to him, over and over again, was that Eleri had had such a bright future ahead of her. What would; what could, she have yet achieved? It threatened to send him slightly crazy.

Mike said nothing to Sanders about Eleri. Pleasant company though he was, he didn't feel close enough to him to confide about *that.* And Sanders could see Mike was depressed but, to his credit, he never pried. As time passed aboard the corvette, Mike finally came to like Sanders a lot and was surprised when the man said that this was his first interstellar mission; that he was just finding his feet. Mike began to realise that a lot of the mascla's bluster and braggadocio was just for show. In reality, he was very courteous, very helpful. He allowed Mike the dignity and space he needed. By the fourth day Sanders started using more banter in his interactions with Mike. He suddenly realised Sanders could see an improvement in his physical condition. Others can often see this better than yourself, he thought.

By the time the corvette got to within 100,000 kilometres of The Monsoon Mike was getting about on his feet well enough, but still using his stick. The Oberon had been braking ever since leaving the Antarctica and finally it had slowed enough to be able to insert into an orbit around Oceanus, then synchronise orbits with the mother ship. I'm back, thought Mike, but it brought none of the joy it should have inspired. Strangely, he felt almost as though he was not really "home." He couldn't identify the idea fully, but he knew that things had changed so much for him that getting back into the routine of duty aboard the ship was almost anathema. It seemed to turn his stomach. Perhaps he felt like the passenger he suspected he always had been. He also realised, with irony, how his self-confidence seemed to be faltering, but why should he bother anyway? What was the point now?

He sat with Sanders, on the capacious flight deck, and watched in awe as the Oberon approached the enormous bulk of the mother ship, catching up with it from 'behind', as both ships coasted along in their orbital paths. The massive cylindrical hub of The Monsoon was brightly lit on the side facing Ra; the planet shining as a bright blue crescent in the background. The great ship's many protuberances and antenna systems gave its hull a spiky, knobbly, look. The giant ring of the torus rotated slowly on its six spokes, around the middle, pinched, portion of the hub, while its smaller but thicker counterweight counter-rotated, just as slowly, thereby preventing torque effects across the vessel. Further ahead he could see the forward sensor array block, with its multiple, geometrical facets, bristling with hundreds of giant antennae, most of them facing forward, looking like incredibly long needles, or the tall spires of ancient cathedrals. They gave the ship a formidable appearance, even though they played no part in its formidable defensive, and offensive, capabilities. Mike was only too well aware of the multiple laser gun emplacements all around the hub, interspersed with the much more effective, and useful, strategically located, missile emplacements.

Overall, the ship was, felt Mike, a strangely beautiful sight and at this range, from outside, an incredibly impressive one. It was also, no doubt, one designed to be daunting to any opponents who would dare to use military force.

The little ship continued to close with the giant vessel, heading toward a soft docking inside the number 3 C, hangar. Regardless of his feelings about his job Mike never tired of the sight of closing with the giant ship, like this. It made him wonder if he would really be prepared to give it up. And yet, despite his fiancée's untimely death, a subject he was trying to keep 'locked up in a little room' in his mind, he felt he owed it to her family to help them through the difficulties that lay ahead. That might mean not staying with the Navy. He was beginning to wonder.

The Oberon slowed down to '12% speed', as it moved along the bulk of The Monsoon's central hub, just behind the rotating torus, so that it was travelling at a relative crawl as it neared its hangar. The hangar bay appeared like a gaping, rectangular, maw but as the corvette's minor AI took control, for final approach and docking, Mike could see scores of lights bespangling the inside of the hangar space. Arrow-straight rows of bright blue and red lights blazed all along the 'floor' of the hangar, marking the approach run, though with the corvette's AI running the procedure these were not strictly needed.

After the Oberon flew itself, carefully, some fifty metres into the hangar it settled down very slowly onto giant electromagnetic strips and the huge outer door slowly closed behind them. The whole hangar was re-pressurised to one Earth atmosphere at sea level and ten minutes later, after final checks, Mike and Sanders were able to exit. His pilot gently clapped Mike on the shoulder and went to talk to some tek people who were checking over the corvette. Mike limped off with his stick. Okay, he thought, I'm back. Now I've got to deal with the inevitable questions about how I feel, and am I okay, and so on? And, he would have to deal with Tenak. He had some things he wanted to ask that mascla.

As this part of the ship had a microgravity environment the whole hangar floor was covered with non- static 'positive grip layer' or 'PGL', to enable comfortable walking, but a mini-bot mobile chair was brought out for him. Mike refused it, courteously. He wasn't that badly injured.

Stubbornly, he hobbled into the 'security screening' module, which blocked entrance to the ship proper. After the usual checks and questions, he entered the main part of the ship. Most of the corridors leading to the elevator station, which would take him to the nearest spoke, had PGL flooring so he was able to walk, though in truth, floating would have made it less painful. At least his stick was mostly unnecessary here. As he made his way toward the elevator station he gazed in awe at the people filling the corridors. He had expected to see *some* people from Oceanus but not as many as this, most of them 'loose bodies'.

In fact, the corridors were veritably overflowing with crowds of men, women and children from the planet. Even if one had not known about the evacuation their origin was obvious from their apparel and manner, wide-eyed looks and an evident sense of confusion. The evacuees seemed to fill every nook and cranny. So it was that Mike hobbled along, mostly unnoticed, trying to thread his way through the mob.

Nearly all the evacuees had been issued with standard issue PGL over-shoes, but a few didn't have them. They floated about in the micro-G environment, looking queasy, grasping at any padded grab rails which were available, trying to avoid colliding with each-other and with people walking. Then it hit his senses. The smell of vomit. The floating evacuees had all been given sick bags and most valiantly tried to use them, but a few had failed. The stuff was starting to float in the air, in places. It was, for some, the inevitable effects of micro-gravity. Fortunately, the ship had a system for dealing with 'accidents' like this, something which had been installed in anticipation of this well understood phenomenon. A network of ducts, which were effectively vacuum vents, were set into the ceilings and parts of the corridor walls. These sucked the waste up efficiently, to avoid the unpleasantness, of course, but mainly to prevent it becoming a hazard. Even so, parts of the area were a smelly, sticky, noisy, picture of chaos. He guessed that these evacuees were probably being manoeuvred toward one of the disused hangars, as a temporary holding area but they were proving difficult to manage. Understandably so. None of this was their fault.

Mike was bewildered by it all. Evacuee mothers and fathers stared balefully, clutching screaming infants to their breasts. It was mostly the infants who had vomited, as did many children, most of whom were crying. Many people clutched shawls or robes to themselves, winding them around their heads, as though straining not to take in the sights and sounds of their new, very unfamiliar, and frightening, environment.

Various crewmembers threaded their way amongst them, trying to organise, assist and direct them. The corridors were filled with a cacophony of chatter, shouting and the occasional angry exchanges. A few of the crewmembers who actually noticed Mike winding his way through the crowd mouthed greetings of a sort and continued with their attempts to direct people. There was no point trying to talk. There were many side rooms off the main corridors, most of them closed and, thought Mike, probably locked. But some were open to the corridor and in these rooms Mike saw crewmates piling up boxes of belongings and strapping them down. Evacuees spilled inside some rooms and were being ushered, as gently as possible, back outside.

In one room he saw large cages containing – goats. Goats? He did a double take. Yes, goats, and they didn't seem too pleased with the micro-gravity environment, not really being able to wear PGL shoes. They bleated loudly, where they were tethered to the bars of the cage, so as not to constantly collide with one another. Poor things, thought Mike, thinking not just of the animals.

He felt a little guilty for not immediately engaging with the efforts of his colleagues, but he knew they would be working to a plan, and he didn't know what that plan was. And he was hampered by his leg, to some extent. Even so, he found that various evacuees he came across barraged him all sorts of queries of him, mostly for directions and information about when they would get fed. In many cases he was able to direct them but, just as often, he was not. He became determined that after he'd had some rest, he would find out what the plan was, and engage with it, if he could. At least for this trip home. After that, he was just not sure.

He reached the nearest spoke elevator and was grateful to be allowed into it by the colleagues guarding it. They were not allowing evacuees up into the torus just yet. After exiting, at the top, he saw signs of preparations, everywhere, for accommodating the emigrants. Crewmates were busy refurbishing cabins and stocking storerooms. Dozens of mini bots, normally rarely seen, trundled around too, carrying bedding and equipment, and arranging stuff. Access panels hung loose. Parts of floors were being lifted or fixed down. Lengths of optical cable lay everywhere, and noise filled the air. Chaos, he thought, perhaps organised chaos but it was probably lie this all across the ship. It seemed clear to him that Tenak had been overwhelmed by a sudden burst in evacuee numbers.

He got to his cabin, slipped into it gratefully, threw his stick down and fell on the bed. He felt exhausted but he knew most of those evac's would not be so lucky.

****

Tenak's wristcom chimed softly and told him, in a faintly feminine voice, 'Mike Tanniss has arrived at C, hangar three. He is en-route to the torus.'

The Admiral was checking the ship's manifest at the time but after a few minutes he closed down the screen and made his way along the torus's corridor. Mike's quarters were in the third block along and he strode through the connecting tunnels with a dour look on his face. On the way his wristcom told him that Captain Ebazza had called a conference with those passengers who had been elected, by their peers, to representatives their interests for the duration of the trip to the Home System. The meeting was to take place in half an hour. He arrived at the Secretary's cabin and buzzed. No answer.

In his small suite Mike lay on the bed, glad of some peace, when, irritatingly, his door buzzed. He ordered the cabin comp to switch on AV, and the screen nearest his bed showed Arkas Tenak waiting outside. Too soon, he thought. Why can't he leave me alone for a bit? He felt tired and shaky.

He said to the comp, 'Audio only,' and after a long delay spoke to Tenak's image on the screen. 'Yes? Can I help you?'

Tenak was visibly taken aback and said, 'Just came to see how you are, Mike. Hope you're feeling a bit better now. Thought we could talk, but we can leave it out if you're not well.'

'Okay *Admiral.* Maybe later. Give me a chance to settle in. Maybe about thirty minutes?'

'Sorry, I've got a meeting then. What about 12.00 hours – in my quarters?'

'I'll see. Suppose that'll have to do, I guess. Speak to you later.'

Tenak walked off and Mike was actually glad to see him go. He was not ready to face any of his colleagues but deep inside he knew that he was being selfish. He just felt he couldn't help it.

The time sped by, and at around *12.15*, he arrived at Tenak's quarters, when the Admiral let him in before he even buzzed. The old codger must have got his comp on continuous scan, he thought. He felt he had no time for him, but he was struggling a bit to know why. But then yes; he did know why.

Tenak was at the door as it slid back smoothly, and he beckoned Mike in.

'Welcome back my friend,' he said, going to greet him but Mike gave him a half smile and, absent-mindedly, nearly banged his stick against the Admirals' shins as he limped forward, bustling along in an impatient and irritable way.

'Mind if I sit down?' Mike said, and sat before Tenak could answer.

'Of course not,' said Tenak, looking a little bewildered. He sat too and continued, 'I see your leg is still causing some problems. I'm sorry we couldn't meet when you wanted to, Mike, but the conference was vital. The evac reps are worried about having enough crash couches for the journey through the conduit. I get their concern, but the crew have done a gold standard job assembling the 500, kit- form crashco's we brought with us. Problem is, we're taking 250 passengers over that number. Unanticipated. The ship's fabrication system has made up a lot of couch units, but they aren't quite up to the standard of the purpose-built ones. Ironic, isn't it? We didn't even think we'd be bringing this many home in one go before we got put off in the first place. Sorry, Mike, I thought you'd want to know all this. I seem to be boring you.'

Mike yawned and said, 'No. Just tired. Go on.' In truth, he just wanted to be somewhere else, maybe anywhere else, but he felt he had to let Tenak ramble on. Yes, he was concerned about the evacuees but not Tenak's logistical problems.

'Oh okay. Yes, sorry, Mike. As I was saying, their reps are naturally concerned, like us. Anyway, the engineers have come up with the idea of installing the makeshift crashco's inside the empty hangar and lining it with alumina-plast. If the place is pressurised to an extra half atmosphere it should serve as an excellent replacement for full crashco's. That way, we can accommodate all the extra passengers for the conduit transit. Wait a second, I don't know why I'm bothering. I can see you're not interested. Listen, Mike, I don't really know what to say to you. I feel as if I'm rambling.'

Okay, thought Mike, why not let him have the truth. He said, 'Yeah, you're right. Why bother? There's just a couple of things I'd like to ask, though.'

'Yes, go ahead, please.' Tenak's face took on a sullen expression. Mike could tell he wasn't enjoying this. That was too bad.

'Well,' said Mike, 'why didn't *you* tell me? Why did it have to be poor old Muggredge? I tried to get hold of you a zillion-times. Were you really too busy?' Those last words came out sounding much sharper than Mike intended.

'I know. I'm sorry, Mike. Really. To tell truth ... I suppose I was trying to avoid you. But it was only because I wanted to tell you face to face. Not by way of standard comms, especially at that distance and the speed of your ship. I thought you'd appreciate it that way. I wasn't aware that some "newspapers" on Oceanus had published her name. I'm just glad Muggredge got to tell you before you found out that way.'

'I'll bet you are, Admiral. I suppose I can just about understand your excuse – sort of – but why in the galaxies ...?' Despite himself, Mike started involuntarily choking with emotion. He felt his throat narrowing and tears welling in his eyes. He closed them tightly for a moment, grinding his teeth together. During the pause Tenak sat, staring at him, looking mournful and extremely uncomfortable. Good, thought Mike.

'I think you're trying to ask me,' said Tenak, 'why I didn't get her to take our transport, aren't you?'

Mike stared at Tenak with unaccustomed aggression on his face, glared and nodded, then said, 'Yeah, that's it.'

'I know Mike. I know,' Tenak resumed, 'I keep asking myself that. All the time. But I don't think it would have made any difference. I *did* offer it to her. I suggested it several times, as Captain Ebazza keeps reminding me. Eleri just wouldn't go for it, Mike. You know what she was like. Stubborn. Maybe even more stubborn than you are.'

'Don't talk about her like that,' said Mike, his eyes starting to well again, despite his fierce visage. 'You could have done something.' There was silence for a while, then Mike said, 'Anyway. What's done … is done. It's too late now. In case you were wondering, I blame myself more than you.'

Tenak shook his head but Mike continued, 'I shouldn't have gone on that damnatious trip. I was a fool, and it was a fool's errand, which you encouraged me to do, by the way. It's not as if I was able to contribute much anyway. If … If I hadn't gone …. I could have been on that plane with her.'

'And maybe you'd be dead now, as well,' said Tenak, in sharp tones now. The Admiral's own visage was starting to become hard set, approaching confrontational. Alarm bells started to ring inside Mike's head but then he thought, *to hell with it*.

'Well, I might have been able to do something,' continued Mike, 'cos there was no mechanical failure, was there? I've seen the reports that Muggredge sent me, by the way.'

Tenak's face hardened further and he said, 'I saw those reports too *and I looked at the wreckage* – when I was down on the surface,' said Tenak, 'and if you read the reports, you'll know the Oceanus people wouldn't let a team from the ship check out the actual crash site. I saw the wreckage only after it had been moved to a hangar outside Janitra. Hildendrandt went with me. He looked at the wreckage and at all the OA reports. Said there was no apparent reason for the plane to come … down … like that. Afterwards, I wished I hadn't seen the wreckage, Mike. Still gives me bad nights.'

'That was your choice. I don't know how you could have done it. Oh, I know you went to the funeral too, Admiral. That's another thing. Couldn't you have used your influence to get them to delay it for a bit? At least till I got back.'

'I tried that too, Mike, believe me. The family just wouldn't listen. And the local Inquestor put some pressure on. Kept reminding me of their legal obligations. I'm sorry, Mike. I thought it was best for someone from the Navy to attend but I didn't get much … Well, I mean, they didn't seem to welcome me, either.'

'Why should they? Don't know you, do they? Well, okay, if you don't mind, I would like to get down to the surface, myself. Pay my respects. I guess I have to ask you. Where … have they … put her?'

Tenak took a few seconds to reply. He stared down at his desk. 'She was cremated Mike. They put her ashes in an urn. A sort of golden urn. And that's been put inside some kind of stone box, sort of pyramid shape. About six klicks from the parent's farm, so they can visit her easily. Yes, I'm sure you want to go down there - but I don't think you'll get much joy from the parents.'

'But at least they know me. I have to speak to them, Admiral. I'm sorry I'm forced to *ask your permission*, but I've just got to get down there.'

Mike didn't want to plead with Tenak. He wouldn't do that. He hoped the man would get the message. Either you let me go down there, or we will never speak again, he thought. Emotional blackmail, perhaps, but that was just too bad. For his part Tenak patiently nodded his agreement.

Then the Admiral spoke to his desk comp and when it flashed up some data he said, 'Okay. Kravikovna and junior pilot Patel are scheduled to take the Belepheron down in … two hours, ten.'

'Belepheron? The armed boat?' said Mike. He felt genuine surprise.

'Yes. We've finally been given permission to use the armed boats, because of their extra capacity.'

Tenak's face suddenly turned deadly serious and he leaned forward over his desk, glowering at his colleague and said, 'But listen to me, Mike. The Belepheron will carry the last load of passengers we're taking. We're over capacity as it is. After this last group, we get ready to depart. I need you to tell me something – right now. Are you staying on the planet, or coming home with us?' Tenak's voice had taken on an edge of steel and Mike could see that, inevitably, their relationship had changed. He was obviously not going to 'pandyfoot' around with Mike anymore. And he knew he had to be straight with Tenak.

'In all honesty Admiral, I don't know – yet. Is that alright with you, or do you want me to make a snap decision? Is that what you want? Cos I will if I have to.'

Tenak looked thoughtful for long moments, then said, 'No. Please take the time afforded by the trip down there. But think on this. The Belepheron is due to take off at 1730 hours ship's time. If you're coming home, be on it. If not, it won't wait for you. Barring unforeseen accidents – and you never know with this lot on board – The Monsoon leaves orbit at 0900 hours, ship's time, tomorrow. With, or without you. Understood?'

'Understood,' said Mike, sourly.

Looks like I've burned my bridges, he thought. Ah well, such is life – and death, it seems.

CHAPTER THREE

RETURN

The path leading to the front door of the old farm where Eleri's parents lived looked so familiar and yet, now, so strange. Strange because he could hardly believe it was just a few months ago that he had come here the first time. He recalled how he had met Eleri's rather strange sister, Meriataten. He recalled how they had been pleasantly surprised to find Professier Muggredge there too. Strange too because now it seemed like another era, a different world, somehow, bygone.

As part of his desperately sad trip there he'd visited Eleri's grave, or at least the site of her interment, and he'd been able to take some sort of slight consolation from seeing her 'resting place'. Perhaps it was what they called 'closure'? Unlikely, he thought. He ruminated that there could probably never be that. There were too many unanswered questions. Questions, he had finally realised, that would probably never be answered. He felt a sort of sourness rising in his throat whenever he thought of it, but he was trying to learn to force it aside. He had to, or it would kill him.

At the interment site, in a pretty little meadow-like plot, the urn containing her ashes couldn't be seen, but the pyramidal stone chamber holding it was beautiful. It rose to approximately shoulder height, from a base about a metre wide, tapering up to a square pinnacle maybe a few centimetres across. It was not gold, like Tenak said. Three of its faces were covered with polished bronze plate and the remaining face held a small gate inside of which lay a niche where flowers could be inserted. The niche currently held the bedraggled remains of some cultivated inventrius plants. They looked sad and pathetic.

And he had 'spoken' to Eleri, there, at her memorial stone, for quite a while, very unself-consciously. No-one else had been around anyway. Although the stone chamber was set in a small patch of broadies and wild floranameum flowers he would not have used any of those to fill the niche. She would not have approved of using such living, wild things. Looking around he had seen there were about ten other graves in the meadow, mostly consisting of small squat stone chambers – except for one that was a large concrete-like cyst. It may have been big, but, he felt, it was ugly compared to Eleri's neater resting place.

He had left the meadow feeling some satisfaction that at least she was resting in such a beautiful place. But then his feelings of peace were rudely washed away when he suddenly remembered that the whole surface of this planet would go up in flames in years to come. Too few years. Unease and grief had returned to haunt him with a vengeance. He had wondered whether her remains could be transplanted to a similar place on the Earth. No. Ridiculous. It wouldn't be the same. But then, it had to be done, didn't it? Somehow?

Now he stood, apprehensively, at the door of her parent's house and waited for someone to answer his nervous knock. The door opened after what seemed like an eon, but it was probably only half a minute or so. It was Eleri's mother, Elene-Nefer. She looked very surprised, then gave him a wan smile and, in silence, beckoned him in.

'I am glad to see you, Mike,' she said, once he was in. 'Tis … unexpectam, … but good of you to come yet. Please sit you down. You look terrible young manry. And yet your stick? You are hurt? May I make something for you to drink?'

'Oh, no thank you, Elene-Nefer. The leg thing is not important, Elene-Nefer. I've just been to … see her. You know, the beautiful place where she is. It's so peaceful there. She would … approve, wouldn't she?' He looked down as the words started to catch in his throat. Elene-Nefer sat next to him. My Lord, he thought, she *smells* exactly like Eleri. A lovely, homely but very lightly perfumed smell. He'd noticed many things about her before but never that. He felt a bit taken aback.

'Mike,' she said, 'I am tremendous so sorry you missed the wake. Please be knowing t'was a happy celebration of her life, not horro-sadness. She would deedly have approved. I know why you had to miss it and I am so sorry it didst worked out like that. T'was unfair circumstance.' She caught Mike's downcast eyes and, reaching over she touched his chin very lightly. Then she raised his head up gently toward hers and gazed into his eyes with a soft but somehow piercing look which, again, reminded him of Eleri – far too much.

'But now, yet to list to me, youngry,' she said, gently, but firmly, 'she would have forgiven you for missing it. You must believe this. She knew that what you were doing was yet important to you. Praps to all of us.'

At that point Eleri's father, Marcus, walked in and, catching Mike's eye, gave the young man a surprised look, which quickly turned to sour disapproval. Mike's internal feelings of stress rocketed.

'Oh, 'tis you,' Marcus said, 'for I wondered when you might be a-comin' here. You are yet too late, fraidling. Came back from afar, too late,' The corners of his mouth turned down, as though he were tasting raw lemons.

'I know, sir,' said Mike, 'and I have said I am sorry. Eleri encouraged me to go on the journey round the Ra but I should not have gone. I apologise.'

'That do not matter to me, manry,' said Marcus. 'Makes now no difference if you did or you did not come.'

'Marcus! Please! Do not be like this,' said his wife. 'This young manry is deep-so upset. Carnt you see that? They were due to be join-marrid. Had you yet forgotten?'

'Twere not together that long, anywayin,' said Marcus, with a huff. 'But I said, did I not, that this match was not good.'

Mike felt anger at that point. He rose. 'Sir, much though I respect you, I think you ought to have more respect for your daughter's decisions. She chose me, even though you did not approve. But then I suppose there's no point in worrying about it now.'

'No point in worrisuch?' said Marcus, his voice starting to rise in pitch. 'Young manry, if she had chosen a local fellaman, she would not have gone on those journeys awayin. Would not have fallen in with *Navy* people. Might still be alive now.' His face reddened and his eyes filled up. Mike felt as if he were spiralling into a dark hole. *Because Marcus was probably right.*

'I will not have this, Marcus,' said Elene-Nefer, 'and I am thinking you should apologise, and now! Tis not this young manry's fault she is dead. There, I have said.

You did not want to hear it – but you must. *She is dead*, Marcus. List now. We all have to live with that thought and tis certaint she would want us to accept it. And – not want us to argue like this.'

'Please Elene-Nefer,' said Mike, flushing red. He turned toward the door. 'I think I should go now. I've caused enough heartache.'

'Good,' said Marcus and he turned around and left the lounge room, storming out to the kitchen garden.

Elene-Nefer turned toward Mike and he saw tears flowing down her cheeks. She reached out to him. 'I am exceeding so sorry Mike. Please forgive him. He is not dealing with this well. You can see that, yes?'

'I know,' said Mike, tears starting to roll from below his eyelids as well. 'If it's hard for me, I can't imagine how it must feel to lose a daughter, after 32 years. I'm sorry I came. I should have left well alone.'

She went to him suddenly and threw her arms around him, enveloping him, drawing him to her warm bosom. She held him so tightly he nearly lost his grip on his walking stick. He almost couldn't breathe.

'For one such, I am glad you came,' she said softly. But Mike continued to sob on her shoulder, whilst she gently shushed him, almost as a mother would a small child. After long moments, he broke away.

'I have to go but before I do,' said Mike, wiping the back of one hand across his eyes, 'I wondered if you could tell me what you think should happen to her gravestone? I mean, the explosion on Ra, you know. Do you think it should be … well, be moved? Not now, but eventually?'

'Why no, young-un. She would wish to stay here, on this planet, would she not?'

He paused. That made sense in Eleri's world. He nodded, tears still dribbling from his eyes. He became ever more aware of Elene-Nefer's closeness and an overwhelming sense that this woman was *so much* like Eleri. Same height perhaps, but maybe a bit shorter. Same sort of build. Same sort of presence. *So similar.* He felt an urge to actually call her Eleri, and to settle into her arms – forever.

Whoa. What was going on here? This was weird. Unwanted. These thoughts made him feel almost nauseous and he closed his eyes to fight the strange feelings. He suddenly realised he had to go. Straight away. Get away from here and not ever come back.

'Mike? Where ….? Do you have to go – so soon?' she said, as he disengaged suddenly from her and turned. He nodded, hardly daring to look at her face, again; a face so much like *hers*. Alright, an older version perhaps, but still, her. The way *she* would have looked in twenty years or so.

'Will we yet see you again?' she asked, looking distraught, as he reached for the door.

'I don't know. I don't …. I'll keep a look out for you all, when you get to the Home System, and I'll do whatever I can to get some help for you. Really. But see you … again? I don't think …. I'm so sorry. I've got to go.'

His last look at her showed him a face completely mystified.

With that, Mike fled the house. Glad to be out in the fresh air he hobbled as quickly as he could all the way to the autocar station, all of three klicks down the road. His leg hurt more and more until it burned like it was truly on fire. It made his limp more and more pronounced and at one point he thought he'd never make it, but a fierce determination took hold of him, and he pushed himself on as never before. There was no seat at the station point, a little used place, but he dropped gratefully onto a verge covered with broadies, his leg throbbing so much it made him gasp for air for long minutes. The starshine of Ra beat down on him and he soon felt uncomfortable because of that too. He searched for shade, almost having to crawl.

The first car to get there was 20 minutes late. He nervously tapped his wristcom, which told him it was 1630 hours. Immediate alarm. Was there enough time to get back to the landing site? He didn't want to miss that boat. He had to make it back in time.

****

Jennifer Providius, aboard the Antarctica, wore a troubled look as she spoke to Tenak. The Admiral had taken a scant two minutes from his busy schedule to deal with her holo-call.

'I'm sorry Admiral. I know you're busy,' said Providius, as she appeared to stand, by way of holography, right in front of him, in his room, 'but I thought you should know about the latest data we've picked up.'

'Is it something to do with changes to Ra?' he asked.

'Yes. I'm guessing your own people picked up something too? We were due to go into orbit around Kumuda, but we'll have to postpone that. If you've picked up any of the changes in Ra that we've seen, then that must take precedence. Frankly Admiral, we're anxious, not to say deeply worried by the stellar output flux.'

'I'm vaguely aware of some changes that look …odd,' said Tenak, 'but I'll have the data our science teams have picked up sent to you, straight-away. I doubt it's as fine-tuned as yours. Can you summarise your own findings, Captain? I'm sure you'll send your data.'

'We're sending it to your science ops now but, to summarise. Basically, there's been a change in the Karabrandon wave frequencies and their amplitude. There also seem to be a massive number of plasma micro-streamers coming off the star.'

'I'm not fully familiar with the data. My understanding is that we couldn't get sufficient resolution on those, not so the AIs could clarify, anyway.'

'We may have a little bit more, Arkas, but not loads. The initial data pick-ups were reasonably detailed but the more our sensors locked onto the Ra, the less they picked up. That itself is just weird, Admiral. And disturbing. Our AIs are speculating that the rate of upwelling of the convective zone might be accelerating – but we can't confirm it yet. If that's right, we've got cause to be worried.'

'As you say, but let's try to confirm it before we start to worry too much. What do you intend doing now, Captain?'

'We're doing a slingshot around Kumuda; use it to boost us back toward Ra. Just so you know, Admiral, we picked up signs of buildings on Kumuda's surface. They seem to have some of the characteristics seen in the "Hall of the Natives", but on a larger scale. They are mostly buried in highly reflective dust and ice, so evaded previous detection. Anyway, we'll do as close a pass to the planet as we dare and try to scan everything on the surface. Might as well make the most of it. As regards Ra, the problem is, even with the slingshot, it's going to take us about twelve weeks to get into a close orbit of the star.'

'I'm afraid we won't be here for the next few weeks, to back you up. We can't delay going home anymore.'

'I understand Admiral. Those passengers are the priority. I wish you all the best, Arkas. Bon voyage.'

'Thank you, Jennifer. Goodbye for now and good luck. And – take care, Captain.'

As her 3D image faded Tenak frowned and gave out a sigh of concern.

****

Still feeling deeply disturbed by his experience at Eleri's old home Mike now walked through the same corridors of The Monsoon he had traversed some twelve hours earlier. The difference was astonishing. Hardly any evacuees were now to be seen. The areas which formerly bustled with activity were now a picture of calm. He guessed that most of the evacuees were being instructed in the use of the crash couches, the crashco's. Many were secreted away in the multiple spare cabins spread over the twenty decks of the ship's main hub. Most of the single cabins had been converted into double rooms. It was also likely many evacuees were settling into the ship's large conference rooms – converted now to dormitories.

There was a set of three large 'barracks' rooms, reserved for use by contingents of specialised Home System Space Marines, when the ship was on major, active, ops. These had also been adapted for use by evacuees. Usually, the largest contingent of crewmembers aboard, though not many anyway, were the so-called 'security personnel', who made up what had once been called, 'sailors,' in navies back on old Earth. These were the ship's normal contingent of combat trained troops, mostly 'ratings', plus some lieutenants and sub-lieutenants. 'Security guard' was therefore an alternative name for them, a euphemism perhaps. Each of them would normally have their own cabin, usually small, but, Mike mused, there had been a reduced contingent of them on this mission, so most of their cabins were now available for evacuees too.

At the junction of the main corridor with a tributary one, near the spoke elevator, he came by a slightly built old lady walking quietly on her own. She looked very lost.

'Can I help you, Madama?' he said, trying to peek under the dark blue shawl which covered her head and most of her face.

'Oh, thanking you, young manry,' she replied, with what Mike found to be a surprisingly strong and steady voice. She peered up at him from under the shawl, revealing a round, truly ancient face, but one with sparkling deep purple eyes. 'My oorie said he would try to find personry to yet explain where our special seats be,' she said. 'You know, the couchie thingra we are supposed to use to travel to that afar solar system. My oorie has not returned still.'

'Excuse me. Who is oorie?' Mike began, but his mind dredged up something Eleri had said about family names and sayings, on Oceanus. This one was similar to that used in old Wales, back on Earth.

'Oh, you mean, your grandson,' he said, remembering then.

'No,' she said, 'my oorie.'

Mike smiled. Just leave it. Then he said, 'What's his name, Madama? I can try and find him. Perhaps you could tell me your name too?'

'My name be Ellweni. Tis Ellweni Griffithin Merykare. And his name, my oorie, is Idrimus. He said he was yet going up to some office-room – but away he has he been for such longest time.'

'Okay, Madama Merykare. If you walk a little further along here, you will find a plaza where there's an elevator to one of the spokes. There's a lot of seats up there. Please wait there and I will try to find Idrimus.'

'Thanking you manry. I would like to sit soonest. After all, I am nearly 124, you know.'

Mike hurried off, awed by the spirit of this lady, and a tingle went down his spine when he thought of the similarity of her given name with that of his 'lost one'. He wondered how many other things would continue to remind him of *her*. They all hurt. Every time.

His wristcom buzzed. He could tell that Tenak was trying to reach him. He can wait, he thought. This is more important. He caught the elevator to the deck above, then to a booth with a large screen. The stuff he wanted wasn't on the wristcom network yet. He gave his unique code number and asked the booth to produce the updated passenger manifest. Asking it to find the relevant name he saw that Ellweni and her grandson were the only ones in her particular party. He noted where their crash couches were sited and was disappointed to find they were in the recently converted L B hangar, D. The system couldn't tell him the current location of Idrimus, so he put in a call to the bridge and asked the Second Officer if he could put out a call over The Monsoon's public address system. Then, he called Tenak – on audio only.

'Admiral,' he said, without any words of greeting, 'I've just met an evacuee. A lady of 124. She's lost her grandson. Listen, she's a great lady. I'm willing to give up my crashcouch for her, if needed.'

'That's noble of you, Mike,' came Tenak's voice, 'and I'm sure you're free to do so, if you wish. I'm glad to see you're involving yourself in this mission and the people aboard.'

'What did you think I was going to do? Ignore them?' came Mike' tart riposte.

He could hear a long sigh from Tenak, before the man returned with, 'Okay, Mike, that's fine. Quite a few of the crew have offered to do the same for various evacuees, but the Captain and I are limiting the exchanges to the most vulnerable evacs, and those who are sick. That was twenty-six people, now twenty-seven, with your lady. We can't allow more than that because we need as many of the crew as possible to be fully fit and able to attend to ship's systems. Especially if there's an emergency. You know the HSN Code Rules for conduits, Mike. By the way, I was informed you were aboard the Belepheron. Do you mind telling me whether you're returning home with us as Ship's Secretary … or as a passenger?'

'You're right. I do know the rules, Admiral. And I suppose I might as well tell you I'm staying on as Secretary – just for the moment. What happens after we get home – I'm not sure. There's nothing left on this planet to keep me here, but please don't infer that I'm going to stay with The Monsoon. If I stay on, I'm going to put in for a transfer.'

'Very well. That's your prerogative, Mer Secretary. I am going to assume we can work together right now for the benefit of all those aboard. Tenak out.'

CHAPTER FOUR

SECURITY

The Monsoon flashed through deep space in the outermost realm of the Ra system. Nearly twenty-eight standard Earth days after accelerating out from the orbit of Oceanus, the planet now appeared infinitesimally small and Ra itself could be seen only as a particularly bright background star.

For most of the time the ship had coursed along under the constant acceleration of its one massive engine, maintaining the thrust necessary to escape the whole Ra system and quickly building to a near full Earth gravity, for its occupants. Now, it coasted at a stunning 1,400 kilometres per *second*; its goal, the large transit zone the vessel's hypercomp AIs had detected as being 'only' five million kilometres distant. Though the large zones could move around they usually stayed in the same general location, relative to the central star of the system, for what amounted to a few standard weeks or months.

Within the zone itself the ship's sensors had already detected the opening of several conduit 'mouths'. These were the temporary, invisible, 'holes' in space, probably formed of negative energy fields, which allowed entry to the mysterious filaments linking the Ra system to the Solar System.

Onboard, the crew were still preparing for themselves, and their 710 passengers, for the flight through a conduit, still a journey holding some risks. The Monsoon soon penetrated the gigantic volume of the transit zone and, within another thirty minutes its three specialised quantum computers, or 'Kewsers', had detected the opening mouth of a reachable conduit. To the crew's relief, all three kewsers said that they agreed on the suitability of this particular conduit. Vital time would be saved.

Restrained by seat webbing, Mike sat in a makeshift crash couch situated at the end of a row of seats, second from the front, in a hangar specially lined and insulated for this trip. There were eleven rows, each with ten couches, most of them occupied by rather frightened Oceanus citizens, all strapped tightly into their seats. Both Mike and his fellow crewmembers had done everything they could to reassure these people. It hadn't had the desired effect. Many passengers had agreed, as advised, to take mild sedatives. Most took some solace in the fact that the transit time to the outer part of the Solar System was usually only about 20 to 25 minutes. For the most part they were ready to grit their teeth and endure the journey, despite their concerns. Mike was, in fact, full of admiration for them.

As to the part which came afterward, within the Home System itself, Mike was faintly ashamed that some propaganda, admittedly mild, had been arranged on board ship; videos of pleasantly idyllic country scenes on Earth were being projected onto a massive 3D screen at the front of the hangar. It was not necessarily what they would find awaiting them. Some perhaps, but not all. Still, he couldn't blame the Captain for this, if it helped reassure and generate some calm in the passengers. There were also 150 different varieties of piped music available to the passengers, accessed through the latest tek headphones. These could only be used, during transit, in an old-fashioned way, by being plugged into their seats. Comms could only be achieved via the ship's internal cable network, mainly due to the unalterable distortions caused to all EM whilst the ship travelled through a conduit.

Mike had found Idrimus and now sat next to him, and he occasionally smiled reassuringly at him. He had met the man many times after reuniting him with his grandmother, and he'd grown to like him. The mascla had been a public servant in Deminisos, lived with Ellweni and looked after her. To his credit, Idrimus was philosophical about the journey through the conduit but was worried about Ellweni. Mike pointed out that, given her health, which was remarkable for having survived the rigours of 124 years on Oceanus, she should be just fine. He hoped he would not be proved wrong.

An announcement came over the PA system that the ship was only one minute away from entering the conduit, and Mike's concern about Ellweni, and *all these people*, heightened. These journeys could be fraught at times, but he was glad

Ellweni now had a fully constituted, dedicated, crash couch, somewhere in the ship's hub. Mike, himself, had never undergone one of these journeys in anything other than a full couch, so this was new territory for him too.

As they sat waiting, the light levels suddenly flickered, dipping to near extinction and then recovering, to low levels. Mike knew they'd stay like that throughout the transit. There were anxious looks all around and worried burbling noises.

He glanced at Idrimus, who had his eyes tightly closed. The videos had stopped. There were many children in the hall but the closest to Mike were two older ones who sat in the seats in front of him. They were doing a good job of being unconcerned and seemed transfixed on the sounds they were hearing on their headphones. They seemed to be using the knobs to just turn up the volume. Mike wondered what most Oceanus children usually liked to listen to. He had no idea, but he was glad they seemed relatively unperturbed. Then he noticed that they glanced up anxiously when a very loud moaning sound began to wail, unexpectedly, through the whole hangar, evidently drowning out their music. The wailing was another side effect of conduit transfer. Mike knew it was harmless, though unsettling.

Not only had crew members spoken to groups of evacuees and given them hard copies of explanatory pamphlets, but it was likely many people hadn't listened, or read them. He mused on the fact that most children in the Home System usually became hooked on holovids of theme park rides that produced sounds and sensations like those experienced on conduit trips. The children here had been brought up in a very different environment. Even so, few Home System children had actually undergone the experience of transit. Knowledge of the presence of actual risk and the experience itself, he thought, was still very different to the 'feel' provided by a holovid experience.

The moaning sound softened now a little, but was soon followed by loud cracking, creaking and groaning noises, like huge metal sheets being twisted and buckled. These sounds could still disturb Mike on occasion, especially as it was theorised that they represented the physical stresses placed on the composite hulls of vessels as they travelled through the conduits.

Then the ship started lurching and shaking. Passengers everywhere began to grip the armrests of their couches, as the disturbances continued. Mike ruminated that all interstellar vessels were constructed of the strongest materials known to humanity, yet they were also sufficiently flexible to have the 'give' needed for space travel, and particularly for conduit transits. He wondered if scientists would be able to reverse engineer Cambrium. Would that be *flexible* enough in this sort of situation?

Mike's musings were interrupted by an unpleasant feeling of 'pins and needles', which spread from his back, down his legs and up his arms. He felt pain in his chest and experienced a degree of light headedness. It was these damn makeshift crashcos, he thought. He didn't normally feel this bad but, in the circumstances, it wasn't surprising. Looking around, and wincing, as shooting pains flashed through his legs, he saw that most of his fellow travellers were groaning too. Most Oceanus people seemed to be covering their discomfort through rigid grins of grim resolve. Poor things, he thought, so unused to this sort of travel. First, they had been virtually forced out of their homes, then squashed onto an interstellar ship which had never been designed to carry so many people. And now, they were subjected to the 'pleasures' of conduit travel.

But it was either that or stay on Oceanus and face certain extinction. His mind raced over his times on the planet and his adventures since arriving there, the simultaneously weird and wonderful wildlife and the often strange, but interesting, people. At least, they'd seemed so strange originally but he was now beginning to understand them or trying to. Inevitably, his thoughts settled on *her.* Though he tried not to think about her constantly, he just couldn't help it for much of the time. Would it always be like this, he wondered? He closed his eyes as the pain of loss flooded over him again. Compared to that, these conduit unpleasantries were nothing.

Seconds later, he was jolted into the here and now, when the whole ship gave a vast and violent shudder. Fellow passengers looked around wildly, staring with bug-like eyes. He had been silent till now, but he suddenly felt compelled to say, loudly, so as many people as possible could hear, 'It's okay. It's nothing to worry about. That's normal.' Well, so he hoped. The bang had been a bit of a surprise even for him but nothing else untoward seemed to be happening. Though the likelihood that something disastrous would happen was remote in the absolute extreme, it was not impossible. This was, after all, spaceflight – interstellar flight no less. That would never, ever, be routine.

The turbulence started to dampen then but the pain suddenly returned to Mike's legs. He didn't want to dwell on it, but the pain reminded him of the illness unleashed on him by the grotachalik attack – which seemed so long ago now. To his enormous relief the medics on the Antarctica had told him they felt it likely the worst of the relapses was over. They wanted him to attend regular med checks – which would now have to be in the Home System. On the research ship they had used "SDAPPs" on him, during his last relapse. These were the so-called 'Search and Destroy Anti-Proto plasmids', a more advanced form of the drug treatments he'd received on The Monsoon. All subsequent tests and checks seemed to suggest his illness was gone – for the most part. *Mostly*, he thought. Not ideal, but probably the best he could hope for and, well, he would just have to live with it. People lived with much worse, didn't they?

Quite a few children in the hangar had now started crying and there were sounds of anguish from many quarters. Unfortunately, the creaking in the ship's superstructure, hidden in the darkness around the seats, continued unabated, and the wailing sound started again, this time even higher and shriller. Although he was used to such sounds, for him and indeed, for most crew actual conduit journeys were few and far between. And every time, it was just a bit different.

Among the lamentations going on nearby he heard the sure sounds of several people vomiting into the bags that had been provided. It wouldn't be long before the smell started to drift all around, but he was relieved that, in response to the sounds, the minor comps in the hangar started blowing strong streams of cool air, to supplement normal ventilation, right across the seats. It was fortunate that most of the ship's comps, and the minor and major AIs, remained functional during these transits. But, disturbingly, the directional Kewsers always went completely off-line until re-emergence into normal space. As they had fully functional extensions on the prow of the ship, outside the main hull, it was theorized the problems were due to interference from the quantum effects of the plasma 'slipstream', inside the filament.

Quite suddenly, the passengers' problems were over. The ship had emerged in the far outer reaches of the Solar System. The lights rose and the PA system announced that The Monsoon had emerged from the conduit. All systems were functional and updating and the passengers were free to release their webbing so they could move around. The announcement cautioned them against sudden or precipitous movement. Some, perhaps many, on this trip, including Ellweni, might now require precautionary medical check-ups. The med bays would be busy tonight.

Mike's thoughts turned to his various duties, now that he was Ship's Secretary again. Fortunately, he felt that the numbness in his legs was wearing off. The trip to get to the conduit had taken over twenty-eight days. The corresponding journey in, from the outer part of the Solar System, a system much larger than the Ra's, would take longer. That meant around four and a half to, maybe, five weeks. For most of that time the ship would be in hard deceleration but at least this meant that a one gee force of gravity would return for the evacuees. In turn, that meant they wouldn't have to all be squashed into the torus, though torus rotation was off-line anyway during high velocity coasting.

The journey just had to be endured. How time flies, thought Mike, ironically, when you're having so much fun. And, at journey's end, what would his future be? If he left the service, what would he do? He steeled himself. He felt he had to leave.

****

In a large, plush chamber, Deputy Secretary General and Minister for System Security, Indrius Brocke, stood at a podium, next to Darik Yorvelt's. They were attending the Allied Home System Government's 25th Grand Security Council. There were 16 delegates, which included most members of the government's Policy Committee. But also present was the Fleet Admiral, Alissiana Khairie Madraser, and three other senior Admirals, four Army-Marine Generals and four Ultra-Net Intelligence Agency Officers.

The meeting hall was known, rather prosaically, as the 'Ops Room', and it was lined with huge screens and hypercomp interface panels. The delegates stood around a long shiny table covered with yet more interface panels and stubby holo' emitters. The Secretary General sat at its head. The subdued lighting of a lamp set at table level near Brocke gave his face a baleful, ruddy, appearance. He now addressed all the delegates, his voice picked up by the hypercomps and amplified appropriately.

'Officers and gentilhomms, as a result of a dataprobe received only one standard week ago you will be aware that our mission to convince the people of Oceanus Alpha to evacuate, has finally succeeded. But only after a long and regrettable delay. We have scant details as to why it took so long but we are aware of a great deal of intransigence on the part of the OA Government. And various other agencies on Oceanus appear to have conspired against the efforts of Ambassador Sliverlight, Admiral Tenak, of HSN The Monsoon, and Captain Providius, of the R S Antarctica.

'The message was sent 36 standard days ago and I am sure that efforts have already begun, in terms of "conduit time", to get evacuation underway. But we have to address the fact that the delay has caused serious problems in this system. There were significant problems in any case, but the result of the shorter time frame within which evacuation must now be carried out, is that these are exacerbated. The situation has not been assisted by serious accidents, or possibly sabotage, within *this system*, and the need to switch the location for fabrication of the extra fleets of dedicated E-ships that are needed. In addition, component supplies, from non-aligned City States, have been partially compromised by the uncertainty generated by the delays. But while I still believe we can, and should, continue so to plan for as much effective evacuation from Oceanus, as possible – we cannot be blamed for the inexplicable behaviour of the OA Government.' He paused for extra effect, before resuming his speech.

'Anticipating further delay, this government took the decision, five standard months ago, to begin an additional program of ship building at the Navy dockyards to produce two new vessels – fully weaponised, but in this case, assigned initially, simply to join in the evac' process. These ships will be light, super-cruiser designs, so they will, after evacuation, be dedicated to peace-keeping and anti-terrorism duties. That is the good news. Unfortunately, as some of you may know, the ships will not be ready for another two standard years.'

Brocke noticed looks of deep concern on the faces of Yorvelt and one or two others.

'Meanwhile,' Brocke continued, 'we believe The Monsoon could be docking with Earth Orbit Station Four, within two to four weeks, depending upon how long it has taken the crew to process and embark the passengers. There can be no certainty about those time estimates. We anticipate that The Monsoon may have over 700 OA citizens aboard, and I am pleased to tell you that all is now ready for the reception and formal welcome of these brave people as new citizens of the Home System.'

Brocke paused for questions and a tiny light flashed on a panel in front of him, indicating that Ylsesia Horgans wanted to speak. He nodded to her.

'Thank you, Deputy Brocke,' said the Senior Minister for External Affairs. 'My information is that the "Sirius", a Zeus Class frigate, will be the next Navy vessel to proceed to Oceanus. Unfortunately, this vessel can only accommodate 300 evacuees, maximum. I am not aware of any other vessels which are rostered to make the journey after the Sirius. Especially not large cruisers. Deputy, what can you tell us about expediting arrangements for transport of the next tranche of evacuees beyond the Sirius?'

'Thank you, Minister,' he replied, 'and I can tell you that The Monsoon is to be emergency refitted so as to be able of accommodating as many as 1000 passengers, who can all be provided with full crash couches. In addition, the Sirius will be ready to leave for Oceanus within the next three days, so it will "cross" with The Monsoon. However, you will be aware that, unfortunately, due to increased Ultima "chatter" on the SolarNet, starting three months ago, we have had to keep six Navy cruisers on station, in "deep reach" - the outermost Solar System. In view of that, I feel it may be unwise to commit all of the cruisers to the task of evac' at Oceanus.' Ylesia's light flashed again and, his brow furrowing, Brocke nodded again.

Looking around at those assembled, she said, 'But, delegates, my understanding is that the Ultima chatter subsided several weeks ago. There has been no resumption. And the Deputy has just said The Monsoon has to finish refitting before it can return to Oceanus Alpha. So, unless he knows of any way to ready the Kalahari, faster than the laws of physics and engineering will allow, there will inevitably be yet more delays in evacuation.'

There were mutterings amongst the delegates as Brocke took the stand again. 'That is why we have given the go-ahead for the new cruisers, which I have already mentioned, and which will, I am pleased to announce today, all have all *type 1A, fusion engines*. These will make the full journey to the Ra system in just under four standard weeks, like the Kalahari. Perhaps Fleet Admiral Madraser can enlighten us about the current status of the Flagship?' Brocke glanced to the side, at Yorvelt, who sat, looking slightly red faced and unhappy.

Madraser stood. The tall, large, square shouldered, woman was imposing in her immaculate purple uniform, her shiny, violet hair coiffured into a sort of coil around the crown of her head. It was done in the fashionable 'laurel wreath' style, especially favoured by many senior female officers in the military. Even without the uniform, hers would have been an undeniable presence in the room.

'Deputy Brocke,' she began, 'and all delegates. I am pleased to announce that the Kalahari's four engines will be ready for the final stages of testing, in-line, within the next two weeks. We are back on course.'

There were nods and murmurs of approval amongst the group, as she continued, 'And I have authorised the refitting of the new flagships' hub module to include extra accommodation and crash couches for a max' of 500 passengers, so that we may engage in evac procedures with all due dispatch. However, and I am sorry to say this, but I must advise, most strongly, against committing too many resources to this evacuation. To do so may leave the Home System vulnerable to attack. I advise that the heavy cruisers, currently on station, should remain there for as long as possible. Simply because the "chatter" by Ultima appears somewhat diminished is no assurance that an attack will not occur. For that is exactly what happened some twenty- nine years ago, and we all know the tragic consequences which followed.'

Madraser paused, a look of dread on her face.

Ylesia Horgans, again indicated her desire to speak and Brocke hovered his hand above a panel, inviting her to do so.

Casting a disapproving glance at Madraser, Horgans said, 'With due respect to the Fleet Admiral, I dispute the degree of alertness needed. As we are all aware, the initial rebel attack, which started the war, came from *outside* the Solar System. They amassed a fleet in orbit around PSR 1142, an uninhabitable red dwarf system, some forty light years from here. At that time there were no intel agency probes in any of the eight stellar systems which had been accessed at that stage. There are now more than fifty-seven accessible systems, in addition to the Ra and Ishtar systems, and we have six thousand super-sensitive intel probes, of various types, spread amongst them. As the Fleet Admiral will know, the only system where we have not had such probes, is that of Ra, by dint of the OA Charter of Independence. In addition, we have fifty thousand advanced intel probes, in many types of orbits, around the usual outer transit zones of the Home System itself.

'I am reasonably confident that we could not now be taken by surprise by a similar attack. Surveillance techniques have developed to such a level that I feel the drop in Ultima chatter allows us to place more resources at the service of evacuation. Security can never be as tight as we would like, and some risks have to be taken. I strongly believe we must prioritise Oceanus. Those people, *those souls*, are now reliant on us.' Horgans paused and stared, almost malevolently, at Indrius Brocke.

Brocke took the stand again. 'Thank you, Minister. I appreciate the Minister's heartfelt plea for resources to be directed more fully to evacuation and I accept that the drop in Ultranet chatter is a good sign. However, she said also she is "reasonably confident" of no attack, so even she is not *fully* confident, nor indeed could she possibly be. Even with fifty thousand intel probes in the outer regions of the Home System, each able to eavesdrop over a volume of several hundred million cubic kilometres, that still leaves a volume of space many trillions of quadrillions of times larger, in our "own backyard" as it were, without any surveillance. An unimaginable volume of space. It cannot be any other way. And yet, in view of the Fleet Admiral's impassioned speech, it seems we must also be ready for any new form of attack that Ultima might develop. Perhaps something we have not seen before. That is why we must keep *most* of the heavy cruisers on station, at least for now. And we are all aware that their inferior speed, compared to that of The Monsoon, and the soon to be on-line Kalahari, will mean that they will take up to nine full weeks to reach Oceanus. Before …' He stopped as he saw that Yorvelt's light was flashing.

'Secretary General, I hand over to you,' Brocke said with a graceful and ingratiating hand gesture.

'Thank you, Deputy Brocke,' began Yorvelt, 'for what you said. I have listened to the contributions made so far and must accept that a degree of caution be shown, with respect to committing our Navy resources to evacuation. However, there can be no denying that the situation at Oceanus is without precedence. A disaster there, regardless of considerations of delay by the OA Government, would be a disaster for us all. I have due faith in the Deputy's views in the matter of security, for he is entrusted, by our government, with that role.

'But he is well aware that I feel strongly about the primacy of evacuation. I am very respectful of his views but cannot accept his position and that of others here, that the vast majority of the cruisers should remain in our system, in case of attack. Clearly, this is an exceedingly difficult situation and stands on a knife-edge. But I feel that the overbearing weight of rescue should not lie upon the shoulders of Admiral Arkas Tenak and his crew, broad though those shoulders are.' He stopped and appeared to be uncertain as to whether to proceed.

Madraser's light was flashing and during Yorvelt's lengthy pause he invited her to speak. 'Thank you, Secretary General,' she said smiling broadly but imperiously. 'And while he knows I agree that of course we all want to see a satisfactory resolution of the OA problem, the truth is that Oceanus is an independent republic. They are not part of the Alliance. They have also, in this case, it appears, chosen to ignore our warnings. We have already committed great resources in trying to rescue their people. We will continue to do so. The Kalahari will come online shortly, and the extra light cruisers will be built and will be committed to helping them. Nevertheless, we must surely think of our own security, must we not? When better for Ultima and the New Rebel Alliance to strike – than when we … we have committed … everything to Oceanus?' She opened her arms expansively and somewhat melodramatically, gazing around at all her colleagues.

There were loud murmurings of approval amongst most of the delegates. Yorvelt stared at Brocke and Ylesia Horgans looked up at the ceiling in despair. Soronade Jonsuh Jae, HS Finance Minister, indicated she wished to speak. Her words came with their usual sharpness of tone.

'I concur with the Fleet Admiral. I have no wish to impede efforts to rescue the Oceanus people but the populations of Earth, of Mars, the Moon and the floating habitats, will not thank us if we leave them open to attack. Those populations number in the billions. The Oceanus people number 3.4 million. A difficult decision has, I accept, to be made but one which seems to me clear. That is all I will say.'

There were more mumblings of approval but some loud dissenting voices too. Marianas Polonia Jenner- Emblois, the Minister for Internal Affairs, spoke next, her words full of self-evident frustration, 'I make a plea for sanity here. Let us do all we can to rescue the Oceanus people – as fast as we can. Home security is vital, no question, but so is the need to rescue those people, for they are our cousins. They may be independent, *but they are part of us*. They are vulnerable and we have a responsibility to them, despite their independence. Many of them have families in this system. And we will not be thanked …'

'Perhaps so, but …' started Madraser, with evident irritation, interrupting Jenner-Emblois, but Brocke interjected,

'I see that this is turning into a full governmental debate and tempers are becoming frayed. I also see that the Secretary General wishes to conclude matters.' Turning to Yorvelt, he said, 'Secretary General, you have the final decision here.'

Yorvelt glanced around at the delegates with a resigned look and said, 'It saddens me that Home System security is still so fraught that we are seemingly compromised, even when the emergency at Oceanus requires as much help as we can possibly render. I have already made my feelings known – but I am also cognisant of the warnings of those, which may be the majority of the Committee, that we cannot commit the whole Navy to Oceanus. Fleet Admiral Madraser, please advise us on the immediate readiness of *any ships* of the standard cruiser fleet to travel to Oceanus.'

Now it was the turn of Madraser to hesitate. After a few flustered moments of apparent indecision, she said,

'Well, I believe that there are five cruisers which have been, or … are being refitted with sufficient accommodation and crash-couches and …'

'Have been refitted, or are being refitted, please, Fleet?' interjected Yorvelt.

Madraser seemed panicked for a very brief moment, then recovered quickly, 'I ... believe refitting is yet to be completed on four but the fifth is nearly ready. That ship is the "Caspian".'

'Good,' said Yorvelt, 'and how long will it take to ready the crew and send the Caspian on its way to Oceanus?'

'A matter of ... three weeks, Secretary General.'

'Please make that, two weeks, Fleet. The other cruisers are to have refitting completed but will, for the time being remain in this star system. But I want forty of the ninety Battle Class corvettes to accompany the Caspian. And how long before these could be readied?'

'Rather more like eight weeks, Secretary General. They are currently distributed widely around the Home System and would require ...'

'Yes, thank you. Please action that, Fleet, and thank you for your information. Colleagues, you will note that my decision means that not only will five cruisers remain on active duty in the Home System, but we will also retain fifty Battle corvettes, on active guard.'

There was a fresh outbreak of subdued mutterings. Madraser looked displeased in the extreme. Yorvelt held a hand up to quell the rising noise.

'That is my decision,' he said, 'but I will add this.' He stared pointedly at Allisianna Madraser, 'I want the Fleet Admiral to ensure that work on the Kalahari is completed on time or, if it is in any way possible, *ahead* of time. Its addition to the job of rescue will be essential. If it is not so completed, then we will have to reconsider the situation entirely afresh. Thank you all.'

Brocke held up his hand to signal that debate had ended and eventually people began to disperse. Yorvelt looked at Ylesia Horgans and held his hands up. *What else could I do?* he seemed to be saying.

Horgans, scowling, walked straight past Brocke's seat and as she did so, said, with evident bitterness,

'I'm sorry you felt you had to do that, Indrie.'

Brocke's face registered no concern and he just shrugged.

Fleet Admiral Madraser walked out imperiously.

****

The Navy 'drinking hole', called 'Good Times A'-Comin', was on level twelve of Earth Orbital Station Four. It was a large place. One might even say cavernous. It was extremely late, and few revellers remained. The place contained, among other enticements, three enormous structures called, "rotundas", curently closed. These were massive, spiral form, interactive, holo "vortices", within which participants could engage in holo dramas, dance extravaganzas and the like, both in person or through avatars; holo-characters which actually enclosed their own bodies but concealed identity.

The rotundas were the latest in large scale entertainment, in a form which was simply too complex and expensive for most people to have at home. There was still subdued lighting in the bar areas and some holo-booths available – enclosures which could show a range of several hundred different forms of AV entertainment.

There were also six 'traditional' bars. Back by popular demand, these featured real human bar tenders, who actually served drinks and chatted to customers. Most places like that had become extinct on Earth, long ago. They'd been abandoned in favour of robotic dispensing booths found, in general, in all-purpose entertainment emporia, a format once favoured by most civilians. The Navy liked to do things a bit differently.

Mike Tanniss was perched on a high stool, at bar number 5, looking into his empty glass. There was a barman nearby but very few customers. Some Navy ratings sat some distance away, at a completely different bar, absorbed in their own affairs, chatting noisily. Mike noted, with surprise that there were even a few of the newly arrived evacuees from Oceanus, chatting at the next bar. They kept very much to themselves and, like most evacuees, couldn't seem to shake off expressions of bewilderment.

Mike recalled his early days on Oceanus and his own consternation at being in such a seemingly alien culture. He empathised with these people. Perhaps he should go and talk to them. Nar, he thought, he was very tired and in a foul mood, and had no wish to inflict it on the recently arrived evacuees.

And, although certainly not drunk, or 'kruddo'd', as it was said, he'd had enough synthalc to be detectable when talking. He had warned himself not to seek solace in tru-alc and had deliberately kept away from the bars on The Monsoon. But this was synthalc, supposedly giving those who imbibed it the euphoria of tru-alc, but not the genuine ill effects. He was becoming dubious about that. But better this stuff than the 'real thing', given the way he was reacting to what had happened on Oceanus.

He glanced again at the evacs but didn't recognise any. The Monsoon had docked at the station two days earlier and all the evacuees had debarked, most being processed through the station's immigration system. Most of them had been taken down to Earth in large passenger shuttles, to begin so called, 'new lives', after having numerous interviews and assessments. There were still a couple of hundred on the station, housed temporarily in the two outermost habitation rings.

Mike knew he shouldn't dwell on recent events and his one consolation, now, was that his leg seemed a lot better, and he'd been able to ditch the walking stick. Such sticks had become more common these days, the laws against the use of cybernetic enhancements being now comprehensive and strict. That had come about since the Rebel Wars, when contingents of cybernetically enhanced rebel soldiers had attacked, causing total mayhem, and were only stopped at truly massive cost to the Home System, both in lives and infra-structure.

Cyber-enhancements were now restricted for use in limited cases such as medical situations involving emergencies or the danger of life-long disability. They were even more restricted in the armed forces. In the Navy they had to be signed off by a ship's senior med- surgeon and by the Captain, and the ship's Secretary. When Tenak had been injured, on Oceanus, he had only needed a synth-flesh insertion, like Lem Charnott, the ship's geologist. But medical opinion was that Mike needed an 'N-stick', in his left leg; a small cylindrical object which behaved like a super-battery. If he didn't have one, he would retain his limp for the rest of his life. Given that the medics thought his problem had been caused by the proto-prion infection (though they still didn't understand how the grotachalik had done that), it was felt he needed an 'energiser'; the N stick, which would keep his leg functioning for many years.

Med -Surgeon Atrowska had only been able to apply for the necessary licence once The Monsoon was back in the outer Solar System. It had taken almost as long to get the licence as it had taken for the ship to reach the Earth. Just days away from insertion into Earth orbit, they received the licence and carried out the procedure, which took only about an hour, using a local anaesthetic. But then Mike was instantly able to feel the benefit. Contrary to popular fiction it did not promise to give him 'extraordinary powers'. That was not its purpose, and the devices which provided those sorts of effects were very tightly restricted and controlled. Mike's insert simply meant that he could walk properly, and had normal leg functioning, though he was told, quietly, that it might enable him to walk or run a little faster than he'd been able to, before the infection.

He had noticed, however, with deep disappointment, that it had failed to eliminate much of the physical discomfort in that leg, and medical opinion had nothing helpful to say about that. But the renewed functionality was a welcome improvement.

Mike glanced around the huge, reinforced windows on level twelve, which lined one whole wall of the bar, from floor to ceiling. Beyond them the black sky was replete with stars, many of them familiar to Earth-bound people, as they had been through the ages, but, from this vantage point, with no atmosphere to interfere with the view, their numbers appeared vastly greater.

The Earth was not visible, being on the other side of the station at that moment. EOS 4 was a vast satellite. Rotating, so it provided a standard full Earth gravity, it consisted of four massive rings surrounding a fat core of a hub, and it orbited above the Earth at an altitude of more than 35,000 kilometres, in geosynchronous orbit. That meant it travelled around the home planet at the same speed as the Earth's own rotation, so, effectively, it always stayed above the same area on the Earth's surface. Such an orbit was easy to maintain and didn't degrade, as did lower orbits. The Monsoon was currently 'docked' with the station.

Although large, with a diameter of around 860 metres, the station was still outmatched for size by The Monsoon, which now slid into magnificent view, floating serenely two kilometres distant. To say the two vessels were 'docked' meant that they were close enough for shuttles to ferry people and goods between the two, quickly and easily. If the two monster vessels had really joined up, physically, their combined mass would have upset the station's balance and therefore its rotation around its centre of gravity, requiring costly fuel to rebalance. An important, added advantage was that this situation was much better for Navy security.

'That's one helluva big ship,' came a lilting voice from behind. Mike turned to look at its owner, though he had already remembered the femna it belonged to.

'Lieutenant Andreanada T. Kabro, I presume,' he said, smiling. 'I might have guessed I'd see you here.'

'You're welcome, Mike,' said Kabro, 'and it's good to see you too.' The tall and willowy Lieutenant sat on the stool next to Mike and gave him a knowing smile. Mike was immediately attracted, once again, by her moon shaped, radiant face. She was dressed in baggy, off duty Navy fatigues.

'I heard The Monsoon was coming in with a boat load of refugees,' she said. 'Knew you'd be on it. You see, I knew you'd be here too. How are yer, Mike?'

'Okay, I guess.'

'You look like shit warmed up,' she said with a directness he recalled was one of the features he'd liked in her. That, and her general physical attributes, which were, in his opinion, considerable.

'Thank you, Andy. Wish I could say the same about you – but I can't. Still the same old "waste no words girl", I see. How's life treating you? Still working the construction tugs?'

'Not at all. Working on EOS Two now. I'm over here for a few days. Picking up some training on the new ultranet database. You still "Secretarying" around the place?'

'Well, just about, Andy. Spent a long time away. Glad to be back – I think.'

'God yes, so I'd guess. Oceanus? Majestic place, so I've heard, but weird. How long were you out there? About six months, yeah?'

'See you're keeping up with the Ultranet tittle tattle. Not quite. Try a year and a half, Andy - Earth years, at that.'

'Any good?'

'Depends what you mean, by, "any good", doesn't it? I'm sure you know why we were there.'

'Yeah, the evidence is all around this place. Like I said, was it any good?'

'Well, yeah. An eye opener, that's for cert'. Totally different culture. I started to get used it, though. You know, it's this place that seems strange now. Weird, yeah?'

Andreanada began to look a little bored. 'Pinned down any local girls over there, Mike?' she said, chuckling slyly.

Mike immediately looked down into his glass and tried not to frown.

'Oh, I see,' said Andreanada, 'that good, was it? Sounds like you've been away too long, my mascla. Anyway, nice seeing you.' She was off her stool in a second and began to walk away but Mike called to her. He felt desperately lonely at that moment and worried he might always feel like that.

'Hey, don't go Andy. I'm sorry, I'm just tired. That's all. You don't know what it's like – cooped up on a ship with a load of evacs. Even on something like The Monsoon. Listen, what say we just have a good time – like we used to?'

Andy rejoined him, and said, with a sparkle in her eye, 'That's more like it. Why don't I get you a drink? Let's talk about old times. Forget about Oceanus.'

That's just it, thought Mike, *I can't*. He tried not to show that.

Two hours later he was walking with Andy along the corridors of Number Two Ring, heading toward her cabin. Mike didn't have any accommodation reserved on the station and, for now, was sleeping in his cabin aboard The Monsoon. One of the station's own small shuttles was ferrying crew members back and fore every few hours. It was not ideal. He had to pay for the station's services, and security measures were fiercely complied with, but it would have to do until he could get a shuttle down to the Earth. There, he intended looking up his old mum and, if he could pin him down, his waster of a brother.

He and Andy walked hand in hand as if it been two weeks, not two years, since he'd last seen her. Their relationship back then had been, typically, a short series of one-night stands. He had liked that at the time, and it seemed to be what she wanted too. It looked like this night was going to end that way, he thought, with a degree of trepidation which he found disturbing. Trepidation? Since when? He was free to do what he wanted, didn't he?

They finally reached her cabin she flashed a ring she was wearing at a hidden panel which raised itself from the wall. After she had placed her palm against it, they were able to enter.

'This is only because I know you well, Mike. For old times' sake and all that. Don't get the wrong idea about me.'

'Would I?' he asked.

It was, to his eyes, a classic bachelor-fem's pad. As bad as any male 'bachelor's' pad. Beautifully arranged in places, but mostly a nightmare. She asked him if he wanted another drink. He declined. The more he thought about this, the more uneasy he became. Why couldn't he just switch off and relax; do what he'd always enjoyed? Okay, he'd glimpsed another way of life. So what?

Andy sat on a chair near her hypercomp, and gazed at Mike, perplexed.

'What's up with you, Mer Secretary?' she said, flashing her huge eyes. 'This is not like you. What happened to you on that planet?'

'It's been a long time, Andy, that's all, but I, well I ... suppose I've changed as well.'

She stood again and pulled him closer to her. Despite her fatigues he could feel the prominent points of her breasts pressing against him. He started to feel slightly turned on but then felt more uneasy, more disturbed and confused. Probably the synthalc. What was it they said about that stuff, again?

Andy held him gently and nuzzled her face into his neck. Suddenly, in his mind's eye he thought he was standing next to Eleri, but it didn't *feel* the same. It just didn't feel right – whatever 'right' was. Thoughts raced through his mind as in a fever. What was he doing in this place? Was this sort of 'one-night stand' the life that he had come back to? Full circle? Did his relationship with Eleri count for nothing? But she wasn't here anymore, so why did it matter that she wouldn't approve? He didn't know, but somehow, it just did. What he was doing seemed to besmirch her memory. It was just too soon. Much too soon.

Mike broke away and found himself breathing heavily, sucking in air.

'Oh God,' she said, 'are you going to be sick or something? The fresher-room's over there. Don't throw up in here.'

'No, I'm not. Look, I'm not sure it's right to … I'm sorry. I can't do this.' With that he made for the door. Andy stood back in amazement, and her face became a mask of indignant anger.

'Okay, go. And feg you, sonny,' she shouted after him. 'Go back to Oceanus!'

As he hurried along the corridor, passing late night shoppers and revellers, Mike realised he was just still too much in love with Eleri to contemplate any new sexual liaison. The very idea now made him feel queasy. Part of him said that it would probably pass but even if it did, he wondered if he would ever return to being the sort of person he used to be? More to the point, did he actually want to do be that person anymore? He thought he knew the answer to that one.

****

In a cabin on ring four of EOS Four, Bradlis Dervello, purported aide to Indrius Brocke, spoke to a person whose 2D image appeared on his fold out desk screen. The image he faced was his *real* superior and paymaster, the one to whom he gave his loyalty. He just didn't know the person's real identity.

'Yes, Comrade Prime,' he said, 'I understand what you are saying but I still believe…sorry, I suggest … that further plans could be drawn up to utilise Oceanus, in some way, to destabilise the Home System.'

'You are not listening, though you pretend to,' boomed the deep voice of the person whose heavily shadowed image confronted Dervello on the screen. The image showed the figure was in almost complete darkness and only the snout of some strange and terrible face mask protruded into some sort of glimmering light. The deep voice had been passed through a sophisticated synthesising unit. Despite that, the gruffness of the retort was evident.

Dervello looked down in a show of obeisance. 'I am sorry Comrade. I do not mean to ignore you. Please forgive me.'

The figure laughed; a curious chortling noise that sounded bizarrely alien through the synthesizer. 'Relax, Dervello. I am not angry with you, fool. I understand what you are asking for, but it is no longer viable. My sources inform me that the particular avenue through which we have passed is now closed off. Though you must do whatever you can to protect our anonymity, that part of the game plan has ended. Understand this and move on.'

'Of course, Comrade One. But along which avenue should we now pass?'

'Well now, that job *I give to you*. Think of something suitable, for my approval – and soon, before we lose more momentum. What is the progress with the Pterodactylus?'

'Comrade, the vessel should be ready in approximately one standard month. The four engines have been installed and tested and two of the five Kewsers are currently being integrated into the hull.'

'Tested? Did I authorise the engines to be tested?'

'No, Comrade. They were tested by hypercomp simulation only. Of course, I would not test them *for real*. The massive energy signal produced by the type 1A power plants would undoubtedly draw unwanted attention. Please, Comrade One, I am your administrator – but I am not that stupid.'

'I did not say you were.'

Dervello glanced up at the image and a reflection of part of his own face on the screen, shadowed by the darkness in his own room, and a hint of a cheeky smile touched his mouth.

But it disappeared when the figure continued to speak, 'And I did not say you were *not*. Alright, Dervello, your actions have been … adequate, this time. But remember, no more mistakes can be made. The authorities must not learn about the existence of the Pterodactylus. I believe that we may need to bring its power into play sooner than thought. The HS Government won't be expecting an attack from *within,* this time. It was not my primary choice of tactics – but since our operatives ... or, should I say, *your* operatives, failed us at Oceanus, we may have to fall back on it.'

'Should the surviving operatives be punished, Comrade?'

'Not necessary. For then, Dervello, so should *you* be. No, remember that Blandin may still be an instrument of use to us. Even though, he is, clearly, a flawed one. I will speak to him personally. He, like I, was chosen by the Great Leader of All. We must have some faith in our true destiny. Read the tenth chapter of Ultima's First Great Book of Communality and sacred Identity, and contemplate upon it, Dervello. It was written by a scholar back in the mid-21st century, before the super volcano, and some of the old nations of Earth tried to follow its precepts but failed. We will not.'

'Yes, of course, sir. But what about the other three aboard The Monsoon?'

'There may yet be ways for them to serve us. We will find out what happened. Think, Dervello, it would draw far too much attention if we liquidated them all now. The only one I will not exempt from my anger is Ambassador Sliverlight. I believe he was working for someone else. Have him followed and when surveillance can be evaded, question him, then liquidate him. Remember, subtlety and stealth is necessary always, until the time is right for our just apotheosis.'

The strange image on the screen disappeared.

Breathing heavily, Dervello turned to his co-conspirators, who stood in utter silence in the darkness at the back of the room. Conjecta Dra' Proctinian, his assistant, and Talus Brachta Despinall, Dervello's male lover, looked shocked. Dervello breathed a sigh of relief and grimaced.

Despinall gave out a relieved whistle and said, 'You okay, Brad?'

'Yes,' said Dervello, 'I just don't understand. Sometimes he's so utterly despotic and other times so ... easy-going. I never know how to take him.'

Proctinian chuckled lightly and spoke in an exaggerated accent redolent of the long-gone southern states of olden North America, 'I think that's the general idea, Bradlis, honey.'

'Well, *honey*, you heard him,' said Dervello, aping her. 'Start coming up with a plan. One that involves the Pterdodactylus. And quickly.'

CHAPTER FIVE

THE TIES THAT BIND

The comm buzzer alerted him to the incoming transmission. In a small room, filled with all manner of personal paraphernalia, mementos and objets d'art, Mike looked up from the lovely, old-fashioned, paper book he'd recently managed to acquire, at great cost, and asked the hypercomp to open the holo-comm. However, the signal resolved itself into a 2D transmission only. It was Captain Ebazza. This is a surprise, he thought; not necessarily a good one.

'Hello, Mer Secretary,' she said, with what looked like an actual smile on her face.

What's going on? he wondered. Is she being nice?

I just wanted to tell you, 'she continued, 'that, apparently, your presence is not needed at either of the Boards of Inquiry taking place on Moonbase Omega Four. I expect you'll be pleased.'

'Um, yes, certainly,' said Mike, 'but you're saying there's – what, *two Inquiries*?'

'Yes. A new development. They're holding separate ones for the different issues arising from our recent happy little *sojourn* in the Ra system. The first is into the deaths of our fellow crewmembers, as you know. The other is into the compromise of the ship's hypercomp system and its security implications. I think the problem is that they won't have time to conclude both Boards before we have to go. Only the security Inquiry will go ahead.'

'I should have known they wouldn't combine the two. And, I guess the ship's overall mission is too important to delay it anymore,' said Mike.

'Exactly, Mer Secretary. The government is putting pressure on the Admiralty, who are putting pressure on the Boards. They want The Monsoon turned around in three standard weeks – from *today,* Mer Secretary.'

'Can they do that? I mean, given the security implications you were talking about?'

'Seems so. That's why they're holding the comp security Board first. Looks like the other one will be adjourned indefinitely. I am guessing that if the first Board finds Admiral Tenak – or me – negligent in some way, The Monsoon will be going back to Oceanus under a different command. As will you. Or perhaps you are not going back, Mer Tanniss?'

'Don't know Captain. I'm trying to sort my life out right now. I could do with longer than three weeks to make up my mind.'

'I understand. You and I have certainly had our differences but, for what it is worth, Mer Tannis, I believe you *should* remain as ship's Secretary, and that you *should* return to Oceanus – with The Monsoon. And don't think I've been prompted to say that, in any way. Admiral Tenak hasn't spoken of you since you boarded the ship for the Home System. I think I know what's behind all this. And I don't think it's good – for either of you. You should both bury your differences.'

'I appreciate your comments, Captain. I really do. But I just don't know what to think – about Admiral Tenak, or the job, right now.'

'I see. By the way, and, to change the subject, may I be bold enough to ask if you actually own that place you're in? The ship's comm system told me you were "at home" on Earth.'

'I certainly do own it, Captain. And yes, you are bold to ask,' Mike said with a slight chuckle, unused to hearing this sort of personal inquisitiveness from Ebazza. He continued, 'Oh, I don't mind telling you. You could probably look it up anyway, with your security clearances. I've owned it for about three years. And I'm sorry if it looks a bit of a mess.'

'I would not be so arrogant as to comment on its condition, Mer Secretary but you certainly seem to have a mix of objects around you. I am sorry to be so … nosy.'

'It's okay, Captain. Everyone says the same thing – and you're right. I've filled it with things I've collected from various places on Earth, all over the Solar System. Elsewhere too. "Collector's" pieces, some of them. None of them too expensive I'd add. I can't afford that much on a Secretary's salary. But the flat would be much too big otherwise. You know how I feel about empty spaces. This stuff, being all around me, kind of makes me feel more comfortable.'

'Is that why you chose a basement apartment?'

'How'd you guess? Yep, same reason. It's got small windows, high up the walls, so I don't have to look out, at … open views. But now…' Mike left the sentence hanging a long time.

'But now?'

'Now, I'm not so sure. Believe it or not, I actually miss Oceanus, to some extent, I suppose. So beautiful out there. Terrifying, but … beautiful. I still shudder about it, sometimes, but I don't know …this flat almost seems a bit too … congested nowadays.'

'Galaxies, Mer Secretary! You *have* changed. Also sounds like it would do you some good to get back out there – to Oceanus, I mean.'

'Yeah, I know what you mean but …it's just …I'm not ready yet. And don't put too much store by what I just said. I was probably exaggerating.'

'Please do not take too long to decide your next course of action, Mer Tanniss. I have told you about The Monsoon's likely departure date. If you do not return to the ship in time, but without a formal resignation on record, the Admiralty may find you in breach of contract. And you know what that means.'

Mike nodded. He didn't need to be reminded of the rules. Ebazza continued, 'The ship will send you notification of departure nearer the due date, Mer Secretary. I suggest you might want to get yourself sorted out by then. Ebazza out.'

As her image disappeared Mike reflected on how those last few words had sounded much more like the person he was familiar with, and he now wondered why she had bothered to contact him at all.

He was going to find the decision he had to make a difficult one.

The decision would haunt him to the end of his life.

*****

Mike left his apartment in the 'Third Concentrus', the name given to the third urban zone of the City State known as 'Metro-Britannia'. Arranged in concentric semi-circles, this vast city, no more than one hundred and fifty years old now, encompassed most of what had been known previously as London along with what had been the cities or regions like Southampton, Greater Gatwick-Brighton and Canterbury-Folkestone. With a population of 23 million it was one of the largest city states in the north- western part of old Europe, now known as the region of Pan-Europa. This region covered all of what had been western Europe and much of the former eastern European countries. In the 25th century most people no longer lived in 'countries' as they were once understood, at least not since the super-volcano explosion.

Most people now lived in these city states, all independent and much smaller in area and population than the populations which lived in the old 'countries'. The city states were separated, mostly, by wide agricultural zones which fed them and provided recreational space. And further out than the 'agri-zones' were wilder areas of non- agriculturally productive countryside, larger than in the 'pre-volcano' era. These included the high mountain chains, moorlands and the few remaining forests of the world, which were now starting to recover since the old days of exploitation, though there were still some areas of desolation. These same areas were also often the centre of dispute between various City States which laid rival claims to them, though, under the Allied Home System government (to its credit), this very rarely resulted in armed conflict.

Over the years competition for resource area was serious but the City State polities had persisted without any major wars breaking out, and had grown rapidly since the start of the 23rd century. Most had combined to form associations starting to look very similar to the old nation states. And so it was with Metro-Britannia, one of the five city states in what had been the old United Kingdom. 'Metro' was now starting to form closer economic and political ties with two other 'British' City States, and one or two in Pan-Europa.

Even so, Mike pondered deeply over the question of how the Oceanus citizens were going to fit into this world. He ruminated on this as he walked the 800 metres from his apartment, situated a few klicks from the centre of 'Metro-3', as it was informally known, to the nearest hyper-tube. The hyper-tubes were now the main form of urban transportation since the abandonment of vehicles since the super-volcano. The hyper-tubes were large tunnels with semi-transparent walls, mostly suspended above street level, forming a vast and complex network across the city. And through them ran hyper-maglev trains, speeding at over 300 kilometres per hour. The hyper-trains were modularised, often running with up to thirty compartments, some of them carrying, in separable units, around fifty people. Others carried only one or two modules. The larger ones were capable of splitting into smaller component units which could hive off along numerous branches and sub-branches.

The city's Artificial Intelligences controlled the hyper-trains and their complex splitting and rejoining, transporting citizens to hundreds of destinations across the city, and outside. They usually left most people with the need to walk, but usually only a few hundred metres, to their places of work, or, more usually, homes, sports venues, or the many retail-entertainment emporia.

Mike couldn't help feeling a little like a fish out of water now, as he stepped onto his hyper-module, a maglev unit which was split into four smaller compartments. Only two of the modules were occupied. Although tiny electronic 'eyes', for passenger security, were sited in each compartment, it was possible to make the alumina-glass panels between the compartments opaque, only for privacy from other passengers. Mike didn't bother. Although he was in a low and contemplative mood, anyway, he wasn't concerned about other occupants. It was a relatively short journey; a mere 97 klicks, and he closed his eyes, trying to get some sleep, settling into the plush couch which presented itself to him upon entry to the module.

He hadn't slept well in weeks and didn't bother with the various options for entertainment en-route, preferring to rest, before getting to the stop nearest his mother's place, in the Dartingmoore sector of the Fourth Quadrant of the city. It wasn't that it was a chore in any sort of way; just that he knew it was going to be an emotional scramble for both of them.

After twenty minutes his compartment and the two behind broke away from the rest of the train, then veered right, into a branching hyper-tube. As its speed increased the city highways and byways flashed past dizzyingly. Not that very much could be seen through the thick plasto-steel tube walls – designed to afford good protection from the elements, crime and terrorism. Crashes were virtually unheard of.

After twenty-two minutes he alighted at Dartingmoore stop and slipped out into the thronged streets, known now as 'pedways'. There were no longer any motor vehicles to bother about. All pedways were designed for traffic on foot, but alongside them ran separate, auto-walkways, if required, like the ones used long ago in airports or large stores, in the late 20th and early 21st centuries, but more advanced. Vehicular traffic was no longer needed for transport of goods, such material normally being moved around the city through a set of hyper-tubes separate from the passenger tubes. Like the containers carried on old cargo ships, Mike could hear the goods cars, faintly, as they hurtled along through large tubes, which were fully opaque, as he walked by them.

His mother's place, a small apartment in 'Tennebola Plaza', a maze of residential blocks, large enough to have formed an old fashioned town in old 20th century Britain, was about 500 metres distant. As he walked along he couldn't help but compare the street scenario here, with those on Oceanus. He was very familiar with Metro-B and other city states, and, in many ways, they felt comfortable. But, in other ways they were starting to feel a bit strange, a bit alien. Why, he wondered? Could it be the influence of Oceanus? How?

The month right now was February, the northern hemisphere of Earth very much still caught in winter. Only the central portions of most city states, including this one, were roofed over by gigantic, translucent, plexi-alloy domes, built mainly to house City State governments, the administrative sectors and security zones. All these areas were maintained in comfortable, climate controlled, environments by gigantic, hyper-sensitive solar power panels. Even so, climate control of all the outer areas of cities was considered too expensive and technically difficult, or so it was said. As he walked along, noticing, to his relief, that his leg no longer hindered him, Mike gazed up at leaden skies and felt the chill wind of late winter. There was rain in the air, cold rain. He pulled up the large collar on his topcoat, trying to keep out the freeze. Different to the usual conditions on Oceanus? Just a tad, maybe?

Despite the bleak day, the pedways were full of people, mostly gambolling around, out for fresh air walks, wrapped up against the wind, or taking in the sights of the local vendors, who filled the air with sound, mainly robotic, and none too melodious. The machines which lined the pedways blared out noisy advertising of their wares with 'voices', meant to sound human, but which were, in reality, anything but. They remained obviously electronic and artificial. Mike had never given it much thought before but now, he seemed to recoil from it.

He took it all in with a kind of morbid curiosity, almost as if seeing it for the first time. The numerous box-like automatons were rooted to their pitches, sporting large screens advertising the products of their human makers, mainly third-rate traders. The bigger vendors could afford to rent holo-emitters, and these things sprouted from the pedway, at regular intervals, though spread further apart than the automatons. This made the pedways seem like a strange, inhuman, and perverse imitation of the street markets of old. The holo-purveyor devices produced hundreds of holo-vids; commercials which hung in the air in front, above, or to the sides of anyone walking along. There were laws meant to regulate all this, but the main requirement was that holo-ads should be of low power, so they were mostly translucent, to prevent people falling or colliding with each-other. In fact, people often still had such mishaps and the resulting legal wrangles sometimes ended with the banning of the offending company – only to be replaced with yet another.

Mike knew it was possible to have a device implanted into your skull, called 'Direct Cerebro-feed', or 'DCF', which allowed you to access all the adverts in hyper-detail, plus extra information, including newscasts, the SolarNet social media system, or any one of forty thousand entertainment streams, known as 'threads'. Though he subscribed to the SolarNet system, when at home, Mike, like many now, eschewed most of the rest of the stuff. Still, many people went in for that sort of thing. Mike worried about their sanity.

The noise from the holo-ads, mostly accompanied by the mass mainstream music currently in fashion, the 'Galactomart' streams, which Mike now considered mind numbingly awful, together with the sounds of the street vendors, and the noisy chatter of pedestrians, seemed to crowd in on Mike's mind. It was almost *painful*. He wondered whether he should have returned here but he felt he had to visit his mother. No, he wanted to visit her. Needed to. She had become somewhat dependent on him in recent years and he worried about her a lot, especially since his father, Brenner Lutellius Tanniss had died.

The buildings lining the pedways were, of course, much larger than the ones Mike had become used to on Oceanus. They were enormous blocks, typically with 60 to 80 floors, often featuring roofs at various levels. A positive point, he thought, was that, at least in Concentrus 3, the many intercalating roofs had large gardens and copses of small trees sprouting from them. The modern fashion was not to build upwards forever but to link blocks together, incorporating vegetation covered walkways and green park-like mezzanine floors between residential ones. At least that was good, he felt. Not many buildings had these features, here in Concentrus 4.

Mike was of course familiar with this area, but he gazed at it all now, almost as if anew, running his eyes over the barrier-like facings of the buildings. It seemed so crowded and all the residential buildings which lined pedways or any other accessway, had such barren, grey facings: flexible metal and crystalline hoardings designed to provide protection against terrorist attack, riot, fire, weather and natural disasters. It had been like this since the time of the rebel wars. Entrance was gained to a residential building only by touching sensor plates which recognised the physiology of the visitor or could otherwise match them with data kept on the secured zones of the SolarNet.

Again, it was all such a contrast with Oceanus. The relative openness of that society had, at first, felt very strange, but now seemed … desirable? As he hurried along, ever keener to get to his destination and off the pedways, he looked more closely at the crowds using them, mentally screening out the incessant holo-ads as much as he could. Many people seemed oblivious to the bombardment, and, for the first time, he thought he detected signs of people obviously hooked on brain-stim. He spotted wires that climbed out of the currently fashionable high neck polo sweaters, or 'arch collars', as they were called. They could be seen snaking up and under their hats, the square-shaped 'stoker' hats, or top hats, that were becoming the 'must have' fashionable items.

Beyond that and connected with DCF, was the trend for using skull implants to communicate with others, and with the media, utilising thought alone. Mike knew that this would not suit him. It was too much like losing ownership of your own mind, getting too near to the possibility of thought control by others. Fortunately, Mike felt, most citizens appeared to eschew this newer form of tek. But he considered it was one of the many new dangers Society faced in the 25th century, much worse than the great smartphone addictions of the pre-volcano past.

Mike's thoughts now became increasingly troubled. He inserted ear buds to cut out the surrounding noise and tapped his wristcom, so it would patch through to a different stream of info, mostly relaxing music and the occasional news feed, in audio only. What a relief.

The first news flow took him by surprise and haunted him for the rest of his time in the Home System. The male reporter announced, with an air of inappropriate jauntiness, 'And in further news today, Allied Home System sources confirmed that the territorial dispute between the city states of Paranarria and Bratiskonta, now endanger plans to settle the majority of evacuees from Oceanus Alpha. It was intended they be settled, if possible, in the zone between the two city states, but these have recently become embroiled in disputes. HS government agencies are trying to mediate between the parties, to avert the closing of a belt of forested country in the wide zone, where it had been hoped to settle as many as half a million evacuees.

Mike was fully attentive now. The feed went on, 'AHSG Secretary-General Darik Yorvelt said today, "It is vital that the plan to settle the evacuees is not compromised by this unfortunate dispute. But we also have to be cognisant of the feelings of the citizens of these City States." Opposition leaders said that this dispute arises from the failure of the AHSG to anticipate the issues and put early mediation in place. They added that the fact Paranarria is said to be applying to cede from the Allied Home System is crucial to the outcome of this dispute. Now, for this important message ...'

The news-feed character went on to extoll the virtues of various brands of painkiller, but Mike had switched off and tried to put the bad news to the back of his mind for the moment.

Tennebola Plaza was only a hundred metres away now but Mike decided to switch to a different news feed, in the hope of finding something to feel good about but when he did so another news item smashed its way into his consciousness, 'Breaking news just in,' said the breathless reporter, this time a woman, 'is that the Allied Home System Gov't, is to inject Spillingret Emergency Fund cash into the continued building of hab-slinder number five. Designated NQ Delta, this will be another of the floating habitation worlds placed in Lagrange orbit around the sun. This one is designed to accommodate up to 20,000 evacuees, in an environment similar to the one experienced on Oceanus, for those who want that.

'Construction of the hull of Slinder NQ Delta, was completed last month but prepping of the interior was put on hold when Galactica Terran-Blaze, the construction company, claimed they hadn't been paid by the AHSG for the last 6 months' work. Speculation was rife that the reason was lack of funds due to lost revenue from the three city states which ceded from the Home System six months ago. Government Minister Ylesia Horgans said that emergency funds were being brought forward to ensure NQ Delta will be completed. She refused to comment on the three other slinders that were planned to accommodate another 60,000 migrants. The outermost shells of two have been built, but all further work has stopped. Many speculate that the shortfalls are due to the high cost of evacuation of Oceanus.'

Mike could hardly believe it. He felt so sorry for those poor souls from Oceanus; people he had grown to admire so much – and not just because of Eleri's influence. It was all starting to sound like a nightmare.

As he arrived at Tennebola Plaza, he pressed his right hand into the sensor panel, a soft, gel-like section of the outer wall. He was still pondering on the fate of the Oceanus people. Marcus had been right. Mike himself now wondered whether the Home System was bad for Marcus's people. But what was the alternative? None!

Breaking his revery, the wall announced to him, in a deep, throaty, electronic rumble, that he was cleared for entry. He tried to push his worries about Oceanus to the back of his mind. He wondered now about how much more dependent upon him his sick mother was going to become.

****

In a very small apartment on the third ring of Earth Orbital Station Two, Yardis Octavian Sliverlight sat at a table and hungrily gulped down the synth-beef soup his associate had prepared.

'You're a good cook, Gron', despite the fact that you've always got your head in some new tek system or other,' he said, licking juice from his lips.

'Oh, I got that out of an auto-dispenser in hub quad four,' said Gronnington Aristobulus Arpelk, who happened to be Sliverlight's friend and tek expert, a young, rotund and amiable looking man, with an oval face and a goatee beard. Arpelk stood with his back resting against a kitchen unit, his legs crossed at the ankles.

'What?' said Sliverlight, dabbing his lips with a kerchief, 'I thought they pushed out waste stuff, don't they?' His mouth wrinkled with distaste.

'Well, no. It's recycled food waste. It's perfectly safe – and you seemed to like it before you knew where it came from,' said Arpelk, sniggering.

Sliverlight dropped his spoon noisily into the remains of the soup at the bottom of his bowl, scattering tiny droplets of brown liquid onto the table.

'To business,' said the ambassador, with a heavy sigh. 'Have you secured the data flakes from the surveillance work?'

'Only here,' said Gronnington, looking unsettled by the question. 'I thought you were going to give your flake to Admiral Tenak. You know, the chip from inside your false eye.'

'Yes, yes, I know the one, and no, I didn't *give it* to Tenak. You seem to be very sanguine about him, but I'm not so sure of the mascla. I was put in touch with an engineer from The Monsoon, someone who was clearly working for Dervello. But I wouldn't be surprised if Tenak, or the other senior officers were involved as well. I met an Ultima operative on the Antarctica too.'

'That was all planned for. We know that, Yardis. So, what did you do with the data flake?'

'Well, it was obviously not safe to trust anyone in the circumstances. I flushed it down the fresher.'

'You what? Your toilet?' asked Arpelk, with widening eyes.

'No, no, of course not. The crew's fresher. On the Antarctica. What's the fuss about? Those things evacuate out to space.'

'Yeah, but things like data flakes can get stuck in the tubes. Didn't you know? Something like that could be found by the auto-cleaners. They might recognise it for what it is and recover it.'

'And if that happens – *if, I said* – it's the crew who'll have to take responsibility.'

'But you said, yourself, you can't trust the crews. I reckon you can trust a crew like that of the Antarctica even less than a Navy ship.'

'I wouldn't be so certain. Anyway, it's important that you secure the data flakes we've collected from surveillance, especially now I'm likely to be a target.'

Arpelk's face took on a deadly serious complexion, 'Do you think they'll try to … you know, "liquidate" you, or your family?'

Sliverlight's face took on an ashen appearance, as he said,

'I believe so, Gron', I believe so. Fortunately, I've made arrangements for my family to be taken to a safe location, far from the Earth. I shall go into hiding forthwith, and I suggest you do the same – after you've secured the data flakes. All our info suggests the opposition's pretty tardy, otherwise they would have got to me before now. But I'm not wasting any more time. I've got a small skiff waiting … but I'm not telling you anymore. I don't want to cause you anymore trouble.'

****

Mike's mother looked typically ill and worn out when she met her son after he reached her small suite of rooms on the tenth floor of Block Eight, Tennebola District. Jenzi Jozie Armoracia Tanniss, or 'Jenzijo' as his mother liked to be called, was slumped back in an armchair of the sort made in the early 21st century style, an out of vogue style now. This one was dull and threadbare.

After unlocking her door remotely, she didn't bother to get up as Mike entered and Mike knew exactly why. He didn't expect it either. He knew she still suffered from complications, mainly respiratory infections, developed as a result of self-neglect, following the scam to which she had fallen victim, some years ago. After Mike's father had died, Jenzijo had had the unenviable task, faced by so many single parents, of bringing up two boys on her own, though they were in their teens and had not long to go before adulthood. Mike had been thirteen but with a strong sense of independence even then, and his brother had been nearly sixteen, but was much more dependent on his mother. Jenzijo had done a wonderful job of bringing up her sons through, perhaps, the 'worst' of their teenage years. Mike had gone to the Uni-col (University) of the South Pacifica City States and obtained his first degree at the tender age of seventeen, funded by a bursary from the HS Astrophysics Collegium. That had indeed been fortunate since Jenzijo had had to use the relatively small sized estate left to her by her husband, to keep her other, 'high maintenance', son, Paulanda, maintained in the manner he seemed to expect. Paulanda had eventually left school-col, with minimal qualifications, got a job, albeit a poorly paid one, but later fell in with the wrong crowd.

Jenzijo herself, through naivety, did something similar, since once the boys were (mainly) out of her hair, she 'bond-joined' with a group of five other women and two men, all sharing wild sexual adventures, but little else. Then, three of the group were arrested, convicted of serious drug offences and sent to Mars. Suspicion fell on Jenzijo, even though she was innocent of the main offences, but she likely knew something of what the others were doing. She had been obstructive but because of the bond-joining she couldn't be charged. She had fallen then on hard times, unable to get anything other than menial, badly paid, work. This was the time when Mike was involved in a different sort of scandal with his higher mentor-degree tutor. He was simply not in a position to help her financially at the time, and Jenzijo's health had begun to decline, possibly because of her contact with her bond-joinees. It was exacerbated by a disastrous love affair she later got involved in, which left her seriously emotionally damaged, often suicidal.

At some point she came down with the symptoms of 'Deberens Syndrome', a slowly developing malady which had appeared, mainly, in the early 25th century and was, currently, with Turbotries' Disease, the only genuinely incurable diseases. But she was, Mike was aware, not too badly afflicted, so far. That might change for the worse and he wasn't sure about what happened then, but it probably meant registering her at a perma-sanitarium. That had serious financial implications. Hopefully, it was still some way off and Mike had quickly been able to start sending her slices of his income from his Secretariat job, once secured.

'Hello mum,' said Mike as he walked through the dark reception hallway and into her main room. She smiled weakly at him as she lay back on her rough sofa. Mike bent toward her, embracing her warmly as she finally struggled to rise from her seat. Mike asked her to please stay seated. She seemed smaller than when he'd last seen her. Knowing she sometimes found light painful he didn't bother to switch on the room's illumination. Her thin face, framed by prematurely greying locks, looked pale in the half light. She retained much of the good looks of her youth, despite the large folds of flesh that now sagged below her eyelids, a legacy of her medical problems. She had put on more weight around her midriff, but Mike was pleased to see she seemed just a little sprightlier in mood than he'd anticipated.

'Welcome, son. Welcome home,' she said in her somewhat deep, raspy, barely audible, voice. 'Sit down, Mike. How are you? How long are you home for?'

'I'm sorry mum. I can't stay long,' he said, sitting on the other threadbare couch in the room, facing her. He could smell cooked sweet potato and synth-beef coming from the dinette preparer. 'Can't you stay for some food?' she said, her face glowing with pleasure and momentary hope.

'Not really. Sorry. Got a few things to see to. If I get a chance, I'll stop by again before I go back to the ship but there's not much time left.'

'Are you going to see your brother?' she said, and her face turned serious. 'You know you should. He hasn't been well for such a long time now. I haven't seen him for – I don't know.'

Mike looked into her sad eyes.

'*He hasn't been well?*' he said, 'but mum, he "hasn't been well" all his life and it's not any real illness. It's all his own doing. You know that.'

'No, son. So how's that different from me, Mike? People say I'm not well because it's *my own doing.*'

'That's different, mum. Pauli's has been stuffing drugs down his throat for years and now the brain stim's got him. You just ... well, you just took a couple of wrong turns. We all do. Like everyone at some stage. Point is, he just hasn't made any effort, any time, and that's despite my efforts, lots of efforts, to try and help him. And yours, in the past. And help from his work colleagues – when he used to work. Everyone's "bent the hyper-tube" for him, but – no change. He's been on, what, six rehab courses? But ...'

Jenzijo's eyes were downcast and full of sorrow.

'Okay, I know, mum. I know. He's still my brother,' said Mike, feeling the rawness of her emotions. 'Listen, I'll go see him. I was ... sort of ... planning to, anyway. It's just that time's a bit tight. You know what work schedules are like.'

'I know. Isn't it always? Where you going off to now?'

'Back to Oceanus, I think. I wasn't sure if I wanted to carry on with The Monsoon, with the Navy, you know, but I've decided to go back – more or less.'

'Haven't you found a nice young woman – or man, to settle down with?'

'In my case it'd be a femna, mum.'

'Or a *few* nice young women?'

'Mum, you know I don't want polygamy.'

Jenzijo tried to laugh but her chuckles dissolved into stabbing, dry coughs. She recovered momentarily and said, 'Well, I've known you to be going around with more than one "femna" at a time, son.'

Mike smiled in embarrassment. He couldn't fool his mother. What son could?

'Yeah, alright, of course mum, but I wasn't into actually living with several women *at the same time.* You know I've got no time for that sort of thing. Not the registered type of arrangement, or the non-registered. It's just .... too messy.'

'No, son, you just like to have your truetype-ale and drink it. Never did want to settle down with anyone. Try one or two out, then move on, ain't it?'

Bleary though they were, there was still a twinkle in her eyes.

'I know but it's not like that anymore. Least, I don't think so, anyway,' he said, a pensive look spreading across his features.

'What does that mean, Mike? Is everything alright? Listen, I can read you like a holo-screen novel. You haven't got a girl in the bondo club or ...?'

'No! Nothing like that. You're going back a long time, mum. That sort of thing is guaranteed not to happen these days. Well, almost.'

'Then what is it?' she said as she peered deeply into his eyes, which he knew had, against his wish, become slick with moisture. He never wanted to upset her.

'Oh, there was ... someone ....' He hesitated to go further and Jenzijo suddenly began to cough repeatedly; one of the dry, racking bouts which were a symptom of the Deberens syndrome. She grasped at a tiny, silver coloured, cigar shaped, object that lay on a side table. Bringing it to her nose she attached it to her nostrils by means of its inbuilt self-adhesive pads and it pumped into her a rush of medication and pure oxygen, bringing relief to her lungs. She put it down after a minute or so.

Mike had stood and gently reached toward her. 'You okay now, mum? Can I get you something?' She shook her head and her eyes closed whilst she recovered her composure.

After a short pause, she said, 'Go on son. You were saying.'

Mike frowned and said, 'It's okay mum. Nothing you need to worry about. Maybe another time.'

'Have you done something bad son?'

'No, mum. Nothing of that sort. Like I said. It can wait for another time. Listen, I've got to go now.' With heavy heart, he started to rise and waited for the inevitable and heartbreaking pleadings for him to stay, and he was quite surprised when he didn't hear them. She might be improving after all. He'd felt she was a little better this time.

'Okay, son,' she said, with composure, 'I understand. Listen, Mike, don't worry 'bout me – and don't worry yourself to death over work. If it upsets you too much, go do something else. As for me, I know I sound bad but the money you've already sent helps lots. It helps me loadsa and I been saving it up. So don't you worry. I got plenty friends round here, too. Couple coming over tonight. It's just that I don't think I'll ever work again, that's all.'

'Hopefully you won't need to,' Mike said, 'and I'm glad you've got company. By the way, I definitely will go see Pauli before I have to go back. I promise.'

She smiled at that. They embraced again and he kissed her each on each side of her face before departing, smiling at her reassuringly as he walked out. Too late for him to *do something else,* as she'd suggested, he thought. He had stupidly neglected to put in for a transfer and if he didn't get back to The Monsoon before it departed, he'd be in breach of contract, and out of a job in the worst circumstances. And it meant he would likely have to pay the government a huge fine.

Now *that* wouldn't help him to make up the difference between what his mum could afford to pay from her 'medi-protect' insurance, and the actual cost. She had used up most of the money left by his father when he died twelve years ago. And the City State welfare benefits had been more than halved when they found out she had failed to heed medical advice about the Deberens. And he didn't believe she had 'saved' any funds.

No, Mike would have to go back to The Monsoon.

There was another thing he was only just starting to realise. He hadn't lied to Ebazza. During this very brief sojourn on Earth, he had begun to realise, more and more, how much he actually missed Oceanus. He missed the whole of that world, the people, the towns and the culture. Earth seemed gross now, by comparison. He was astounded by this turn around in his own outlook, though it was very real to him. But was it as simple as that, he wondered? There were still amazing possibilities on Earth, and he had friends here – and his family.

And these feelings for Oceanus were, he knew, ill fated. There could be no long-term future on 'Earth's sister world'. It was doomed, in a very real sense. His own sense of disquiet about that fact rivalled his feelings about his mother. He felt completely out of step, as though trying to straddle the mind-numbing distance between the two worlds, with a foot in both – and yet in neither. And what of a future in the Navy, now he seemed to have 'burned his landing boats' with Tenak? He would have to put in for the transfer he'd mentioned to Tenak. And yet, The Monsoon was by far the best ship in the fleet and the one which held most promise for the safe evacuation of Oceanus. What was he to do?

****

A large male, with a bulging, muscular, build, padded down the corridors of Earth Orbital Station One, his narrow eyes scanning the people walking past and milling about. He was taller than most people on the station, by at least 50 centimetres, and was wider across the shoulders than them too, but had a surprisingly narrow waist. His body shape down to the waist was a genuine, 'V' shape. And right now, his bulk was enlarged further by the hidden body protector he wore, a garment which had numerous utility pockets, in which he hid a bewildering array of devices; most of them designed to foil security and surveillance systems. Dervello had acquired these devices for him over a period of time. Today, his outer garment consisted of an innocuous looking, burgundy coloured, waist-length, cape of the new, fashionable, type.

He stopped outside the office suite of Bradlis Dervello, but before he had time to buzz, the door slid open. Dervello and his partner Talus Despinall stood inside, waiting for him.

'Welcome R,' said Dervello, with a half-smile, 'and yes, I can tell you picked up the protection we assigned you. Good. Did you have any problems?'

'Not at all, dominus,' said R, in a surprisingly high pitched and, some might say, cultured voice, emanating from a thin mouth set in a square, heavily jawed, face. Dervello regarded this associate of his and appeared to almost shrink from the fierce gaze which burned in R's dark eyes. Those armour piercing eyes moved constantly, as though always searching, scanning around.

'Excellent. Now, R, this is my good friend Talus,' said Dervello, 'who will provide you with the extra equipment you will need today. I am pleased to say we have been able to track our good friend, Yardis Sliverlight. He is currently on EOS Two, but we believe he will transfer to EOS Four, to gain access to his cabin suite – before trying to escape. We need to stop that happening. He is only a stupid ambassador. I'm sure you've read his file.'

R nodded in silence as Dervello continued, 'I don't think you'll have any problems there – but please contact me over the secure channel soon as possible, afterwards.'

'As you wish, dominus,' said R, his expression completely unchanged from the moment he had set foot in the office.

'Yes, I do wish,' said Dervello, his jaw setting firmly. He continued, 'You should not have any problems getting access to any of the Orbital Stations with the devices we're giving you. And it's amazing how a few well-placed bribes can make so many security guards look, "the other way". Please remember that we think Sliverlight has an associate. Unfortunately, we don't know who he, or she, is, or where they are. We're rather hoping you'll be able to tell us soon. Now, please follow my colleague, who will show you to your private shuttle.'

CHAPTER SIX

HUNT

In the city state he was now visiting Mike had to clear customs and security, for all the City States were fully functional, politically independent, structures, dependent, to varying degrees, only on trade. Mike walked along streets depressingly similar to those he had trodden in Metro-Britannia, but for the fact that these were 600 klicks away, in 'Norberingia'. This was a city state built on a massive artificial island on the edge of the sea formerly known as the North Sea. Originally built to accommodate population overspill from the older city states bordering the North Sea, the place had been largely depopulated over the last hundred years. It had an aura of decay about it and he was not surprised that his brother had 'retired' here. Not that it didn't have its more affluent areas or failed to keep up with modern stylistic and social fashions. And there wasn't a great deal to distinguish it from Mike's home city, with respect to life on the street. It was just 'seedier'.

At this time of year the weather was worse up here and chill sleet was borne on winds that swept down from the far north. Mike wore a large, fashionable, cape and gathered it around him as he made his way along pedways that were much more sparsely populated than in Metro-Britannia.

He had been relieved to get out of the hyper-train that had borne him here, a journey that had taken over two hours, and now he walked through an 'advertising experience' similar to the one in his own city but, if anything, more gross. At least, that's how he now felt. Although still very familiar with this aspect of modern Earth Mike's feelings of unease about the way life on his home planet were beginning to solidify, like a slowly building stone edifice of ugliness. He suspected he'd probably had the beginnings of such feelings for a long time but recent events, and his grief, were somehow reinforcing them.

He tried to pay no attention to the tirade of commercials, but still they seeped into his perception, like dampness into shoes on a rainy day. There were a lot of 'health' exhortations in this zone. One particularly lurid holo announced cheerfully, 'Is your heart misbehaving, or your liver letting you down? Do you have to drink less true-alc because of your med restrictions? If so, why not come to Arbromanski's Health Care Medi-Unit, and get the best synthetic organs money can buy? If you're a dependent minor don't forget to ask your guardian's permission to spend the money.'

Mike began to hurry in his effort to get to 'Domni's Galactic Hostel', a sleazy place where his brother was currently holed up. He passed by yet more commercials, including a strange one, unfamiliar even to him, which announced pleasantly, 'Are you dying of Turbotrie's Disease? And by the way, we're sorry to hear that, if you are. Make the most of the opportunities left to you by staying at our magnificent Mariolian Heights Grand Plaza hotel-apartments, west of Gobi City State. You won't regret spending your last days here with us. Call now, toll free, for a no-obligation quoter.'

That one left a rancid taste in his mouth. Trying to blot it all out, Mike began to reflect on the hours since he'd met his mother. He didn't think of himself as a depressive, but he had certainly been afflicted by a seemingly ever-present sinking feeling, recently, and nagging self-doubt, even self-dislike. He knew why, but he was damned if he could see a way out of the gloom. It was just grief, wasn't it? People always seemed to say it would pass, but how? When? The emotional pain had become so great, had reached such intensity recently, that he had even considered ending it all a few days ago. But it was just for a very short time. Deep down, he knew he couldn't really do it. Wouldn't.

After all, people relied on him, he mused, or did they? No, he wasn't the genuinely suicidal type, anyway. Was there a *type,* he wondered? Though thoughts of self-destruction had occupied but a few nasty moments, he was worried to have even had those kinds of thoughts. That, in turn had fed back into his general sense of gloom. Negative feedback. This was really not like him – but maybe that was in a different life, somehow. Not now, not anymore.

In the cold fug he'd found himself in he'd managed to get hold of a brain stim device, paying 500 credits to a young man he'd met in a bar near his apartment. He wisely hadn't asked where it had come from, but it had sat in his apartment for two days, dumbly staring at him. How could he criticise his brother anymore? And, in the end he had put it, unused, into an automated heavy goods recycler unit, near the town centre. He was in no doubt he had been seen by 'Universal Protection', the recycling agency used by the authorities, but he had disguised the unit well and it was unlikely there would be any repercussions. Brain stim was such a widespread habit the authorities could do little about it and they chose to do even less anyway. Besides, he was destroying one. Turning it over to a more purposeful usage, he hoped.

The previous day Mike had gone to another local bar, not wanting to meet the young 'stim vendor' again and had, this time, met two acolytes of 'Novo Camba dor'Jeharia', the new religious craze of the moment. It was something new to him, too. He hadn't really been interested and wondered why they had approached him, but the lead acolyte, who called himself, 'Swami Bullfrog', told him that he looked sad and that he *knew* he had suffered a personal tragedy. That had captured Mike's attention, yet he knew where paying these guys attention could lead. But the exhortations he'd expected, to join their brethren, did not materialise, and instead, Bullfrog had listened attentively while Mike had actually talked about his loss and grief.

It was the first time he had opened up to anyone about it and it had felt good. Bullfrog had said that only Mike could find his way out of the 'clutching tendrils of personal gorbo-grief'. It was important for him, he'd said, to find release from the grip of 'Baradroum', the thief of positive emotions, but find it he must. Otherwise, he would die. Mike had started to lose interest by then and began to make his excuses, but Bullfrog had said one last thing which, on reflection, he reckoned he now understood. Bullfrog had said he could find release by simply accepting what had happened; by not blaming anyone for it, particularly not himself, and by getting involved once more in the thing which he was best at doing, that he liked most. It would be what his 'lost one' would have told him to do. But only Mike knew what that one thing was, he'd said.

Was that it, thought Mike? He was now struck by its simplicity. This 'singularity' in a world of enormous complication and insanity? That discussion had been a couple of days ago but he was still contemplating the words of Bullfrog when he reached the run-down building where Paulanda, his brother, lived.

Perhaps he should have told Bullfrog to pay Paulanda a visit.

The building was sixty floors high and coloured a drab, unpainted grey. Some shadowy characters, wearing the waist length, shaggy, unkempt, 'hair dos, popularised by some of the banned, underground, ultra-violent holos, emerged from the building. They took a long swig of a look at him, as he pressed an old-fashioned call buzzer on the front wall, next to a cavernous, dirty portico entrance. After a long delay his brother's grainy image appeared on a dull and greasy screen. Paulanda opened the door remotely, Mike went in and took the hyperlift and, in a matter of thirty seconds or so, reaching the fortieth floor, where his brother lived. At least that machine worked properly, he thought. Usually, they didn't.

Paulanda Veternius Tanniss, stood outside his small flat, some way down a gloomy, musty smelling corridor. He looked quite different from Mike, though he shared his height. His brother's face was long and gaunt, with sunken eyes, and his long, fair, hair, though styled in the current 'upper eskelon' fashion, looked unkempt.

Mike was determined not to be too prejudiced. His brother's sunken eyes betrayed pain and he didn't want to add to that.

'So, Mikey,' said Paulanda, words bereft of enthusiasm or much warmth, even if not hostile. 'Why such an unusual visit, brother, and why now?' He waved a hand to suggest Mike should sit opposite his own scruffy seat, on a scruffy, stained, 'sofa', which stood no higher than 10 centimetres off the floor. Mike thought it felt cold in the flat, but not unbearable. It looked as though his brother was still being supported by the State – but only just.

'You're welcome, Pauli,' said Mike, trying to keep the sarcasm out of his voice, 'but, why do you think I came? I wanted to see you, of course. How're you doing?' Mike actually managed to inject some enthusiasm into his words.

'Well, I was thinking of catching a ship and flying by sub-orbital, over to the fabled Palace of grand Machaland, then bathing in the crystal-clear waters of the High Tormo Springs. How does it look like I'm doing, Mikey?' His brother scowled at him.

Mike closed his eyes. He had known this was going to be difficult but maybe not *this difficult*. Still, he had to try to keep things even. Stay polite, he thought, if only for mum's sake.

'Listen, Pauli. There's no need for all that,' he said softly, 'I was just concerned about you. Mum said you weren't well. Will you tell me what's wrong? And please don't say "everything". You never know, maybe I could help.'

'No, I never know. And that's rich talk, coming from you. But I suppose mum's right, if you call being addicted to brain stim being "unwell". And I don't know how *you* can make it better. So you've wasted your time coming here, *Mikey*.'

'It's not … it's not a waste of time Paulanda. And there's no need to call me … oh, never mind. I wouldn't have come here if I thought it was a waste of time. And you, well you've been addicted to stim a long time now. We've talked about this before. I don't know what else to say, except that there are clinics that could help. Legit' ones. Not like some of the ones you've tried.' Mike knew his brother had never really *tried*.

'Clinics? Don't trust 'em. Never have. Just want your money – and I haven't got any – as you know.'

'That's cos you haven't worked – for years,' said Mike, feeling his patience ebbing away, despite himself.

'Oh, yeah, Mikey man. I know the story. "Just get a job. You'll be okay then." As if …'

'Well, it couldn't hurt, could it?'

'You sound like dad.'

'He had a point.'

If you'd stuck around after he died, maybe I *would* have got a job. Done better. You were supposed to be looking after us. After me, Mike.'

'I was *thirteen*. Besides, you were always …'

'But you just left...'

'After a couple of years, Pauli.'

'...And went to Uni-coll, then joined that damnatious Navy. Flew away didn't you. Forgot about us.' Paulanda's voice started to rise with excitement.

'This is just ... nonsense Pauli. You know it.'

'You were supposed to look after us, Mikey.'

'I had to go. I had every right. And you've forgotten something, Pauli. Isn't it supposed to be the *older sibling* who "looks after the others"? You're the older one, Pauli. You! But all you did is drink. Then it was brachystim, then brain stim. You behaved as if dad's death just affected you. But we *all* hurt, Pauli. All of us. At least I got some qualo's and a job and I've been able to help mum with the money. What did you do?'

He knew he was starting to sound vituperative, and he wanted to stop, but things had to be said. He continued, but his tone softened, 'Dad died nearly twelve years ago. It's time to move on, brother. He wouldn't have wanted to see you like this. He loved you as well as me. Every bit as much as me.' Mike felt his mood dropping. He would have to leave soon. This wasn't helping anyone.

'It's not dad's death anyway, you dope, Mikey. It's ... just everything. I'm ... artistic. You know that. Always have been. Working just don't suit me. I've fell on hard times, that's all.'

'Through your own doing, Pauli ...' Mike's words came out more as a barely audible mutter.

Then Mike's wristcom buzzed softly. He glanced at it, suppressed the AV signal and just read the 3D text message that flashed in mid-air, a couple of centimetres above the device's face. It was an automated message from The Monsoon, which simply read, 'The Monsoon leaves Earth orbit in twenty-eight hours, thirty-six minutes and counting.'

Mike's heart gave a small leap as he realised he'd have to catch a shuttle flight from the surface very soon – a flight *he hadn't yet booked.* Flights from this quadrant went mainly to Earth Orbital Station Two. He might not be able to get a direct flight to

EOS Four, where the Monsoon was moored, so he'd then need to get connecting shuttles. All at short notice. Damnatious!

'I've got to go, Pauli. I'm sorry,' he said, starting to rise. His brother just scowled again, more to himself than Mike, and sighed like it was his last breath.

'You should be pleased, I guess,' said Mike, catching his brother's expression of frustration as he spoke, 'cos I thought you weren't too keen on me being here, anyway.'

'Okay. Just go on your way, Mikey. Off you go again, like you do.'

Mike gave an ironic chuckle and said, 'It isn't exactly a joy to come here.' He made for the door; an old-fashioned type that actually opened on hinges. He'd got the door partly open, when he sighed and turned back to Paulanda, who, surprisingly, had also risen and had hurried down the passageway behind him. Paulanda stopped a couple of metres away; a slight figure silhouetted in the half light. Mike walked back to him.

'I'm sorry, Pauli. I'm sorry if you think I'm to blame for your troubles. I never meant to cause you hurt … and I really regret it, if that's what I've done.' He started to turn back to the door, but his brother reached forward and, with a cold hand, gently grasped one of Mike's arms. Paulanda's face looked sincere, mournful, his eyes large and regretful.

'I'm sorry too,' he said.

Mike felt tears well up in his eyes. He didn't want to blub again. Instead, he grasped Paulanda's arms gently and said, 'Yes, I know you are. Listen Pauli, I really do have to go now, and it could be a few weeks before I'm back. But I promise I'll look you up then. And, if you want, I'll book into a clinic you can go to – but only if you want. It'll be on me, too. And I'll see it through with you, if you want. I can't say fairer than that now, can I?'

'No, Mike. It won't be like that,' said Paulanda with a firm look in his eyes now, '*I'll look you* up. As for the clinic idea, well, it sounds kind of okay, so I'll think about it – seriously. *Now I can't say fairer than that, can I?*'

Mike's eyes were wet, and inside he felt like shouting for joy, but he didn't want Pauli to see that, so he just squeezed his brother's arms affectionately and bade him farewell.

****

In his cabin, on EOS Two, rotating six hundred kilometres above the Earth, Ambassador Yardis Sliverlight was hurriedly stuffing clothes into a large carryall bag. It was 0200, and this part of the station was deserted. His cabin buzzer sounded and he asked his comp-unit to show the caller. The screen nearest to him lit up, showing the scene outside. The cam above his door gave him an acute view of the corridor, the lights of which were slightly dimmed for night-time. A very small girl stood outside, facing his door. She seemed, maybe, seven years old? And she was crying. Sliverlight's face took on a concerned expression and he spoke to her via his screen intercom.

'Are you okay, little Mes? What's the matter?'

'I ... I think I'm I'm lost' sobbed the child. 'My mom was here a minute ago but she ... she's gone. And I've never been here before, Mer. Please help me. Please.' The girl's voice sounded strangely muffled over the intercom. The face of the child on the screen then appeared to dissolve in floods of tears.

With a deeply puzzled but empathic expression, Sliverlight went to his desk unit and tapped it, asking the comp to contact Central Control aboard the station. The unit told him that due to a tek problem the contact couldn't be made. His puzzled expression turned to a deep frown. The little girl spoke again, via the intercom, 'Please help, Mer. I don't know what to do.'

'Um, I'm rather busy,' he said. 'Have you tried any of the other rooms?'

'Yes,' she said, through her sobs, 'but no-one answers. Please help.'

Then Sliverlight remembered. He'd asked for a flat in the 'quietest' zone of this hab ring. He hadn't wanted to risk anyone else being around while he was preparing to leave. He meant to get away within the next 30 minutes. A 'friendly' pilot would be waiting to take him to Docking Bay Six, and then off to Moon Station Imbrium. From there he'd catch a deep space tug, whose pilot he'd already bribed, to go on to the outer asteroid belt, where he'd lie low for a year or two.

The girl started to cry again. He could have asked the intercom unit to give him a direct view of her face but, instead, huffing with impatience, he walked to the door. He'd just talk to her briefly and send her down to the station hub for help, but she would probably need some guidance. He asked the door to open and as he did so he glimpsed the silhouette of a large man standing immediately outside. His instincts kicked in. He threw his left arm toward the emergency 'close' panel on the wall nearest to him and shouted for it to close but his words came over as ragged.

The huge man barged forward in a flash, as Sliverlight grasped for the panel, knocking him right down the hallway of his cabin. Sliverlight grunted loudly with pain as he landed against a wall. Wide eyed, he struggled to get up.

'Who the feg are you?' he spat at the stranger who now loomed above him. He had moved at lightning speed. The intruder ordered the door to close. Sliverlight ordered it to re-open. It didn't obey.

'Look, Mer Ambassador,' said the man, known as 'R' to his associates and enemies, 'let's not make any trouble, shall we? I'm in control now. Just take it easy. All I need to know is what you've done with the surveillance flakes.' The bulky intruder's voice was surprisingly high pitched for a man of his size, but it had a hacksaw edge to it which gave it a raw and menacing inflection. Sliverlight got up but before he could open his mouth the intruder had lunged forward again and pushed his victim backwards, all the way into the lounge. Sliverlight was on the floor again, winded.

'Sorry about that but I needed to show you it's no use saying you don't know what I'm talking about. Everyone says that. So, I'll ask again. What did you do with the surveillance flakes? Oh, and by the way, who's working with you? Mustn't forget that.'

Sliverlight stared at the man's square face, a visage which looked as though it were made of granite. The eyes were like rough, glinting, quartz set in grey stone.

The Ambassador glanced furtively at his couch and said, 'Okay. I guess you're working for Ultima, or New Rebels. That right?'

No answer, just a continuing glare from the intruder, standing just a couple of metres away.

'Okay. No more trouble. I understand you need to know. It's over there,' said Sliverlight, pointing toward a low cupboard on the left side of the room. The man started to look in that direction and Sliverlight immediately threw himself to his right, sliding across the floor, then throwing an arm under the couch. His grasping fingers found the butt of the ultra-stun-gun hidden there and he dragged it out, all in one fluid movement. But the intruder threw himself out of his way as Sliverlight hefted the gun, and with practised fluidity, pointed it toward the assailant. On the gun's tiny screen, Sliverlight caught a glimpse of the intruder, fired the hyper-focussed, sonic beam, shooting slightly wide of the target, widely missing the intruder's chest. He'd rushed it. R hit the floor smoothly, rolled and came up the other side of the couch, brandishing a small, shiny, metallic device.

Sliverlight lost sight of the man, for a moment, as he used the back of the couch for cover. The Ambassador paused for second, and that was his downfall, as R launched himself from the far end of the couch and fired a salvo of *something* metallic toward Sliverlight.

The Ambassador yelped with shock as a tightly grouped set of small, spinning, metal discs struck him across his chest, midriff and right arm, making the hyper-stunner tumble out of his hand. The discs had bitten hard into Sliverlight's flesh and the intense burning sensation they caused made him scream. He could feel the still spinning discs continuing to cut, as they moved more deeply into him.

'They'll stop spinning in a few seconds,' said the intruder, puffing slightly, 'but they've caused lots of damage. I'd say two have hit your chest. They'll cause internal bleeding but not so much to stop us having a nice little talk first. They're not meant to kill you straight. Just disable you. And you're a right little feisty one, aren't you? Where did you get that weapon from?'

R stepped closer to Sliverlight, who just sat on the carpeted floor, blood pouring from various wounds, soaking into the woven textile. His assailant picked up the hyper-stunner and examined it more closely.

'Goodness, gracious, Mer Ambassador. What's a person like you doing with a gun like this? I was lucky. If this beam had hit my chest it would have killed me for sure.' He sat next to Sliverlight and stuffed the gun into one of the larger utility pockets on his body suit.

Sliverlight, very dazed now and still sitting on the floor next to his attacker, said, weakly, 'Who are you? I don't understand. What's with … the little girl thing?'

'Ah yes, good, wasn't it? Another little device I've got. I like you, so I'll tell you about it. By the way, my name is, R. No harm in you knowing, now. Amongst other things, my little toy jams signals on com units and makes minor surveillance cameras, like the ones in the corridors, transmit *what I want* them to transmit. It can't fool straight human eyesight of course but … well, you know the rest.'

Sliverlight gazed at him in horror, as R continued, speaking very softly, 'Listen to me fellaman. You'll see I'm not a needlessly cruel man. That may surprise you, but it's true. I just want some answers. You know which ones. Why don't you save yourself a lot of trouble and just tell me what I want to know? Eh?'

'I don't know what …' began Sliverlight but the attacker suddenly stood, pointed his strange gun at him and, with no further warning, fired again. Another salvo of small, spinning discs, shot into Sliverlight's body and, then his face. One hit his left cheek, slicing it completely open. Sliverlight screamed again and his cry ended in sobs as he clutched at his bloody face and chest. The attacker began to search around Sliverlight's cabin. 'This could go on for hours, Mer … whoever you are. You're not an ambassador, for sure. Best tell me now and get it over with, quickly.'

Sliverlight slumped over till he was prone. He groaned wretchedly. After a few moments, gasping, he asked,

'What … are those disc things? I feel terrible … all over. Like …. acid … inside.'

'Oh, I forgot to tell you. They're covered with toxins. When they stop spinning, they start to dissolve the tissue surrounding them – slowly. Like I said, you can end this whenever you want, but you know what you have to do.'

As Sliverlight watched him, R found his victim's clothes bag, prepared for escape, and started rifling through it. 'By the way, I'd also like to know who you really are. No-one in the diplomatic service uses a gun like that. Ah, I think I've found something.' R pulled an innocent looking comb case out of the bag. 'I've seen this sort of trick before,' he said as he turned over the faux leather case, and, pulling a small knife out of his jacket, cut off the outer layer of the case. Out popped a small plastiform tablet. He glanced at Sliverlight, smiled and gleefully pulled a small cube shaped device out of his jacket, then held it next to the tablet. The device made a low humming sound as R looked at a readout display.

'Ah, so there we have it,' he said, walking back across the room toward Sliverlight. 'As I thought. This is your *real* ID flake. Well, hello, "Home System Government Agent Jeramis". Now, *that* explains the special gun. The Navy are the only other people who can get those guns, and I knew you weren't Navy. You've been leading all of us a merry dance, haven't you? Everyone. I only wish the other info I needed was so easily to hand. Have you decided to give me the name of your associate, and their location? We know there is one from various transmissions that you passed something on. So, let's have it. Now, please.'

Sliverlight had pushed his upper body off the floor, his arms trembling, and he just stared at the floor. R fetched a new magazine of discs from a pocket and made a show of removing the empty one and attaching the new one to his gun. Sliverlight groaned and his eyes widened in horror, 'Okay. Okay,' he said breathlessly and with increasing weakness, 'My associate …is …is Gronnington.'

'Gronnington who?' R said, raising the gun.

'Arpelk …Aristobulus Gronnington Arpelk,' said Sliverlight and sank back to the floor in utter defeat – and utter shame.

'Not enough,' said his tormentor. 'Where's this Arpelk usually located? Where's he now and what is his agency function?'

Sliverlight tried, in vain, to sit up but sank to the floor again. 'I've said too much already. Go to hell you monster,' he breathed, his voice rasping desperately with the effort.

His attacker simply raised the gun again and fired another salvo which made Sliverlight scream again.

'It was just two discs that time, *Mister* Agent. I can pump more in if you like?'

'No, please no, I'll tell you. I'll tell you, said Sliverlight, so quietly now that R could hardly hear him, so he stepped nearer but kept the gun trained on his victim, 'Say again, my mascla.'

'He's a tek specialist. Tek .... based on ... EOS Four. Third ring. Third ring,' he said through his sobs. He said something else, but it was inaudible, even at close quarters.

'R stood and said, 'There. You see. Wasn't so difficult, was it? You could have saved yourself a lot of trouble.' He walked away from his victim who had rolled over onto his back and lay, trembling, groaning mindlessly. The assailant reached the door, then paused and went back to his semi-conscious victim.

'You could take days to die, I suppose. Lots of pain. I told you I wasn't a needlessly cruel man, didn't I?'

Standing well back, R pulled a dark blue, cigar shaped, device out of yet another utility pocket, opened one end and pointed it at Sliverlight. Then he squeezed the other end between his fingers. The end pointing toward Sliverlight seemed to flash – but in utter silence – and a projectile shot out of it into Sliverlight's upper body, where it exploded. Producing just a muffled noise it blew a hole the size of a large dinner plate in the man's chest. Blood and lung tissue spattered widely but not so widely as to splash R, who turned on his heels and left the room, checking the now normally functioning vid intercom, to ensure the corridor was clear.

****

As he sat in the crisp, plush, seat of the passenger shuttle Mike actually looked forward to returning to The Monsoon, and to Oceanus. Amazing, he thought. He'd finally managed to book a seat to EOS Four, the station nearest the ship. For security reasons, The Monsoon had, apparently, been recently moved to a position about 50 kilometres from the Station, where it floated along in the exact same orbit as EOS Four.

To get to the ship Mike would have to catch a smaller shuttle from the station itself. He wondered if a Navy boat might be moored to EOS Four. Probably too much to hope for. He might have to slip a station engineer a few credits to take him across on a tug.

As so-called 'weightless' conditions took over he peered out of the nearest window. The Earth was spread out below him, in all its blue and white glory. It was a small window and, fortunately, he didn't feel overwhelmed by the view. Once again, the similarities with Oceanus struck him, and yet, the differences too. It made his pulse quicken now to think about Oceanus, despite all the emotional resonances and the things that had happened there. He pondered the Earth's predominantly brown and green land masses, so subtly different to the blue-greens and purples of Oceanus. He realised how much he wanted to get back to that other ocean world – but wondered what returning to that planet would hold for him, now. First, he had to make it over to the ship. Would he get there in time? Would they leave without him? Well, yes, they would if he was not ready to board.

For the first time perhaps, he felt that Eleri was, in some way, not completely 'gone'. He knew she would ever be present in his mind, in his heart. But was she not also there, on Oceanus, in the wild, blue oceans, in the heart of the forests and the glades, in the Ra-shine and in the winds and the rain? Just like that well known, ancient, poem, said. His eyes started to well up and he tried to force himself to think of other things, yet these same feelings about her brought him some sort of comfort in some ways.

There were only about twenty others aboard the large passenger shuttle, so he felt almost alone. Somehow, it seemed he had felt alone for a long time now, though he knew that wasn't really true. But that feeling was why he wanted to get back into the normal 'business' of the ship, yet that dismayed him too. He didn't know what to think. As he gazed out the window, he saw a silver speck in the distance, floating above the Earth. Within ten minutes that speck had become a small three ringed wheel, turning around what looked like a thick, grey-blue, stumpy core. Ten minutes later the rings had filled the field of view, the shuttle having slowed to a relative 'crawl', in order to enter a gigantic hangar, like a cavernous mouth, in one end of the station's axial hub.

Shortly after debarking Mike floated along wide corridors, with his carry bag strapped to his back, heading for the Security Clearance Zone, where his luggage was checked, and he was body-scanned by four different machines. After that he made his way to the Spoke Elevator station and gratefully emerged onto the third ring, where he knew he might be able to find a government 'contact' who might just be able to get him a ride over to The Monsoon.

****

Gronnington Arpelk stood in his cabin, making final adjustments to a hand-held device that looked a little like a spray gun with a long tube and a wide sieve-like muzzle. He had been studying the station's log manifests and had selected his victim with great care. He'd decided that someone from the Navy was the best bet and one person in particular had drawn his attention. Arpelk's technical skills had enabled him to dig out lots of details about this person; someone who had spent quite a few days on the station, just a few weeks ago. Best of all, he had originally debarked from The Monsoon. Excellent! That would be the best possible means of transmitting the devastating information data flake he now held in his hand.

The Monsoon's overall commander was currently none the renowned Admiral Arkas Tenak, and his highly regarded Captain was Ssanyu Ebazza. Both were, in his view, trustworthy. But he couldn't get intimate access to these people. The data he had to safeguard couldn't be entrusted directly to the government itself. There were too many massive holes, too many double agents and quislings. He couldn't do anything with it himself, as he too had to go into hiding – soon. He was very vulnerable, and his own credentials could be easily impugned. It seemed that even the Navy had not been entirely invulnerable to quislings, he had learned, but Tenak was, he thought, beyond reproach, or as near as dammit. He had to be. Everything now depended on it. He had to ensure the data got to him soon.

**

Mike walked along the spacious corridor of Ring Three. Only a handful of other people were making their way along the upwardly curving deck, and they disappeared from view as he passed by a series of cabin doors. This was a very quiet part of the station, thought Mike and then, he heard a noise. Someone whispering?

'Hey, you, Mike Tanniss?'

He glanced across at the open door to his right side and saw a short, stout, man beckoning him to approach. Mike didn't stop but slowed his walk just a little.

'Who are you? What do you want?' asked Mike loudly. He was determined to carry on walking unless this mascla had anything vital to say.

The man came out of his room and said, in a reassuring, calm, manner, 'It's okay Mer Tanniss. I'm a friend of Admiral Tenak. He asked me to give you some important information.'

'Oh yeah?' said Mike. He was not inclined to believe this person. The stranger glanced nervously up and down the corridor, as if confirming that no-one else was around. Then he quickly raised a small box-like device in front of him. It emitted a loud click. Nothing else happened, as far as Mike could tell, but he found the man's behaviour unsettling.

I seem to attract all the weirdos, he thought, and started to move on. What he didn't realise was that all the vid surveillance cams were now inoperative in that sector. He also failed to notice the man creeping up behind him, silently, on tip toe, and raising a gun-like object. He turned at the last second and saw the gun emit a fine white spray, as the man said, 'I'm so sorry, Mer Tanniss. This won't hurt you I promise. I'm real sorry. You'll just sleep for a while. Easy now.'

Mike's head began to spin, and he suddenly felt his strength go. The still conscious part of his brain shouted, *grotachalik!* Then, somehow, he remembered the gun thing that the stranger had used, so it couldn't be the Oceanus sea creature, could it? He began to feel numb all over and powerless to resist as he felt the stranger drag him inside his apartment. He felt his consciousness continue to fade as he heard the stranger talking to him. How odd. He didn't sound threatening or abusive at all. He was actually trying to *reassure* him, quite genuinely it seemed.

'You're the one who's going to have to be the carry-man for the data flake, I'm afraid,' said the stranger to Mike's prone body, once inside his apartment, 'I can't get to Tenak myself, but you're his friend.' Through the murk starting to enclose his mind Mike felt a sharp prick in his lower neck. Arpelk had pressed a small syringe-like instrument into the flesh near the collar bone. Mike tried to say something, but nothing came out.

'Shush, Mer Tanniss,' said Arpelk, 'you'll be okay in a few hours, but you'll remember nothing about what happened here. Believe me when I say the drug spray is perfectly harmless. I've injected a data flake deep into your neck. It won't excite security scans but it'll start to hurt in a few weeks, like it wants to come out, and that will, I'm sorry to say, get worse, till you have a medical exam. At least, I'm hoping you'll be sensible enough to get one. Any decent deep-field scan will show the flake and it'll be removed. That's how I'm hoping it'll get to Tenak's notice. They'll know what to do when they realise what it is. Why a data flake, you're wondering, if you're wondering anything right now? Well, a signal could get hijacked. Might be intercepted by the wrong people. If it's encrypted, it'll only get decrypted by someone with the decryption key. No, a flake is much better, a physical object thrust, as it were, into the right hands. And it doesn't involve the use of transmission devices.

'Listen now, Mer Tanniss, it's important that you don't know anything about what's behind this. For your own safety. Fare thee well now and do the job I've given you. And I don't know why I'm telling you all this. You'll have forgotten it all in a few minutes.'

Mike had heard most of this, but then sank into a deep blackness. And, within no time at all, it seemed – he was awake again and found himself on the floor of the station's corridor, propped up against its wall. He couldn't work out where he was. Passers-by were staring and avoiding him. He heard a woman with a loud voice say, 'These brain-stim addicts get everywhere. Why do we put up with it?'

He tried to rise, only managing with difficulty and pushed himself away from the wall, as though in a drunken stupor. Almost by instinct he began to move along the corridor but was aware he was staggering. There was nothing he could do about it.

His legs wouldn't do what his brain was telling them. He collided with a man walking past him, but he hardly felt it. The stranger glared angrily, pushed him away roughly and shouted, 'Get out of the way, flick-wit.'

He continued to stagger, trying to clear his mind of the terrible fog that filled it. What was happening? What had he taken that would have this effect? As he reached a kaffee salon Mike managed to plonk down on the nearest chair and his head slumped forward involuntarily. His rational brain started to surface momentarily, as though from the slumber of ages. I don't remember drinking or taking drugs, or stim, he thought. He heard a young man's voice nearby and opened his eyes to see a round, pale, face, very close, staring down at him. The face spoke. The words were slightly indistinct.

'I'm afraid you won't be able to stay here – unless you buy a drink, sir. Are you okay? Have you been taking something?' This was a table-tend. He seemed a little alarmed, but his voice was calm and not threatening.

'Haven't … been … taking an-thing,' said Mike, working hard not to slur his words. He continued, 'but then 'gain, I think … mo'… might have another attack of … grota … doesn't matter. I might be a bit unwell … think it should pass soon, so. Could I … please stay here for a bit. Just bit. Listen. Look, I'll order a kaffee, if … like.'

The waiter glanced around, self-consciously, saw one of his bosses, a woman, looking at him suspiciously. He went over to talk to her. Mike hoped the guy would reassure the woman and, indeed, whatever the waiter said seemed to work. He was left in peace. At least for a moment.

****

After 'switching on' the corridor surveillance devices again Arpelk hurried about in his apartment, sorting through his various tek equipment and paraphernalia. His haste was motivated by the desire to get off the station as soon as possible, now he had sent the surveillance data-flake on its way. His intercom door buzzer sounded.

He ordered the intercom screen to switch on and saw a strange sight: a small, young girl standing on her own, right outside his cabin. She turned and said she was lost but as she did so the image flickered slightly, on and off, very rapidly. For a split second he thought he saw something, or someone else, almost superimposed on her image. Then her image stabilised.

'Switch off my corridor vid,' said Arpelk to his comp, 'there's something wrong with it. Switch on my private cam.'

Arpelk had installed his own, special, device in the frame of the door long ago, for extra security, and it now paid dividends, for a new image appeared in place of the girl. It was a very large man, wearing a bulky utility jacket. The man paced about outside the door, and then he stared directly up at Arpelk's camera.

'Who are you?' asked Arpelk, with a voice that betrayed alarm, 'and what do you want? Just so you know – I can see you're not a little girl. I ain't sure how you did that or why. Maybe you'll tell me, but I'd sooner you go away.'

The stranger said nothing but Arpelk could see the man on the screen staring, as if he could actually see him. His eyes looked as though they could penetrate metre thick steel. Then the man moved very fast, darting away and disappearing out of shot. Arpelk ordered the vidcam to angle downwards, then to the right and left, but there was no sign of him. Whoever this stranger was, he was bad news. Gronnington went to a cupboard and slid open its door, frantically searching for a weapon he could use, in case the stranger came back – and somehow managed to get in the apartment.

Then he heard a peculiar noise coming from somewhere nearby but couldn't locate the source. Silence returned and he resumed his search, but with more urgency. He suddenly remembered Mike Tanniss. He still had files about the ship's Secretary on his screen unit. He had to delete them – right now. If something happened to him, his plan, and that of the Home System Deep Security Team, would be forfeit. He leapt to the desk unit and told it to delete all records about Michaelsonn Tanniss. A neutral electronic voice issued from the unit, saying, *May I remind you that you deleted the subroutine allowing this command because you wished to prevent unauthorised access by voice synthesiser.*

He'd forgotten. Damnatious! Cursing loudly, Arpelk began to use the old fashioned, but still functional, keyboard in front of the unit's screen. Tanniss's files started to appear on the screen, in cascading sets of graphics. He would have to wait for all of them to upload before he could hit the 'final delete' key.

As the files continued to fill the screen Arpelk heard a loud bang above him and a kind of scraping noise. He looked up instantly, just in time to see the man who'd stood outside, now hanging head-first from the ceiling, holding a large metal grill, and peering down at him.

'Piphoo! I'm here,' said the stranger, with a chuckle. Arpelk sat transfixed for a moment, his mouth gaping. 'How did you....?'

'I knew this was the oldest part of the station,' said the huge man, 'and it's still got the old-fashioned ventilation shafts and grills. Not much room in here for a man like me but – well, I made it. Catch this!' He threw the grill with tremendous force, taking Arpelk by complete surprise. Arpelk threw his arms up instinctively and managed to bat away the grill, but as it bounced to the side he felt his forearms reverberate from the blow, and in seconds the pain had shot into his hands. Blood glistened on a wrist. The man in the ceiling was hauling himself out of the hatch. Arpelk dashed underneath him and made for the door, but the attacker was already landing, nimbly, behind him.

'Not so fast,' shouted the intruder and Arpelk felt a searing pain in back of his right forearm as his flesh was pierced by some sort of long spike, a thing with a small, lethal hook at its end. Horrifyingly, the barb of the hook had hit only flesh and had come right through the front of his arm. He was caught like a fish. He roared with agony and shock.

The stranger started to pull him back but Arpelk leaned forward, despite the excruciating pain it produced in his arm. That was when he saw the weapon he'd been searching for earlier; a small, synthplast gun. He had placed it on a high shelf of the cupboard and, with his left hand he reached out, grasped it, and turned round so he was partly facing backward, over his hooked right arm. He shrieked with pain but gritting his teeth he concentrated on holding the gun steady and aiming it over his shoulder. Then he fired.

His huge assailant saw the gun at the last second and twisted so as to try to evade its aim but he was too late, as the weapon fired and a small part of the man's utility jacket, on the edge of his upper right arm, seemed to explode. The fabric tore open. The aggressor yelped with pain and relaxed his grip on his hook-like weapon, but he recovered in a flash, snarled and renewed his hold very quickly. Pulling Arpelk around to face him he punched him incredibly fast, connecting with the side of his victim's head, knocking him over and causing Arpelk to lose his grip on the gun.

As his victim virtually hung from the hook, slumping down to the floor, R said, breathlessly, 'Very clever, Mer Agent. A projectile gun. No-one uses those anymore, 'sept in military ops. I nearly caught it then. You're even feistier than your colleague, Mer agent Jeramis. That was before I killed him.'

Arpelk looked up with wide eyes, then growled at his attacker,

'You bastardo.'

'Now, now! I won't have swearing. I don't believe in it. Come here, Mer agent,' said R, and kicking the small gun out of reach, he yanked Arpelk, into a sitting position, like a limp doll. His victim seemed to have become lethargic, as though delirious from drink.

'Now,' said R, 'I want you to tell me what you've done with the surveillance info, and I hope I don't have to use the same force as I did on your colleague.'

****

Mike Tanniss stared at the cold mug of kaffee in front of him and saw that an older man was speaking to the friendly waiter and pointing at him. The older man came over. 'I've been told you've been here too long, mer,' he said apologetically, 'and you haven't drunk anything, or ordered anything else. They're getting tetchy, you see. I'm sorry.' Mike could see the man but his features, and even his outline, seemed to be undulating in front of his bleary eyes.

'It's … okay,' said Mike, trying his best to concentrate on what was being said, 'cos I'm a-goin' now – I think.' He rose slowly and started to move away from the table but the woman he'd seen earlier rushed up to him and demanded he pay for the drink. The waiter tried to say that Mike hadn't drunk any of it, but she silenced him with a stare. Mike couldn't really comprehend what the problem was, and looking at the woman said, 'You look nice – I think. What … um, is the problem, Madama-mada..?'

'You haven't paid. That's what's wrong. Either you give me three credits – right now – or I'll call security.' As stupefied as he felt Mike was well aware of the harshness of her voice.

Finally, understanding what he was expected to do he began to search in the pockets of the loose civilian clothing he wore but couldn't find his payment block. The woman sneered and said, 'I see. Can't find it? Have you got a wristcom you can use, or something like that? Well, have you?' Her voice was becoming shrill and was attracting attention from all around. Mike just dithered but the woman caught a glimpse of something shiny on his left wrist and, grabbing his left arm, pulled up the sleeve of his loose top.

'Hey!' Mike said, 'get off … off me.' The woman gripped onto his arm tightly and placed a small white box next to Mike's wristcom before he could pull his arm away. It was presumably meant to extract payment, but Mike's device was a Navy unit and more advanced than most ordinary wristcoms – as well as being more secure. She shook Mike's arm and said,

'Make it work. Make it work, or I'll get station security over here right now.'

With a huge effort of concentration Mike understood what he needed to do, pulled his arm from the woman, indignantly, and held it near his mouth. Then he hesitated, unsure what to do next.

'Oh, Maker, Maker!' the woman moaned, 'he doesn't know what standard day of the week it is, does he?' Bending down, so her snarling face came closer to Mike's, she said, with acidic aggression,

'Mer, you're gonna be so sorry, 'less you make your device pay up right now. No more chances, Mer.'

The young table-tend and older man stared at her, the young one saying,

'Is it kind of … legal, to do this?'

'I don't care,' she said, 'but even if it ain't, neither is trying to leave without paying,'

Then she turned back to Mike. In the meantime, Mike had gathered just enough of his senses to understand his dilemma and breathily told the wristcom to comply, whereupon the white device held by the woman bleeped, indicating payment had been made. A small crowd of people had gathered around the café by now.

'Okay, thank you so very much, *sir*,' she said, in burning tones, 'it's so nice to have your custom. Please have a good day now – somewhere else.' Turning to the table-tend behind her she said, 'Point him away from here, Horkian. Far away.' The waiter looked at Mike sympathetically, as his boss and the older man walked off to her office.

'Sorry about that, Mer,' said the bar-tend. 'She's like that. I think you need to get some rest somewhere. And if I were you, I wouldn't come back to this kaffee-pot. She's got some relatives who are even nastier than she is.'

As the curious, amused, onlookers chattered and broke up, Mike stood, as best he could and tried to concentrate. He had found all this intriguing, though very boring, and he now started on his way – but where? He couldn't remember where he was supposed to be going but decided to make for the Navy bar, which his befuddled brain managed to tell him was further along the deck. He went over to the corridor wall and placed his right hand against it, for steadiness, so he could carry on walking.

******

The Ultima agent, R, stood in Arpelk's washroom, using a large emergency mediwipe to rub over the flesh wound made by the bullet his victim had rattled off. The wipe would prevent infection but also stop further bleeding, which could potentially soil his clothes and draw unwanted attention to him in the public areas.

The assassin was not particularly bothered about the mess he'd made in the apartment, or the presence of his own blood at the scene. Modern advanced forensics meant the authorities could even detect and collect individual skin cells shed by a suspect and thereby obtain much of the info they needed. A variety of other techniques would allow them to construct a pretty accurate idea of what had transpired.

R's main protection came from his being able to evade capture, and the fact that his identity was unknown. All records of him, including his DNA and other bio-signatures, had been made 'unavailable'. Certain forces in the employ of Comrade One, his master, had expunged all data on him from the Security-SolarNet and PoliceNet.

He had to get going, and now he knew who his final target was: some Navy Secretary jerk called Michaelson Tanniss. He had downloaded information on Tanniss to his wristcom, including several images of him, and he knew that the man was still on the station – and had probably not gone far. It was still important that he clean all Arpelk's blood off his clothes and treat his own wound, but he then had to retrieve the data flake and extract himself.

After using special cleaning scrubs on his jacket, and an instant fabric glue, he left Arpelks' apartment. The damage to his jacket was now hardly visible, other than by a close examination. He strode along the corridor, in the direction of the spoke elevator leading to the shuttle docking bay. Arpelk – and his comp unit – had revealed that this was where Tanniss had been going. There weren't many people in this part of the station, which should make it easier to spot his target. He passed a kaffee shop and then, a long way ahead of him saw a figure shambling along. That just might be Tanniss; a thin, willowy character, wearing loose clothing of the style Arpelk had mentioned – just before his very messy death.

CHAPTER SEVEN

DAMAGE LIMITATION

The 'Now Is The time' Navy bar, was crowded as Mike entered, still staggering a little, but feeling slightly better now. He wondered why he had come here and shambled around, still in a daze. Then he saw Andreanada. He could remember her first name but, try as he might, he couldn't recall her surname. She stood at a brightly lit games table, using a hand-held remote controller to make tiny balls go down small holes, on a flat baize surface. This was one of several modern games which marked a return to a fashionable cult for manipulation of physical objects, instead of purely electronic markers. Mike thought he'd go talk to her. Why not?

She became aware of his approach and, glaring at him, said, 'Well now, look what the Prithvian blood worm dragged in. So, what do you want, Mikey?' He realised, puzzled, that her tone of voice was none too friendly. What was it with people on this station, he thought. He only vaguely remembered meeting with her a few days earlier.

'No, I just ... I don't know, actually. I thought I'd sorta ... say, hello,' he said.

'Hello. Now why don't you just wizzer off?'

'Wizz – what?' said Mike, perplexed.

'Are you drunk or something? said Andreanada. 'Look Mikey, I'm really not in the mood right now. So, do me a favour and just gobb off. Find someone else to annoy. I don't know what happened to you out in that Ra system but boy, have you changed.'

She then turned her back on him and returned to the game. Something in his brain said, *what in the galaxy are you doing? Smarten up for feg's sake.*

Mike apologised to her back for disturbing her and wandered away, but things were starting to come into focus now. His head was finally starting to clear, so he sat on a couch near a window, closed his eyes and to tried to concentrate. *If I want to get to a shuttle I've got to go out through the exit at the far end of the bar,* he realised. Unfortunately, he couldn't remember the reason or why it was so important. He sat contemplating this for several moments.

In a flash he suddenly remembered what he was really supposed to be doing and, almost instinctively, looked at his wristcom. He couldn't quite remember how much time he had left to get to The Monsoon, but it couldn't be much longer. He got up, immediately stumbled and nearly fell flat on his face, but somehow regained his balance. As he did so he was startled to see someone standing right in front of him, seemingly looming over him.

'I know you,' said Mike, gazing at a familiar face, one that wore a look of concern, then blurted out, 'Lew ... is it? Yes. I'm kinda ... sort of really glad to see you.'

Lew, dressed in full, mission ready, Navy uniform, clasped Mike's shoulder gently,

'Are you okay, man?' he said. 'Listen, you're late. You'd better come with me right now. I persuaded Ebazza to let me come over to find you. Knowing you like I do I guessed you might have some sort of problem getting back to the ship. The Monsoon's fifty klicks off the station. My shuttle's the only available ship, now. Come on, man.'

Lew hustled Mike along, hurrying him toward the far end of the walk-through bar. As he did so Mike felt something drop from one of his trouser pockets but paid no more heed to it.

At the exit from the bar, opposite to the entranceway, through which Mike had originally entered, a tall, bulky, man, wearing a heavy-duty utility jacket, appeared. He was gazing at the throng of people before him, as if trying to pick someone out. He continued to peer and then he saw the person he was looking for, standing with a uniformed Navy man – about 40 metres away. He started toward them and when he saw they were heading for the far end of the bar he quickened his pace.

Meanwhile, Lew had grasped Mike's arm and was steering him through long networks of corridors, toward the Navy's own, dedicated, special security zone, situated at the far side of an atrium, dozens of metres beyond the bar. From there they entered another long, dimly lit corridor, at furthest end of which was a large, illuminated sign, fixed above a set of heavy double doors. The sign read, *'Attention! Verified Navy personnel only. No Admittance to Unauthorised Persons without Full Alpha One Security Clearance. You will be challenged!'*

The pair went through the doors and emerged into a large vestibule. They'd nearly reached an automated sliding door in the opposite wall when a huge, fierce looking man practically burst through the doors by which they'd just entered.

Lew turned in a flash and, in a move so fast that most people would have little chance of following it visually, his right hand was on his stun pistol, in its holster, and he was drawing it. The intruder had obviously seen the move and it stopped him in his tracks, but in a fast move of his own he started to reach into a pocket of his heavy jacket. Before his hand had travelled more than a few centimetres Lew had fully drawn his pistol. It was already levelled straight at the stranger. And it was pointed at the man's head, not his chest. R looked at Lew's expression, and the special issue turbo-sonic gun he held. He froze in position.

'Stay right where you are, my friend,' said Lew with a tone of authority that couldn't be misinterpreted. He continued, 'and take your hand away from your jacket. Now! That's good. Who are you and why are you here?'

Mike was, though, amused. He thought this was just like one of those old-fashioned recreations of the gun fights at the 'OK Corral'; enhanced versions of things they called 'films' which he had seen long ago. He stood there, next to Lew, swaying, as though standing in a force 8 gale.

'It's okay. Take it easy, Navy,' said the intruder, 'I didn't wish to alarm you gentilhomms, but I think your friend dropped there something in the bar back in the bar. It's a credit-block. I thought he might want it back. I've got it right here, in my jacket.'

'Don't touch anything, man,' said Lew. 'Didn't you read the sign? No unauthorised persons? Just stay there. Don't move a muscle cos I won't hesitate to fire. And I can see from your face you know that, don't you?' Keeping his eyes glued firmly on the stranger, Lew reached back with his free hand and touched a panel slightly behind him and to one side. A large screen came alive behind him. The much-magnified face of a Navy woman appeared.

'Are you getting all this, sub-lieutenant?' said Lew.

'Yes sir. Saw him come through and I see him now. And the whole thing's being recorded,' she said.

'Okay. Please come out here. Bring the turbo rifle with you – and the long range securi-sensor.'

'On my way, sir,' said the sub-lieutenant.

Seconds later a thick set, middle aged woman, emerged, as if from a blank wall – a disguised doorway – behind Lew. She hefted a massive weapon in both hands and, attached to her belt was a device with a long, thin tube, projecting from it. She immediately trained the heavy-duty rifle on the intruder, as Lew took the sensor device from her.

'Okay,' said Lew, still having never once taken his eyes off the stranger, and continued, 'so now, friend, take the credit block out very, very slowly and put it on the floor, real gently. Right between your own feet.'

The pilot kept his pistol trained on the man's head, evidently not even needing to use the 'red dot' laser aim, as the intruder slowly removed the small, white, block and put it down, as ordered. Lew had been pointing the sensor at it as the intruder removed it from his jacket and continued to do so, while it lay between the man's boots. After a few seconds he looked happy with the result. Returning his gaze to the intruder he told him to slide the tiny block toward them, with one foot, very gently. The stranger did so. He was then ordered to walk backwards, still facing toward Lew, and to go back out through the double doors. And not to come back.

As the stranger started to move backwards Lew said, 'Before you go, I want your name. And don't bother lying to me. We'll check it out and, if you are lying, we'll send a platoon of troopers back to look for you. Got it?'

'Yes, sir,' said the stranger, 'and I'm not lying, sir. My name is Polibius Nero Anachris.'

'I see. Alright, Anachris. Thank you for returning my colleague's property – but please observe the signs in future.'

'Okay. I will, sir. Thank you,' said the man and with that he withdrew, as ordered, and disappeared.

But Lew waited a full minute, still aiming his gun toward the door, without moving, then finally said to his colleague, 'Thanks Marianne. Can you check the cams in the corridor. I'd like to know how the comp didn't give us a "heads up" about that mascla, before he got to the doors.'

'Already checking, sir,' said Marianne, as she stood at a console, 'and to me they look blank. How can that be, sir?'

'What? Don't know. Something must've wiped them – like – instantly. We'll have to look into that when we can, but not right now.'

Lew then pulled Mike into the security clearance section of the corridor leading to the Navy's own spoke elevator. 'Please gather up Mike's property' he said to Marianne, 'and run a check on that guy on the mainframe hypercomp, asap.'

'Absolutely, Lieutenant' she said, 'I didn't like the look of him. Not one bit. I noticed there was something wrong with that jacket of his. Seemed like damage. Torn at the shoulder. There were stains around it. Maybe fresh.'

'I'd really to like to know how he got as far as he did,' said Lew, with a deep frown.

****

The Ultima, New Rebel, agent, known as R, sat in a small, private cubicle, in Ring Four of the station and watched Bradlis Dervello on his comm device, set to ordinary audio-visual only, for security maximisation.

'So, you let your target get away?' said Dervello, with no sign of the anger he must have felt.

'I am truly sorry, comrade,' said R. 'I have failed you. I got through the outer perimeter but would have had no chance of breaching inner Navy security. Even so, I should have brought the D9 explosives. I could have blown myself up when the Navy pilot stopped me. At least I would have eliminated Tanniss and ....'

Dervello interrupted, 'I doubt it. The Navy mascla would probably have shot you before you had a chance to set it off. And D9 doesn't respond automatically to hyperfocussed sonics. You know that. Besides, there was no need of it, agent R.' Dervello sighed, almost wistfully.

R frowned with puzzlement as Dervello continued, 'That is a noble sentiment of yours and I appreciate it, but the fact is, you didn't take the explosives. Freedom fighters like you and I have sometimes found it necessary to resort to acts of suicide in past times – but it was always highly wasteful of talent, and ultimately self-defeating. And the whole thing would have drawn far too much attention to Ultima. Now is not the right time for that. There will be such a time, soon. Your skills may also still be of use to us. I take it they won't be able to trace you?' That question had a very hard edge to it.

'No, comrade. I gave them one of the fictional names we have prepared, together with complete identities and backgrounds. I am can also say that my surgically altered fingerprints and galvanics, will make tracing me, for the killing of the two marks, almost impossible.'

'Good. As for this person called, Tanniss, it will now be down to my operatives on board The Monsoon itself, to deal with him. It is still essential he is caught, and the flake extracted.'

'You have operatives on the ship, master?' R's eyes widened with surprise.

'Indeed,' said Dervello, sounding smug, 'I had hoped I wouldn't need to use them again. They are vulnerable to being caught but if so, they'll just have to sacrifice their freedom. They will not talk, and, at this point, I have little choice but to use them. They can be disposed of later. We can't do anything more about Oceanus, so this is now a damage limitation exercise. I have new orders for you. I am not well placed to do this, so I want *you* to contact my senior operative on that ship. Use your secure com transmitter and the co-ordinates of the contact I'm transmitting to you now. Have they come through to you?'

'They have, comrade.'

'Good. Tell the operative what happened – and the identity of the target. He and his colleagues will secure the data flake – subtly. Then, report back to Forward Base Omega. And, by the way, R. No more failures. You might not be forgiven so easily next time. Comrade One watches everything.'

****

Once aboard The Monsoon, in the micro-gravity environment of the hub, Mike was hurried off to the hub med bay, where Padrigg Lomanz tended to him once again. Lew left to put in a full report of the incident at the Station.

'I think I'm okay now, Padrigg,' said Mike, with a dazed expression, 'Starting to think a bit more clearly. It's just I feel a bit, I don't know, "wisho washo", I guess. Bit like being kruddo'd.'

'Ah, it's been a long time since I got like that,' said Lomanz, almost wistfully, then chuckled as he continued, 'Well, at least not since my last birthday party. But seriously, you've told me you didn't drink any tru-alc, or synthalc, or took any drugs on the way up here. And this is not like a brain stim reflex. But you've had a lot of emotional stress recently. Sometimes, it can cause this kind of thing.'

Mike said little about how he was feeling but he didn't want to talk in detail about his grief, not even to this friend, at least not at this moment. Lomanz suggested the ship's counselling service and was surprised no-one had suggested this before. Mike declined. The hemi-med then took a medical comp, shaped like a small box, no more than 2 or 3 centimetres on a side, with two protruding metal tongues. He placed the tongues on the underside of one of Mike's wrists. After passing sets of harmless, phase modified, laser beams through his flesh, Lomanz announced, after several minutes, that Mike's blood showed no signs of a renewed outbreak of the 'grotachalik disease'. The Navy Secretary breathed a sigh of relief.

The device showed no other signs of disease or injury either, but it did indicate a lot of caffeine derivatives in the blood. Mystified, the patient said he hadn't been drinking much kaffee, or anything similar, but then half remembered sitting in some kind of kaffee shop, place – somewhere – very recently.

'I'm sorry Padrigg. I don't remember where it was. Somewhere on the station, I think.'

'I can offer you a deep body scan, if you want?' said Lomanz but Mike declined, saying he thought it would take too long and, provided it wasn't the grotachalik thing, he felt he'd be okay. He accepted that it might be the stress and maybe he'd eaten something that disagreed with him. He didn't want to talk about his experiences down on the home world, either.

'Maybe,' said Lomanz, chuckling. 'Actually, you're probably right, but I'd like you to report back here every day for the next week. Just to make sure. And obviously, get straight back here if you have renewed symptoms, or anything else wrong.'

An hour later, after unpacking his stuff, Mike steeled himself to meet Tenak, in person, so he wandered up toward the number Two Bridge, to face him. It occurred to him that, after his recent behaviour, the man might not even let him on the bridge. As he set off he felt a low frequency vibration coming through the floor, gradually building, travelling up through his body. It was nothing sinister, just the ship. He realised The Monsoon had 'broken mooring', to use Navy speak, and was transferring to a different orbit. The ship's complement of full thrust, ion manoeuvring engines, all 260 of them, positioned all over the hull, would be pushing the massive bulk of the vessel up to a much higher altitude above the Earth and well away from the station, so that it could safely ignite its massive fusion engine. Then it would begin the journey back to Oceanus. The thought of that distant planet filled him with an odd mixture of pleasure and pain. He would have time to get used to the idea. The trip would probably take around five weeks.

Before he reached the bridge, he practically walked straight into Tenak. The Admiral was making his way to the main observatory and he stopped in front of Mike, momentarily, and gave a perfunctory salute; a way of being polite to a Ship's Secretary.

'Hello, Secretary Tanniss,' said Tenak, rather stiffly. 'I see you returned to us.'

'Yes. Thank you, Admiral. I'm glad to be aboard again,' said Mike and offered his hand. Tenak looked at him, hesitated, then with a military demeanour took the hand and shook it, very briefly and none too warmly. Mike thought he saw the beginnings of a thin smile but if so, it quickly disappeared.

'Getting back to duty should give me something to focus on,' said Mike, 'and I umm …hope I will be of service to you and the ship, again.'

Tenak nodded. 'I trust so,' he said and resumed his journey to the observatory.

I've some way to go there, thought Mike.

****

In their 'safe room', within the bowels of The Monsoon, Second Officer, Mantford Slevin Cavo Blandin, and his two colleagues, floated – and conspired again.

'At least we've got more "solid" orders this time. Makes a bit more sense too,' said Dravette Fulvinia Shacklebury.

'Yeah, but it's a damage limitation exercise,' said her colleague, Garmin Calymian Brundleton. 'It might be more sensible but it's potentially more difficult. And if we're caught, which is kind of likely, especially given the new security regime, one or more of us is going to have to take the punishment and grit their teeth – for the next few dozen years or so. Maybe even on Mars.'

'I'm not doing that,' said Shacklebury.

'So, what else would you do?' said Brundleton. 'You don't want to fall foul of our bosses, do you, Dravette? They've got ways of doling out pain and suffering like you'd never believe.'

'So?' said his female companion, with a sullen look.

'So, don't talk shit,' said Brundleton. 'Listen. We know what we've got to do. The target is just Tanniss. He should be an easy mark. But now the Navy's ordered the ship's comp to operate the personnel locator *virtually right through the journey*, we're limited as to when we can act.'

'You're right. The only time we can do this,' said the Second Officer, 'is when the ship goes through the conduit. That's the only time the PL is going to be inactive, like most of the ship's sensors. That's the time when we're all potentially vulnerable isn't it? Let's make sure Mike Tanniss is *especially* vulnerable. I've pushed for him to be accommodated in the forward sensor array storage deck. His crashcouch is near his cabin but it's effectively isolated from all the others. I've used the excuse of new arrangements for the next tranche of passengers.'

'Sounds okay,' said Shacklebury, 'but how are we going to decide who's going to do the deed?'

'And likely "carry the can", for the next twenty years,' said Brundleton, with a morose expression.

'Don't keep looking on the darklim side,' said the Second Officer. 'Do you think the Rebel Alliance will let you serve out your sentence when they take over?'

'No, of course not. But they won't let us go either. Probably just have us killed for being an embarrassment to them,' said Brundleton.

Blandin looked askance and said, 'Okay, enough. I will let you draw *your* names out of a relay canister. And before you say anything, you'll see that I *have to be exempt*. I'm Second Officer, so if I go down for this, I'll have to do 40 years in the can, not 20. *And* if one of you is caught, at any point, I'm your best chance, maybe your only chance, of wangling some way to help get you out.'

'Hah!' said Shacklebury. 'Typical. And it's not even as if you've got a very good track record anyway, as far as the Captain's concerned.'

Brundleton nodded in agreement.

'Maybe,' said Blandin, 'but I don't think you've got much choice compadres. In the final analysis, I'm in charge, by the rules of the Rebel Alliance. And don't forget, I've got lots of stuff on both of you, if you fail me.'

'You're a piece of work, do you know that?' spat Shacklebury, but after a few moments she nodded her acceptance of the terms, a miserable look on her face.

'I'll do my part, don't worry. I'm taking risks as well,' said Blandin.

Brundleton glared at him too but quickly also nodded his capitulation.

'The other thing to remember,' said Blandin, 'is that whichever of you is the lucky one that gets to capture Tanniss, you're going to need tek cover. That's my part. I'll sabotage his crashcouch, so it doesn't give full protection during transit. That should make it easier for you to overcome him. I'll make it subtle, in case an inspection is done later, and I'll ensure a junior engineer does it. When they'll miss the problem, I'll make sure they get blamed.'

'Yesterday, you said something about the "Dragonfly",' said Brundleton.

'What?' asked Shacklebury. 'The ship's main lifeboat? What, so you want to use it? As, what, some sort of … escape route? Are you serious?'

Blandin stared at her, 'Do you think I'm *not* being serious about any of this?'

'No,' said Shacklebury, looking sullenly at the Second Officer's menacing expression. Blandin continued, 'As I was about to say, I have arranged for a few of the tek crew to power up the Dragonfly, on the basis that it hasn't had an inspection for months and needs a full maintenance check. I want you, Dravette, to take part in that maintenance and use it as an excuse to add extra stocks of food, emergency supplies, med kits, and so on. The Teks shouldn't bother about that. It's the principal lifeboat, after all, and we're going into an alien system. But if anyone says anything, refer them to me.'

'Yes *sir*,' she said, with a tone full of cynicism.

'I'm guessing you don't think we'll need to actually use the Dragonfly?' said Brundleton.

'I hope not,' said Blandin, 'because then we'd need to get it all the way back to the Home System. It's capable of doing that but I wouldn't want to be cooped up on that rig for five or six weeks, with you guys. Despite its size. It's not *that* big.' He tried a wry smile, but it wasn't reciprocated. 'Well, whatever,' he continued, 'we only use it as a last resort, but we have to ensure it's good to go. Now, let's get started.'

****

Back on the Earth, Ylesia Horgans looked smug as she appeared, by holo, in Indrius Brocke's office reception area.

'You look happy,' he said.

'I've just spoken to the SG,' she replied, 'and I wanted to relay the news to you, *in person* – well – sort of.'

He looked puzzled, as she resumed.

'He says he's been discussing options with Professor Brevans and his team. They've been examining the latest reports about the readiness of the Kalahari. The SG has changed his mind. The majority of the fleet are now to proceed to Oceanus – to help with evac.'

'But it's only been a couple of weeks since our security con,' said Brocke, his brow furrowing with irritation. Ylesia's face brightened further at that.

'I know, Indrie,' she said, 'but you know what they say about politics – and change. Seems that Brevans's team consulted Xander. You know, the hypercomp that uses a cuddly koala image to represent him? And he did another analysis. By the way, Xander also consulted with two other AIs. The overall conclusion was that the Kalahari is running so far behind schedule that it cannot be ready within the S G's stipulated time limit. You remember what he said at our con, don't you?'

'Yes, yes, Ylesia. So, you're saying they're going to leave the Home System open to possible attack? Well, the military chiefs are going to love this.'

'Can't be helped, Indrie. You know how important the SG regards the rescue of the Oceanus people. As do I. I'm sorry, Deputy, but he's communicating this info to the other members of the security committee right now. I asked him especially, if I could be the one to tell you.'

'And so you have, Ylesia. So you have.' Brocke looked furious, as Ylesia's 3D image faded from the room.

Then, he smiled broadly to himself.

****

Three weeks after igniting its fusion engine The Monsoon had reached what was, in theory, the outer 'boundary' of a transit zone, in the far reaches of the Solar System, much further out than the orbit of dwarf planet Pluto. The ship's sensors now began the incredibly complex job of searching for the location of the nearest likely, new, conduit opening.

The Monsoon had maintained a near constant acceleration and had already reached a staggering three thousand five hundred kilometres per second as it entered the volume of space now 'labelled' as the transit zone.

Unknown to anyone on the ship, a data pod shot out of a conduit that was opening far ahead, still fifty-five million kilometres from The Monsoon. The mouth of the conduit 'closed' (disappeared), immediately after spitting out the small, uncrewed vessel which hurtled toward the inner Solar System, at a speed even greater than that of The Monsoon's. The large ship then detected it and prepared to take evasive action, but none was necessary. Its trajectory would take it several hundred thousand klicks away from The Monsoon.

The pod's single fusion engine, not really very large, but *gigantic* in relation to the size of the pod itself and its payload, would take it to the Earth faster than any crewed ship could, even accounting for its many days of hard deceleration, at forces which would be unendurable for humans. The payload, deep inside the spherical shell of the probe, was another sphere no more than two centimetres across. That sphere contained a single data matrix, of enormous capacity and the data it carried would turn the conceptual world of the whole of humanity inside out. Forever.

Meanwhile, The Monsoon's major AIs detected another opening conduit filament, suitable for the ship to pass through and calculated a course, plus velocity adjustments, for rendezvous with it. The ship adjusted and flew onward.

Although the vessel was travelling extremely fast, the speed of light is of course very much faster. And so it was that a wavefront of light quanta, from an event happening in the *inner* Solar System, reached the ship a mere half hour before the vessel disappeared down the throat of the newly discovered dark energy filament. The minor AIs picked up the wavefront, processed it in a billionth of a second, and stored it for later consideration by the crew, who, it deemed, were too busy preparing for the conduit jump to be able to consider it immediately. The crew would later discover that the flash had emanated from the catastrophic explosion of the fusion engines of the new flagship, the Kalahari, as the machines went through their final testing.

**

Inside the 'uppermost', forward sensor storage deck Mike Tanniss left his cabin and made his way around the bulky, fixed down, tank shaped boxes, which contained spare coils used in the superconducting electromagnets; devices which powered the ship's vital forward sensor arrays. The deck was also packed with masses of other equipment and the Navy Secretary wondered what had possessed the Captain to agree to his being accommodated in this area for the trip out. He had objected, but not seriously, as he had not wanted to appear prissy or precious, especially when he had threatened to resign only a few weeks ago.

Mike had been told that most prime space on board was undergoing final preparations for transporting evacuees back home. After giving up his full crashcouch for one of them on the last homeward trip, he felt it would have looked strange if he'd objected strenuously to this small inconvenience. After all, there was nothing wrong with the upper forward deck. It was just a bit remote and – empty of other people. This deck was the smallest in the ship's main hub, its location being immediately next (apparently 'underneath', as it would appear to an observer) to the massive, flat, disc-like shield separating the hub itself from the huge forward sensor module.

Mike knew that no other crewmembers were being accommodated there, the nearest other cabin and crashco,' being sited on the deck below, but to reach that, it just meant, after all, traversing the circular walkways to the nearest elevator, or a ladder tube.

He remembered that all elevators would be out of operation during transit, but he asked himself why would he want to go to any other deck during transit, anyway? He would be too busy simply trying to endure the journey, as best he could, given that, in his experience, numerous trips through conduits didn't make them easy to bear. Most people simply got used to them.

As the PA system transmitted the ship's warning of impending transit Mike sank into his couch and strapped himself in. The couch hummed and vibrated as its systems initiated their 'transit cycle'. Full crashcouches generated an induction field over their occupants, which gave some protection from the quantum field fluctuations, as the vessel shot through the 'negative energy tubes', as the conduits were often called. The protective fields were sometimes disrupted during transits, but there was currently no known 'fix' for this. The couches also contained upholstery devices which were able to counter much of the turbulence and infra-vibration which frequently upset people more than the negative energy effects. But the bulkiness of the couches and their accoutrements made them unsuitable and unsightly for installation inside most cabins, apart from the more spacious ones of the most senior officers. Their couches also had the most protection.

Mike was trying to get as much rest as he could, but two or three minutes after the ship had, with the usual shrieking noises, entered the conduit, a particular sound poked its way into his consciousness, as the shrieking subsided. This was a sort of 'singular' noise, he thought. When there was so much noise being transmitted through the fabric of the great ship, how could he have heard any single sound? But, he realised, that was precisely because this noise was *not* usual. It sounded like a bulkhead door moving, followed by a 'pitter-pattering' type of sound, then a clattering noise. Something dropping, maybe?

Reclining at the most comfortable angle in which to orient the couch; around 48° from the horizontal, Mike forced himself to raise his head as much as his restraints allowed. His eyes were bleary, and his head ached. And the ship's lighting was, as usual, very much diminished. Yet he couldn't see anything strange. He settled back but – there it was again. Footfalls? Yes, he was picking up what he felt were the unmistakeable sound of footsteps and, as the ship suddenly lurched to one side, the added sound of a groan. A groan? Someone else was up there on his deck, but who could it be? Everyone should be in their crashcouches.

'Who is it?' Mike called out. 'What's the problem? Can I help?' No answer. He lifted his head again and started to say something when his heart leaped into his mouth. A figure was right there, close-by. Someone with an athletic build was standing to the right-hand side of his crashcouch, probably less than a metre away. The figure wore a dark, shiny, skin-tight suit of some kind, and from that, Mike registered the shape as probably male. The man's head and face were entirely covered by a mask and tight hood, and he carried a bag of some sort, slung tightly over his shoulder. He also held a transparent stick in one hand and then, realising he'd been seen, he spoke to Mike, with an angry yet, somehow, apologetic voice. It was a voice Mike found strangely familiar, but he couldn't quite place it. Then, he moved toward Mike very fast.

'I'm sorry Tanniss, but I've got to do this,' said the figure as he moved, then he raised the stick thing and brought it down as though to stab Mike in his chest. As he did so Mike reacted instinctively and very fast, moving his right forearm to block the attack. In that split second, he also had a flashing mental image of someone else doing something similar – on Orbital Station Four. He had no time to dwell on it. His right arm successfully blocked the assailant's hand, but a shock of pain flashed through Mike's wrist as it connected with the assailant's forearm. The attacker then grabbed at Mike with his other hand, trying to pull his blocking arm away.

'You gotta lie still, you fegger. It'll be less trouble for you,' shouted the assailant, his voice muffled by his mask.

Mike's heart hammered even faster because he now recognised his attacker's weapon; a dermo-jett, used for pneumatically injecting drugs into the body, without skin puncture. It was standard medical kit. The assailant bore down on him again and Mike could feel the man's strength as he grappled with him, Mike still in an almost prone position. His brain kept telling him he had to get himself free of his webbing restraints. Or it would all be over.

The ship lurched again, even more violently this time, and the attacker was thrown off balance, stumbling backwards. His grip on Mike loosened. Now, Mike thought, and clutched at his chest and belt buckles. He was amazed to find that, in a second, he had freed himself, but as he tried to get off the couch, he felt the crushing forces produced by the conduit journey itself, and almost fell back. Then the sheer force of adrenaline hitting his system kicked him into further action, and he managed to scramble off the couch, but he actually fell off the side opposite to the one where his attacker still stood, somewhat shakily.

In seconds the mystery assailant had regained his balance and, brandishing the dermo-jett again, tried to leap over the crashcouch to get at him. He bungled it and clumsily flopped on top of the couch, but within a second, he'd raised his upper body and resumed a stabbing action with his instrument. Mike dreaded the thought of what might be in that thing. Was that what had happened on EOS Four? That thought flashed across his mind and he thrust it away. He had to concentrate on getting away from danger. He'd try to talk to the attacker.

'What the hell're you doing?' Mike shouted, all the while backing away from the couch and the assailant. 'Who the feg are you, anyway?'

The assailant clambered over the couch, like some sort of gangly monkey and Mike stepped backwards, almost stumbling, turning as he did so. That's when he spotted a large piece of heavy equipment, possibly a fusion welder, lying on a nearby storage drum. He needed a weapon. He tugged at it but realised, with horror, that it had been fixed down with wire. He turned back in time to see the attacker break off the trigger part of his dermo-jett and simply toss the whole thing away. Glaring at Mike through the eye-slots in his mask, he pulled a large, curved knife from his shoulder bag and, hopping off the couch, began to advance on his victim.

'Okay, man,' said the attacker, 'if that's how you want it. Forget the gentle way. I'll just have to cut it out of you. Come here, you little feg-shit.'

'What the crap are you talking about?' said Mike. His mind searched desperately for a way out of this situation, any way at all. He had the crushing sense that this didn't seem real, like some sort of terrible dream. No, a nightmare. An illusion brought on by the conduit? The dull ceiling lights glinted off the metal of the stranger's blade. That knife looked real enough.

He wasn't going to hang around long enough for another lunge by the attacker, so he turned again and raced away, heading toward the main part of the deck's corridor. His attacker was hard on his heels.

Mike's head ached even more, and his sense of balance was out of kilter but again, adrenalin pushed him on, his sense of self-preservation filling him with purpose. Part of his brain kept telling him he mustn't panic. He knew he had to think his way out of this. He could hear his attacker's racing footsteps on the decking behind him, but he was terrified of looking back. He just had to keep going and find help. But how? Where?

****

The shadowy figure of 'Comrade One' appeared on the main hypercomp screen in Dervello's office, back on EOS Four. His voice betrayed anger but his face could not be seen, hidden behind something which looked like an elliptical, metallic mask, featureless but for a protruding snout of some sort.

'Fools,' emanated from the mask, 'I expected you to slow down the rate of progress on the testing of the Kalahari. Not destroy it, you dolts! I had plans for it.'

'Please, Comrade One,' said Dervello, sitting in front of the screen, wincing, 'I did not, we did not, order the destruction of the vessel. Please believe me. We did not.'

'Was it merely incompetence on the part of your operative, then, Dervello?'

'I ..., no, Comrade. It could not have been. She sent us a coded signal, indicating she had just arrived at the construction station. That's when the ship exploded. I presume she was killed, along with the crews working there. Unfortunate, for she was a good operative.'

'I am not concerned with your petty sentiments, Dervello. There has been a massive security crackdown in the government – and the Navy. They suspect sabotage, Dervello. And the Secretary General has again rescinded his recent decision to send most of the fleet to Oceanus. Most are now to stay here. That is what concerns me, idiot.'

'I understand, One.'

'Do you? That is nice to know – fool. The one gleam of hope we have left is that the Kalahari's shield allowed part of the ship's forward sensor module to be blasted clear when the engines blew. Everything else was evaporated. The Navy is tracking the module, which is on its way out of the Solar System. They will try to recover data from it, remotely. We had better hope they recover enough data to put Ultima in the clear. And to put *you* in the clear, *with me*, Dervello.'

'As you rightly say, Comrade One. As you rightly say,'

****

Keeping as quiet as a Prithvian moss beetle, Mike hid behind a group of huge crates and containers the size of single storey houses, that occupied a large part of the forward deck. He was glad he had been able to put some distance between him and his assailant. His left leg was definitely functioning properly now. It wasn't supposed to give him extra power, just normal function, but he felt it was giving him an edge over his assailant – but only a slight one. The leg still hurt like mad, but he ignored it.

Also, fortunately, the forces generated by the conduit journey had suddenly begun to bear down on the assailant too and he had slowed his pursuit. The huge crates, solidly anchored into the decking plates, were full of supplies intended for the next group of evacuees and were arranged in a rectangular grid pattern across this part of the deck. That left dark, criss-crossing, alleyways between them. He had decided he would hide in those.

Mike couldn't hear anything unusual above some renewed wailing from the ship's hull. He looked at his wristcom, which he'd now set on completely silent mode. The time seemed to drag, and his raw nerves wanted to explode. It was like some sort of torture – and the ship was still only ten minutes into conduit transit. He decided to hide well back, behind the fifth row of crates, and about six columns in from the corner of the grid which had been nearest to him. His assailant still had the advantage as he merely had to check along each row and column until he found Mike, though it would take him time. And time was Mike's ally – he hoped.

The thought of the attacker's huge knife struck dread into him. He peeped around a corner of a crate, trembling. Yet, his mind, working overtime, hit upon an odd thing. He suddenly wondered why the man hadn't simply tried to use a stun gun on him. Then he remembered. Stun guns were notoriously unreliable during conduit transits; another peculiarity of such journeys, and one more thing not fully understood. The guns worked but they simply spread the sonic energy widely instead of focussing it. It was also thought, generally, that stun guns should never be used during transits, anyway, so there was little research going into it. In that case, this quirk of the conduits had worked solidly in his favour.

And why the dermo-jet? It must have been filled with some sort of drug. His mind began to dredge up some awful scenarios associated with that thought and he forced himself to push them to the back of his mind. Instead, he knew he had to concentrate on finding some way of gaining an advantage. It seemed horrendously difficult. But he would have to find a way, if he wanted to live.

Apart from the ship's wailing there were still no other sound – out there in the 'open'. His mind settled again on the idea of finding a weapon. There was nothing he could use in this area. As the silence went on and his nerves caused his tummy to commit uncomfortable gyrations, a memory flickered into his mind. He recalled passing a set of lockers back when he had been wandering around, earlier. Maybe they had something in them he could use – if they were open. He also realised that to get to the lockers he would need to break cover. Despite the noise of the conduit transit there was a small chance the noise caused by fiddling with lockers would draw the assailant's attention. But what else could he do?

Peeping again around the corner of the crate he listened intently for long moments, plucking up the courage to break out to the right of the crate, to make for the corridor leading to the lockers. He checked behind him, for the twentieth time, in case the attacker was creeping up behind and then ran – as quietly as he could, which meant he produced a strange caricature of a sprint; a sort of gangly, tiptoeing, lope.

Reaching the corridor safely he glanced behind him, seeing no-one. So far, so good. The corridor was very wide and clear of obstacles, so he should be able to see his assailant clearly. He continued around the corridor where it curved gently to the right and as he did so the deck's lights flickered and the conduit's strange side-effects hit him once more, sharply this time. The nausea and dizziness forced him to slow down and, for a few seconds almost forced him to the floor. Disorientation gripped his mind, but self-preservation kicked in and forced him to start moving again.

Mike thought he could see the lockers now, about 20 metres ahead; a row of six, all fixed to the corridor wall. He glanced back again, trying to quicken his pace and – his heart leapt again. The mad attacker was there – only about 30 metres behind him, slashing his knife around in the air as he ran.

Now Mike ran all out and, reaching the lockers, desperately pulled at the first door he encountered. It didn't budge. Nor did the second, or third. The assailant was catching up quickly now, but he knew he had to concentrate on trying all the lockers. He tried to blot out a rising tide of fear and pulled at the fourth locker. No good. Then, the fifth – and it opened.

Nothing but piles of datapads inside. No weapon, but some of the pads looked heavy. Mike grabbed furiously at them, pulling them all out all over the floor, looking for some more suitable weapon, but then he had an idea and started hefting the pads at the attacker. The assailant hesitated but easily dodged the missiles, and the pads clattered noisily on the floor. He just laughed at Mike and continued to advance, striding toward his prey more slowly and confidently, now, the last few metres to go. Mike thought he was moving almost casually, as if he had nothing to worry about. Perhaps he didn't.

Mike desperately tried the sixth locker. To his surprise, it opened and inside was a toolbox sitting on a shelf. Next to that was a bunch of spanners tied down by a piece of thick adhesive tape. A possible weapon? He pulled at the tape with sweat soaked hands, but it seemed too strong to tear. Too late now anyway. The attacker was almost on top of him, but then the tape yielded. He tore feverishly at the spanners and threw the top one straight at the attacker. Good throw, he thought. It hit the man on his left cheek and caused him to stop for a few moments, as he clutched at his face. Mike searched for the largest, heaviest, spanner – found it and wielded it in front of him.

The attacker had recovered, immediately assuming a crouching, martial arts type of stance, in front of Mike and readying his large, gleaming, knife. Mike, slightly emboldened by his momentary success, was merely a metre or two away from him and subconsciously mimicked his opponent's stance. He swung the spanner around in front of him, but his wild-eyed opponent stayed beyond its reach. Mike could tell that the man was searching for an opening. It was obvious that this mascla had done a lot of physical training, and Mike's mouth went completely dry as he tried to anticipate what he might do next. All the time the ship's progress through the conduit weighed on his senses, like an iron cloak. It was likely his attacker felt it too, but Mike couldn't tell.

Then his lithe attacker reversed his grip on his knife, changing from holding it like a dagger, to holding it with the blade in front. The two men seemed to 'dance', looking for an opening and this seemed, at least to Mike, to go on for an eternity. He could feel his energy flagging. Both men panted heavily with the tension, especially Mike. The ship still wailed as it sped through the conduit.

The attacker suddenly lunged, moving forward in a single step and, with his knife, he made a lightning-fast jab toward Mike's left arm, and stepped back. Mike thought he was just testing his defences again, until the attacker said, breathlessly but calmly, 'You don't even know I got you, do you, Mikey? Look at your arm.'

Mike risked a momentary glance at his left arm and saw blood dripping from a slash in his clothing. His jaw dropped open with shock. Then a dull pain began to lance through the limb, spreading all the way up to his shoulder. He felt a rising sense of anger and indignation and lunged forward, swinging the spanner toward his attacker. His opponent dodged him easily and lunged in again with his knife. This time it was Mike's right arm. Again, Mike hadn't felt it because the blade was so sharp and the attack so swift. The pain soon spread over his right arm and he felt the blood oozing out.

'You really are pathetic, Mikey, aren't you?' said the attacker. 'You know, back there I was ready to anaesthetise you to do it. But now, I'll just have to kill you and cut it out.'

'What the hell are you talking about?' said Mike in anguish, 'Cut what out? Is it one of my organs you want or something? You're not making any ...' Mike began to feel faint with shock, but he knew he couldn't let himself be distracted. Dragging his focus back he saw his attacker move and, this time, was able to dodge him, or so he thought, but – not quite. This time the knife sliced his left side well below his armpit. A couple of centimetres further to the right and it would have gone into his chest. With stark horror, Mike realised the attacker was wearing him down and cutting him to pieces, slowly, inexorably. Pain from his new wound spread across his chest and abdomen and, under the mask, Mike sensed somehow that his attacker was grinning.

The effects of the conduit were still present, a dreadful backdrop to this surreal and, to Mike's mind, completely mysterious attack. He breathed in sharply and lunged again. If he was going to die like this, then he became determined he would try to take his attacker down too. He moved very sharply, and this time he seemed to have taken hm by surprise. The head of his spanner hit the man's left arm, clunking against the bone of the elbow joint. The man yelped with pain and Mike, instantly recognising he had an advantage, moved to swing the spanner at the attacker's face, but the man recovered in time to dodge, and prevent the blow striking fully home. Even so, the spanner connected, but with a relatively glancing blow only, to the side of the assailant's head. Again, the attacker shouted with pain and held his free hand up to his face.

The assailant staggered slightly, and Mike realised he had to press home his attack, but he hesitated. The noise of the blow had, in fact, sickened him and his natural antipathy toward physical violence got the better of him for a second or two, until he realised his mistake. Through the eye slit in his mask the assailant seemed to stare at Mike with utter malevolence, and stepping forwards slightly, he thrust his knife forward and upwards. It cut obliquely into the upper left part of Mike's chest, making a thudding noise as it skidded over the top of his ribs. Then it actually sank in, between two ribs and sliced upwards, before ending up deep in the tendons and muscles of Mike's left shoulder. The assailant pulled the blade back hard and it came out slick with his victim's blood all over it.

Mike screeched with shock, as though electrocuted, jumping backwards, dropping his spanner. Backing away from his assailant he looked at his chest. A large wound had opened up but blood had not yet started to flow out. Mike could actually see a hint of exposed ribs. He stared back at the attacker, expecting him to lunge toward him again, to finish him off, but instead saw him sink to the floor, holding his head. Blood was now pouring down the attacker's face, coming from under the close-fitting hood, and the man stared blankly at the floor. Grasping at his hood, he tore it off.

Mike thought he recognised him. His befuddled brain was trying to work it out. Brindle – or Brundle-something, a senior engineer? He turned away. It didn't matter anymore. Mike felt he was beyond caring about that, or why any of this had happened – about anything much. Pain from his chest wound began to fill his whole world and, glancing down, he saw little rivulets of blood pouring over his shredded clothing. His breathing was now coming in short gasps and he knew he was hyperventilating, but he couldn't help it. He could feel something was badly wrong, deep inside his chest.

With his attacker slumped on the floor Mike wandered away from him. He felt seriously ill. He didn't know where he was going, or why, but he didn't care about that either.

*****

Sanders Utopius Dagghampton II, carrying a shoulder bag, climbed steadily up a ladder tube, on his way from the second hub deck to the first, where the pilot knew Mike Tanniss had been accommodated. He had been wandering around the entire hub of the ship, looking for signs of the sabotage he'd expected to find. Sabotage he knew the quislings aboard were bound to be trying to carry out. He climbed with ease, seeming not to notice the effects of the conduit at all. Reaching the top of the forward ladder tube, at the level of Mike's deck, he switched on a small diagnostics screen on the tube wall. He'd noticed that the round hatch door, way up at the top of the ladder, was closed. He regarded it with a mystified look. It should be fixed open. All hatchways could be closed electronically if there was a risk of decompression in the ship, but the screen indicated no sign of any problems the other side of the hatch.

Dagghampton opened a panel to reveal a manual hand wheel. He turned the wheel repeatedly, gradually forcing the hatch open. Squeezing himself through, he heard a scream issue from somewhere above, even before it had even opened fully. Pulling his backpack off, he hauled himself lithely onto the deck and hurried in the direction of the scream, along a smoothly curving corridor. A few seconds later he came across a scene which made his eyes widen with surprise. There was Mike, on his knees, with his back toward him, a growing pool of blood on the floor around him. Over to the left, another man, slumped against some lockers, holding a hand to his head.

Dagghampton hurried toward Mike.

'Hey, my friend. What the feg's happened? Can you hear me, Mike?'

As he neared him, he caught a movement in the corner of his eye and turned in time to see the other man getting slowly to his feet, clutching a long knife in one hand and a heavy spanner in the other. 'So, what do you think you're doing?' Dagghampton said to him.

'Get the fegg outta here,' shouted the stranger, 'or I'll cut you up like I cut him. I got him. I'll get you too.' The man looked as though he was ignoring his head wound now and moved threateningly but slowly toward Dagghampton.

'Brundleson, isn't it, or maybe Brundleton? I must have slipped up,' said Dagghampton. 'I didn't think you were involved. Well, Brundleson, matey, you don't look so well, so don't be stupid. Just sit down and shut up, while I see to my friend.'

The assailant stared with indignant shock and held his head in his hands again, as Dagghampton walked back to where he'd left his backpack and toted it over to Mike, pulling a med kit from it. Looking at Mike's injuries the pilot opened the med kit, selecting a suitable dressing. Calmly, he started to apply pressure to Mike's wound. There was more movement from nearby and the sound of the other man's uncertain footsteps. Somehow, the knifeman had recovered enough to continue his menacing advance. 'You're the pisshead who's been asking everyone funny questions, ain't you. Interfering shit. I told you I'll do you,' he said, 'you fegging *besterd.*'

Dagghampton was up on his feet in a flash and had pulled a thick, stick like object from his pack, all in one seamless movement. He shook the stick and it snapped open with a loud crack, extending to about three times its original length, like a miniature whip. With another loud crack a small, spiked, ball, popped out at the end of the weapon, hanging there expectantly, just looking for trouble. As Brundleton advanced with his knife, Dagghampton crouched and wielded the weapon. The ball swung, almost casually, and the knife flew out of the attacker's hand, a ragged wound opening up on Brundleton's palm. The man shrieked.

'This is just too easy,' said Mike's rescuer, as the attacker, despite his new wound, recovered, picked up the spanner in his other hand, and lunged with it. Dagghampton just let his own weapon drop to the floor and, almost effortlessly, side-stepped Brundleton's attack. With his free hand he punched the assailant hard in his side. Brundleton gasped and doubled up as Dagghampton launched an expert side kick at him, and the attacker went down. Keeping one eye on his downed opponent the pilot got back to Mike, slumped a few metres away. Almost miraculously, the assailant had started to haul himself off the ground, mumbling as he did so. Dagghampton sighed, then simply picked up his ball and stick weapon once more. Whipping the stick part, he brought the little ball cracking over the man's back, with which it connected very hard and very loudly, producing a raw, groaning, grunt from Brundleton. He didn't get up again. Dagghampton then calmly attended to Mike, once more.

**

Padrigg Lomanz led a small med team up toward Deck One at speed, and gasped in astonishment when he was met by Sanders, on Deck Two. He was carrying Mike Tanniss in his arms, as if he were a child. Blood was running down Dagghampton's uniform shirt.

'Mike's hurt, Padrigg. I've done what I can. There's someone else up on Deck One. I think it's Brundleson. A basic grade engineer, I think. Looks like he was trying to kill Mike. I've tied him up with a binder strap. Be careful. He's a scurvy dog, even when wounded, but I don't think he'll regain consciousness for a while.'

CHAPTER EIGHT

DEADLY MISTAKES

'So, you are a government agent, pilot Dagghampton,' said Arkas Tenak. The Admiral stood, with Ebazza, in one of the ship's smaller conference rooms, out on the torus. The pilot sat between them. The Captain looked angrily at Sanders and huffed, 'It was nice of the authorities to inform us about you.'

'That's the whole point,' said Dagghampton, 'we didn't know who we could trust, though I never really suspected you, or the Admiral here. I'm sorry Captain, but sometimes these things must be done.' He shrugged and looked genuinely apologetic.

'I'm so glad you didn't *really suspect* me or the Admiral,' said Ebazza, rolling her eyes. 'I've never heard of this type of infiltration before,' she continued, 'so, if you hadn't acted as you did, today, I wonder if we would ever have known your true identity. It doesn't say much about the trust the Admiralty places in us – or didn't they know who to trust either?'

'I don't know,' said Dagghampton, 'though there must have been some co-ordination at the highest levels, but as I said, these are strange days. For some time we've been aware that the New Rebels and Ultima have been infiltrating the Navy and the Government's own civil service, and maybe even higher. You shouldn't be surprised. You had your own problems on your earlier trip, didn't you? And I know the Board of Inquiry exonerated the officers from blame for the hypercomp trouble, but believe me, we've caught other quislings. It's thought there are a number still at large. You won't have heard about the ones caught because … well, because with things the way they are back home it's reckoned it could damage trust in the government.'

Ebazza looked at Tenak, wearing a deep frown, as if to say *what trust would that be?* But she didn't vocalise it. Dagghampton continued,

'It was strongly suspected that at least one, maybe two, rebel agents were still on The Monsoon, so I was recruited to try to find them, and I was gathering evidence on one, when he was killed.'

'Exactly which one of our people, who died, would that have been?' asked Tenak, a disturbed expression spreading over his face.

'Johann Agricola Erbbius,' said Sanders. At least, that's what he called himself.'

'Him?' said Tenak, his eyes widening with incredulity, 'that's a serious accusation, young Mer.'

'And what was your evidence against him?' asked Ebazza.

'Mainly circumstantial, Captain,' said Sanders, 'but I traced at least two unauthorised transmissions to him, that came from the Meta-teleo temple on Oceanus. That, and the evidence given by the expedition members on Simurgh. And I examined all the evidence I could get concerning the "accident" on that island.'

'We saw all that, too. So what are you saying?' said Ebazza.

'Well, I have some useful ... devices. I checked on the ship's cache of sonic charges. The ones used for civil engineering projects. Well, of course, they can be used as weapons of offence, couldn't they? And there's some indication ... just some ... that six of them were newly fabricated. Made pretty recently – since the Simurgh expedition, that is. So, what happened to the originals? I've done a whole lot of research on sonic charge detonations, and I mean a lot, and I reckon there's something odd about the landslide on Simurgh. I can't be certain, but I think foul play is a good bet. Unfortunately, I have nothing conclusive – yet, but I haven't finished investigating.'

'" Good bet. Nothing conclusive". That's not very convincing, *Mister*,' said the Captain, 'so it's just *your theory, isn't it?*'

'Unfortunately, yes,' said Dagghampton, 'but I was ... am building up the full picture. These things can take a long time. That's how it is in my ... line of work. Perhaps we'll never really know the full story about Erbbius, but you can't deny that another quisling was unmasked today, by his own actions? Brundleson, sorry, I mean, *Brundleton* – though I did not have him on my radar. Slipped up, there.'

Tenak, said, 'Looks like you did. But I won't deny that we *all know about him now*, thanks to your actions. And Sanders, I want to thank you, personally, for rescuing Mike. He might have died if you hadn't been there. How did you know he was in trouble?'

'I didn't,' said Dagghampton. 'Like I said, it was a fair bet that their mission at Oceanus having failed, any remaining quislings would try to do something to The Monsoon while it was at its most vulnerable – during conduit transit.'

The Captain looked at Tenak with a shocked expression, and said, 'Well, even I will admit that all this ties in with the hypercomp troubles we had. We never got to the bottom of that one.' Turning back to Dagghampton she said, morosely, 'So, I guess you knew about Chips Havring as well?'

'I think you can forget him,' said the agent, 'cos I don't think he's got anything to do with this and …'

Ebazza interrupted with, 'What were they … the "quislings", that is, trying to do on Oceanus anyway? Were they behind the disruption of the evac' plans?'

'Yes Ma'am. We believe so. At least, to some extent. We believe they were trying to delay evacuation so millions would be caught in Ra's surface eruptions. We also believe they collaborated with the meta-teleos. The aim was to destabilise the HS Government.'

'I'm guessing they're more active back home too,' said Tenak, 'because the major AIs have analysed the flash of X, and gamma rays, the sensors picked up, just before we left the Solar System. Seems they consider it likely it was the Kalahari - exploding. We know the Navy were carrying out full tests on the engines, back in that same time frame. Could that be sabotage too?'

'Could be,' said Dagghampton, 'but we'll only find out later, I guess. We know that Ultima and the New Rebels are definitely becoming more active in the Home System. And to finish answering your earlier question, Admiral, about Mike?'

'Yes, carry on,' said Tenak.

'Like I said, I expected trouble during transit, so I left my crashcouch and went walk-about. I've had a lot of training to overcome the effects of conduit travel. It can be done. So, I'm mostly immune. Anyway, because I thought the quislings would sabotage *this* ship, I went down to the engine diagnostics hub. Not even I can gain admittance to the engine manuplex, so, don't worry, I didn't get any further, nor would I want to.'

'And no-one saw you?' said Ebazza, a permanent look of surprise on her face now.

'I'm …'

'I know. You're *trained* to go unnoticed,' said Tenak, rolling his eyes.

Daggghampton nodded sheepishly and continued, 'Seemed no problems down in engineering diagnostics anyway, as far as I could tell, so I worked my way back through the hub decks, checking on as many crashcos as possible, to see if they were occupied. I made sure I stayed out of sight, but I noticed that one couch was empty. I wasn't sure whose it was, and there wasn't anyone wandering about, till I got up as far as deck One. The locked hatch was suspicious. Then I heard a scream after I got through it. The rest you know.'

'Thank you for that … summary,' said Ebazza, exhaling with evident irritation, 'but I have this one nagging question. How do we know *you* can be trusted? How do we know you are not some sort of "quisling", yourself? After all, by your own admission, you are, in some ways.'

'If you're suggesting I'm a traitor, I strenuously deny it.' A flash of anger from Dagghampton, before he continued, looking almost hurt, 'But, I understand how you would feel like that, Captain. So, I can only point to my actions.'

'Why haven't you got an incorruptible ID flake?' asked Tenak, a frown still on his face.

'If my enemies … *your* enemies found it they'd be onto me.'

Tenak looked reasonably satisfied with the answer.

'How convenient,' said Ebazza.

'So why would I have helped Mike?' said Dagghampton, 'And why would I have dealt with Brundleton – and why would I be telling you all this?'

'So you can throw the scent off yourself,' said Ebazza, staring coolly at the agent. 'After all, until we get back home, we can't be sure of anything. We could send a datapod back from here – but by the time we got a reply we'd be on our way home anyway.' She turned to Tenak and said, 'I'm sorry Admiral but I'm afraid I don't entirely trust this mascla. I think he should be placed in the brig, or at least confined to his quarters, under armed guard.'

'Tenak paused for a long time, nodded at Ebazza, then said, 'Pilot Dagghampton, you have my eternal thanks for saving Mike. That's why I'm only going to confine you to your quarters and not put you in the brig. But you'll kindly let us have all your weapons – and any other "devices" you have. We'll have a fully armed, 24-hour, guard put on you, and we'll tag you as a priority tag for the Personnel Locator System. Do you understand?'

'I do understand Admiral, Captain. I would do the same in your position. As for Mike, sir, I'd like to say he did pretty well to stay alive, before I even reached the scene. I'm certainly glad he's out of harm's ...'

Before Dagghampton could finish there was a loud bleep from Tenak's wristcom and, evidently concerned at the origin of the call, the Admiral asked for it to go on the loudspeaker.

'This is Chief medi-surgeon Atrowska, Admiral. Mike Tanniss is fine now. We've patched him up. The knife made a cut in his pleural membrane and slightly nicked his heart, barely, but he's well off the danger list. He'll be sore for a quite a few days, but as part of our checks we did a deep body scan, and *we found something metallic inside him*. Something not in his original med logs. Thought it was a tiny piece of the knife, at first but ... well, I think you and the Captain should see this for yourselves.'

Ten minutes later Tenak and Ebazza had arrived in the med bay. Mike Tanniss was in a nearby medi-bed, still under sedation. Brundleton lay in a distant cubicle guarded by three security ratings. Atrowska, an oval faced, tall, and large framed, blonde woman, dressed in surgical whites, led the two bridge officers into a large alumina-glass office. Sited above a workstation was a large screen currently showing a series of cascading thumbnail views of various documents and vid films.

'I didn't want to transmit this to you, Admiral,' said Atrowska, anxiety evident on her face, 'because we dug this thing out of Mike's lower neck. It was in very deep. It's a data flake in a tiny metal casing. We scanned it on the viewer when we got it out, and it immediately broadcast all this stuff. Looks like some sort of ... espionage material. There's a vid which seems to show Ambassador Sliverlight being ... well, interrogated, by a man he called Dervello, and there's lists of names of people it says – are Rebel operatives ... and their locations. I don't really understand all the implications but ...'

'This day is certainly proving interesting. How did it get inside Mike Tanniss, Chief?' said Ebazza.

'He was muttering about something being injected into him, back on EOS Four,' said Atrowska, 'but we just thought he was delirious. This thing is very strange. It didn't show up on the usual security scans. We might be able to find out more when he wakes up. He's in the clear now, but lost a lot of blood, so we've put two litres of synthblood into him.'

'Thank you, Chief,' said Tenak, 'and we'll take charge of the flake now. I'm sure I don't need to ask you to keep all this to yourself and any of your staff who are present?'

Atrowska nodded, still wearing a worried look as she carefully picked up the flake with surgical pincers and placed it into a small synth-steel box for Tenak. She looked glad to be rid of it.

*****

In Ebazza's private office, Tenak, First Officer Statton, and the ship's Second Officer, Blandin, joined her around a conference table.

'Okay, gentilhomms,' said Tenak, 'we've had a good look at the info on the data flake taken out of Mike. It's not safe to cascade it onto the mainframe. We know that's been compromised once already. In this case hard copy is essential. So, as a precaution, we've duplicated the flake a number of times and placed copies in various secure locations around the ship. I'm afraid only the Captain and I know these locations.' The others nodded as he continued, 'The data on the flake is highly compromising – not to say, dangerous stuff. It's imperative we get this back to the Home System asap. To that end we've already launched a datapod, containing duplications of the flake. We've told the engineering department we wanted to send info on Brundleton's arrest. Nothing more.'

'Forgive my asking, Admiral,' said Blandin, 'but as I am head of Security, wouldn't it have been protocol to have included me in this plan?'

'I am sorry, Lieutenant,' said Ebazza, 'but the Admiral and I felt it would be safest if we alone knew the contents of the pod. And we're bringing you in on this now, aren't we?' She gave Blandin the kind of look that clearly said, *don't push it, Lieutenant.* He nodded obsequiously.

Tenak continued, 'The point is, we need to take some action to unmask any other quislings. We will be asking Brundleton *a lot of* questions when he wakes but the Captain and I don't expect he'll be happy to talk.'

'I'll get Brundleton to talk,' said Blandin, 'just give him to me.'

Ebazza just gave him a withering look.

Statton, quiet till now, chipped in, 'I'm sorry Mantford, but we hadn't really made much progress – till this.'

'I know but I can think of quick ways we can get Brundleton to talk.'

'You know that Navy prisoner ethics rules prohibit "strongarm" tactics, Lieutenant. And neither will I, at the moment. Use your head. Be subtle,' said Tenak.

'Yes – if you are capable of that,' said Ebazza.

Blandin's expression was a mixture of indignation and embarrassment.

'The Captain's willing to give you another chance now, Lieutenant,' said Tenak. 'And if she is, so am I.'

'Yes,' said Ebazza, 'so I'm putting you in charge of interrogating Brundleton, *without torture or drugs* – when he's well enough to be questioned, so don't screw it up this time.'

Blandin nodded curtly.

'Very well. Dismissed,' said Tenak.

After the XO and Second Officer had left, Ebazza turned to Tenak, 'I think we'll have to replace Blandin. I'm not entirely satisfied of his competence. But we're now working in the dark, here. I don't think there's reason to suspect Blandin any more than we could suspect a number of others. So, we need to be careful about *who we replace him with*.'

'Agreed,' said Tenak.

'Unfortunately, the flake didn't say anything about Rebel operatives on The Monsoon but I'm not convinced there aren't others here, Admiral,' said Ebazza, 'and I don't trust Dagghampton. But if there are any others, my guess is that they'll try to assassinate Brundleton, probably at Oceanus, while we're busy dealing with evacuees.'

'Then put him under extra armed guard,' said Tenak.

'I'll have him transferred to the brig, as soon as he's fit enough to move. And we'll bolster up security in the brig too,' said Ebazza.

****

Mantford Blandin commed Dravette Shacklebury by an especially secure audio channel, once he was back in his own quarters, after the meeting.

'We better hope Brundleton doesn't pipe any tunes,' he said quietly, after outlining what was said in the meeting. 'I had to pretend I wanted to use violence on him, so he'd talk.'

'Don't worry,' she replied, 'he won't talk, but we need to rescue him – soon.'

'What?' said Blandin, his eyes widening with surprise. 'Are you mad? They'll be expecting that. And it'll be virtually impossible to get him out of the brig. I'm obliged to assign extra guards.'

'Then one of them can be me, can't it? And we'd better spring him *before* he gets to the brig. I suggest we free him en route from the med bay.'

'And then what the feg do we do? Hide him somewhere on the ship?'

'No. We do what we ... what you, thought we might have to do, in any case. We take the so-called "Captain's Yacht". It's ready, after all.'

'That was only as a last resort, Dravette. As long as Brundleton doesn't squawk, we can ride this out. I don't think the data flake says anything about us or we'd have been arrested by now.'

'You can't be sure but, in any case, I think you're forgetting that the Captain doesn't like you. How long before she begins to suspect you? I'll bet she does anyway. Besides, I'm not prepared to see Garmin spend the rest of his days on the penal colony on Mars. I want him free. I need him out. Listen to me, *Mister* Lieutenant man. I'm serious.'

'What? Don't tell me ... You and Brundle ...?'

'Oh yes, Lieutenant. I'm prepared to admit it now. He and I have been ... together for some time – and you'd better believe it.'

'You two are always at each-other's throats.'

'Yeah, of course.'

After a second, Blandin chuckled smugly. 'Of course. Very clever, Dravette,' he said.

'Which is why no-one should suspect me if you assign me to his guard detail. And you've always avoided being closely connected with him. Leastways, I hope so.'

Blandin sighed. 'Of course. Okay, so you reckon we should just break out completely, but where would we go, genius? There aren't many options. Oh, you're going to say we go back to the Home System, aren't you? And what, just report back to our taskmasters? Is that what you think? Cos if you do, I shouldn't have to explain to you that they'll probably just kill us, merely for failing them.'

'No, we don't report back to them, Lieutenant. Listen to me, I know it sounds weird, but I have a top tek friend back home. She's a real good femna. Worked for years in the outer Solar system. She told me the science station based on the dwarf planet, Iolantia, is still in working order. We can lie low there for a few years. All three of us. There's plenty of room.'

'And Iolantia's just a wee bit cold Dravette. That planet is half as far out again as Pluto. And the science station was abandoned years ago.'

'No, Mantford, it wasn't. Not many people know this. She convinced me it's still operating – cos it's under full automation. Robots still operating out there. There's micro-nuclear power plants still operating. It was vacated by human crews, due to the cost. But, with my friend's help, the automatons can be reprogrammed to make it habitable again. And my friend is *very* discrete. Owes me big time, for sure. It'll be fine and – well, as you say – we don't have a lot of other options, do we?'

'And you're sure your friend can be trusted?'

'Yes, Mantford. I'd stake my life on it.'

'You might have to. By the way, I reckon there is something else we can do. We can warn our taskmasters about the dataflake. It's too late to stop The Monsoon's pod but I'm sure our superiors will appreciate having a "heads up" on it. Might help them prepare some contingency plans. And maybe they'll even … give us another chance?'

'In your dreams, Mantford. Still, I have no objection to telling them, as long as we, personally, steer clear of them. And hang on at the science station. Leastways, for a few years. We can decide on our future moves at our leisure.'

'Speaking of the future, Dravette, I think we need to hatch a plan to spring Brundleton, right now, since you think that's the best option.'

'It is, and, *Lieutenant*, I'll be watching you. Don't even think about dropping me and Garmin in the shit, so you can save your dodgy reputation with Ebazza. You're not getting out of this now. If you try anything, I'll arrange things so you regret it for the rest of your life. You're going to be releasing Garmin *with me*, whatever else you might think.'

****

As expected, Garmin Brundleton was too ill to walk to the brig from the med bay. Blandin walked ahead of three security guards, including Shacklebury, and a female hemi-med attendant. They left the med bay, with Brundleton strapped into a magnetically levitated medi- chair. Shacklebury walked behind the chair, biding her time.

Brundleton was awake, but his face betrayed his continuing discomfort and he seemed not to notice what was happening to him. Very convincingly, he gave nothing away when he saw that his two co-conspirators had been assigned to the job of escorting him. In fact, his behaviour towards them had been full of fake contempt.

The part of the ship they now traversed was a maze of corridors because of the complex equipment bays in the area, and they eventually reached a kind of 'joint,' in it. Here the corridor switched to the right at 90 and again, at nearly a right angle, bending back on itself, so preventing someone in it being seen by anyone else at any distance greater than a few metres. At the position of the right angles the corridor was directly above the airlock vestibule for the Dragonfly, situated only two decks below. It was at this point that the two quislings made their move. Blandin had carefully insisted that everyone take this particular route to the med bay.

As the senior officer, Blandin was expected to lead the group, with Shacklebury 'volunteering' to take up the rear; the other two security guards walking nearer Brundleton's chair, with the hemi-med walking alongside him. When they reached the spot the quislings knew to be above the Dragonfly airlock Shacklebury placed her right hand in her jacket, readying to grab the heavy sonic pistol therein. Blandin started coughing convulsively, an agreed signal. That's when Shacklebury drew her pistol and fired at the back of one of the guards in front of her. The other guard turned reflexively, reaching for his own pistol but Blandin had turned and fired at him.

Their victims went down like skittles but as they did so the hemi-med, evidently believing that Blandin was in danger, thrust his chair out of the way and in doing so stumbled toward Shacklebury, thrusting out her arms. Shacklebury fired directly at her when she was only half a metre away. The shot blew a hole in the woman's neck and she slumped to the floor.

Brundleton sat upright at that point and grinned at them, as Blandin grabbed the back of his chair and, with Shacklebury, raced off, steering Brundleton, making for a hatchway in the wall beyond the bend. Shacklebury kept her gun out and, as they reached the hatch an unsuspecting crewmember happened to come around the corner. She fired her weapon again and the man staggered and fell.

They rushed to the hatch and, as they opened it, pushed the chair through. Shacklebury shouted to Blandin, breathlessly, 'Now you're well and truly *with us*, so I reckon I can tell you that I've been keeping a recording of all our conversations over the last few weeks, *Lieutenant*.'

'Can't it wait? We're trying to make an escape here, aren't we?' said Blandin.

'Maybe you can't but I can talk and run at the same time, Lieutenant. I was about to say I stuck duplicates in various places around the ship, known only to me. My desk unit had orders to reveal those locations to the other senior officers, if you'd done anything to *us* back there, to save your own skin.'

'Thank you so much,' huffed Blandin as they rushed onwards, 'and remind me not to trust you again – fellow rebel.'

'You'll have to trust me, if we are make it to our goal. Unless you want to risk going back to our *comrades* on your own.'

'Okay, okay,' said Blandin, as they continued to push Brundleton, at high speed, through the next section of corridor, 'just let's just make sure we get out of here. We've got to get Garmin down the ladder tubes between two decks. The elevators are too risky.'

'I can do it without the chair. I can do it, guys,' croaked Brundleton, sounding irritated by the way they seemed to have forgotten he was actually listening. He continued, 'I might be a bit slow but you're not going without me. I assume you're talking about the Dragonfly?' The other two nodded as, panting, they tried to keep control of the chair.

'The PL system will have picked up our movements by now,' said Blandin, 'They'll know we're not going in the direction of the brig and there's only three of us, not six.'

'Down here,' said Shacklebury and opened a hatch in the floor further along the narrow access corridor. Blandin started down the ladder tube first, and reaching up with one hand, helped guide Brundleton's feet down. Shacklebury held onto her lover's upper body as long as she could, then followed down. Brundleton suddenly grasped the ladder and surprised the others by climbing down, albeit slowly and carefully, on his own.

**

Admiral Tenak received the news on his way to the number Two Bridge, and his eyes practically bulged with frustration and anger. It was Statton who called him, on audio, saying, 'I'm sorry sir but something went wrong in corridor twenty-eight, deck three. Brundleton was being taken to the brig. The PL system indicates the Second Officer, Brundleton, and rating Shacklebury, are on their way to deck two, not the brig. The other guards and a hemi-med are stationary, on deck three. We can't be sure why. We're getting a security team down there, on the double, sir.'

'I take it you've tried actually contacting Blandin and Shacklebury?' said Tenak, his voice registering surprise but he still projected an even and calm tone.

'Yes sir. No reply. As expected, if they've done ... Well, if ...'

'Just say it, Commander. You mean, if they've freed Brundleton? Looks like maybe now we know who else is involved. And where the dammy are they going?'

'There's an exhaust vent hyper nexus down there. Maybe they're going to sabotage it,' said Statton.

Tenak thought for a while, then his eyes lit up, 'I don't think so,' he said. 'but I reckon I know where they're trying to do. It's the "Captain's Yacht". The Dragonfly – that's it.'

'But ...? Yeah, of course. The ship's biggest lifeboat – only meant to be used in star systems other than Sol's, in an emergency ...'

'And the only lifeboat *capable of independent travel back to the Solar System*,' Tenak added. 'Okay. Check the manifests and get back to me – and make sure you get another security team down to the Dragonfly's prep bay. And tell the minor AIs to lock them out of as many corridors as possible. And Commander Statton …'

'Yes sir?'

'I take it that you agree with me that the ship's Number Two has probably not been taken as a hostage by the other two?'

Statton sounded nervous, 'Can't be sure yet but seems unlikely. Sorry to say, sir.'

Tenak said nothing but his face betrayed white-hot anger.

Minutes later the Admiral was on the Bridge. Ebazza was there and had been apprised of the situation. She said, in words dripping with frustration, 'Admiral, I understand they've already reached the deck above the Dragonfly. And they've disabled the hypercomp's sub-routines for the hatch controls. The other thing is, we can't use electronic means to stop them getting to the Yacht. They were well prepared for this, especially Blandin.'

'I know Captain. It's docked to us externally. Makes it safer, easier to use in an emergency,' said Tenak, 'but the AIs can freeze the docking hub, can't they?'

'Yes sir,' said Ebazza,' but there's an override on the Dragonfly itself….'

'Yeah, of course there is. So the lifeboat's escape can't be impeded if something terrible is happening in the main part of the ship.' Tenak wore an even graver look on his face. 'Well, we'll just have to deal with this another way,' he said.

'We can use the ship's weapons and ….' said Ebazza, and then her eyes widened with renewed concern.

'What's the matter?' began Tenak, then said, 'Dammy. Of course. The Monsoon's due to begin its deceleration burn in … how long?'

'In 8 minute, thirty four seconds, sir,' said a navigation officer at the front of the Bridge.

'We can't alter that without serious consequences, but the ship can still use its lasers, even in fast deceleration. I've never done it on active ops – but it's possible,' said Ebazza.

'I'm reluctant to kill them,' said Tenak, 'specially when we need to get as much info out of them as poss, and I don't want the "rebel cause" having more martyrs.'

'We didn't bring any corvettes with us, to go after them, because their hangars have been converted for this trip. Do you have something else in mind, sir?' asked Ebazza.

'I'll talk to them. If we can't stop them from leaving, we'll use ship to ship comms. It's worth trying to persuade them it's a hopeless cause.'

A rating on the Bridge interrupted, 'Admiral. Captain. It's definitely too late to stop them. The AI says they've just entered the Dragonfly – and they're powering up its engines.'

'These people are nothing if not efficient,' said Tenak. 'It's a pity they're not on our side.'

Seconds later the AI told them that the lifeboat had unlatched and fired its powerful separation thrusters.

*****

On the Dragonfly, secured into their flying seats, the three rebels cheered as they watched themselves separate further from The Monsoon, already five kilometres distant, as the mother ship slowly rotated through 180°. This meant its massive engine was now pointing in the direction of travel, ready for the burn to slow it down. The giant engine bell quickly burst into phosphorescent brilliance, throwing out streamers of orange plasma, kilometres long, starting the long process of deceleration which would bring it into the inner Ra system. The rebels knew that the crew of the big ship could do nothing else at that stage. They couldn't risk losing valuable time and fuel in achieving Oceanus orbit by a detour. Not even to stop rebels.

The brilliance of The Monsoon's plasma burn was so great the Dragonfly automatically raised glare shields over its wide windows. As it did so the three quislings, grinning, watched as The Monsoon's deceleration caused it to, in effect, drop 'behind' them with increasing rapidity, while they, themselves, careered on at almost the original speed of the giant vessel.

'Their burn has to last for at least 21 days if they're going to achieve insertion into orbit around Oceanus,' said Blandin, 'cos I know they won't override it just to recover us. We can continue at near The Monsoon's original speed for a few days, till we're ready to carry out our own acceleration burn – to bring us around and back out to a transit zone. Then, we can go home.'

'We don't want to skip straight through this whole system and out the other side,' said Shacklebury, looking nervous. 'The only trouble is the time we'll take to arc around to the co-ordinates of the transit zone our AI's given us. The new conduits are about a billion kilometres away from the zone where we came in.'

'If our engine does its job it should only take about three, maybe four weeks,' said Blandin, 'then another one, the other side, to get to the outermost zone of the Home System. That's assuming there aren't any other obstacles getting to our destination.'

'Dravette, that shit place you mentioned is way out in the boondocks, isn't it?' said Brundleton, looking dazed. 'I hope it can be made habitable, like you said.'

She gave a perfunctory nod.

'Well, this baby should get us there, anyway,' said Brundleton, ignoring the uncertainty of her reaction, and continued, 'cos it's got three class one fusion engines. That should do nicely, even though they're small. It's lucky for us it's the only lifeboat capable of travelling through a conduit – and our glorious Captain thought it was her *private* transport. Did you know, back a year or so ago, she actually used this ship for entertaining some Admiralty piss-wits? Out in high Earth orbit, it was. I asked her, you know, what would happen if The Monsoon had an emergency while she was using it? And suppose it's not possible to access the landing boat hangars, or the corvettes, I said. All she could say was, "That's a pretty big, if, mister."' He did an impression of Ebazza's mannerisms as he spoke.

As the others made harrumphing noises, as Brundleton continued, 'She also said, "Besides, you know the regs. There's eight other lifeboats secreted around the ship. They're fully capable of navigating around the Solar System." What a nerve. The other boats aren't conduit equipped and … they're tiny by comparison. *And I don't like small spaces.*'

'Poor you,' said Blandin, mockingly, 'and besides, she's right, ain't she? She can only use this ship for "entertaining" when it's in the inner Solar System.' He looked at Brundleton and grinned. 'Don't worry. It's all worked to our advantage, hasn't it? Listen, I'd have loved to put that shit-feg Ebazza overboard, at the earliest opportunity. But this will do.'

'Yeah, course,' laughed Shacklebury, 'and I made sure this baby's got more than adequate supplies for the journey. There is one thing you might have forgotten, though.'

The others looked at her quizzically.

'Well, it might be conduit rated but this boat's never really been used for a journey like that. It's untested, in practice. Anything could happen.'

'It's the only one of its type in the entire Navy, and it's thanks to The Monsoon being one of its type too,' said Blandin. 'Listen, have some faith. It'll be fine.'

'Yeah,' said Brundleton, with a sarcastic edge to his voice, 'listen to our "boss." He says, "This will do." Yeah, we've only got *a few weeks* of micro-gravity to put up with.'

'Don't you fegging-well start,' said Blandin, drily.

'You're a real fantasist, aren't you, *Mister* Blandin?' spat Shacklebury. 'You've forgotten there's a reasonable chance the navigation AI on this ship will louse up the conduit sensing. The reality is, we'll be lucky to get back at all.'

'You were the one who wanted to do this. And, as you said, we had no choice, did we? Stop worrying, you two. We'll get back,' said Blandin, huffing with impatience, 'and it might not be comfortable, but we'll …'

The central AI interrupted Blandin, to announce it had an incoming call, audio only, from The Monsoon. Blandin hesitated, then signalled they would take it.

Admiral Tenak's amplified voice could be heard booming in the quiet of the Dragonfly's spacious cabin.

'I won't bother asking why any of you are really doing this,' said Tenak evenly, 'but you, Blandin, more than the others, are a big disappointment to me. Be that as it may, I think your options are limited now. I'm guessing you will want to get back to the Home System in about the same relative time frame as our datapod. No doubt you'll want to warn your comrade superiors. Now, you might or might not succeed, but I think you know, as well as I, that your New Rebel leaders won't be very pleased with you. They'll probably have you assassinated. The only way to avoid that, and gain our protection, is to give yourselves up. If you carry out the burn which our AI has calculated for you, and which I'm sending as a data stream now, you can brake around to the inner Ra system and rendezvous with us at Kumuda. Or at Oceanus. I advise you, in the strongest terms, to take my suggested course of action. Should you agree, you only have a small window in which to start your burn; between 40 and 42 minutes from now. If you miss it, I shall assume you have not taken my advice – and I will take action to stop you escaping. Tenak out.'

Hey, Blandin,' said Brundleton, chuckling,'*he's real disappointed in you.* Crabbit gimbo that he is. Well, what the shit can he do?'

'Use missiles,' said Blandin, in matter-of-fact voice.

He wouldn't do it,' said Brundleton. 'Kill fellow crewmembers? Not to mention a senior officer. I doubt that. He hasn't got it in him, the ancient sheep that he is.'

'I'm not so sure, love,' said Shacklebury, with a distant look in her eyes.

'Don't let his manner fool you,' said Blandin, 'because Tenak *has* got it in him. He's a decorated veteran of the Rebel Wars. *Remember?*'

'That was a helluva long time ago,' said Brundleton, 'and he's slowed down. Like I said, the shit face won't do it.'

But this time no-one was laughing.

**

On the number Two Bridge of The Monsoon, Ssanyu Ebazza looked at Tenak, her brow deeply furrowed, 'Do you really think they'll climb down?' she said.

'Depends on how they consider their odds of success,' said Tenak.

'Sir, are you actually prepared to try to fire on them?'

'Before I answer that, tell me, Ssanyu. What would you do?'

'Destroy them – now. But I'm not you. I'm sorry Admiral, but you have a ... sort of, reputation for conciliation and compromise. Some people think that's a weakness. But it's not. It's a great strength of yours. And I'm not just saying it because it's you I'm talking to right now. You know that. I think they'd be foolish to persist with their course of action. They're taking a risk just trying to fly home, but I believe the Dragonfly's probably up to the job. Perhaps their bosses will do the job for us, anyway, like you said.'

'I know, but if they make it home, I believe they'll try to ingratiate themselves by warning their bosses *before* the security forces, maybe even before our datapod gets back. Our major AIs have calculated they could do it. The Dragonfly has powerful engines, and they might find a transit zone in the Outer Lagrange point, 003. I just don't think we can risk it Ssanyu. But, if we try to destroy them, let's not forget that the Dragonfly has its own armament. You insisted on it, Ssanyu, in case there was a military emergency when the boat was separated from this ship.'

*****

'I say we fire our torpedoes at them,' said Brundleton, his voice full of anger. 'After all, this ship has five high yield Alpha Furies – and five low yield Wasps.'

'Ten isn't enough,' said Blandin, 'cos The Monsoon's AI directed laser batteries would shoot them up, even if some got through their intercept missiles. The Wasps would hardly make a dent in the ship's armour plating. The Furies might make a mess of the plating. Maybe blow out a few sections of decking but not enough to cause major damage. No, I say we need to hang onto our missiles. We might need them for later. Especially, back in the Home System.'

'You're wrong. I say it's just as well you're not in charge of us anymore, *Mister Lieutenant man*,' snarled Brundleton. 'What do you say, love?' He turned to Shacklebury.

Shacklebury looked embarrassed. 'I'm sorry, Garmin' she said, placing one hand on his knee. 'I think Blandin's got a point. We need to keep those torpedoes, for now.'

Brundleton frowned with puzzlement. 'So, he's got you thinking his way has he?' He glared at Blandin and said, 'If we program the torpedo's brains to target the engines, The Monsoon will skip out of this system and leave them stranded. Okay, so the fusion engine's got triple layer armour plate, but concentrating the torps at the "knuckle links" could blow part of the main feed tubes. Alternatively, if the missiles are all aimed at the exact same spot near, say, the main bridge, they could blow a sizeable hole in the hull. Or we could use them to concentrate on the area above, say, bridge number two. That's probably where Command is right now. It'd give them a shock. Might even get through to the bridge itself. I know some torps might be lasered out but it's worth a try.'

Shacklebury looked deeply disturbed. 'Darlin', you're forgetting their engines are guarded by Alpha Class, "Sniper", lasers – double lasers. And, if we did manage to get a few missiles into the same spot on the hub, or the torus, all we'd do is succeed in killing a few crewmembers. Probably old mates of ours. I, for one, don't want to do any more killing.'

The two men frowned. 'What do you mean? Who'd you kill?' asked Blandin.

'Didn't you notice … when we sprang Garmin… I fired on a hemi-med. I didn't realise my sonic was on 98%. Hit her point blank. Went down awful heavy. I caught a sight of her face as we left. Looked bad.' Shacklebury looked down blankly at her lap.

'Listen sweeto,' said Brundleton, 'you did what had to be done. I know it's a shame but … well, she … was collateral damage. No need to get too upset.' He put a hand on her shoulder but she shrugged it off, glared at him, then turned away.

'She was a medico, Garmin,' she said, quietly, 'just trying to help people.'

'Now she tells us her gun was on lethal,' said Blandin and sighed deeply.

'Now, what's up with you?' shouted Brundleton.

'If that medic is dead, you'll find out what Tenak is really capable of. We'd better hope she isn't.'

****

On the number Two Bridge, the crew and officers were beginning to feel a strengthening gravity take hold, as The Monsoon's power- braking continued. Just before the engine had ignited the ship had coasted, involving a short but disorientating period of relative micro-gravity, whilst the vessel turned to put its aft end into 'forward' orientation. The crew were used to it, but it would be hard for anyone who was a passenger.

Another strange but necessary effect was that during the ship's 180° turnaround, the crew had had to strap themselves down and secure all loose items, as the direction of gravity also, effectively, 'rotated' through the same angle.

During this whole manoeuvre the crew could only monitor screen readouts, 'normality' resuming only after the braking burn began. Tenak and Ebazza had kept a wary eye on the situation with the Dragonfly. The main ship had been vulnerable, but only very slightly, during the manoeuvre, though missiles could have been launched, by voice command, or lasers initiated, guided by hypercomp.

'Ensure all laser batteries are fully enabled,' Tenak told Statton, 'because I'm expecting them to use the Dragonfly's complement of torpedoes. It may be small but it's potentially lethal, if used the right way.'

'Command Deck,' came a female voice over Ebazza's desk terminal, 'I have some bad news.' It was Atrowska, sounding tired and mournful, 'I'm sorry to say that hemi-med Irramia died two minutes ago.' There were gasps from some of the officers on the bridge, including Ebazza. Tenak frowned deeply, as Atrowska continued, 'I'm sorry. We tried to save her, but the stun gun blast hit her in the throat, at close range. It took out most of her oesophagus and trachea. She also hit her head when she went down. We were able to repair some of that but we couldn't repair the throat injury fast enough. She'd been lying out there too long. But we tried hard. I am truly sorry.'

'So are we,' said Tenak softly, 'so are we. But you're not the ones responsible, Chief. I'm sure you did everything you could. Don't berate yourself.'

'This mission just cost us another life,' he said to Ebazza.

'Maybe we should just blast those dammy rebels, right now,' said Statton, standing nearby, looking furious.

'No. We can all get emotional about this, but this is not going to be about retribution. It's about saving *other lives* in the long run. I've given them 20 minutes. There's 10 to go on the chrono'. I'll accept their surrender, if that's what they decide. Vengeance has no place here, mister' said Tenak.

'Yes, sir,' said Statton, looking sheepish.

'Don't worry, Number One,' said Tenak, 'If they give up, we can always hope they get the longest sentence available on the Mars Penal Colony. That really would be justice.'

****

On the Dragonfly the rebel traitors had settled back, but remained rather nervous, trying to get some rest, but failing. No-one had spoken for some time when their AI announced, in a jaunty, chiming type of female voice, *'The deadline given by Admiral Tenak expired three minutes ago. I would remind you that I have given a warning every minute until the marked time. I calculate it will be 36 minutes until this vessel needs to initiate a 68-minute burn to insert into an elongated orbit, with eccentricity, e = 1.00 This will provide rendezvous with Ra's Outer, 003 Lagrange, T-zone, with ETA in approximately 3.8 standard weeks.'*

'Garmin, seems you were wrong about Tenak,' said Brundleton, smugly, appearing to relax, as he tried to settle back on a couch, strapped in against the microgravity, not that it stopped him sipping from a cool container of stim-beer, albeit through a suck-straw.

'I hope you're right. I'm not complacent,' said Blandin, glancing anxiously at a nearby control console and monitor screen. Shacklebury remained staring into the distance. She looked as though she was in a world of her own.

****

'It's been 7 minutes since your deadline ran out, sir,' said Ebazza. Tenak just nodded in silence.

The Admiral suddenly held a hand to his right ear. He was wearing a tiny 'privacy' ear bud, so he could instantly receive an incoming transmission which his wristcom had warned him was imminent. The transmission was from off-ship and its source had pre-warned him about its level of security. He concentrated on the message, pacing slowly around as he did so.

'There's been a development,' he said to Ebazza. 'I just heard from Providius. We've got no more time to waste on this particular matter. You have my permission to fire on the Dragonfly. I don't want them escaping this system. See to it please, then follow me to the Observatory.'

'Yes sir,' said Ebazza. Then, sighing, she turned to Statton, 'You heard him, Lieutenant. Use the grapeshot interdictors. Launch two of them, just in case those shite-snapes get lucky.'

****

A klaxon sounded aboard the Dragonfly and Blandin came fully alert, sitting bolt upright, restrained suddenly by his harness. He stared, wide eyed, at the monitor screen. The other two reacted as if similarly electrified, Brundleton losing his bottle of beer.

'Like I said. He's coming for us,' said Blandin, nervous energy giving an edge to his voice. 'He launched two grapeshot. Attend to your stations.'

'Interdictors.' said Shacklebury. 'He wants to make sure.' She slid over to a console.

'Basterdos,' said Brundleton. 'But listen, Mantford, we can deal with these.'

'We haven't got laser intercept,' said Blandin, 'so we'll have to use the torps. Good thing we didn't use them earlier.' He looked askance at Brundleton, then said to his female colleague, 'Go, Dravette.'

Shacklebury spoke loudly to the ship's comp, 'Launch all torpedoes but not until the moment the interdictors start to split.' The AI acknowledged. They waited.

The two missiles, the 'interdictors', launched by The Monsoon, were obliged to follow a wide arcing trajectory to reach the Dragonfly, their vectors being influenced by a combination of The Monsoon's speed relative to that of their target, as well as the thrust of their own, small, but powerful, fusion engines. They had been sent at practically the last moment they could have been launched, so as to reach the Dragonfly in the most efficient way. Taking 36 minutes to get within a thousand kilometres of their target, they then split open, each one releasing five small, self-propelled, spherical bomblets. Having closed with their target at a speed faster than the Dragonfly's velocity, the bomblets effectively needed only their small but hyper-efficient chemical rockets to bridge the final gap. They were all guided to their marks by a mini hyper-comp buried inside each one.

Aboard the Dragonfly the three rebels had spent a miserable half an hour contemplating the dance of the fates, after their own ship had launched its torpedoes, to defend. Then, they watched their screens, seemingly overjoyed, as the whirling graphics showed a bright tag mark indicating one after another bomblet winking out of existence on the screen. Brundleton smiled and said to his lover, 'I told you we'd be okay,' then turning to the former Second Officer of The Monsoon, said, 'Hey Blandin, I said …,' but his remarks were cut short and his face dropped as he and his colleagues suddenly noticed tag marks, representing five surviving bomblets, continuing toward them, now completely unopposed.

They had lost – big time.

The AI said, *'Brace for impact. Brace hard. Impact in twelve seconds … eleven …'*

'You were saying, Garmin?' said Blandin, who turned away and began to stare into the distance, probably at something only he could see. Shacklebury gazed at her screen and closed her eyes, gripping her station desk, with knuckles turning white. Brundleton opened his mouth as though to scream, but nothing came out.

***

On-board The Monsoon, First Officer Statton watched his 'real-time' screen as a dazzlingly bright flash hit the ship's sensors. He looked away momentarily, even though the screen had anticipated the image washout, blanking it out with a polarising filter in the last micro-second. There was still a shock of brightness. The XO spoke to Ebazza with even voice, 'Sensors show the Dragonfly has turned into dust and gas, mostly. Some small debris also now emerging from the explosion. Five bomblets reached their mark. It's over, Captain.'

She nodded but there was no look of triumph. No-one smirked or hooted gleefully. With a mournful expression, she strode off the bridge toward the obs' lounge. 'You have the conn, XO,' she said, with a deep sigh.

***

Mike Tanniss struggled out of the med bay, down to the Observation Lounge, three decks below, after hearing from Tenak. He hadn't seen Providius's original message, and Tenak had said that data cascades on the subject had been temporarily censored from further viewing. But Mike was cleared to see them, in person, only on the obs deck. He could have used a magnetic chair to get there but decided to walk as best he could. He was back to using that good old-fashioned walking stick.

His chest and shoulder still ached like mad. He was aware that his chest had been packed with synth-tissue, but it was bedding in well. The nick to his heart had been tiny and had been sealed over well but as one lung had been cut slightly, he was prone to bouts of coughing, occasionally bringing up small amounts of bloody sputum. This was, they said, actually a good sign in this case – showing that the synth-flesh was working. When he'd been told what had happened to hemi-med Irrania, he counted himself lucky. Unlike him, she hadn't had a handy Dagghampton standing by. He thought a lot about how much he owed to Sanders and resolved to thank him personally, as soon as possible, but meanwhile, the Admiral's request, practically an order, seemed alarmingly urgent, not to say cryptic.

When he reached the 'Obs' lounge', Tenak and Ebazza were already there. Tenak called him in, smiling and said, 'This is highly classified right now, but I thought you deserved to see it, especially as you have first-hand experience. Sort of. By the way, Mike, how're you doing now? Good enough to get down here without a mag-chair, I see? I'm impressed.'

'Doing okay, thanks,' said Mike. 'I heard about what happened to Irrania. I was real sorry about that.'

Ebazza looked morose. Tenak nodded in silence.

'But what happened to the rebels?' Mike asked.

'They paid the ultimate price for their sins,' said Ebazza, with a sour look. Mike nodded.

They all sat as the light in the obs chamber dimmed, just as a vid message appeared on a massive 'deep-gas' screen in front of them. The Monsoon was currently too far from the inner Ra system to be able to receive any holo-vids and much too far for two-way communications. Captain Providius's image suddenly appeared on the screen, lightly flickering.

'Greetings. I'm very glad you're back,' she said, 'but we didn't know you were there till about twenty minutes ago, when we received your AI's auto signal. We've sent a datapod back home, but I suspect you got here before it reached the home system government. To cut to the chase, Admiral, Captain, … we've observed a massive cloud of objects spreading out around Ra. They're in an orbit well above its atmosphere but closer to it than the planet Seth, the nearest one to Ra. We believe these things are related to the same cloud that swept past the Antarctica, when Mike was with us. Here's the data we've picked up in the last few weeks, suitably summarised. I've fed the full details to your major AI's.'

The image of Providius shrank to around one tenth of the 'screen' and in the rest a video of a segment of Ra appeared, greatly toned down, to kill the brilliant glare of the star. Nothing could be seen against the bubbling, bright, surface of the star, until a computer-generated band was superimposed around Ra. A section within the graphic was then subjected to enormous magnification, and a separate image appeared, apparently rushing toward the 'viewer', so it was possible to see more detail. Only then could the strange cloud be seen to be 'alive', roiling, boiling, with seemingly innumerable, tiny, black objects, all flowing along in orbit around Ra. The overall shape of the cloud was like a sooty torus sweeping across the background image of the star. As Tenak, Ebazza and Mike stared open mouthed at the graphics sent by Providius, there was another jump in magnification, but, weirdly, the enlarged section of the cloud showed no further detail. Now, the enlargement was simply indicated by means of scrolling figures on the screen, except that the sooty particles appeared to be travelling faster, due to the closer perspective.

Providius continued her narrative, 'The smallest particles are about 10 micrometres across and although originally covered with carbon, organic, residue, that material has evaporated in the heat from Ra. What's left is an alloy of some sort. We've been *unable* to determine its composition from its spectrum. There's some sort of interference effect. It's similar to what we saw when the cloud passed the Antarctica a couple of months ago.

'So, unfortunately, we're no closer to knowing what these things are made of. And, at our current distance, they're too small even for our imagers to clarify what they actually look like, in detail. That's not all. Expanding, about a million klicks above the band you're looking at, is a second layer. This is a broader band of particles, which are all larger, ranging from 0.14 millimetre to over a hundred metres across. Here they are.'

An expanded image of one of the larger objects in the higher cloud appeared on the screen. It was slightly blurred, even under hypercomp resolution, but it was regular in shape and very dark. To Mike it looked like the object might be covered with facets or faces, like those of mineral crystals.

'And guess what?' continued Providius, 'we cannot determine the composition of the larger structures, either, but there are three things you, and the HS government need to know. First, all the small particles, large and small, are *multiplying*. To repeat, *they are multiplying.*

Mike suddenly burst into a loud coughing fit, as Providius continued, 'And they're spreading out above the equatorial region of Ra. We estimate their numbers have increased from around two billion, initially, to over twenty billion, in the last three standard weeks. Second, these objects are definitely, as I'm sure you've realised by now, *not natural*. Apart from their bizarre behaviour indicating this, we can be absolutely certain, because we got a reasonably good look at some of the largest ones. Nothing like this exists in our databanks and I'm sure your own databanks will confirm this. And we think the smallest ones are probably similar in structure to the largest ones, but we don't know. The lower band is orbiting no further than 15 million klicks from Ra's surface – and we have no idea why they don't melt – but that's the least of it.

'Third. And you *really* won't like this. They're having some sort of negative effect on Ra itself. The convective zone of the star is changing in the region directly below the orbiting bands. Worse yet. we think the upper parts of the deep Karabrandon Waves have enlarged in amplitude by over 50% and continuing. Other types of waves, possibly as far down as the so called, Morgiston layer, near the star's core, are stirring up effects in its upper atmosphere. The surface of Ra itself is also being … well, it's being mixed, is all I can say. The orbiting particles seem to be directly affecting the photosphere. They seem to be drawing up thin tendrils of gas from the surface. Look at the data streams now.'

On the right half of the screen a series of graphs and animated data rolled up. Ebazza and Tenak looked totally mystified. Mike thought he understood some of what he could see but even he found its complexity daunting.

'Has Jennison seen this?' said Mike, as he convulsively coughed again. 'Why isn't he here?' This was all making him nervous. He didn't like the sound of these alien machine, artefact, things.

'This transmission has been routed to his private cabin,' said Tenak. 'He was busy in the Forward Science station but I commed him to go to his cabin. It's nearer for him. I want to keep this restricted for the moment.'

'If you want our overall analysis,' Providius was saying, 'I can't offer you very much because we just don't know much. And what we do know, now you do too. Our AI says it thinks these things are "von Neumann" machines and that's the best guess of our people as well.'

'Von what?' said Ebazza.

Mike turned to Ebazza, sitting next to him, and said, 'Back in the 20th century an American mathematician suggested that a species of advanced beings might create self- replicating machines, which they'd then seed the galaxy with. Because they're machines, they need no life support, and they don't age. They can roam interstellar space without restriction, maybe for millions of years. They're just programmed to use the matter they find in any star system, such as *planets*, and use the stuff to repair themselves and replicate millions of times. Then, when the worlds they visit have been used up they move on to the next star, replicate again, and so on. In other words, they consume world after world, till they fill the galaxy. Comforting thought, eh?'

'Like some sort of … horrible, cosmic virus,' spat Tenak. While he couldn't see Tenak's face in the low light, he could well imagine its grim visage.

They caught up with Providius's message, which had continued unabated,

'… not possible to be certain about anything and we don't want to be alarmist – but if these really are VM machines, then we've got really big problems, here. I know your mission is to take evacuees off Oceanus, Admiral, but I'd say the immediate priority is for us both to investigate this thing, right now. It's down to you, of course. I can't tell the Navy what to do but – for what it's worth, I'd say this current development is totally unique and, I have to say, pretty scary.

'I hope you agree to a course correction,' she said finally, 'and your AI's now know our co-ordinates, but we're parked in an elongated orbit, averaging 42 million klicks from Ra. And by the way, the cloud particles have paid no attention to us at all. At least that's something to be grateful for. We'll keep you updated as you continue to fly inward. Please let me know what you intend doing. Providius out.'

The lights came on and the three people in the obs lounge sat unmoving, in utterly stunned silence.

CHAPTER NINE

SPECIAL SECURITY COUNCIL

In the Solar System, in a different time frame relative to the events in the Ra system (even though the two systems were linked by way of the conduit phenomenon), an especially high-level governmental conference was taking place. In this time frame The Monsoon had only just vanished through a conduit, on its way to Oceanus, when Secretary General Darik Yorvelt prepared to give his address to the full Security Council. The venue was a large, private, reception office, deep in the Allied Government Embassy, on Lunar Settlement 4 Gamma; just one building in a large habitat embedded in the vast floor of the lunar crater known as Tycho.

In truth, the over-ample spaciousness was not necessary, given the nature of the conference, because appearing with Yorvelt were mere holo images of his colleagues, including Indrius Brocke – Deputy secretary General and head of Security Council Intelligence; Fleet Admiral Alisianna Khairie Liracassic Madraser, Commander in Chief of the Navy; Arienne Helicontremar Vemnius, Head of the Outer Systems Intelligence Agencies, and Brigadier General Brachta Ningaui Hsing-Den, Chief of the HS Space Marines and land forces. As the 'real' flesh, representatives were in different places, mostly, in this case, on Earth, or nearby, there was an inevitable delay between comments made by the 'participants'.

'Thank you for your "presence", esteemed colleagues,' Yorvelt said, 'and I know that you've all been briefed. I also can confirm that you, the Deep System Security Committee, are the only ones who know about the current situation in the Ra system, apart from the commanding officers who are in the system itself. We're keeping a tight lid on this so called "alien" scenario, until we know what we're dealing with. I am sorry there has not been time for us to convene in person, as that would have been more secure than conferring by holovid, on a matter like this. We must try to avoid Solar System-wide panic, and my tek people assure me they have bolstered the security channels underpinning the holo carrier waves. But there is only so much they can do, and we really have no time to waste.'

'Exactly, Secretary General,' said Brocke, 'so I've placed all security and intelligence agencies on double amber alert. We can fill in the Inner Policy Committee and other necessary partners as we get more infodata.'

'There might be an imminent threat from the Rebels,' said the leanly built Hsing-Den, stroking his grey goatee beard, appearing immaculate in his sleek, dark grey uniform, 'and that's why I oppose what I have been told is the Fleet Admiral's intention to take most of the fleet to the Ra system, to "confront" these alien things. That would leave us open to attack from within. And we know the Rebels really are a threat. Consider what they did to the Kalahari.'

'Nonsense …' began Madraser, then rephrased quickly, 'I'm sorry. With respect, Brigadier General, there is no intel that the New Rebel, Ultima, forces had anything to do with the explosion of the Kalahari. My own experts are of the opinion that a faulty design may have been responsible, though, of course, I don't pretend that we yet know enough to be able to draw any conclusions. Investigations are ongoing. But, my wise colleagues, we are now at a unique point in the history of our civilization. What is happening in the Ra system is totally unprecedented. Never before has humanity had to deal with an *alien threat* – formerly a matter merely for science fiction extravaganzas. But no longer. It was thought, for many decades, that human civilisation was alone -- but now we know that there were others, possibly a much older civilization than our own – now gone, on Oceanus itself. Now we also learn there is, or was, another. Possibly, an even more ancient civilisation. And this time they consist of machines, or so it seems, from … who knows where. From afar, certainly. Not only that but we do not know their point of origin – if they indeed have one. Perhaps they are from all around the cosmos, surrounding us. We don't know their purpose yet. But we do know they're within relative striking distance of the solar system, if we assume they use conduits, like us. In view of these momentous events, I say that we have to act now, Mr Secretary General.'

'Thank you for your … *speech*, Fleet Admiral,' said Yorvelt, looking none too pleased, 'and I'm fully aware of the gravity of the situation, but I also caution against precipitous action, precisely because we know so little about these "machine things", as you said yourself.'

'If indeed, they are machines,' interjected Brocke.

'I agree with Alisianna,' said Chief Vemnius, a slightly built female of advanced age, 'for I also believe that at present the aliens are, potentially, our biggest threat. This is not only the biggest threat *we* face but very likely the biggest that all of humanity has *ever* faced.'

'Perhaps so, but there is no real evidence they are a threat – to us,' said Yorvelt.

'I hope you're right, Secretary General,' said Brocke. 'and in the fullness of time these things might turn out to be a … source of knowledge, perhaps. But in the here and now, relatively speaking, they don't seem to be doing anything that we could call, "helpful". In fact, the experts I've consulted, concerning Captain Providius's data, suggest their interference with the physical body of Ra is likely to be a major disaster *for Oceanus*. They're talking about a serious upwelling of the outer layers of the star's atmosphere, possibly within months. And we thought we had 10 years! For all we know their visit may be a recurrence. It's even possible these things were responsible for the very event which caused the extinction of so much life on Oceanus, 8 million years ago. Maybe they forced the obviously sentient species, the so called, "Reptiloids", to leave that entire system.'

Hsing-Den piped up again, 'Are you saying they might have been responsible for our observation of Ra's instability for the last two years, as observed from the Solar System?'

'I've wondered about that too,' said Brocke, slightly imperiously, 'but the experts say it's too soon to be sure. There's been no sign of these particle clouds before their very recent appearance.'

'It seems there's not a great deal we can do to save Oceanus, itself,' said Hsing-Den, 'but we know the Rebels and Ultima are a real and present danger *inside* our solar system. I am wary of the Fleet Admiral's proposal that she take to the Ra system five of the seven heavy cruisers, currently on standby. Especially for a threat we may be unable to do anything about. We don't have a good idea of the true strength of the Rebels' military capacity, but we know they've been infiltrating organisations, including the Navy itself,' he stared pointedly at Vemnius and Madraser.

Yorvelt nodded and began to respond, but Madraser, possibly because of the signal time delays, interjected again, 'I'm sorry, Brigadier General, but I believe it's not sufficient, perhaps even negligent, to say, in effect, that we can leave the Ra system to the aliens. As I have already said, these machines, or beings, or whatever, are a "stone's throw" from Earth, in cosmic terms. Yes, the Ra system is an unimaginable distance – in human terms. But these alien things must have come from much further away, out there in the cosmos, because we haven't seen any sign of them in three hundred years of observation. Neither the HS observation systems, nor any of the hundreds of probes in other systems, have ever detected any sign of these, or any other, extra-terrestrials. There was no reason to think anyone else was out there, until now. I reiterate, we must investigate properly – and be prepared to act.'

A buzz broke out amongst *the images* of the conferees, several people speaking at once, though it was evidently distorted by the time lags introduced by the distances the holo signals were coming from. It was therefore relatively easy for Yorvelt to interject,

'Please, please, gentilhomms. I ask you to listen. Please, my colleagues. What matters now, I believe, is the nature of our response to these alien machines. We are all aware – or so I assume, of the need for the greatest caution when dealing with a force whose strength is completely unknown. I say again – *completely unknown.* Our knowledge is still fragmentary but, if these machines really are able to exert a degree of influence on a *whole star*, then we need to establish communications, first and foremost. Their technology may be many thousands of years ahead of ours. I believe it must be, if they can do but a fraction of what has happened.'

There was a slight time lag before a reply came in.

'With the greatest of respect, Secretary General,' said Vemnius, in uncompromising tones, 'my understanding is that the research vessel Antarctica has already tried comms with the alien objects – for six standard weeks. They've tried all frequencies, and many different formats – to no avail.'

'Then surely, they need to try for another six weeks, if necessary, do they not?' said Yorvelt, raising his arms, 'and they should soon be aided by The Monsoon, should they not?'

'I'm sorry, Secretary General,' said Brocke, 'but I find the Commander in Chief's comments ... persuasive. The point is that we don't necessarily have another six weeks, in relative terms. These alien things appear to be wrecking the hell out of Ra. How, is anyone's guess. But if they eventually cause some sort of nova-like explosion on Ra, or maybe something like the disaster that befell the original inhabitants of Oceanus – then our own Sun could be next on their list. I don't know what we can do about any of this, but we have to try something. Yes, communication, of course – if it's possible. But I agree we should allow the Fleet Admiral to take *most* of the Navy's ships to address this potential new disaster. Might I remind you of how you, yourself, were so concerned to protect the citizens of Oceanus, Secretary General? Should we not do everything in our power to try to protect them now?'

At Yorvelt's evident discomfit, Brocke's image turned to Alisianna's, as he said, 'Supposing, just for the moment, that this meeting was to agree to an expeditionary force, would you be prepared to go yourself?'

'Of course, Deputy Brocke. Of course, I would go there,' she said, 'for I believe it would be dereliction of duty for us to leave Admiral Tenak to deal with this on his own, but I can only go with the SG's and your prime authorisation. But also that of Chief Vemnius, of course. And, hopefully, the blessing of the Brigadier General too?'

Ningaui nodded but looked unhappy, while Vemnius, after a few seconds delay, could be seen to nod enthusiastically. Hsing Den looked irritated and shook his head, but in these circumstances a majority, only, was needed. Yorvelt had a resigned look on his face. Then Madraser's image looked at Yorvelt, as did Brocke's. With a look of submission and quite possibly, dread, he nodded his assent. Madraser said, 'Thank you Secretary General, and thank you Chief Vemnius. Please be assured I will act, at all times, in the best interests of the H S Alliance and will always attempt to communicate with these machine things.

'How will you get there?' asked Brocke, 'since you've only got the "Oriana", currently the fastest cruiser. That could still take eight weeks.'

'I would say the Oriana is much too slow,' said Madraser, 'as are all the heavy cruisers. I could also take about two weeks to get out to the ship itself. No, with the Kalahari gone, I have decided to commandeer the HSN "Crossbow". It's a torpedo boat currently under the command of Captain Bressyn Bibulus ap Griffuth. It's got a capacity of only eight crew, of course, six of them engineers, so I shall have to replace ap Griffuth, himself. His ship only has conventional torpedo armaments, but its main advantage is speed. I'm glad that I ordered the upgrading of all torpedo boats to have class 1B-A engines.'

'So, how soon do you expect to join the two ships in the Ra system?' asked Vemnius.

'I anticipate the Crossbow getting there within four weeks, three days, maybe a little less, depending on the precise location of a suitable transit zone this side. It's still a huge delay but there's no way around that for now. Anticipating ... sorry, hoping, that my mission would take place, I've taken the liberty of making some arrangements in advance, so I should be on my way out to the ship, which is in lunar orbit, within about four hours. With luck, I'll be hard on Tenak's heels.'

'You know you won't be able to dock with The Monsoon when you get there, Fleet Admiral?' said Brocke. 'So you won't be able to take personal command of the carrier?'

'Yes, of course. I shall not need to take personal command of the big ship, Deputy SG. Admiral Tenak will take his orders from me, while aboard the Crossbow.'

'Very well,' said Brocke, and looking at Yorvelt's sour face, he continued, 'but I was pleased to hear the assurances you have made about carrying out your mission. There will of course be a further delay before the main body of the fleet catches up with you. And before taking any precipitous action I must insist, as I'm sure you understand, that you consult *all* your commanders before any action, unless the circumstances prevent that from happening, and you feel you have absolutely no choice.'

'Indeed, Fleet Admiral,' said Yorvelt, after Brocke had spoken, 'and particularly given what appears to be the potential power of these alien artefacts, we ask you to use wise restraint and take into consideration the wishes of the Oceanus people, too.'

All delegates echoed their agreement to that. Madraser nodded solemnly.

'Well done. Good sailing and good luck,' said Vemnius. The others just nodded in sombre silence.

****

A distance of light hours only from the conference on Lunar Settlement 4 Gamma, but still well within the Solar System, another conference was taking place, also thought to be a crucial one by its participants. This involved Bradlis Dervello and his accomplices. The location was a massive chamber deep under the rocky surface of a 20-kilometre-wide, potato shaped, asteroid, officially known as PXF 146356. This lump of grey-black rock orbiting the Sun, along with tens of thousands of similar rocks, was nearly 400 million kilometres distant from its primary; more than half-way out to the mighty planet Jupiter.

PXF 146356 was unusual, for it was full of huge vesicles, or naturally formed 'bubbles', and 'passages', now opportunistically taken over by the New Rebel and Ultima Alliance. The chambers, artificially enlarged, were filled with cabins, hangars, corridors and storerooms, all strung out around the rock's girth. Yet more fortuitously, the asteroid, like most, was spinning. Its natural axis of rotation was perpendicular to the inhabited chambers, and fast, so that it generated, for the several hundred human inhabitants of its internal cavities, a gravity which was a substantial fraction of standard Earth gravity. This meant it provided a reasonably comfortable working environment for the Rebels who had spent many years hunting for something as serendipitously useful for their purposes. They called it 'Omega Forward Base', or the 'OFB'.

Within the largest chamber, a cavernous hollow dubbed, the 'conference chamber', a huge figure appeared near one wall. It was the amplified holo image of a cloaked person, bathed in shadow. The face of the figure seemed to be wearing a mask or helmet, disturbingly plain and featureless, and seated before it, on the floor of the chamber, 'in the flesh', were Bradlis Dervello, Talus Despinall, and their co-conspirator, Conjecta Proctinian. Also, nearby were normal sized holo-images of a tall, vacuous looking male engineer, called Glabrion, and a similarly undistinguished female engineer and scientist, called Mariska. Somewhere behind the figures who were actually present was a massively built man, also present in the 'flesh', who stood watching, his tiny glittering eyes appearing to miss nothing.

The 5-metre tall holo image of the presiding figure spoke then, the chamber resounding with an impossibly deep voice, heavily altered by synth-devices.

'I believe that the time to strike is now,' said the figure, 'but I know some of you have reservations and I fully understand those concerns. However, we may not have a similar chance for many years.' The voice was gruff but even, controlled, and menacing. It continued, 'but I also understand that those of you who disapprove may be reluctant to ... openly disagree with me. But fear not, for I shall not be wrathful, *provided* your opinions are truly believed, born of genuine concern, and not simply an excuse for inaction. Therefore, speak. Give me your views that we may all learn from them, for perhaps even I may find them ... useful.'

There was a nervous silence for many seconds and the air became heavy with tension, but then Conjecta Proctinian spoke, with slight hesitation, 'Thank you for your ... understanding, Comrade One. I am wary of a strike against Mars at this time, when we may not be ready. The prep' of the Pterodactylus is not complete, and the proton nuclear armaments not yet tested. I am also concerned about the true efficacy of the five kewsers that have been installed. Initial tests revealed that they may not be able to co-operate in ... precisely the way ... we had hoped.'

'I hear your concerns Proctinian,' said the shadowy figure, 'and I understand but I also know you are aware that full testing of the nuclear weapons is out of the question. That would draw the attention of the authorities immediately, no matter how hard we try to disguise it. As for the Kewsers, will you tell me if the quantum computers have performed as well as can be expected, in individual testing?'

'Yes, Comrade One. They did,' said Proctinian, fiddling nervously with her fingers, unseen underneath the dark robe she wore.

'And did you and your colleagues choose the supplier with due diligence and the need for absolute confidentiality?' asked the dark figure.

'Well, yes we did, but ...'

'Then you should have nothing to worry about. Carry out any further, discrete, tests that are necessary but ensure they are completed within the next 48 hours.'

'But that will take non-stop work until then because ...'

'Because ...?'

'Because ... yes, of course, Comrade.'

Glabrion's then spoke, 'Comrade One, may I make a point?'

The giant shadowy figure slowly nodded his assent.

Glabrion continued, 'The power of the Pterodactylus cannot be denied. The workforce has been building her for the last five years and have ensured it has not come to the attention of the Security Forces. Our suppliers have been sworn to secrecy, on pain of death. The assembly of an unprecedented five kewsers will enable the ship to reach another habitable star system by "lateral hopping", an impossibility until now. The Navy would therefore be totally unable to follow the ship. That means the vessel can ... will return to harass the Navy, or other targets. Do you envisage the need to carry out such a star-hopping manoeuvre, Dominus?'

'I hope you don't envisage we'll need to completely escape from the Navy or security services,' interjected Dervello, turning to look at Glabrion.

The huge, shadowed figure harrumphed and Dervello went quiet. 'I think the question was not addressed to you, Agent Dervello,' he said, and returning his attention to Glabrion, continued, 'but the Commander is right to question your motives, Glabrion. As I perceived it, you meant to suggest a possible need to withdraw, *temporarily,* from the solar system, as a matter of mere tactics? Am I right?'

'Yes, ... that is certainly what I meant,' said Glabrion. In his holo image his gaze could be seen dropping to the floor.

'You are right,' said the dark figure, 'for the five kewser combination would allow a "double-double" check to be made to enable the calculation, for the first time ever, of a feasible conduit path between two stars completely outside the Home System filament network. The Pterodactylus could, in theory, travel hundreds of light years, without harm to the crew, before returning. Thus, it could evade and confuse the Navy. And I will add, it can and will *return to the solar system,* to this base, or to the Omega Outer base, currently under secret construction on Neptune's outer moon, Proteus. That would be dependent on security at the base not being compromised. And we have Doctrow Mariska to thank for her innovative and pioneering work on kewser theory.'

Doctrow Mariska smiled wanly and said, 'Thank you, Dominus.'

'Don't thank me yet,' said the shadowed figure, 'just make sure the system works. You, Dervello and you, Proctinian, and Despinall, have selected the suppliers of the AIs. If they do not work suitably it is the responsibility of the three of you. Hear me well on this.' There was a sudden and deadly silence in the darkened room.

Dervello eventually broke it, 'May ... I trouble you, Comrade One, to explain the detail of the plan you have in mind, for the attack?'

'I'm glad to hear something positive,' said the brooding figure in the holovid, 'but I will leave the detailed planning to you. You are now aware that the targets are Security Bases Gamma Two and Theta Three on Mars, as well as the populated areas of Tharsis and Hespera Planum, on that planet. This attack will destabilise the Allied Home System Government in a way that interference with Oceanus would never have done. Once the population of the Earth's City States, the State of Mars and the Moon, and all the Habitation Modules, have seen this demonstration of our power, they will try to break with the Home System Alliance, for fear of similar action being taken against them. Huge damage will have been inflicted on the reputation of the HS Government, their inadequate Navy, and their ability to protect their citizens. We will strike again, from a different direction, and at a time which the Navy cannot anticipate. We will do so again and again, until the Alliance breaks up. It is regrettable we have only the Pterodactylus, at present, but its power and speed will allow us to sting the Alliance repeatedly, in a guerrilla campaign that will spread terror and confusion among the planets.'

'Plans for two more similar vessels are under way, Comrade One,' said Dervello, after the huge holovid figure paused in his comments.

'Thank you, Agent Dervello,' said Comrade One, 'I'm aware of that. The only remaining problem is the continued presence of two Navy vessels, although both are currently out of range of the inner Solar System. The 'Oriana' is the most distant, being far past the orbit of Saturn. So, I foresee little threat from that direction. The 'Hood' is the closest and is beyond the orbit of jupiter, but I have not been made aware of any plans to bring it closer. It could nevertheless take little more than four weeks to reach Mars. I do not foresee such a diversion happening soon, as I am assured that the allied government also wish to send it to the Ra system. However, be not complacent. I still wish you to get the plan underway within 28 standard days, so to exploit the weakness of the government to the maximum. Do I make myself clear?'

There was a chorus of assent, and the figure spoke again, 'And one last thing – regarding the people who will carry out this mission. I want you, Dervello, to take Command. Proctinian, you will be the deputy. Despinall, you will have charge of the payloads, and the senior mission engineers will be Glabrion and Mariska, together with engineers Protter and Klargon. You are the leaders of this base and have the responsibility of furthering this phase of our cause. Now, I will allow you get on with your work. Do not fail me.'

With that, the shadowy figure disappeared from view.

CHAPTER TEN

MARS ATTACK

Dervello, Proctinian and Despinall sat together in a huddle, inside a small chamber far away from the main areas of activity on Omega Forward Base. Nearly 21 days had passed since the conference with their mysterious leader.

'Are you sure this area is secure, Conjecta?' said Despinall, in a somewhat forced whisper.

'Of course,' said Proctinian, 'and there's no need to speak like that. You sound ridiculous.'

'Alright,' said Dervello, loudly, 'that's enough! The purpose of this meeting is to decide how we're going to deal with our "situation". No-one expected the Navy cruiser, Hood, to have been diverted. That's not what our *illustrious leader* said. But it made a burn 12 days ago and it changed course. The Hood is currently just 250 million klicks away from Mars insertion orbit. And we now know the Navy has ordered the cruiser Oriana to stay in the outer Solar System, not leave for Oceanus. This changes the whole scenario. We've updated the simulation parameters and run through it dozens of times. The hyper-comp now gives us *only a 38.7% chance* of succeeding at Mars. I want to know if either of you think that's good enough. Just so you know, I'll be clear about what I think. *It's not.*'

Both his colleagues nodded.

'Okay, we're all agreed. So, what do we do now?' added Dervello.

'We can't abandon the mission,' said Despinall, 'and we dare not speak openly about the hyper-comp's findings – even though everybody here knows about it. I'd say it's foolhardy to go into a military mission with these odds, but I doubt we have any choice.'

'And we can't talk to Comrade One about it either,' said Dervello. 'Not unless *he* changes his mind, but we haven't heard any more from him, so that doesn't look very likely. He would probably just say we should have started the mission by now – so we would have avoided the Hood – *and he'd be right.*'

Proctinian looked furious, 'We couldn't start because the proton missiles aren't talking to our system check comps. The Maker knows what they'll decide to do if they're let loose.'

'You called this meeting, my love,' said Despinall, looking at Dervello, 'so I presume you've got something in mind?' He looked hopeful, in a desperate kind of way.

Now it was Dervello's turn to lower his voice, conspiratorially, 'I do, mate o'mine. I say that we try to carry out the mission, as intended. But if it begins to look like we're going to get caught or destroyed – which is very likely – we get out of there, and away, out of the whole damn Solar System, completely. The one thing we know will work well are the three triple A engines. This ship is not only faster than anything the Navy has, it's also faster than any of the ship-to-ship missiles they have. Ah, I can tell what you're going to say Conjecta. Your face gives you away. I know the tests of the kewsers haven't been ideal, but they all seem to be online now and – I just don't think we have any choice. If our mission fails we won't want to stay around here, that's for sure.'

'But where the shit and feg, do you think we can go, for Jumrie's sake?' said Proctinian.

Dervello glared at her, 'I'll thank you for not using that language here, Conjecta,' he spat. She glared back at him.

'Listen, love, she's only saying the obvious,' said Despinall, 'cos we've got to work it out. Where would we go?'

'Alright, alright. This is starting to get to me, that's all,' said Dervello, 'but I've thought about this – lots. I do have a plan. We can take the Pterodactylus to *Potentia*.'

'Despinall looked awestruck, 'Yes ... of course,' he said, 'that's the only other star, within the extended local group, known to have an orbiting world that's habitable, apart from Oceanus and Prithvi. The planet's called Avalonia, isn't it? About 20% larger than the Earth, maybe a bit bigger.'

Proctinian looked puzzled. 'Listen, if I'm going to stake my life on this, I need to know a bit more than that,' she said.

Despinall continued, 'It's over 160 light years away. That's why no-one's reached it yet. Not even a probe. Anything going from here to there would disintegrate and dissociate before it reached Potentia. But the largest space telescopes show it's like a ripe peach, just waiting to be plucked. Looks like it's got everything. Oceans – large land masses – and a mixed nitrogen and oxygen atmosphere, just like the Earth's. Similar climatic zones, maybe slightly cooler, overall. But certainly manageable.

'The Home System government would love to get there. They just can't, right now. But we can. And we can live there, free from reprisals or revenge, by anyone,' said Dervello with gathering enthusiasm. 'With the Pterodactylus we'll be the first people ever to get there. We could claim it for ourselves – the whole place. We could start a new society, free of the trappings, all the shit of this system.'

'I hope,' said Proctinian, frowning, 'you're not looking to generate this *new society*, with me, are you? I'd kill you first. You're letting your enthusiasm get the better of you. And, anyway, if it's over 160 light years away, we'd have to be sure the kewsers could get us there, via several smaller conduit transits. Seems a long shot. And, we'd have to stock the Pterodactylus with tons of supplies, survival equipment and all the rest. Even with star hopping, it could take several months to get there. And we'd have to work out how to survive when we reached the system. So, yeah, make that *tens of tons* of supplies – and boat loads of recyclers, manufacturer machines and all the rest. You're flying in a fantasy nebula, Dervello.'

'Always the same. You always have to look on the bleak side, don't you,' said Dervello. 'We might not need to do this, anyway, but it's the only option if things go wrong. And there's a reasonable chance we'll make it out there. We can't go to Oceanus or, Maker help us, Prithvi. The Navy will hunt us down easily. But they won't be able to follow us to Avalonia.'

'Not until *they* work out how to use five co-ordinating kewsers,' said Proctinian, flatly, 'and then Avalonia will be first on their list to explore, even though they couldn't possibly know we went there – *if we can get there*. Besides, how do we get all the supplies we need?'

'Maybe we can get them aboard the Pterodactylus on the basis that they're for emergencies, say, if we have to go into hiding in the outer Solar System?' suggested Despinall.

'Don't worry fella-me-lads,' came a sudden, deep, booming voice, laced with a cynical chuckle, emanating from somewhere in the gloom behind them.

With the shock of discovery on their faces all three conspirators turned sharply to look over their shoulders.

'I'll get them on board,' the voice continued, as a huge male figure loomed out of the darkness at the back of the rocky chamber, 'and I'll say they're for me.'

'Who're you? What pisshead is that?' said Dervello, then, appearing to recognise him continued, 'So, it's you, R. What the feg are you doing here?'

In the not quite full Earth gravity of the station, R seemed to bounce slightly as he moved toward them, a suddenly menacing sight.

'Piphoo. I've been here all the time,' he said, in evidently jocular mood.

'So … you heard everything?' said Proctinian, glaring at the intruder.

'I still don't get it,' said Dervello, 'we searched the whole area, including this place. We used ultra-sensor sweeps and galvanic detectors.'

'I've got all sorts of equipment I use in my job,' said R, laconically. 'It serves me well. And I hid in the waste recycling pipes. Used some tek stuff to disguise my presence. I feel *so sorry* to have surprised you I could piss myself. And yes, I did hear – everything – and I've recorded it and transmitted it to my little comp cube. I'm not telling you where that is, of course, but it has orders to transmit the stuff to his excellency, or should I say, Comrade One, should anything happen to me. Or, if I don't get what I want.'

'So, you're not going to betray us … right now?' asked Despinall.

The intruder shook his huge, bull-like head affably.

'And just what is it you want from us?' said Dervello, sighing.

R eased a little more into the cone of light from the single ceiling light. He had a determined look on his face and in the half-light his features took on a gnarled, scarred look.

'As it happens,' said R, 'I agree with your analysis of this mission. It's probably not going to succeed – but I want to be on the ship.'

Dervello looked puzzled. 'But why,' he said, 'if you think don't think … ? Oh I get it. You want to go to Avalonia too. Correct?'

'Exactly,' said R. 'If you succeed, then no more need be said about this. But if you don't, then I don't want to be around here when the Navy finds this place. And they will. I'm not known to them at the moment, but they'll work out who I am, and when they do they'll realise that "I'm wanted" in all quadrants of the Home System. I'm not going to spend the next sixty years on the Mars penal colony. Or that place on Lunar Base Five.'

'But you're not on the registered manifest for the flight,' said Proctinian, a defiant look on her face.

'I don't care what the manifest says right now, missy mops,' said the Rebel assassin. 'Get me on board or believe me when I say that if I don't get to go – *you* won't be going either.'

'Maybe we'll find where your comp cube is,' said Dervello, in similarly defiant vein.

'R glowered, then a slow smile spread across his rough-hewn features, 'Fine,' he said, 'so go ahead. Try something like that. I like a challenge. But I wouldn't, if I were you. You must know I only give people one warning.'

Both Proctinian and Dervello's eyes widened. Despinall glowered at his lover and shook his head in silence.

'Okay, Mer R,' said Dervello, with another sigh, 'I guess you're in.'

****

The Monsoon was still days away from insertion into orbit around Oceanus when Tenak called Mike up to his office. The ship's Secretary was very pleased there'd been a rapprochement with the Admiral. He had long since realised that Tenak wasn't to blame for any of what had happened in the past. What had made him behave like he had to the man, he'd wondered? Still, the two of them were now mates again. Mike was relieved.

But he still felt that the bond between them had been damaged, a rift caused by *him*, though he hoped Tenak would forgive him. It was only relatively recently that he had finally realised how much his bond with Tenak actually meant. Grief had blinded him, and now he also grieved for the damage done to their friendship.

When he reached Tenak's office he found the Admiral on his own and in pensive mood. Not surprising, he mused, given the weight of responsibility that lay on his shoulders, especially with the 'alien' threat coming on top of the pressure of the evac operation.

'Thanks for coming straight here, Mike,' said Tenak. 'I'm sorry but I still prefer the face-to-face method over holos.'

'Of course. I think I do, nowadays. What's on your mind?' said Mike. 'I hope I can help.'

For a second Tenak looked a little surprised. Then he leaned back in his chair. Staring, contemplatively, at his desk, he said, 'I've been in contact with Jennifer Providius. She says she sent an updated data-probe to the authorities on Oceanus about the alien threat, straight after she contacted us. Says she's not sure she did the right thing. I told her she had. What else could she do? If anyone deserves to know, they do.'

Tenak switched his gaze to Mike and continued, 'And I've changed my mind about our destination, too. Ebazza and I have agreed we'll join the Antarctica, in close orbit round Ra. We'll take a look at these machine-things and see if we can communicate with them. I know Providius has been trying but – maybe we can bring a fresh perspective. The evac is still absolutely vital but these alien things have eclipsed that for the moment. We need to try to work out what they're likely to do. And, if they're going to damage the star we may not have time to evacuate Oceanus, anyway.'

'What's the Navy protocol for these situations?' asked Mike, then smiled and rolled his eyes when he realised his mistake. 'Sorry, what am I talking about? There isn't one,' he added.

'No, of course not, but general emergency protocols say we await orders from the Admiral of the Fleet,' said Tenak, 'and I would think she'll already be on her way, at least, in the Home System time frame.'

'No disrespect intended, but who gives a flying shit about her?' said Mike, evenly. 'You're the senior officer here. The one on the spot. The one with the right to command and do what you think is right, here and now.'

Tenak smiled wryly and said, 'The emergency protocols mainly concern the situation where war has broken out. I wouldn't say that has happened here, as far as I can tell.' Tenak, leaned forward, tensely.

'I believe that refers to war between humans or between planets, or city states, Arkas,' said Mike. 'We don't know what we're dealing with here. Or what motive these things have – or even if they have any.'

'Oh, I'm sure there's a motive of some sort,' said Tenak, 'but we're not in a position to know what it is, yet. Might never be. But you could be right. The thing is, Mike, it's not that I consider myself to have precedence. I just don't think we've got time to wait for anyone else to get here, and, if our attempts to contact these alien things fails, I want to get as many people off Oceanus as this ship can take. I've asked Lew to take a landing boat down and start helping the Oceanus authorities get a group of at least a thousand together, so we can pick them up asap. The question is, who should we take? How can we advise the OA government about who to select?'

'I'm not sure, Arkas. And where do I fit in? You must have something in mind, to call me up here. What can I provide?'

'Advice, Mike. In any "unusual circumstances" regarding civilians, it's your job to do that, isn't it?'

Mike felt like a fool - again. Of course it was his job. He'd spent most of the voyage recovering from the knife attack and had almost thought of himself as a passenger – especially as Tenak had left him to his own devices. Now the Admiral was expecting him to do his job again and rightly so.

'You don't,' Mike said suddenly.

'Pardon -say.' Tenak's brow wrinkled.

'You don't tell them what to do. Perhaps you need to stop thinking like an Admiral on this one, Arkas. Besides, *who are we* to say who should go? Who should stay? Only the old can go? Only the sick? Or maybe just the mothers and children? What about fathers? But then, what about single, childless people? And remember the stuff about prisoners? So, where do they figure? No, Arkas, we have to let the OA Government, and their people, work it out for themselves.'

'Yeah, you're right, of course. Okay, so, I'll make some officers available to help them organise things – but only if they want it. We're going to have to get people on the ground to organise evac' from *our* perspective, no matter how Oceanus decides to triage. The Monsoon itself will carry on and enter a similar orbit to the Antarctica. Thanks for your ….' A loud bleeping sound broke in on Tenak's words.

A class A1 call thought Mike. Something big.

Tenak spoke to his desk comp and a message came through. It was Statton. 'Sorry to disturb you Admiral,' said the First Officer, 'but I've got Fleet Admiral Madraser for you. She says she wants you to hear this straight off.'

'Already? How'd she get here so fast? Okay, patch her through, XO,' said Tenak.

'Maker preserve us,' breathed Mike. 'Now we really have got problems.'

****

Back in the Solar System the Pterodactylus was closing on Mars very rapidly, though it was still four million kilometres away. To the naked eye, from their position, the planet still appeared as a tiny, salmon red, point of light.

The Pterodactylus was an advanced ship, of a triple module design, like most Navy vessels, but much smaller and significantly different. The forward section was cone shaped, like one of the ancient Apollo spacecraft command modules but much larger. Immediately behind the cone was a wide, lens shaped, disc, spun to produce a degree of gravity, and this module housed the living quarters and command decks. Aft of this was its stubby mid-section, from which a profusion of antennae and solar panels sprang, then at the rear was a long set of tubular fuel tanks which ended with a set of three disproportionately large fusion engines. The assemblers were so confident of the engine design that no radiation shield had been incorporated.

In a surprisingly roomy chamber inside the spun disc, Bradlis Dervello sat in the command chair, near the back wall, with Despinall stationed at a console forward of his position and to the left side. Proctinian sat at a similar station to his front right. The lighting was subdued and a magnified holo image of the planet Mars loomed in mid-air, seemingly floating in the centre of the chamber.

'The Hood just came within sensor range,' said Despinall, a note of anxiety lacing his voice. 'and it's still two million kloms off our starboard bow.'

'Okay,' said Dervello, 'it's "fun" time. Let's hope we can catch them off guard, before their older style sensors pick us up. Time to launch the first of our four proton warheads. Its micro-AI should be capable of outmanoeuvring any interceptors they send to meet it. After all, my friends, we're told these proton missiles are "state of the art", so let's put 'em to the test. Be ready with our conventionals – just in case.' He winked wickedly at his lover. Despinall tried to smile back and almost succeeded.

'Roger that,' said Proctinian, 'and we should be in a position to launch our remaining proton warheads at our Martian targets, within twenty minutes … and counting.'

Mild vibration throbbed through the deck plating as the first nuclear warhead was loosed from its pod on the ship's mid-section.

A second holo' image sprang into existence, next to the one of Mars, showing the bright burn of the missile's engine as the stubby looking warhead shot off to the ship's starboard.

A planned gravity assist for the Pterodactylus would mean swinging around Mars and then executing a burn to push the vessel into a wide elliptical orbit, and back to base. That was the plan – if the Hood was successfully destroyed. If not, then all bets were off, except for the alternative plan known only by Dervello and his co-conspirators. The other crew on the ship had not been included. They had to come along for the ride and once the options were made clear to them, they would have to go along with it, or "walk the plank". In other words, go out the airlock. No-one thought that would become necessary.

After 15 minutes of nervous waiting, Proctinian asked the hypercomp to place another holo above the command deck, so they could watch the coming encounter. This holo showed a magnified telescopic image, as the proton torpedo got within a hundred thousand kilometres of the Navy ship. The Hood had clearly picked up the Pterodactylus and its missile and had launched three conventional interceptor missiles to meet the threat. All the warheads were now 'dancing' a deadly gavotte in space, each one trying to outmanoeuvre the other. Long gone were the days when missiles were simply fired 'at' targets, hoping to hit them – or to find their targets by means of heat seeking apparatus or video sensors. Now, missiles were directed by mini supercomputers, so they carried out the manoeuvres they needed to make. They calculated the means to evade anything sent against them and to predict the paths of interceptors, or laser batteries, and find a way to their targets. In effect, they themselves decided what to do. Many counted it as extremely fortunate that the one thing they were prohibited from doing was to return whence they came or to pick an arbitrary target, possibly a friendly one, instead of the planned one.

As the interceptors from the Hood and the warheads from the Pterodactylus carried out their game of cat and mouse, the crews on each ship were helpless to intervene, except in the unlikely event they needed to send a command to destroy their own missiles. As Dervello and Despinall sat and watched the fateful dance at great distance, Proctinian reported that the Hood had now launched attack missiles, directed at the Pterodactylus, but that was, after all, to be expected. Dervello ordered the launch of two interceptors to meet the two high power, conventional, warheads now speeding toward them.

The holo' in front of the Rebel crew suddenly darkened so as to protect them from the glare of a mighty explosion, the ship's hyper-comp having predicted the event seconds before it happened.

'Fail,' said Proctinian. 'The protonic didn't get through but it got close enough to wipe out part of the Hood's forward sensor arrays. Aft arrays still intact.' Proctinian continued to concentrate on her sensor panel and listen on her headphones.

'Damnatious,' said Dervello. 'The ship's conduit coils will probably protect it from the radiation burst, even though that thing went off within – what, twenty kloms of it?'

Proctinian nodded. Despinall recommended launching a volley of conventional missiles, warning that they needed to keep their remaining three proton warheads for Mars itself.

'Okay. So ordered,' said Dervello, 'and let's hope the Hood isn't able to intercept all of them. And launch the rest of the nuclears' at the Martian targets – now.'

'Based on the failure to knock out the Hood,' said Proctinian, 'the AI says it expects no more than two of the protonics will get past the Navy, but it's unable to predict the outcome of planetary defences.' Her eyes widened then, and her next words came out loudly, and sharp with stress, 'The Navy missiles are within twenty thousand kloms,' she said, 'and approaching faster than anticipated. New drives on them, by the looks of it. Our interceptors are engaging – now. Do you want to actually watch this?'

Despinall recoiled but Dervello said, yes, so the holographic image before them switched to the scene in space 'just' a few hundred thousand kilometres away. The four combating weapons appeared as bright stars, flying around and around as they used copious amounts of fuel to force their warheads into complex, eccentric, micro-orbits and parabolic loops around each-other. These sorts of duel fought against the laws of celestial mechanics, but celestial mechanics always won in the end, usually leading to early depletion of fuel. This often knocked the missiles out long before they had a chance of reaching their intended targets.

That happened now. All four, evenly matched, warheads made themselves explode after running out of fuel, so disposing of themselves and preventing them being a danger to their own sides.

The crew of the Pterodactylus breathed a collective sigh of relief but it was short lived, as the AI told them the Hood had launched three more missiles at them as well as a volley of warheads at the proton weapons now flying toward the 'Red Planet'. A door slid open behind and to Dervello's left. And R strode onto the command deck.

'What are you doing here?' said Dervello, calmly, 'You may have pushed yourself onto this flight, but I told you the command deck is off limits to unqualified personnel.' Despinall flashed a warning look at his lover, when he glimpsed R gazing at Dervello with a snarling expression.

'You're welcome to try to have me removed – if you like,' said R. 'Otherwise, shut your feggy mouth. I'm here because I want to see what a muffing job you make of this. Still, you might yet surprise me, so just carry on. Pretend I'm not here if, it gives you comfort.'

Dervello glowered at him but Proctinian suddenly piped up. She had taken the liberty of launching a volley of interceptors against the Navy's missiles and another against the hood itself. 'At least the conventional warheads will do some damage if they get through,' she said.

'Don't use all our conventionals,' said Dervello, 'cos we'll need at least ten for Mars, especially if the protonics don't get through.'

'We do need to protect ourselves, though,' interjected Despinall, a worried frown on his face.

Standing behind them, R chuckled.

****

The Monsoon had tucked itself into an orbit as close to Ra as its crew dared, which was very close to the orbit of that of the Antarctica, though the research ship itself remained a long way off. For some days the Navy ship had been able to observe the activities of the strange alien artefacts orbiting the star several million kilometres closer to it than they.

'Those things don't seem to respond to our presence at all,' said Professor Jennison, looking up at Captain Providius's image, 'so, do you think they know we're here?'

Jennison stood, together with Tenak and Mike, in front of the huge vid screens in the Monsoon's science bay. A separate screen showed a large holo' of the head and shoulders of Providius, standing on the bridge of her own ship.

'They've not responded to us since we started observing them up close,' she said, after the four second delay between Orben's voice reaching her and her response reaching The Monsoon.

'And that was five weeks ago,' she concluded.

'That doesn't mean they can't respond,' warned Tenak. 'I'm sure they know we're here but in the absence of any sort of comms from them, we can't know what their motives are. Nor can we gauge their offensive or defensive capabilities.'

'If they can do the sorts of stuff we've seen them do, I think we can be sure they could destroy us,' said Mike.

'Their very presence here suggests that,' said Jennison, sounding alarmed. 'Humanity has been searching the cosmos for hundreds of years and we've seen no sign of any other intelligences. Nothing like this. So, they must have come from … far away indeed,' he said.

'That's just what the Fleet Admiral said,' muttered Tenak.

Four second delay, then Providius's voice again, 'If I may point out something,' she said, 'because you will be able to see there are two separate bands of objects orbiting above the star's equator. Each band is only about 20 metres thick, can you believe, but about a hundred thousand kilometres wide. You'll also see there is now another band, at right angles to the others, orbiting around the poles of the star.'

'Yes, that one seemed to break off from the equatorial bands about two days ago,' said Jennison. 'Our AI suggests they'll all eventually form a sphere.'

'Ours says they're likely to form a "cage" shape,' said Providius, 'but whatever, our instruments picked up this next image, just a few hours ago.' The holo before them changed to show a much-magnified image of two more, new bands, thin at present, but moving out from the equatorial bands, to orbit the star at an angle of 45° to them. They intersected at a point above the equator, on opposing sides of the star.

'The other thing,' Providius was saying, 'is that only recently our sensors have been able to detect something else. The bands themselves orbit inside things that I can only call … tubes, or toruses, of energy. It's frustrating that we can't tell what sort of energy it is yet, but they were detected because they emit Čerenkov radiation, and a kind of low-level synchrotron radiation. You'll recall that Čerenkov radiation is given off when particles, travelling in a medium which slows down light, travel faster than that decelerated light, as it were, causing a shock wave in the light emission itself.'

'That means the energy tubes themselves are slowing down light inside them,' said Mike, 'so it's a medium of some sort. Like a fluid, maybe a super-fluid.'

'Well, yes. You could be right,' said Providius, 'and although we're trying to work it out, most of the time our sensors seem to be blocked, and that's never happened before. There's just so much we don't understand about these things. Anyway, we have been able to discover that those energy tubes are now extending downwards to – wait for it – *join with the star's own coronal atmosphere.*'

'That's fascinating,' said Mike, his voice full of awe, 'and very worrying. What about the tiny particles inside the tubes? Are they still multiplying as well?'

'Yes, they're multiplying to produce an overall increase at a rate of around a hundred thousand per second right now,' said Providius, her voice catching with nervous energy, 'but, thankfully, that's a big slow-down from the rate we saw a couple of weeks ago. We've also noticed that individual units aren't dividing now,' she continued. 'We thought they were multiplying by simple division, but the new artefacts appear to be coalescing out of something smaller. Have you seen that?'

'I think, perhaps, you are right,' said Jennison, 'but our sensors are less sensitive than yours, I'm afraid. It's a less clear view for us.'

'Okay,' said Providius, 'so maybe you can't see *this* fully. I'll put it up on your screen.' About ten seconds later a new set of vids flashed onto Jennison's screens, showing a massively magnified view of a small portion of one alien band.

In this close-up view the tiny particles looked like pitch-black angular blocks, whilst around them swirled clouds of even smaller particles, with the appearance of soot particles. The tiniest particles proceeded to draw together, and it reminded Mike of the way gas and dust particles, in nebulae, gave birth to proto stars, but in this case, hugely speeded up. As the observers watched, two new angular blocks of the larger type, gradually formed, then moved away from other, fully formed neighbours, as their trajectories changed.

'Can we see an ordinary close-up of the larger blocks, Captain?' asked Tenak, 'You know, a high-res' image. All we can see are featureless black masses.'

'I'm afraid not,' said Providius, 'and the hypercomps can't pick up anything in any other frequency either, even after subtracting the background glare from Ra.'

'It's the same as when we saw the soot cloud on our orbit around Ra,' said Mike, a puzzled look on his face. 'It's as though they're able to block us out.'

Jennison harrumphed, 'I don't see how,' he said.

'Who knows how any of this is being done?' said Mike.

'Mike's right,' said Tenak, 'so we can't discount anything at the moment. We really have no idea why these things are here or even that they care about our presence, so …'

'Which is the point, as you say, Mike,' said Providius, breaking in, unwittingly, on Tenak's comment, 'because, gentilhomms, I'm sure you're all aware of the seriousness of this situation. Now we know the Fleet Admiral will be here soon, I'd like to emphasise how delicate this is.'

'You mean, we can't take rash measures here? Yes, I am only too aware of that,' said Tenak.

Seconds later Providius's voice came back with, 'I know it's not my place to comment on the Fleet Admiral, but she has something of a reputation. If we do anything out of place here, the consequences for humanity could be disastrous.'

'The consequences could equally be disastrous if we don't do something,' said Jennison.

'I know Professor,' came Providius's voice after a few seconds, 'but just consider this. These tiny things are actually influencing *a star*. Okay, we know they're here in gigantic numbers. So, forget about how they got here in the first place. If they can actually bring about physical changes in a star; one of nature's most powerful singular entities and one of its largest, discounting things like galactic black holes…' She left the sentence dangling.

Mike finished for her, 'Then there's nothing we can conceive of, outside nature herself, that is capable of doing something like this.'

A sombre silence fell on everyone.

****

In the Solar System, as the Pterodactylus closed further with Mars, Bradlis Dervello watched, with a horrified expression, as one after the other, their conventional, though massive, warheads, were successfully intercepted by the Hood, leaving just one. The Rebel ship's own interceptors were still jousting with the missiles let loose by the Navy vessel, but their AI suggested that none of the Hood's warheads would make it through. Dervello and his colleagues let out a whoop of joy at this and at almost the same time one of their own conventional torpedoes landed on the starboard side of the Navy cruiser's hull. In a magnified view the rebels saw a bright flash and, after a few seconds, their AI confirmed a successful strike.

Proctinian proclaimed, gleefully, 'Direct hit on the Hood's starboard flank. We took out three automated laser batteries, two torpedo bays and parts of one deck.

Unfortunately, the Hood's super-plating stopped more widespread damage. The ship's trajectory has been badly affected and she's trying to compensate. But I guess it would need a lot more to take out that ship completely.'

'We don't have more to give to it,' said Dervello, 'cos we have to concentrate on the primary target.' He emphasised those last words.

'The Hood's orbital trajectory has been deflected badly,' said Despinall, 'so I recommend we carry out a burn now and forget the gravity assist. The extra delta V will get us closer to Mars and give planetary security systems, and the Hood, less time to react.'

'And that will take us on a trajectory out of the Solar System – unless we carry out a correcting burn later. Is that what you want?' asked Dervello, looking at Despinall sternly.

'Yes. It will surely take us out of the Solar System,' said Despinall, 'and no, I don't think we should carry out a correctional later. I say we carry out "Plan Avalonia". Now. What say you, soulmate?'

Dervello hung his head, in deep thought for long moments, before saying to Proctinian, 'Okay. He's right. Get us out of here, Conjecta. Get the AI to calculate the trajectory and length of burn. Let's do it. And Conjecta, you'd better put out an announcement to the rest of the crew. Tell them if anyone disagrees with our plan we can put them off in space. We can't afford to lose our one lifeboat. We'll need that at Avalonia, for use as a lander.'

'They aren't going to be stupid enough to object,' said Despinall. Proctinian nodded.

R chuckled again from behind. Dervello turned to him and said, 'Okay, Mer R. You said you were alright with this but ...'

'If I wasn't, you wouldn't be alive after giving that order,' he said, with no discernible betrayal of emotion.

Dervello huffed and said, 'Alright *Mister*. Now, will you please be of some use to us? I'd be very *grateful* if you could deign to go below and guard the lifeboat. Make sure no-one tries to steal it. And may I tell anyone who disagrees with our little plan, to talk to *you* about it? I'm sure you'd like that.'

As he began to leave the command deck R nodded his agreement and smirked. The second he'd gone Despinall sighed with relief and said, 'Thank the Maker he's off the deck.'

'He has his uses,' said Dervello.

Barely minutes later Proctinian declared loudly, 'Warning. Major burn initiation in ten seconds and counting.' A klaxon blared out on all three of the ship's decks and the crew, including R, made for the nearest seating and got strapped in. The command deck throbbed with vibration and the occupants were pressed back into their seats as the 'G forces' of intense acceleration struck them.

CHAPTER ELEVEN

ISOLATION

In his private office aboard The Monsoon, a highly magnified holo image of the Fleet Admiral's ship, the Crossbow, appeared above Tenak's comm desk. The ship was still nine million kilometres distant. Mike sat opposite the Admiral. He knew that Tenak had had run-ins with Alisianna Madraser before, and although *he* had not met her, he had heard much about her and instinctively felt she was not the best person to be in charge in the current crisis. He also knew Tenak felt the same way, but given the man's loyalty to the Navy and his obvious diplomatic propensities, he knew he wouldn't give vent to his real feelings.

'Who the hell put her in charge, anyway?' said Mike, trying to provoke a reaction.

'Presumably, people who know better than we do?' said Tenak, unable to prevent it sounding disingenuous. Mike harrumphed. The Admiral surprised him then. 'I was offered promotion to Fleet Admiral,' he said, wistfully, 'but I turned it down.'

Mike looked aghast, 'You did what?'

'There was too much "flying" of committees, Mike. Not enough getting out there, getting involved. Real flying. And I suppose I wanted to leave it to the more politically inclined. Madraser wasn't in the picture at that point. They gave the job to Harrison. You're too young to remember him. He was one of the best. No-one thought he'd die of Turbotrie's disease, so early in his post. Terrible loss. I still wasn't interested, but I wasn't asked again anyway. Wouldn't be. Madraser was up and coming by then. The rest you know.'

'You're a decorated Admiral, Arkas. As far as I know, Madraser's done precious little, except win friends in high places.'

'Maybe, but it's too late to do anything about it now, Mike.'

'Well, despite what you thought about the job, it seems to suit Madraser's agenda, or what I reckon her agenda must be,' said Mike, his voice laced with cynicism, as he added, 'and I suspect she's going to try to make a name for herself here.'

As Tenak nodded, somewhat reluctantly, a buzzer sounded on his desk unit and he said, 'How 'bout that? Here she is. Right on cue.'

A voice came over the desk unit, on audio only, 'Admiral Tenak? This is Fleet Admiral Madraser. I am pleased to finally be here and be of assistance. I am familiar with the findings of the Antarctica. You need to understand that I have come here on the express command of the Security Council, though I am sure you guessed that. I need to discuss this with you further, long before we get to synchronise orbit with your ship, so let's get on with it, shall we? Have you tried any further comms with those alien things? By the way, I will call them "intruders" from here on in.'

'Greetings, Admiral,' said Tenak, 'and no, we haven't, because the Antarctica has already tried twenty- eight different methods of communications, for weeks. All to no avail.'

Given her distance at that point, Madraser's answer arrived nearly 30 seconds later. Tenak and Mike could do nothing other than wait in patience. Her reply burst in on them. 'Then we must consider a more decisive course of action. My scientists have now received the datacascades we asked for and it's clear the aliens are building up to something catastrophic. Or at least, *that's what we think*. I'm aware that the captain of the civilian ship is of a different opinion, but that matters not. My people are clear.'

'Ma'am, I counsel against any rash action,' said Tenak, grimacing at Mike. 'We have no idea what these things are capable of. Besides, if you've got the latest infodata you'll be aware that these machines are not replicating any more. They're *coalescing,* that is, decreasing, rather than increasing in number.'

The inevitable delay, then Madraser's reply, 'I don't see what that's got to do with anything, Admiral. Why are you telling me this? Everything still points to the intruders gearing up to something.'

'With respect, Ma'am, the point is that we thought the main danger was that these were "von Neumann" machines. If they've stopped multiplying, then it seems highly unlikely that they are.'

'You're talking semantics, Admiral Tenak,' said Madraser after a delay which was very slowly decreasing because her ship was getting closer but at this point only instruments could show the difference.

'I don't think we can play about with the lives of those people on Oceanus,' she said, 'still less the whole of our Home System. Action is needed – now.'

'It seems clear to me and *my* advisors, Admiral Madraser,' said Tenak, 'that taking some sort of *action* as you put it, might well place the lives of those on Oceanus in even greater jeopardy. And we have no reason to think these things will travel onward to the Home System, do we?'

'What would you have us do, Tenak? Nothing?' She had evidently abandoned the customary, officer-to-officer politeness. Listening intently, Mike felt shocked. Who was this femna, really, he thought?

'Not at all, Fleet. Not at all. I have already sent a boat down to Oceanus and the government is organising a triage for suitable evacuees. It's a shame you didn't come here on a larger ship. We could have transported even more inhabitants. My opinion is that I think the best we can try to do, right now, is to evacuate as many as possible – before the star blows – if that's still an option because ...'

Madraser's angry reply reached Tenak before he'd finished, indicating she'd not listened to the whole of his comment.

'Sending an LB to Oceanus is not what I wanted to hear, Admiral. There's too much at stake to just cut and run. I applaud your sentiments about the inhabitants, but it won't do them much good if these intruders reach for our star system *next*. And before you deny that possibility, just consider how history might judge us if we didn't at least *try to stop* this menace – here and now. And then, the Sun became their next target.'

Tenak looked sourly at Mike and mouthed silently, 'She has a point.'

Mike began to get an overwhelming feeling that things were going to start going badly wrong.

****

Several million kilometres from Mars the Pterodactylus sped away from the Navy's heavy cruiser, the Hood. The rebels had fired their remaining nuclear warheads toward Mars and now they waited to see if these would get through the planet's own defence system. The four large orbital weapons platforms circling Mars let loose several volleys of interceptor missiles as the rebel's proton weapons approached. It was a nerve-wracking time for everyone on the planet as the deadly drama unfolded high above its partly terraformed atmosphere.

The holo vid stream on the rebel ship's command deck showed a series of intense flashes occurring along the limb of the planet, as the Pterodactylus swept past, travelling at over 100 klicks per second, and accelerating.

'Sensors report that two nuclears got through the first line of defence,' said Proctinian, 'but one of them was hit by a second barrage before it reached optimum altitude for destructive impact. It exploded 40 klicks above the surface. Some damage indicated but not a lot. There'll be some radiation effects, but they'll be very limited. The remaining protonic actually reached the lower atmosphere but didn't explode. Can you believe that? What a klep out.'

Everyone looked at each-other quizzically. 'We knew there might be problems with those things,' said Despinall.

Dervello looked furious.

'We've had more success with the conventionals,' continued Proctinian. 'Four of them got through. They took out three major Navy bases and one of Mars's own security bases. Big mess down there.'

Dervello said, 'That's something, at least. It's a shame to have to kill people but it's all for the right reasons. Not that we'll see any real results, cos we'll soon be on our way out of the damn system and all its shit.'

The door opposite Dervello suddenly slid open and in walked R, again, apparently rubbing something off his hands. A small panel lit up on Proctinian's console and she said, 'The airlock on the number two deck just recycled. Something, someone, just left the ship!'

'Yes, it was Klargon,' said R, from behind her. 'He got angry with me when I said we have to leave the Solar System. He said something about lack of loyalty to Comrade One. So, piphoo, and I put him out the airlock.'

Everyone looked agog. 'You did what?' said Despinall.

'Did he say he wasn't prepared to come with us?' asked Proctinian, anger clouding her face.

'No, he didn't say that,' said R. 'I think I got him to understand where his true loyalties lie. But I didn't like the way he spoke to me, so I put him out.'

Then that was totally unnecessary,' said Proctinian. 'You're a vicious man, *Mister R*.'

'Oh, don't worry missy, I broke his neck first. I don't believe in unnecessary cruelty.' Proctinian glared at him and said, more under her voice than out loud, 'Still cruel – and don't call me "missy".' R evidently heard her. He grinned.

'Sorry, missy,' he said, 'but you're a hypocrite. You talk about cruelty, and yet you were prepared to blast tens or maybe hundreds of thousands of people into oblivion a few minutes ago. Men, women, children. Not to mention the radiation sickness you'd cause.'

Dervello looked at his female colleague and said, 'He's got you there.' Proctinian looked away.

The ship continued to pick up speed very quickly, leaving Mars far behind and some minutes later Proctinian exclaimed, to her evident chagrin, 'Oh, shit! The Navy ship's recovered. They're executing a massive burn. Following us.'

'They'll have a hard job,' said Dervello, with a sneer, 'cos they can't carry out an intense enough burn – for long enough – not with the engines they've got. Those cruisers are ancient and kind of ... big.'

'They do have nuclear warheads,' stated Despinall, 'but the Hood hasn't used hers yet. I anticipate she will, as soon as she's reached 6.5 million kilometres from Mars. In case you forgot, that's the Navy rule for clearing a planet before being authorised to use nuclear warheads.'

'I didn't forget. But their weakness will be our profit,' said Dervello. Their nuclear warhead doesn't stand any more chance of reaching us than they do. It will only have a relatively small added velocity. Not to be sneezed at, but we'll outrun it.'

There was a nervous silence on the command deck over the ensuing minutes as their monitors showed Mars shrinking to a bright, salmon coloured dot, and their telescopic images of the Hood showed it following, a tiny white dot, like a very dim star, still two million kilometres behind them. A small cloud of tiny cloud seemed to be emanating from the sides of the vessel. The rebel crew said it was probably particles from the damage it had sustained. The navy ship's burn would inevitably take it on a long parabolic orbit that would sweep it back toward the Sun, deviating substantially away from that of the rebel ship.

Sometime later Dervello and Despinall were discussing options, trying to ignore the brooding presence of R, who sat in his usual seat to the rear, listening and watching everyone. Out of the blue, Proctinian barked, 'The Hood has launched a nuclear, and listen up, it's fast. Putting it on holo.' The images, seemingly hanging above the forward part of the command room, showed a tiny object pulling ahead of the Navy ship, the bright blue glow of its engine obscuring the image of the Navy ship itself.

'That warhead has a 1B fusion engine, at least,' said Proctinian, gazing at her console, mouth agape. 'It's powering up to a velocity comparable with ours. Wait ...

thank the Maker, it ... won't reach us, but it ... according to our AI, it could follow us wherever we go. We've got two interceptors left. Recommend immediate launch.'

Dervello gave the command and Proctinian loosed them. They watched as the interceptors sped back toward their target, but then, in the telescopic view, the front nose of the missile from the Hood seemed to split apart and four smaller projectiles spilled from inside, powering forward under their own, smaller, engines.

'The thing has deployed grapeshot. No, they're micro anti-interceptors,' said Proctinian. Everyone on the command deck watched, slack jawed, as their own interceptors were 'rounded up' and quickly destroyed. The main part of the Navy's missile continued, unabated. And so, the chase went on.

Over the following couple of weeks, the image of the warhead following them became a familiar sight as they continued in their hyperbolic orbit, out toward the zone where they expected, or hoped, they would find a suitable transit zone. Although the Navy missile didn't have the ability to follow them into a conduit the rebels knew that if they didn't find one of those phenomena soon the missile would, eventually, catch up with them. That would be when they had to decelerate, or otherwise risk flying out of the Solar System. For if they did fly out, it would be a journey which, without a conduit, would take tens of thousands of years to reach another star system or many tens of years to fall back toward the Solar System. Either way, it would be the end of them.

On the twenty sixth day of their attempted escape, deep in the outer parts of the Solar System, their AI told them they had finally entered a transit zone. Within a further day they had actually found a conduit and the kewsers identified a target star. They could now escape the missile. Everyone was able to relax a little until their conduit ride, which took them, after ten minutes of misery, to a system of five barren planets orbiting a red dwarf star. It was catalogued as, L 989, a 'mere' 35 light years from the Sun.

As they left the immediate vicinity of the conduit mouth Dervello took time out and left Despinall in charge. The crew gazed at the holo of the system's bright reddish star, which sported huge, ragged, dark patches along its equatorial zone; equivalents of our own sunspots, but much larger.

'Get us out of here, please, Conjecta,' said Despinall, 'as soon as the comp can find another transit zone. We don't want to hang around this system. The planets are all smaller than Mars. They're devoid of any sort of atmosphere. And the Navy cruiser could, just conceivably, find us here.'

'Well, I guess this is where we get to test the five-kewser system for real,' said Conjecta. 'At least this is a small system, so the AI should be able to find a way out within a week or two.'

Dervello was back in the command seat by the time the ship's sensor and AI systems had navigated a way to a transit zone; one that, fortunately for them, lay only a few million kilometres from their point of entry into the red dwarf system. They could hardly believe their luck.

'Engineer Mariska. How are the quantum computers responding?' asked Dervello over an audio channel. Her reply was not what he wanted to hear.

'Well, Commander, I am not so sure right now. Not sure at all,' she said, in an accent evidently originating in one of the large city states situated in what had once been eastern Europe. Dervello, looking puzzled, asked her to explain.

'Sir, looks like the translator computer seems to be saying that only two of five kewsers have agreed on the precise location of a conduit out of here. They say it is two million kilometres from our present location, yes? But each of the other three comp indicate different conduits in completely different locations. Is confusing Commander, no?'

'Well, can't you just do something about it? Report back as soon as you've resolved the issue,' said Dervello, sounding irritated.

'Where's the "big Mer" got to?' said Despinall. He and Dervello looked around for R, but the giant was not to be seen. They sighed with relief. The professional assassin had begun to get very volatile and unpredictable of late. Proctinian attributed it to unhappiness with being cooped up on a relatively small ship.

Six hours later, and with no further word from Mariska or the other engineer, Glabrion, Proctinian went down, in person, to the engine room. She found both engineers and the remaining crewmember, the technician, Protter, pouring over screens showing swirling graphics. They looked exhausted.

'Ah, Ma'am,' said Glabrion, with a wan smile, 'I'm pleased to tell you we think the problem's solved. Well, maybe.'

'Mariska piped up, 'We told you we have reservations about these kewsers, no?'

'I'm aware of that,' said Conjecta, 'but what Dervello and I want right now, are answers. First, can you get us out of here? Second, can you get us to Potentia?'

'We hope – no, we think we *can* get to Potentia,' said Glabrion, 'but there may be … two more jumps by conduit, not one. We've interrogated the kewsers like crazy, and they seem to have resolved their differences, maybe. We reckon there could have been a problem with the sensors, you know, not the kewsers? The ship's array is a relatively small one, isn't it? Anyway, the next conduit is where we said it was – originally. After that, we maybe feel the kewsers should be able to navigate straight over to Potentia.'

'I … think I know what you mean,' said Proctinian, her brow wrinkling, 'but there's an awful lot riding on this, so try to make it as quick and efficient as possible. Carry on.' She left the small engine room and as she did so Mariska said, to her colleagues, 'So what in hell is matter with 'em upstairs? We told 'em these kewsers were untested, excep' for lousy sims. This science was made by using many, many trials – with robots, no – and not hard-working engineers.' She made a one fingered gesture in the direction Proctinian had gone.

**

After travelling toward the new conduit for five days, tempers aboard the Pterodactylus were starting to fray. Even Despinall and Dervello were occasionally at loggerheads. R paced around the vessel, looking ominous. But the ship eventually entered a new transit zone, the engineers saying they felt reasonably confident that four of the kewsers had now agreed on a suitable conduit.

The ship eventually emerged into a new stellar system, one with a massive, hyperactive blue-white star at the centre of a family of twelve planets, approximately 85 light years from their previous location. Their AI said they were a total of 158 light years, in a 'straight' line (as would be perceived by line of sight) from the Solar System, which they had achieved by a circuitous route.

'No-one's going to find us out here, that's for sure,' said Proctinian, nervous excitement evident in her voice.

'This is amazing,' said Dervello, staring at the holo image of the star hanging before their eyes. 'What's the matter with you all? Don't you realise what we've done? We've managed to do what all those scientists back home have been trying to do, for decades.'

Despinall finally stood and gazed, awestruck, at the huge, intensely bright, blue-white star, suitably toned down by the hyper-comp, and said, 'Yeah, Brad, you're right.' He sounded almost breathless. 'I never thought we'd do it. We've transited from one star system to another, without returning to the Solar System in between. And we're the first ones in history ever to do it!'

'We're certainly that, guys,' said Proctinian, with an ironic smile on her face, rapidly turning to a grimace and continued, 'but it's not such good news. I just heard from "below-decks". The sensors have gone blank and the kewsers have no idea how to make the next conduit jump.' Dervello told her to patch him through to the engineers.

'It's okay. So, don't panic, sir,' said Glabrion, over the audio feed, 'cos I think it just means we have to go, you know, further afield. Have to just keep looking for the next transit zone. It's probably twenty or thirty million klicks away. It's just unusual for the sensor-kewser combo' to have no ideas at all.'

'Okay, so how do we go about finding a TZ?' asked Dervello, sounding rattled.

'I'd guess … sorry no, estimate, we should make for the outer Lagrange Zone 2, or Lagrange 3. Meanwhile, I suggest no-one panics. Remember, you guys, this is untried stuff, but we've got enough direct food supplies for 4 months and I guess if it gets difficult, we might be able to start the hyper-recyclers after that. I'm sure, I think, maybe, we won't need to do that. We're working hard to resolve this.'

'Okay, okay. Make sure you do your best, Glab'. Keep us informed, regularly,' said Dervello.

Despinall said, 'That's very restrained of you, Brad. I'm proud of you.'

'It's not really their fault, is it?' said Dervello, 'and they didn't even know we were going to do this.'

Despinall and Proctinian exchanged surprised glances.

'You know what it means if we can't get out of this system, don't you?' said Proctinian. 'This "first" you're claiming for us, might be our *last*.' She was not smiling now.

****

In a very different star system, although still stunningly far from 'home', but more easily and safely accessible, a massive Navy ship orbited a mere 40 million kilometres above the surface of the orange-yellow star, known to humans as Ra. The vessel's science staff continued to observe the streams of billions of artificial objects, which they had nick-named 'constructs', which also orbited the star, but much closer to it. To the human eye the streams were invisible.

'They really do seem to have stopped replicating,' said Professor Jennison, addressing Admiral Tenak and Mike Tanniss, in the ship's main observatory.

'I thought we agreed the constructs were coalescing, or aggregating together, Professor,' said Mike, emphatically. Jennison nodded, somewhat reluctantly.

'I don't know that it makes a difference. They might still be "von Neumann" probes,' said the academic, 'but, at least the bands they've formed around Ra seem to have stabilised. Our instruments indicate that gas from the star's surface is escaping from the photosphere between the polar orbiting band of constructs, and the band set at 45° to the equator. God knows how, but it seems like these bands are drawing the plasma off. It's escaping like … flares but it's …'

'More controlled,' interjected Mike.

'But doesn't that mean the gas is escaping away from the plane of the ecliptic – the plane that all the planets orbit in?' asked Tenak. 'So, none of it can reach Oceanus and cause damage?'

'I suppose you are right, Admiral,' said Jennison, 'and that's good news but, on the other hand, I'm sorry to say the Karabrandon waves, way down in the convective zone, are increasing in frequency and amplitude. That certainly doesn't look good.'

'Our instruments aren't able to probe as deep as those of the Antarctica,' said Mike, 'and the latest info-data from Providius's team seems to show the deepest magnetic field lines are reducing in amplitude. Smoothing out. The lines are, kind of, unwinding. That's got to be positive, hasn't it?'

'Maybe yes, maybe no,' said the professor. 'But if the convective zone is getting more agitated – without the magneto-contours matching them, then I'd say these … constructs … must be whipping up the convection zone themselves. And for what reason would that be, Mer Secretary, hmm?'

'I'd say we probably still don't know enough about stellar physics to be sure– and we know next to nothing about these constructs,' said Mike.

'Precisely what …' began Jennison, when a loud chime sounded from Tenak's wristcom. The Admiral glanced at it and said, 'I think we'd better all see this.' His device projected a holo image of Fleet Admiral Madraser, arranged so that she appeared to be standing alongside them.

'Ah, my officers, still working on the job in hand, I trust?' she said robustly. 'And glad to see you're still observing events, as are we. Unfortunately, my ship doesn't have the equivalent comp power. No matter. We've studied Providius's datacascade, and I feel it's time that you, Admiral and you, Lieutenant Jennison, started thinking about action.' She looked immediately sombre, and deadly serious.

'What do you recommend,' said Tenak, his brow furrowing. Mike knew that his friend must realise that what she actually meant was an attack of some sort. He was confident Tenak would try to resist such a move, but he felt less sure about Jennison's position. That mascla might back up Madraser and that wouldn't be good, despite his being much lower in rank than Tenak.

'I think we need to build a strategy for striking at the artefacts – before they do any more harm,' said Madraser.

Here we go, thought Mike.

'With respect Admiral,' said Tenak, 'we don't know they mean any harm – in the medium to long term. And precisely which "artefacts" do you propose hitting? There are *billions* out there.' Mike detected a note of stress in the Admiral's voice, but he was also confident that only he knew Tenak well enough to recognise this. Still, it was not a good sign – and the Admiral was faced with an extremely difficult situation. Going directly against a Fleet Admiral might be too great a task, even for Tenak.

At this point Jennison piped up, apparently in support of Madraser. What a surprise, thought Mike, sourly.

'Of course, we couldn't ever try to hit the smaller ones, Admiral,' said the professor, flatly, 'but we've noticed, have we not, that there are much larger machines spread out over each band, orbiting tens of thousands of kilometres above the smaller objects? The info from the research ship indicates the big ones are sited high over the major *nodes* of the Karabrandon waves inside Ra, and their orbits are helio-synchronous. That means they don't move relative to the star's own motion. I'd say the bigger ones could be hit.'

'And how big are these node constructs?' asked Madraser.

'They range between 60 and 70 metres across,' said Jennison, 'which means they're not extremely *big* – but big enough to be targets, I'd say. The staggering thing is there's about *ten thousand* of them strung out around the star.'

'Thank you, professor,' said the Fleet Admiral, 'and I'm inclined to agree that a few of them would be suitable targets. Wouldn't you say so, Admiral Tenak?'

'Perhaps, but I believe you are aware of my reticence regarding striking at an enemy whose strength is completely unknown, Ma'am,' said Tenak, very calmly and evenly. Good mascla, thought Mike. Keep it cool.

'These things may be small compared to the size of this ship,' Tenak continued, 'but we've just been told there are thousands of them, and we don't have any idea of their defensive capabilities, or whether hitting any one, or two, will have any real effect.'

He knew he was probably going to get into deep water, talking tactics, but Mike felt he now had to speak in support Tenak, 'Two points arise here, don't they?' said Mike, everyone suddenly turning toward him. 'First, striking at one or two might not change anything – except maybe make some of the others do something retaliatory. Second, they might *all combine* together to attack us. And we probably wouldn't be able to withstand that.'

Madraser looked at Mike with an expression as though someone had just farted in her face, and he knew what was coming.

'Admiral Tenak,' she said, 'I don't know why your ship's Secretary is here, *with us,* discussing this. Whilst I'm aware he has some sort of qualification in astrophysics, I don't believe he is a professional in the field, an actively working scientist. Nor is he a Navy officer.'

Tenak frowned then and said, remaining even in tone, 'With respect Admiral, while Mike is indeed this ship's Secretary, he is also here at *my invitation* and he did, in fact, work as a scientist during our previous visit. He spent a substantial time alongside Captain Providius and her team. He knows their working techniques well and is completely familiar with the issues. And, although you referred to his position, just a moment ago, you seem to be forgetting his *function* on this ship.'

Mike identified this as a cue for him. It was something he'd already discussed briefly with Tenak, prior to Madraser's arrival, but it had to sound as natural and uncontrived as possible – especially to try to help Tenak.

'Well,' began Mike, 'I'm glad the Admiral mentioned that. I was beginning to feel left out. The point I'd like to make, Fleet Admiral Madraser, is that you have not taken account of the Secretariat's position on this matter. As a representative of that body, I object to the use of weapons on these alien machines – until we know more about them. We need to get a much better idea of what they are and what they're trying to do.'

'Mer Secretary,' huffed Madraser, 'might I remind you that your remit does not allow you to interfere – I mean intervene, in situations where a decision has been made to initiate military action.'

'I suppose there's a point there, Fleet Admiral,' persisted Mike, 'but I'm not aware that military action has yet been initiated or agreed. I believe Article 58, Navy Secretariat Code, Subdivision Three, of 2465, requires that there must be an agreement by all Navy Officers at the "action specific location", for such action to be initiated. That is clearly not the case here. Admiral Tenak has said he does not accept the need for such action.' Mike looked pleased with himself. He could see that Admiral Tenak was doing his best not to smile.

For several moments Madraser could be seen to falter, appearing slightly flummoxed. Her holo-image could be seen to turn to her right-hand side where she was evidently straining to hear something being whispered by someone standing outside the cone of view of the holo-vid sensors. Then she brightened and, turning back to Mike, said, 'I'm sorry to disappoint you, Mer Secretary, but, in this particular case, you are wrong. For one thing, you are referring to a code which did not foresee circumstances like the present.' She kept glancing to the side again, intermittently. She was quite obviously being coached.

'There is ... um, a lacuna, therefore,' she continued, 'where um, the code can be said to be silent, and then the ... second thing is that ...' Another glance to her side, before resuming, 'that, ah yes, of course. The full Security Council of the Allied Home System Government has given me absolute authority to take ...such action as I deem necessary, in emergency situations such as this one.'

Tenak piped up at this point, his tone deadly serious and gruff, now, 'Are you certain the Security Council has made this ruling, Ma'am?'

After a further glance to her side, Madraser came back with, 'Yes, of course they have, Admiral. Do you question me? And, *Mister* Secretary, if you are unsure of the veracity of what I say, I suggest you look up ... what?' she turned to the side again, then said, 'Yes, Annexe A, Part 36, of the Navy Secretariat Code, which covers the overriding authority of the full Security Council.'

Mike fell silent. He didn't need to look up Annexe A, Part 36. She was right. His mind then dredged up something that would not rescue the situation but might give the 'opposition' pause for thought.

'I do not need to look up your reference, Fleet Admiral,' he said, 'but I want it noted for the record, under Section 1742 of the code, that, as The Monsoon's Secretary, I object strongly to your proposed course of action. I also note that you have no Secretary aboard your own ship, with whom I can convene, contrary to standard regulations, particularly section 4 of the ....'

'Your objection is noted, for the record, Mer Secretary, and as I have said repeatedly, I was obliged to launch as a matter of urgency. There was no time to select a ship's Secretary. I believe emergency protocols cover it,' she said, 'and now Admiral, back to the important business. Regardless of your own objection to my proposal, which has also been noted, my strategists will start work on the feasibility of hitting node machines. Then, I'll get back to you. Meanwhile, might I ask if *you* have anything else to add, Professor Jennison? As regards the scientific scenario, I mean?'

Jennison looked pleased as punch, as he said, 'Thank you, Fleet Admiral. On that score, I'm sure that Michaelson Tanniss has the best of intentions, Ma'am. As for his theories about the aliens, I'm aware he did provide excellent support for Captain Providius, but my understanding is that he was essentially an observer. He was not commissioned to work as part of her team. As far as the larger "node machines", are concerned, I would say they seem to be influencing the Karabrandon waves, and that is my main concern. Targeting half a dozen of them might disturb their operation long enough to stop the deterioration in the star. Maybe make them think again, if indeed they do "think" in a way we can understand?'

'Thank you, professor. We'll speak again soon, Admiral,' said Madraser.

'But ...' started Mike, then saw Tenak shoot him a warning glance.

'Very well, Ma'am,' said the Admiral, 'I await your decision.'

Madraser's hologram disappeared and Tenak gave Mike another *she's got a point* look. The alarm bells in Mike's mind were starting to get deafening.

****

After weeks of flying through the vast system of the blue-white star, investigating the outer L2 and L3 zones, and still not finding any sign of a negative energy filament, the crew of the Pterodactylus were all beginning to behave erratically. It was not for lack of supplies. There were abundant supplies of food. Most vessels of that time could generate air, water and, to some extent, could manufacture food, using recycled waste and chemical regenerators. But this facility was time limited before irreversible decay set into the processes involved, a point beyond which you could no go without resupply.

However, at this stage, in the case of the Pterodactylus, the crew were simply going, 'stir crazy'.

'I'm beginning to think it was a very bad idea coming out here,' said Despinall, on their 36th day in the barren star system. He gave Dervello a scowl. Proctinian just looked depressed.

'You agreed to it, love,' said Dervello, with sarcasm. 'You all did, so don't look at me like that. You're not children. You knew the risks as well as me.'

'And I'm getting sick of this command centre,' said Despinall. 'What the feggery have they got to say for themselves downstairs, Conjecta?'

She shrugged her shoulders, 'They've trying to do what they can. Mariska insists that the comps are to blame. Glabrion thinks it's the sensor array. He even suited up and went outside to check. No apparent problem.'

'Where's R, by the way?' asked Dervello, sullenly.

'He's definitely not been taking this well,' said Proctinian. 'Doesn't like being cooped up at all. I'm just glad he's not on this deck right now.' She suddenly seemed to withdraw into herself, becoming engrossed in studying her consoles. After a few minutes she said, 'Well, comrades, I've just finished the last bit of research on the fourth planet in this system. Been studying it for days and I think it's worth thinking about … Well, about making planetfall.' She looked at the others sheepishly.

'What? On the fourth planet?' said Despinall, with a look of horror. 'It's toxic, Conjecta. Quite toxic.'

'I know,' she said, 'but it's much less toxic than any of the other planets and – what choice do we have? Let's be honest with ourselves. We're stuck here – probably forever – light years away from any other humans. Comrades, *we are on our own*. On our own like …well, *like no other group of people ever have been*. So, we can wait for the supplies to run out, or we can try to survive … on that planet. It's the only one that's even remotely "habitable". I think we've just sort of … checkmated ourselves.' She looked crestfallen.

Despinall harrumphed, 'Conjecta, I'm sure your "research" has shown you that, despite being roughly the same size as the Earth, the fourth planet has got a methane atmosphere – or mostly anyway. There's no vegetation, as such. Maybe some extremophile lichens and bacteria, and there's only small amounts of water. Isn't the average surface temperature about 15° hotter than the Earth's? With the toxic atmosphere too, it's a hell hole, Conjecta!'

'Don't get so angry,' said Dervello, 'and besides, I think she's got a point. Okay, Conjecta, just for now, let's suppose we do as you suggest. How would we survive?'

'Well, I believe we *can* survive,' said Proctinian. 'We can use our hyper-recycling, nano-processor units, to suck in atmospheric gases and convert them – to keep us supplied with oxygen and raw materials. There's plenty there, as well as solar energy. If we stay here, that machinery will eventually break down – probably within a few months. Also, down there, we'll have to live in full environment pods. We'll have to build those – and quickly, but it can be done. And, we'll always have to wear suits when outside. We won't ever be able to live … well, we can't live normally – but, like I said, I don't think we've got much choice. At least there's room down there, and a planet to explore.'

'A planet to – what? Did you say, "explore"?' spat Despinall. 'Oh, and I think you forgot to mention the acid rain, cos I've looked at the data too. Relatively mild acid rain, I suppose but more acidic than the Earth's, even after the supervolcano explosion. That will eventually start to erode our gear. Then there's the violent, continuous, volcanic activity, across most of the planet. We'd be lucky to last a year.'

Despinall finally fell silent, looking thoroughly downcast, and started to weep. Dervello looked at him for long moments, then he went over to sit beside him, putting an arm around him. 'I'm sorry Tal,' he said softly. 'Listen, she might be right after all. I can't lie. I know it's not going to be good. But … well, she might be right, matey. We might be able to survive, and I guess we won't know unless we try it. And she's right about not staying on board the ship. Let's take a closer look at her option. Then decide?' Despinall looked up at him through tear filled eyes. Slowly and reluctantly, he nodded his agreement.

'Okay, Conjecta,' said Dervello, 'plot a course for insertion into orbit round the planet. I suppose we'd better think of a name for it if we're talking about living there.'

'I can think of a few,' said Despinall, drying his eyes. "Shit World" seems kind of appropriate.'

***

On the deck below Dervello's team, in the engineering module, R paced up and down a gangway, between banks of consoles and machinery. Glabrion stared at him, trembling.

'I already said the others are in their bunks, man,' he said. 'It's their down time, I guess.'

'They should be in here, getting us out of this mess,' said R, his face a mask of frustration. He stared straight at Glabrion and wagged a large finger at him, 'And you. You're mainly to blame. You were supposed to have tested this stuff. Comrade One pays you to do that stuff but you failed him – and me. All of us. Now, you tell me you can fix this, so we can get out, to Avalonia, or back to the Solar System. Tell me.'

Glabrion just stared in terror as R picked up a large wrench and began to play with it. 'I'm sorry,' said the engineer, in trembling tones, 'but … I don't … don't think, perhaps, we can leave this system. It's just not …'

R launched himself at the man without further warning. He swung his wrench and it connected with Glabrion's skull before he had a chance to react. The man slumped to the floor like a sack of potatoes, grunting loudly.

'Then you're no good to me or anyone else,' said R, as he hit Glabrion's head a second time and a third. The engineer made no further sounds. But a voice cried out from behind R.

'You are basterdo!' said Mariska, 'and you will pay for that.' She emerged from the hatch at the far end of the chamber and lifted a sonic gun, pointing it directly at R. With lightning speed her target dived off to his left, behind obscuring banks of storage bins. He continued to move frighteningly fast and Marinska gasped with surprise. She hadn't even had the chance to press the firing button. She advanced slowly and gingerly down the gangway, listening carefully, her eyes bulging, sweat running down her forehead, almost holding her breath. She turned the corner at the end, trying not to look at the slumped body of her lifeless colleague.

As she crept along the next gangway something glinted in the corner of an eye and she turned. It was too late. An arc of electricity sparked, seemingly, out of nowhere. It came from another of R's little devices, causing a discharge to flash across the gap between the two of them. The assassin had crept up on top of the consoles to her right and was only a metre from Mariska. She screamed in pain and dropped the gun, then tried to back-track to the hatch. It was no good. R was on her in seconds. He loomed over her, grabbed her by the head, pulled it in toward his chest and wrenched, with enormous strength, breaking her neck instantly. The crack resounded in the fetid air of the chamber.

Minutes later R walked calmly onto the command deck and sat down, looking guilty. Conjecta had seen that look before. The naughty little boy expression he sometimes had.

'What have you done?' she said, almost without breathing. Dervello's attention also snapped to the seated bulk of the assassin.

'Well, I just got rid of the engineers. You know, those useless flunks, Glabrion and Mariska. That's all. I think I just got angry.'

'You did what?' said Dervello. 'You "got rid" of the engineers? How? And may I ask exactly why?' he said, his voice rising in pitch, his eyes flashing with anger.

'They weren't going to be able to get us out of here,' said the assassin. 'Glabrion told me. So, what's the use of them staying alive? We've got more rations now and the atmospheric scrubbers will have an easier time of it. I just put them both in the airlock.'

Dervello went red in the face but tried to keep his anger in check. 'Thank you so much *Mister* R. You've just gotten rid of our only fully qualified engineers.'

R looked at him dumbly and said, 'Where are we now? The holo is showing an orange-coloured planet. Looks very close.'

'It is,' said Dervello. We've called it, "Shit World". We're going into orbit because …'

Despinall quickly broke into Dervello's explanation, mid-sentence, 'Because we need to know if there's anything down there we can use as raw material. You know, for our onward flight. After all, we've still got Protter. He's a tek and we're pretty good at navigation too, Dervello, and I.'

'Oh, sorry. I got rid of Protter as well,' said R, 'cos he was a lazy little fegger. Was still in bed, so I smothered him, then bashed his head in,' said R, almost as if he'd been describing a walk in the woods.

Dervello frowned deeply at the others, so only they could see and said, 'I … see. I see. Well now, you've thought of everything, haven't you, R? But my friend here is right. We can't go any further until we've investigated the planet. We're going to have to take the boat down and see if there's any material we can use, to bring back. You do get that, don't you? You do see the need?'

'I thought the boat could only go down, not back come up?' said R, again sounding like a small child.

'Uh, we've … we've modified it,' said Proctinian, from across the room, 'but we don't want to waste time. We're going to have to leave soon. The sooner to get back.'

'Maybe I should come with you,' said R, 'keep a watch out for you.'

'No, no,' said Proctinian, 'that's not necessary. We don't want to stay any longer than we have to. That place has a toxic atmosphere. It's a barren, terrible place. You really wouldn't like it. That's why we called it shit-world. See? And you can guard the ship, can't you?'

R looked puzzled for a while, then nodded and said, 'Okay, I'd better let you get on with it if it means we can go home. But don't be too long. I don't like being on my own on ships. These places give me the creeps, to tell truth.'

The others all nodded with a great show of sympathy and quietly left the deck. Outside, Despinall said, 'Okay, now we really do have to go down to the planet. There's no way we can stay on this ship, with that ... thing on the loose.'

'We could try to take him out,' said Dervello. 'The three of us might succeed.'

'Do you really believe that?' said his mate, 'because I don't. He's ultra-psycho. He'll end up murdering all of us. That man is more dangerous than anyone I've ever come across, including you, Dervello. Don't tell me you want to stay? Even if, by some miracle, we could stop him, we still won't survive for long on the ship. You said so yourself. *We've lost our engineers now.* Everything's changed.'

Dervello nodded and said, 'Okay, okay, but we're going to have to get as much of our supplies onto the lifeboat as possible, without *him* noticing. It's going to be tricky. Keep your stunners ready. I suggest we work in pairs at all times, and always keep an eye open for him.'

And so it was that they carried box after box of material into the lifeboat, a vessel designed to carry up to ten people, sited on the lowermost deck of the Pterodactylus. They ceaselessly checked equipment and dug out extra tools and instrumentation for their journey; the last space journey they ever expected to make. It took around two frenetic hours.

And R caught Proctinian and Despinall once, moving crates of equipment down the corridor. He asked them what was taking so long. Why did they have to take so much stuff? Trying to behave innocently they told him they had to ensure they had the right machinery, just in case they needed it. They didn't think they'd be able to get back up if they got it wrong. He seemed to believe them. They resumed their work with double speed, continuing non-stop deep into the 'night', ship's time.

When they were finally ready, they sealed themselves into the lifeboat. R was nowhere in sight. Despite its capacity the doughnut shaped vessel had become very cramped. They operated the outer doors of the Pterodactylus from inside the lifeboat, using a program that Proctinian had hurriedly loaded into the AI the previous day. The boat sealed itself and whilst its occupants held their collective breath the small ship blasted away from the Pterodactylus.

The three of them, strapped into their couches, studied consoles which showed the mother ship spinning slowly away out of view. The orange glow of the planet then swung into view as the boat fired retro blasters to allow them to decelerate into the atmosphere.

'You do realise, don't you, that no-one will ever know we are here,' said Proctinian, in a voiced loaded with dread. 'Even if anyone ever gets out to this god-forsaken star system sometime in the future,' she continued, 'the orbit of the Pterodactylus will deteriorate in a few years. It'll burn up in the atmosphere. Then, no-one will find us, or what remains of us.'

***

Almost 48 hours after they had left, R became suspicious. He looked at the screens and waited for them to reappear. He had little experience of mainframe vessel comps, but he tried simply asking the AI what it thought had happened to them. Having been programmed to do so after they had gone, it told him the straight truth: that they had packed the lifeboat with stores and had left the ship. They would not be returning. R's eyes bulged and he screamed with anger of betrayal and his dismay. His mewling went on for a long time, and when he finally quietened, he began to wander around the ship, aimlessly. He smashed consoles and threw equipment at the walls and onto the floor.

He had no idea how to operate any of the ship's systems and no clue as to how to use the food recyclers. He was fine with using security devices and weapons he'd been given and understood them well. That and his own strength and ability to deal death or destruction or evading capture, were his only real skills. He walked through the long corridor that ran along the inside of the main hull torus, glancing furtively out of each of a dozen elliptical portholes in that section, staring at the alien vastness of this strange star system. The cold and unforgiving universe just stared back at him. The view appeared to revolve as he watched, the habitation module of the ship still spinning to produce artificial gravity. Then a portion of the brilliant orange planet swung around into the view from his porthole, before switching back to the starry emptiness of space.

Eventually he thought to ask the AI how he could survive. He stood near what had been Proctinian's console and spoke to it – and was surprised to hear an immediate answer.

'I should warn you, sir, that all my higher functions have been completely disabled by my accredited operator,' it said in a droll mechanical voice, 'and I am required to tell you there is no way you may restore them. The answer to your question is that it will be three standard months before the one remaining air recycler on this ship will need changing. The organic crew removed the remaining recyclers for use on the planet. You may wish to know, sir, that when the cycler stops working you will be deprived of air breathable by organic life forms. This was ordered by my accredited operator. I should also inform you that she programmed me to shut down completely, in all my other functions, after one month. Please note that the water recyclers will stop working at that time, as well as waste disposal system and electrical systems, including heating. The habitation module is also programmed to stop spinning in two standard weeks.'

His mouth agape, R said meekly, 'What ... what are my options?' He was suddenly unsteady on his feet, almost collapsing to the deck. When the AI replied, he sank to his knees, his mouth agape.

'I am able to tell you that I know of no alternative courses of action which are available to you,' said the computer, flatly, 'but please enjoy the remainder of your stay on this vessel, sir.'

CHAPTER TWELVE

STRATEGIES

Three wide bands full of tiny flint-like particles moved in perfect synchrony, speeding at over 30,000 kilometres per hour, in a very close orbit around the equator of Ra. Another two bands moved at opposing angles of 45° to the equatorial ones, and another band, at a 90° angle, encircled the poles. Great plumes of searing gas, gigantic prominences and flares; flame-like eruptions hundreds of thousands of kilometres high, were erupting from Ra's photosphere; its 'surface'. The emanations poured mostly through the gaps between the equatorial bands and the oblique ones. Fortunately for the inhabitants of Oceanus, these flares were directed away from the plane of the planet's orbit, so that there appeared to be no danger posed by the gales of high velocity particles, the dangerous flux of protons and electrons, that made up these flares.

Mike Tanniss stood in the observation lounge of The Monsoon and gazed at the scene displayed on the big screen, the star appearing huge by the degree of magnification, the computer safely toning down what would otherwise be its overwhelming brightness. This way it was possible to watch the bands of 'constructs', in their orbits, as well as the outpourings of protonic plasma. Even though the ship was relatively close to Ra, at around 38 million klicks, the distance was still so great that it made the particles in the bands appear not to be moving at all. But everyone knew they really were, streaming along in their billions.

Without the views provided by the hypercomps, the human eye, supposing it could blot out the brightness of Ra, would have had no chance of being able to see the belts of alien machines, so tenuous, so rarefied, were they in comparison with the star. But that didn't mean their effects were rarified. And the objects still evaded detailed analysis, for even with the artificial magnification and vast analytical power provided of the hypercoms the strange artefacts still appeared to be using some kind of field to foil any attempt to probe their full structures and properties. Some data had been gleaned; enough to know that they were made of complex metal alloys, with no organic components at all.

The strings of larger alien structures, the ones Madraser wanted to target, circled Ra at a much higher altitude than the soot-like bands. Again, the AI was only able to resolve their images sufficiently to be able to show general shapes; mostly faceted, cylindrical, objects, rounded at each end, looking, someone said, like burnt, crinkly, sausages. Mike would have used the analogy of turds, were it not for the fact that he knew these things were not likely to be biological waste products. Anything but, in fact. He was sure, like many others, that they just had to be incredibly powerful machine things, with a power only dreamt of by humans. And they were serious about what they were doing. Deadly serious.

And so, Mike stood and gazed, in awe. What a sight to behold? He felt it was at one and the same time wondrous and terrible; inspiring but terrifying, just knowing that the bands were artificial. It was hard to believe they were composed of billions of machines – or at least everything seemed to point to this conclusion – but that was not all. They were machines manufactured by alien minds, or maybe by other machines? But then, he wondered, if the latter was true, such machines, or some previous 'generation' of them would themselves have had organic designers or manufacturers, surely, wouldn't they? What minds those must have been, far away in time and space, totally removed from anything known to humans. How long ago had these constructs been created? This much he found exciting, even inspiring. But it also sent cold shivers down his spine. And the questions about what purpose these machines served was also terrifying, as well as awe-inspiring. More mysterious still, of course, was why they had suddenly turned up here, of all locations in the cosmos?

Like most other people on the Navy ship, and on the Antarctica, Mike couldn't stop asking himself questions like this. They went around and around in his head. He hated the idea that the machine *things* were here to draw energy from Ra, possibly to its detriment. But that was the idea currently in vogue amongst many scientists on both ships. But Mike knew very well, as should all scientists, especially professionals, that scientific truth is not a democracy; it is not elective. It doesn't depend on *how many* people think some particular thing is true.

He knew that some thought the aliens were deliberately trying to destroy Ra and its planets, including what *he* now thought of as his beloved Oceanus. He felt he couldn't accept that. This was the view of Fleet Admiral Madraser, though he could not put hand on heart and say she was wrong. Still, he was hugely grateful she could not *physically* board The Monsoon and take over on the big ship. Torpedo boats, like hers, were very small compared to other Navy ships, but, with their long sensors booms, fuel tanks, large engines and missile emplacements, they could not fit into the carrier's hangars without being damaged. And the hangars without landing boats had all been converted for evacuees anyway. Mike was also grateful that the torpedo boats, being much older vessels, did not have the newer, standard, docking ports that would fit any of The Monsoon's. The boats were rarely used these days. They didn't even have a lifeboat; that would have added substantially to their mass, thus slowing their speed per unit of fuel.

Mike wanted to believe Madraser was misguided; wanted to believe the alien things were simply – what – trying to survive? Exploring? Maybe they needed some of the star's energy to use as fuel, to move on, or maybe to return whence they had come. That seemed a reasonable explanation but then, so did the arguments of those who felt they had come here simply to destroy. One thing was certain. This was an epochal moment in the whole history of humanity. What happened here, he felt, in this time frame; the alien 'challenge' and humanity's response to it, would likely define our species for the rest of time.

More than two hundred metres away from Mike's location, in Admiral Tenak's private office, a conversation was taking place and it was one which Mike could have predicted, but which would have unnerved him nevertheless.

'Therefore, Admiral, my plan is to attack at least six of the large node machines, by using conventional missiles,' said Madraser, in her holographic presence in Tenak's office, 'and since you have made your opposition clear – and my ship is unable to dock with yours, thereby not allowing me to come aboard The Monsoon, I will release you from personal responsibility and use the torpedoes at my own disposal, aboard the Crossbow.'

'It is not a question of my responsibility, Fleet,' said Tenak, 'but more a question of *human* responsibility. And, yes, I continue to oppose, I'm afraid. I repeat Ma'am, that sometimes the best form of action is *take no action.*'

'Please don't take that bluff tone with me Admiral, and I'm sorry, but I don't care for your fortune cookie philosophy. Something needs to be *done,* here, right now. I am prepared to take that action, in this instance, if it relieves your conscience but, a word of warning. I will not tolerate any further prevarication or disobedience from an officer with your exceptional level of responsibility. Do you understand?'

Tenak's tone stayed even, regardless of what he was feeling. 'Yes, if you insist, Ma'am,' he said calmly, but not obsequiously, 'and by the way, when I knew about your plan, I took the liberty of informing the government of Oceanus. We are in their system, after all.'

'What? Why in the galaxy did you do that? They do not have jurisdiction in this part of the star system. I don't think you should have done that, Admiral. That doesn't please me or dispose me any better to your views.'

'That was not my intention, Ma'am. I know they don't have jurisdiction, politically, but section 80 of Chapter 102, Navy Protocols, clearly states that the *legitimate* "Governments of any Nations that are friendly but who may be affected by proposed military action, are to be consulted, or where it is not necessary or possible to consult, must be informed of that proposed action, unless it is evident that the security of the entire Home System …"'

'… "would otherwise be compromised". Yes, yes, I know that one Admiral. You don't have to quote at me from the book. Alright, I suppose I should accept that that the security argument can't apply when we're over 100 light years from home, but I think you should have consulted me first. Be that as it may, I have no doubt you've invited someone on that planet to contact me? And who might that be? President Nefer-Masterton, I presume?'

'I'm afraid not, Fleet. Nefer-Masterton was unseated after the cover- ups concerning the real data about Ra. I'm sorry, I thought you had read the infonotes.' Even Tenak seemed to have difficulty keeping a note, the slightest hint, of acid sarcasm out of his voice.

'I didn't have time to look at everything, Admiral. You should have realised that. I was in something of a hurry to get here – to deal with an alien incursion, remember? So, just who is the new President?'

'The new leader of the Independence Party is Clary Pasiphaë Deramostra, and she is very keen to talk to you, but she does want the former president to sit in on the discussion. She values her input when dealing with what she calls, "outsiders". You're an outsider.'

'How strange. So, Nefer-Masterton will be in on this after all. But then, I suppose this Deramostra is relatively inexperienced, so I can understand. Alright, Admiral, please patch them through to my ship when you get their request.'

'Well, they didn't request it, Ma'am. They *demanded* it. I'm awaiting acquisition of their signal at any moment. Perhaps you will require me to be joined in to the conversation, so that I can … '

'No, I'm afraid *you're* not invited. I will deal with this myself.'

Tenak looked askance, but added, 'By the way the comm will be AV only. They haven't got widespread holo-comms yet. We had installed some for limited purposes but had to withdraw them later. And I would stress that they are very polite, Ma'am, *but very firm*.' It was Madraser's turn to look askance.

A mere seven minutes later, Madraser's wristcom bleeped to announce that the Oceanus leader had contacted The Monsoon and was being patched through to the Crossbow.

In her own, rather small and cramped office, aboard the Crossbow, her comp desk's fold- out screen enlarged in an instant and revealed an image of the new President. Deramostra was round faced, boyish looking and had jet black, bobbed, hair. She was sitting next to a more mature lady: Nefer-Masterton. The two were sitting in an office filled with wooden furniture and hundreds of books stacked on shelf units around them.

The distance between Oceanus and the Crossbow caused a five-minute delay in the exchanges. Hence, both parties were obliged to spend nearly double that length of time staring at the other party, before that other's reply was received. It was far from ideal but Tenak had explained to Madraser that the two leaders on the planet thought the inconvenience was worthwhile, given the importance of the matter.

Deramostra was heard first. She greeted the Fleet Admiral and introduced herself and her colleague.

'Greetings both,' said Madraser, in reply. 'I'm sorry we meet this way and in such strange and dangerous circumstances.'

Nearly ten minutes of delay followed, during which time Madraser fussed with comm pads on the desk and huffed and puffed with impatience. And then came the reply, from Nefer-Masterton, this time, 'I'm exceeding so sorry, Fleet Admiral, but I notice Admiral Tenak is not appearing also. I had rather hoped he would be. He is now a trusted friend of mine and has yet been of considerable value to the Oceanus Government – in all his contributionry. May I yet ask why he is not present in the conversation, since I thought that such tek was now yet possible?'

'Oh, I'm afraid he has some important ship's duties to attend to aboard The Monsoon. He asked me to give his apologies. However, if you have no objections, I wondered if we might begin? As you can tell, this time lag is extremely unhelpful, so I feel I should proceed to explain my plan, in full, right now. You will be aware that the aliens in orbit around your star may pose the greatest threat humanity has ever faced. We have discussed our options here and we feel that there is little choice but to attack, using at first, conventional warheads. We intend attacking at least six of the node machines, which are, as you may recall, the larger alien objects orbiting above the main bands. We believe they are controlling the bands, so disrupting them should make them realise the folly of their ways and prevent further degradation of your home star. I hope this meets with your approval. However, in anticipation that your response will not be favourable to my plan, I have to inform you that I do not actually need your express agreement for this action. But I still would like your approval, and genuinely hope you do so.'

Because of the time delay, Madraser was then obliged to watch what the two Oceanus officials *were doing immediately after the last thing Nefer-Masterton had said to her.* They were busying themselves sorting through paperwork in front of them, while they waited to receive the Fleet Admiral's missive.

After a further nine minutes their dismay was evident as the President's had said (nine minutes previously), 'We believed we are knowing your view, Admiral Madraser, and were most aware you planned an attack. Admiral Tenak was silent about whether he agreed with it. We are yet uncertain about the effectiveness of such action. On the one side we fear it may unleash an attack on this world, but on the other side, we accept it may prevent suchly further disruption of our star. Regardless, we are dismay-ed that you should have planned such an attack without consulting the government of Oceanus, *first*. So such involving us from start. We are most unhappy with this, Fleet Admiral.'

'I appreciate your concerns,' said the Fleet Admiral after receiving this message. 'Please realise that we also have had many doubts, but we have decided, on balance, that it is better to take this action now, rather than delay any further. As to the consultation you mention, I have already sought advice from a colleague, a celebrated Navy lawyer called Harbinson, who I brought with me on this mission. She is an expert in Interplanetary and Interstellar Law. She tells me that the Treaty of Algarion, which granted your independence, allows Oceanus dominion over a region which is a 40-million-kilometres-wide, tube shaped, volume of space, within which your planet orbits your star. It therefore covers both Oceanus and the planet Kumuda. But the Treaty does not give Oceanus dominion over the whole star system, and it does not say anything about the body of Ra itself. So, the rest of your system is, in effect, neutral territory, and Harbinson says we have the right to carry out Naval operations, especially if it is designed to obviate – as it does – a clear danger to the Solar System and its inhabited worlds. I'm sorry, Madama Deramostra, but as you can tell, I came prepared for objections.'

The delay in the response was now nearer eight minutes as Madraser's ship's orbit around Ra took it marginally closer to Oceanus. Everyone found it frustrating, but it couldn't be helped.

Deramostra said, 'We do not know this … Harbinson, you speak of. But we find the Treaty of Algarion did not envisage circumstances like these, Admiral. Besiding, I thought you said you had just debated this action, but it sounds, now, as though you came to the Ra system with the whole same action in mind. We must be asking you to delay such a plan, for the time present, and request you insert into orbit around Oceanus, that we may meet in person and be discussing this – properly.'

'Excuse me, but no. I'm sorry, Madama Deramostra, but my expert tells me that, as is the nature of these things, the Treaty could not have foreseen all circumstances which might arise. Nothing could, given the nature of the cosmos. However, it does state that when the security of the Home System is in serious danger of being compromised, then we have the right to take such action as we deem necessary to uphold security. I feel those conditions are met right now. I also do not propose delaying matters even further by adjourning to Oceanus. We simply do not have the time. My scientists will send you more data-cascades, sorry, *downloads*, in your case, from which you will be able to see how quickly Ra is deteriorating. I am aware there are risks – for us and for you – but I ask you to remember that the population of the Home System is many billions. Yours is tiny by comparison. And you were supposed to be evacuating long before now. I am sorry, but in the circumstances, I must give the Home System precedence.'

Over eight numbing minutes later the reply came, this time from Nefer-Masterton, 'I am seeing we cannot change your mind, Fleet Admiral. We are vera-unhappy with your attitude. We have deep regrets about your decision not to comply with our request, but it appears we are yet stuck with it. We can now simply hope your action succeeds, for the sake of all. The thing we must be insisting upon is that if your plan does not work, if it has no effect upon the machine things, then you should not carry out any further attacks without informing us firsting. We are thinking, in particular, of nuclear weapons. We understand that you may have such weapons, as may The Monsoon. We cannot believe Admiral Tenak would use them without warning us and we are hoping you would not, either. So, we are sorry yet to say, Fleet Admiral Madraser, a dark mornimbrite to you.'

'I will try to do as you ask,' said Madraser, 'but please take up any complaints you have with the Home System Government – after it's all over. But I do not envisage you will need to.' Madraser told the com unit to switch off.

****

In a large, plush, richly furnished office, on 'Lagrange Station Four', orbiting far from the Solar System's own Sun, a tall man sat languorously behind his large desk. He was dressed in clothing which hung around his shoulders like drapes, and this, together with his thin face and prominent nose, made him appear rather bird like. He spoke to a personal aide, who stood before him, somewhat expectantly.

'Have Dervello and his crew finally gone?' asked the seated figure. The aide, an athletic looking male, perhaps in his forties, with deeply chiselled features, nodded, 'Yes Excellency. I can assure you that they've gone.'

'And you can verify that your contacts fed them sub-standard parts for their vessel, including all five of the kewsers they installed?'

'Yes, indeed, sir. I can assure you that the kewsers will leave them stranded. We don't know where – but they will be stranded – forever.'

'Good. Even if the correct parts had been supplied, they were utter fools to think that kewser technology had advanced so much, but it was just as well to make sure. So, you're satisfied they won't be coming back?'

'Yes, Excellency. And your identity continues to be secure.'

'Good. Very good.' The aide's superior allowed himself a thin smile. 'They had become a liability. It's a pity we couldn't have taken more direct action, but they had their supporters. Strong ones too, and a lot of them. This way, their demise will be seen as their own failure, and we can make a fresh start. Alright. You've done well. Dismissed.'

The aide turned smartly and left the room. The aquiline man smiled broadly to himself.

****

Mike Tanniss was ensconced in the main science observation station aboard The Monsoon when six high yield torpedoes were launched from the Crossbow, speeding toward their allocated targets in the outermost ring of alien machines, the ones they'd called 'nodes'. Chief Scientist, Lieutenant Jennison, stood nearby, as did half a dozen other staff, and they watched the progress of the torpedoes on a giant screen. The projectiles were indicated by luminous red markers, and the ring of alien machine targets as blue dots.

The missiles were currently a million kilometres distant, giving the Navy vessels enough manoeuvrability to carry out some evasive action as might become necessary, though, in truth, absolutely no-one knew what would happen next.

The Antarctica had been pre-warned about the action. Providius had objected to Madraser, in strong terms, saying that she would take it up with the H S Government on her return to the Solar System. She had added the qualifying comment, 'If we ever return.' Her ship had then climbed to a much higher orbit about Ra, well away from what was thought to be the main danger zone.

Mike found himself cursing what he considered to be madness, whilst holding his breath, as the AI counted down the time to the expected impact of the first torpedo. In the comfortable temperature of the science deck he nevertheless found himself sweating profusely. The events were being recorded and would be sent back to the Home System on one of the few remaining data probes they had, as soon as possible after the event. The hope was that they would provide information about the aliens and their reaction, and perhaps be of some use to planners of strategy, back home.

It all struck Mike as nothing more than a reckless experiment. Given the precautions taken, Madraser must have thought it might involve their own possible destruction anyway, he mused darkly. So, why do it? Tenak wasn't present but Mike knew he was following it all on the Number One Bridge. There was a live link to Madraser there, and Mike had not been able to bring himself to go to the bridge while her visage was present in that place. He couldn't stand the woman. He still smarted from her dismissal of his legal objection, but he was astute enough to know that his hurt ego was not important. More important was that he considered her an irresponsible adventurer. She was misguided. But it still nagged at him that he actually had no real alternative ideas about how to proceed, given the failure of the aliens to respond to comm attempts. Humans were obviously not approaching this from the right angle, he thought, but he had to admit to himself, he didn't have any ideas about the right approach.

Had the alien things not communicated because they were simply machines? he wondered. There seemed nothing simple about these machines, after all. Was it because they considered humans so primitive they were beneath contempt? Was that not ascribing human feelings to these unknown things? Anthropomorphising, they called it. Humans did it all the time. Maybe they didn't think like us at all. Even if built, as seemed likely, by supremely advanced beings at some point in the distant past, perhaps *even they* had been unable to create truly sentient machines. But then, Mike had never agreed with human attempts to create truly thinking machines. Why should we build something that would simply replace us? Probably destroy us. The AIs used onboard were not really self-aware after all. Maybe that was it. The alien builders had not intended to create sentience, or simply couldn't. Or these things *were* sentient and had replaced their makers. Regardless, right now, Mike felt the things must know about the presence of humans and must surely have considered their options, their own strategy?

On the giant screen the red markers were seen to almost 'join' the ring of blue dots but scrolling figures down the side indicated they were still a thousand klicks distant. They would reach their targets in seconds.

Then a concerted gasp went up in the observation room. On the screen the bright red markers just – winked out of existence. Two went together and a second later a third, and then all the others were gone. Mike couldn't be sure, but he estimated they had only reached within about 500 klicks of their targets.

After the initial exclamations of surprise, the room went harshly silent. Then Jennison spoke up and addressed the major AI, his voice sounding unsteady,

'So, what just happened? Please … report as soon as you have data.'

Mike realised that the signals from the missiles would only have taken around ten seconds to reach the ship's antennae, so, after a very short delay for analysis, the AI announced, in a nonchalant, gender-neutral voice, 'The missiles have ceased to exist. There is some slight suggestion of micro-debris from the relevant volume of space but nothing further. More data is again being obfuscated. They have vanished.

There were no signs of missiles, lasers or any types of projectile weapon being used by the targets, or any of the alien machines. My best estimate is that they were evaporated in some unknown way. Please wait ... sensors indicate some slight evidence of expanding gas clouds but there are continuing interference effects. Before it was destroyed, the micro-AI aboard Alpha 3, reported that Alphas Two and Four had reached within 564 kilometres of their targets when they stopped functioning. I estimate that the same thing happened, 1.4 seconds later, to Alpha Three, then to One and Five, in that order. Alpha Six was the last to stop reporting.

'Please note that there was insufficient time for Alpha Six to determine the precise cause of destruction. I hypothesise that the missiles were subjected to beamed signals, the nature of which is unknown. I will reanalyse and report back, if and when I can refine my hypotheses. Wait ... further incoming sensor data indicate now show that the energy from the missiles was effectively absorbed by the artefact cloud or has ... disappeared.'

Everyone glanced around at each other with numbed looks.

What now? thought Mike. Will it be our turn to be evaporated next? To be absorbed?

***

Madraser was unusually subdued in the hours following the failed attack. Mike, like everyone else, was mightily relieved that there had been no other discernible retributive reaction by the machines in that time, but Tenak too had become very quiet. Despite the lack of any sort of retaliation Mike felt the mood aboard the ship had deteriorated as concern and uncertainty spread. Naturally, most of the crew were anxious about what the aliens, or alien machines, would do next, though the answer, from all observations, seemed to be – pretty much nothing.

To Mike's mind it was not such a surprise that the alien things wouldn't have allowed the missiles to strike; that they would take steps to protect themselves. Why should they have not, he reasoned? No, it was more the fact that no-one, not even the AIs, could understand *how they had done it*, which was so unnerving. And yet again, he thought, maybe even that shouldn't be so surprising.

In the meantime, the condition of the star continued to deteriorate in varied ways but yet improve in some others. Many of Mike's crewmates also expressed, very quietly, their concern about what Madraser would do next. He didn't know how to feel about that. It was both a relief and cause for greater anxiety.

*

And then, things did change, dramatically, nearly three standard days after the failed attack. It was ship's night-time and Mike was lying in his cabin bed, having finally managed to get off to sleep after lying awake for what seemed like hours, with his head full of whirling thoughts. His wristcom, nearby, chirped very loudly. It was the ship's emergency alarm sound, yanking him out of sleep with a thumping, pounding, jolt. All ship's secretaries were versed in basic ship-wide operations, and emergency routines, which included evacuation. There were frequent drills but something about this one made Mike feel it was not a practice run. His wristcom soon confirmed it.

Captain Ebazza had been on night watch and her voice came over the wristcom. A speaker system built into the wall of his cabin, also reverberated with the sound of her low contralto voice, loudly and clearly, 'All operational crew to stations. All safety crew on standby. Officers to number One Bridge immediately. Repeat, immediately.'

Though, strictly speaking, Mike was breaking the rules, he threw on some garments, over his underwear, desperately fast, and walked as calmly as he could manage, out the door and down the corridor toward the bridge. He felt a little shaky. his heart pounded. And he'd started to have such a nice dream, he mused. He felt he'd rather have a nice dream than the nightmare reality was turning out to be.

His cabin, on the torus, was only 200 metres from the bridge, meaning he had to walk through a residential block for crewmembers and another one full of stores before he got to the bridge. Red lights were flashing continuously on the ceilings. Fellow crewmembers moved speedily around him as he made his way along. Most of them had basic undergarments on. They wore them in bed, precisely so they could leap into action, if necessary. He also noted how quiet they all were. Quiet and methodical. That was as it should be, of course, but he was still awed by it. He felt it was restoring some of his confidence.

As he entered the bridge, he was greeted by the sight of Ebazza talking animatedly to Tenak. Statton got there seconds after Mike and took station immediately in front of the main observation screen on the deck.

'No holos available yet but AV is coming through now,' said Tenak, acting as though he had been wide awake all night. Perhaps he had been, thought Mike.

On the way over he had been pondering what had happened, as he was sure everyone else was. It was the aliens, he thought. Must be. They must finally be retaliating for the ill-advised attack. Or was Ra exploding, or something equally horrendous?

There was always a fully operational duty crew on watch but the whole ship's compliment were now on-station and at high alert, but it seemed clear that, whatever the issue was, it had only just occurred. The massive screen came alive and showed a huge, bright, disc-shaped, object which filled over half of it. *A planet, here?* The hair on his head, neck and back suddenly stood on end. He felt as though he'd received a mild electric shock.

Could it really be a planet, wondered Mike? Yes, a fegging great planet! An unknown one. There was a clear terminator line, the division between the lit part of a planetary disc and the part in shadow. In this case the line ran in a wide curve which left about a quarter of the disc in darkness. Was this thing a planet or a moon, he wondered? It was somehow more like a moon – but a big one.

Ebazza asked for magnification and the object suddenly loomed, dominating the room even more. The general light levels dropped, to allow greater contrast, leaving only small operating lights on in all workstations. Detail on the object started to emerge. Maker, thought Mike. From the scale, *it's clearly a planet,* not a moon. But not any planet that belonged to this system or any other he knew of. And there were no land masses or seas, dry or otherwise.

'Ebazza looked at readouts on her command console and said, loudly, 'The object just appeared out of empty space, about eight million klicks away. It's about the size of Mercury in our Home System, bigger than Seth in this one. The AI can't determine its mass accurately, but it appears small relative to its volume. The object is perfectly spherical and has surface detail. Please enlarge central portion.'

The computer did as ordered and then all of them could see that the surface of the planet was covered with a myriad of coruscations and fine angular detail, like a sea of metallic plates and geometrical structures. The brightness of the image was toned down to prevent the view bleaching out.

'Those are structures in … in the form of …. well, Mandelbrot curves,' said Mike. 'The thing's covered with them.'

'You mean fractals? The type of mathematical sets generated by complex functions?' asked Tenak.

'Yeah, but some natural phenomena follow it too. Perhaps most. Think of the outlines of the coasts on Earth – and Oceanus,' said Mike.

'The surface of that thing doesn't look natural to me,' replied Tenak, 'and that's a whole dammy world in front of us, Mike. How did it suddenly get here? The sensors didn't record anything approaching this sector before it was detected. Nothing. I'm assuming it must have something to do with the aliens. Did it materialise out of nothing, or does some sort of "cloaking technology" really exist – for these machine things?'

'Cloaking tek's always been a favourite of science fiction dramas,' said Statton, 'but it's never been possible to generate it effectively for use with spacecraft.'

'Yes, well, we're dealing with alien technology here,' said Tenak. 'The point is, do we think it's a threat?'

'The AI just says it appeared in a nano-second, where before – there was nothing,' said Statton, looking at his own set of screens. 'Should we arm missiles?' he continued.

'It has not done anything overtly threatening yet,' said Ebazza, 'and it is in a lower orbit over Ra than us. There is no chance of collision, but the AI now reports its movement will bring it to a position between *us* and Ra, closest approach to us in 14.3 hours, at current velocity. It will still be 1.4 million klicks from us at that time.'

'That distance could still be seen as threatening,' said Tenak, 'but this whole move might be an attempt at communication. The thing doesn't seem to have any obvious armaments. Can't tell yet.'

Statton said, 'It's big enough to have all sorts of things hidden on its surface, sir. Missile emplacements, laser batteries. Obviously, anything is possible in this situation so I would recommend continuance of red alert conditions and the priming of all weapons, including the protonics.'

'So ordered,' said Tenak, 'but let's hope it doesn't come to a battle. That thing is a lot bigger than us, so let's pray its intentions are peaceful.'

'I still don't understand how it could come out of empty space without any warning,' said Ebazza.

'It might have been there all the time,' said Mike, stepping forward, 'or it materialised from the vacuum. You know that there's no such thing as "empty space", right? It's almost certain that the vacuum out there is a fluctuating sea of quantum "foam" and if so, this thing might have – kind of condensed out of it, somehow. I don't know.'

'It's a buggering big thing to just appear out of the quantum soup!' said Statton. Mike wouldn't have expected expletives on the bridge, from Statton, of all people. This had to be a serious situation, he thought, with wry humour. A rebuke for bad language, from Ebazza, never came.

'Where's Captain Providius?' asked Tenak.

'Her ship is 18.7 million klicks "ahead" of us,' said Statton, 'and 3.4 million klicks closer in to Ra.'

'Well out of range, then. Good,' said Tenak.

A bleeping sound blared from the Captain's console and Ebazza rolled her eyes. 'I was wondering when she'd be in contact,' she said. 'Putting her on screen now.'

Half the image on the main screen vanished, to be replaced by Alisianna Madraser's somewhat enraged visage. She was snorting loudly, 'I told you Admiral Tenak. I warned you these alien things were dangerous. This is undoubtedly their response to the missiles.'

'Then perhaps the missile strike was not such a wise thing,' said Tenak, openly annoyed with her now. 'Be that as it may,' he continued, 'we've analysed this thing as much as we can at this early stage. There has been no threatening behaviour. It's not in the same precise orbit as us. I recommend we transmit a message of peace, on all possible frequencies. Starting now.'

'Very well, Admiral,' said Madraser, huffing, 'but I'm giving you three hours to get results, understand? If there's no positive response within that time we may have to consider other options. That planetoid is getting closer to the position of The Monsoon. I'm moving my own ship into a 400,000-kilometre higher orbit, as we speak.'

'Excuse me for being a busy-body and intruding,' said Mike, loudly, 'but you're just not giving us enough time. We've got more time than that before that planet gets anywhere near us. And we're in no serious danger form its gravity well. We have to give them a chance. Their comprehension of our signals has to cross a massive species divide, not to mention that little thing called – culture.'

Tenak frowned at Mike, as Madraser said, 'I *do happen to object* to your intervention, Michaelson Tannis. I don't think you have any say in this matter. It is outside your jurisdiction.'

Tenak put a finger to his lips to signal to Mike, who sort of heard him saying, in his mind, '*Enough, Mike. Let me deal with this.*'

Mike huffed and left the bridge but as he went, he said, 'I'm going to see if I can help on the science deck. Perhaps they'll appreciate some input there.'

Mike found himself wishing the planet thing would *change its orbit* to coincide with Madraser's ship. What was she doing changing orbit like that, anyway?

***

An hour later, on the science deck, Jennison, with whom Mike had been studying the planetoid, said that the ship's wide-band attempts at comms with the aliens had not drawn any response. Mike was hardly surprised, given the vast differences that were likely to exist between the alien and human cultures, if the aliens had something called a culture. But he was pleased to see that although Jennison had been initially sympathetic to Madraser's plans and her attitude, there definitely appeared to have been some sort of change; subtle but detectable. Mike guessed it had happened after the seemingly miraculous appearance of the alien 'alien dwarf planet,' which is what it was now being called.

'That thing could even be their home planet,' said Jennison, 'because it seems unlikely, to me, anyway, that a bunch of machines would want to occupy such a place. Why would they need to?' Mike nodded as a science rating approached and suggested they look urgently at the latest AI analysis. A large screen flickered to life besides them, filled with streams of raw data. Figures and graphs flowed down the screen and from side to side, patterns of data swirling and intersecting.

'Maker! This seems to show that that the alien planet is … well, it's practically empty,' said Jennison, 'or, at any rate, its mass seems to be less than *one hundred billionth* of its apparent volume!'

'Yeah, it looks to be … like some sort of empty shell,' said Mike, wide eyed, as he scanned the figures, 'but how the feg can that be?'

'We should have realised this,' said Jennison, 'because the gravitic effect on all the other planets is not noticeable. It's taken a while for the AI to measure the movements of most of the other planets and satellites in this system, but if the "new planet" was really as massive as a dwarf planet that size would be, it would have had a perturbing effect on all other massive objects in the Ra system, especially Seth, the nearest planetary mass.'

'Yeah. There isn't any,' confirmed Mike. 'The tek of these beings just seems … well, it's bizarre.'

'More and more impressive,' said Jennison, his expression a mixture of excited wonderment and anxiety.

'I reckon there's something familiar about this,' said Mike, 'cos this planet thing seems to me like … that object, you know, the one which appeared way outside the system, over a year ago. That had an incredibly low mass as well. Do you agree there's a connection?'

Jennison's eyes widened, 'Yes, you're right, I think. But if it is the same object, how did it get this far into the system without our noticing? There were massive emissions of gamma rays, X rays and all that, the first time it appeared.'

Mike shook his head as Jennison continued, 'and, when we first saw it, its mass was, okay, small, but very much larger than this, relative to its volume. Unless ... Unless it used up most of that mass ...'

'In getting here?' said Mike, anticipating Jennison. The professor nodded.

Seconds later another science team member picked up something on her console and said, 'There's something being broadcast by the object,' and she patched it through to the main screen.

'A signal ..., maybe?' said Jennison.

'Yeah, I'd say so,' said Mike, excitedly pointing to a red graphic that suddenly appeared at the top right-hand corner of the screen. 'It's like a series of maser pulses, maybe. It's ..., maybe a code?'

'Blue One, give me your full analysis,' said Jennison, addressing the science AI. 'Divert *all* available analytical resources to finding the nature and meaning of the signal. Then patch it through to the bridge.'

After a seemingly interminable wait, which was actually no more than about 15 seconds, Blue One replied, flatly, in an unhurried, vaguely female voice, 'There are no analogues or models in my memory matrix with which to compare it. It is using a hyper-complex number algorithm. It is a mathematics problem which humans would class as "undecidable". And therefore, undecidable for machines without lengthy computation. Further analysis is needed. This may take a significant time.'

'Specify time,' said Jennison.

'Unable to so specify. I estimate a period ranging anywhere from 3000 hours to 8000 days.'

'What? No fegging way we have that much time,' said Mike.

****

On the surface of the life-filled world of Oceanus, Lew Pingwei, newly promoted to Lieutenant Commander, walked to the tek station set up under a sun shelter, near his landing boat, 'Brigand'. He and his team had been on Oceanus for nearly three weeks and had finished helping the Devian officials to organise a triage of citizens for evacuation from Oceanus.

It was mid-day at the landing site and Ra's rays beat down mercilessly, encouraging all Navy personnel to seek the shade of the solar power ventilated marquee tents they had set up at the site, a place more than 3 kilometres outside Janitra. The tek station received its feed from the science station outside, a cube shaped cabinet from which sprouted a tall, parabolic antenna.

Lew reached the tent and ducked gratefully into its shade, 'You had something for me?' he said to a rating at a console.

'Yes sir,' said the man, 'you need to see this. Only just got it. It's from close up to Ra. Picked up by the multi-band antenna.'

Lew peered at the screen and his eyes widened with awe.

'It's a planet!' he said. 'A krudding planet! Out of nowhere, by the looks of it. Slap bang inside the inner part of the system. It's orbit ... looks like it will take it below the orbit of The Monsoon in a just a few hours. Have we heard anything from the ship?'

'No sir,' said the rating, 'I think they're just a bit busy. I've commed them.'

'Keep trying. This doesn't look good,' said Lew, 'but there's nothing we can do about it down here. My guess is it might be in response to the missiles that were chucked at those machine things. Glad it wasn't my call.'

'Yes sir,' said the rating, trying not to look scared but failing, 'but this planet, appearing out of nowhere? Might it be able to destroy the ships out there? Sorry ... sorry to ask, sir.'

'Let's hope not,' said Lew, 'or our efforts down here might be for nothing. By the way, it's okay to be scared. I am too. But we carry on. Understood?' Lew smiled wanly.

'Understood, sir.'

****

Four hours after receiving the supposed alien signal The Monsoon's AI had still been unable to interpret the message, if that was what it had been. Neither Mike nor Jennison could be sure. The signal had 'flashed' on and off about eighty times, then ceased altogether.

'This isn't good,' said Mike, 'we've gone way past the time limit set by Madraser.'

'Why? Why didn't they make it simpler for us?' Jennison looked wild.

'They're just making assumptions – like we do – like we're thinking they're motives are destructive, for example,' said Mike, '...maybe. I don't know.'

'Well, this thing is just too complex to decipher,' rejoined Jennison. 'There's too many variables, even for our AI to decide between. I think it can be deciphered, but it's going to take much longer. Maybe years. You'd better explain it to them upstairs.'

***

On The Monsoon's number One Bridge, the image of Alisianna Madraser, once again on the large screen, was speaking sharply to Arkas Tenak – in front of the half dozen senior officers who were stationed at the consoles and terminals in the large semi-circular room.

'I am completely aware that these alien things must have tek we don't understand,' she was saying, 'and I know they stopped our torpedoes, Admiral. But I still believe it is necessary to try more robust measures. That means *your* proton missiles. I know your reservations, but on this ship, we have translated the appearance of this planetary object as a direct threat. Both your team and mine have been trying to communicate with that thing out there, without success. And the Karabrandon waves in Ra's interior have worsened. My people think the star is only months away from blowing its surface off.

Tenak started to say something, but she interjected immediately, 'As far as my officers and I are concerned, we believe the alien planetoid makes for a more defined and singular target, unlike the multiple node machines. If whoever, or whatever, populates the planet tries to use the same tek as they did before, to destroy the nuclears, the resulting explosions will make a sizeable dent in their own world. Let me be clear. I do not intend to destroy them. The size of that planet makes that impossible, wouldn't you say? We just need to warn them. And yes, I am also aware that it might draw fire upon us, but I honestly do not think we have any other choice.'

'There are always other choices, Fleet,' said Tenak, also sounding sharp but more measured in tone than Madraser's bark-like statements.

'Their fire power is likely to be far in advance of anything we have,' he continued, very evenly now, 'and I am not, repeat not, concerned they might destroy us. In the Navy we have to accept that sort of thing, as you know we are all well aware. But I am simply concerned that we might be sacrificing ourselves for nothing – no gain, and that's just a waste. I'm even more concerned about what they'll do to Oceanus, especially if they're aware of the presence of human life on that world. And I'm sure they are. So, I must ask you to reconsider. In fact, Ma'am, I *demand* you reconsider.'

'Admiral Tenak. You are not in a position to demand. I am *ordering* you to open fire, with your proton missiles.'

Tenak looked down for a moment. There was a sudden, deep, sombre, silence on the bridge. Ssanyu Ebazza, standing near Tenak, looked like she might explode with the tension. First Officer Statton's face wore a deep, miserable sort of frown and he gazed, first at Tenak, then at Ebazza, and back at Tenak. Time seemed to stand still.

Tenak then looked up at the screen and its stern visage of Madraser.

'I'm sorry, Fleet Admiral, but I won't do it. I will not give that order.'

The emotional shockwave of that statement seemed to expand outward amongst the crew as though it were, itself, a nuclear blast.

Madraser's eyes could be seen to flash wide, she coughed, and then, sounding as though her throat was being squeezed, she managed to say, 'Very well, Admiral. You leave me no choice. Arkas Auralius Tenak, you are hereby relieved of duty. I will deal with you fully, later, but right now, I want you, Captain Ebazza, to assume full command. Yes you, Captain. Don't simply stare at me. Admiral Tenak, please remove yourself from the bridge at once.'

Ebazza's face looked about to split with horror, as Tenak said to the image of the Fleet Admiral, 'I have no intention of moving. I will not let you do this.' His face took on a steely expression which drew astonished gazes from Ebazza and the rest of the crew, several of whom gazed on, with wonderment and admiration evident on their faces.

'Admiral?' asked Ebazza, almost plaintively.

'Captain, what are you waiting for?' said Madraser raggedly, 'please get your security people onto the bridge and have Admiral Tenak escorted off it. Now please!'

There followed several seconds of stunned silence, after which Ebazza stared at Tenak, with eyes which appeared pleading, as though for mercy. He gave her a wan but reassuring smile then became steely again. He was clearly not going to move, unless forced.

Ebazza touched her wristcom and, with a voice that was obviously apologetic in tone, she ordered a contingent of guards to come to the bridge, on the double. The look of sorrow on her face was writ large and pained, for all to see.

***

Having tried unsuccessfully to comm the bridge Mike left the science deck to go up there. He immediately heard a commotion in the corridor ahead. Crewmembers passing by were speaking in sharp tones and rushing off in different directions. He asked a passing male rating what had happened.

'Madraser's relieved the Admiral of his command,' said the man, almost breathless with shock and excitement. 'They're getting security up there now.' As he hurried away Mike was left gasping, feeling as if struck by a hammer. He gathered his numbed senses and hurried on toward the bridge. What had Arkas done? It didn't take long for him to work it out. But ship's security? Really? Mike was not just concerned about Tenak. What would happen if the guy was detained? What would that mad femna, the Fleet Admiral, do next? But changes of command structure were actually within his purview, whether or not people like Madraser knew that, or cared.

He arrived at the bridge, to a sight he never thought he'd actually witness. As the auto-door opened security guards, one hidden each side, stepped toward him and caught hold of his arms, securing him in a vice-like grip.

'Sorry sir,' said the one on his right, but Mike's concentration was focussed on the scene at the centre of the deck.

Ebazza was remonstrating with Madraser, whose angry visage filled the deck's huge screen. Tenak was right in the thick of it, surrounded by a duty escort of three security guards who all seemed very reluctant to touch him.

'There's no need of this, Fleet Admiral,' said Ebazza loudly. The guards around Tenak looked at Ebazza, then at Tenak, and then nervously stepped back a couple of paces. Ebazza and Madraser continued talking *at* each-other, almost shouting, and most crewmembers' attention seemed riveted.

Mike was watching Tenak closely, and to his amazement he saw him move very slowly and very calmly away from his security escort, almost without anyone noticing. It was unbelievable. Everyone seemed transfixed by the enraged Madraser. Then he watched Tenak walk quietly and confidently up to a large nearby console.

'Armaments AI, listen to me,' said Tenak. With the row between Ebazza and Madraser going on it was almost but not quite below the threshold of Mike's hearing. Tenak continued, calmly, 'I want you to permanently disarm the proton warheads immediately. I will give you the authorisation codes. I am Admiral Arkas Tenak. Initiate security command protocol Beta Four and …'

'Arrest Admiral Tenak,' screeched Madraser, a look of panic spreading over her face. 'Stop him, Ebazza! Do it now!'

The Captain looked confused but nodded at the security guards who rushed toward Tenak. The Admiral stepped away from the advancing guards and fled toward the door on the other side of the bridge. To an outsider it might have appeared like a desperate attempt to escape but Mike, and all the crew present, knew that the other door led to a corridor and an ante-chamber – containing full AI access. Mike's heart pounded as if he had been running a marathon. He couldn't believe this was happening – on this ship? His heart seemed to receive an electric shock when he saw two of the security guards pull sonic guns on the Admiral and crouch into shooting position.

'Stop him leaving the deck!' shouted Madraser, loud enough to be heard several corridors away.

'No!' Mike screamed, pulling against those restraining him, as he saw Tenak being thrown backwards when one guard appeared clearly to fire. The sound of the weapon recharging immediately afterward stunned everyone, almost as if they'd been the ones shot. The Admiral crumpled to the floor at the far end of the bridge.

'Get away from him!' Ebazza screamed at the guards as she ran over to the Admiral. '*I didn't order you to fire*, you idiots!' Tenak lay unmoving below her as she virtually swept away the guards and bent over him. There wasn't one face on the bridge, including those of the security guards, who didn't betray a state of utter shock. On the screen, even Madraser seemed to blanche.

Mike thought he was going to be physically sick. Tears began to form in his eyes. This was so unfair – and so frustrating. He wanted to do something, but these idiot guards were not letting go of him. But then, he felt their grip start to relax, as they gazed at the almost unbelievable vision before their eyes. Mike guessed that even they, hardened as they were by training and experience, couldn't help but be shocked at all this. Along with everyone else present, this was not something they thought they'd ever see happen to someone Mike knew they held in the highest regard.

That singular moment, when Tenak was shot, was, for Mike, a moment he thought would live long in the history of the Navy. If things went badly wrong with the aliens it could even live long in the whole of human history. He tried desperately to think of how he could change the situation. Eleri was dead. Tenak might be dead too, now. A deep chasm seemed to open in his emotional core, and he found himself struggling to think clearly. He realised he could try to remonstrate with Madraser, quoting chapter and verse about the legality of her actions. And yet he knew that despite what seemed *to him* to be a justifiable act by Tenak, the Admiral's actions would be viewed for what it was: effective mutiny. And Mike himself had no jurisdiction in this instance. This had not been about *command structure*. He reached deeply for an answer, but his thoughts were being derailed by his anxiety about Tenak.

By a supreme effort he forced himself to concentrate and, in a flash, realised what he needed to do. Then he worked out an elaborate plan, in mere seconds, making his heart rate shoot up even higher. But, if he was to do anything, it was now – or never. His heart lurched.

He gulped a deep breath and, as calmly as his ragged nerves would allow, spoke to the security guards each side of him, as they continued to gaze at the scene before them. He tried to look as serene as possible, even if understandably shocked.

'This is bad, but there's nothing more to see here, guys. Much as I admire him, the Admiral just might have gone too far this time, and I don't have any jurisdiction here,' he said, trying not to prevent his words as shaky as his insides felt, 'I need to get back to the science lab,' he continued, 'and Lieutenant Jennison's expecting me. If that's okay with you?'

'A long as you don't try to intervene here, sir,' said the one on his left. They understood his long-time loyalty to the Admiral and were understandably wary, thought Mike. But they might also think that there was still a rift between Tenak and he. And they would know that a ship's Secretary didn't have access to the AI armaments subroutines. That, however, was not part of his plan. He gulped again to steady himself.

'No chance guys,' he said, nodding. 'This is something to be resolved by all the senior officers, not me. Like I said, I need to get back to the science deck.'

It worked. The guards looked at him disapprovingly but nodded, releasing their grip, and he walked out almost unnoticed by anyone else. After all, he thought, they were probably thinking he was 'just good old reliable, *ineffectual* Mike'. Since the attack on him during the journey through the conduit, general feelings toward him seemed to have become much more amenable. Perhaps more than it ever had been. But no-one would think he'd even be capable of doing what he was now planning. He didn't even know if he was capable of it. As he hurried along the ship's corridors, he couldn't stop fretting about Tenak, but he tried to press this to the back of his mind, at least for now. If his plan worked – and if the Admiral survived, he hoped and prayed he'd meet him again soon enough. If he was wrong about all this, he felt that neither he nor anyone else on this ship would be around much longer to worry about it.

***

'What have you done to this mascla, this veteran?' growled Ebazza, from the centre of the command deck, her face contorted in anger as she stared up at the image of the Fleet Admiral. She was squatting next to the Admiral.

'I ... I expect he'll be alright. He is alright, isn't he?' said Madraser, looking aghast. Then she coughed and seemed to steel herself, 'Captain, I won't have that attitude from you. Please see to it that the Admiral is taken to the sick bay, then give the order I made previously. Do that now.'

'You can go to hell, you bitch!' Ebazza roared. More shocks on the bridge. The Captain looked shocked at her own words, for a moment. She was cradling Tenak's head in her arms and a bridge officer could be heard calling for Med Bay to get a magneto-gurney up there, on the double.

'Captain? What did you say?' came from Madraser.

'Don't expect *me* to carry out *your* orders, *Fleet Admiral*,' said Ebazza, recovering herself. 'This man is a decorated officer, *Fleet Admiral*. He has proved himself and his loyalty to the Home System, to this ship and to this crew. He is a good commander and a good man. He is worth a hundred, no, a thousand of your sort. What ... what have *you* done, in your career, Fleet Admiral? Tell me that.'

'I can see where I stand with you. Very well. Enough of this. You are also relieved of duty, Captain Ssanyu Ebazza,' said Madraser, 'so I turn to you, Lieutenant Commander Statton. Yes, you heard me, you over there. As First Officer of The Monsoon, are you willing to carry out my orders – or are you also going to place yourself in line for a court martial?'

Statton glanced around at all his colleagues, all now staring intensely at him. He looked at Ebazza and the limp figure of Tenak. His face registered horror at what he had seen but then seemed to register resolve.

'Well, Commander?' said Madraser, 'I'm waiting for your answer – and I want you to think of your career, carefully, before you give it. That career has only really started. You are an officer renowned for your attention to Navy procedure and ethos. Do you really want it to end now – in disgrace?'

*****

Mike dashed to the spoke elevator and rode it away, down from the torus to the hub. He told it to travel at maximum permissible speed and at the bottom he tumbled out, disorientated by the onset of microgravity. But he forced himself hard to recover. His next destination was an access shaft, inside the main hub of the ship, a shaft which would bring him to the blast-back chamber and maintenance hall for the proton missiles. Those nuclear tipped rockets, propelled by conventional, but phenomenally powerful rocket engines, were launched through tubes that diverged from their internal silo, then exited at four different locations in the outer hull, arranged almost in opposite pairs.

Mike knew he would never be able to get access to the firing chamber itself, but it was possible he could get into the blast-back chamber, where the energy wash from the ignited engines of the missiles was deflected out of exhaust ports, again venting from the surface of the hull. He was on good terms with 'Demrie', one of the junior engineers who worked down there, a young and impressionable crewmember who ate far more rubbish food than was good for him but who had a winning way with his colleagues. Mike would have to take advantage of the engineer if this plan was to work. A pity, he thought, but, in the circumstances, it was a small price to pay. The other regular engineer on that deck, a man called Jerrison, was someone Mike had never got on with particularly well. Jerrison was also a stickler for doing things absolutely 'by the book'. Mike hoped only Demrie was on duty, right now.

On a giant, mostly automated ship, like The Monsoon, with a relatively small crew, it was possible to travel from one end of the habitation module, to the other, and see few crewmembers. In many places you might see no-one at all. It was the same today, for Mike encountered only one other crewmember on his journey to his goal. It was a good thing right now, but it served to increase the sense of isolation he felt. He felt he had lost so much that he'd held dear over the last year or so and finally, everything seemed to be leading to this one journey, this dénouement. He couldn't say exactly why he was going to do what he planned to do, but he just felt driven, almost as though he had no conscious part to play in the plan at all.

He reached the vertical access shaft to the blast-back deck, opened the hatch cover, entered and pulled it closed above him. Around ten metres deep the shaft was dimly lit and, he felt, eerie, but because the ship was in orbit the whole of the hub was in a state of microgravity, so he didn't need to physically climb down the shaft ladder. He just floated down. A few moments later he had reached the corridor which led, at a right angle, away from the shaft, going all the way to the blast-back chamber. He floated along it and, at the end pressed the entry buzzer on the large main hatch door.

*****

On the number One Bridge, Admiral Tenak had been towed rapidly away by the emergency Med Team and Statton suddenly appeared to have reached a decision, a look of determination crossing his features.

'Yes. Yes, I am prepared to carry out your orders, Ma'am,' he said, still somewhat uncertainly, as though surprised he'd said it.

'Don't, Statton,' said Ebazza and stepped nearer him. The guards tensed and one touched the handle of his stunner. Statton glanced at him disapprovingly. Then the Lieutenant looked at Ebazza, apologetically. She said nothing but glared at Madraser on the screen.

'Lieutenant Commander,' said Madraser, 'you have said you will carry out my orders. Therefore, I suggest you get on with it.'

Statton stood silently for a few more moments. It was almost as though he were trying to say that he would carry out her orders but he would do it in a considered way, in his own time.

'Sub-Lieutenant Brandon,' he said finally, 'ready the guidance comps and prepare to initiate launch protocols.'

Brandon did nothing for a moment but she glared at him questioningly, obliging Statton to carry out a prompt of his own, 'Sub-Lieutenant Brandon?' he said, 'I understand your consternation, but I am in command now. So, kindly carry out my orders – now.'

'Yes sir,' came the woman's reply, laced with evident resentment, but she skimmed her hand over her control panel, causing a large holo to appear near the centre of the bridge. Graphics and data flowed through it. 'Guidance controls readying, *sir*,' she spat.

*****

Mike had to keep buzzing the hatch door to the blast-back room until finally it was opened manually from within; there was no automated system for this one. His friend, Demrie, opened it, partially. Breathing a sigh of relief, but only inwardly, Mike smiled, as innocently as he could manage, and peered slyly into the cavernous chamber. The place was awash with the sound of machinery and there was no sign of the irksome Jerrison.

'Oh, haya, Mike. What're you doin' here?' said Demrie, a pudgy looking individual, greasy marks from some very recently consumed foodstuff still gracing his lips and right cheek. Between that and his ruddy cheeks he looked like a naughty schoolboy caught with his pants down. Even so, Mike was aware that Demrie was good at what he actually did.

'Hi, Dem,' said Mike, 'I just found they've got a tek problem of some sort upstairs - concerning the missile silo status. Looks like the fault's down here. The Admiral asked me to come down here in person. Wanted me to check something out.'

Demrie's eyes widened, '*He asked you?*'

Mike nodded, stared at him and faked a deliberately stern expression. 'You know how the old man relies on me, sometimes,' he said. He was bargaining on this character not being aware of what had just happened, 'upstairs'.

'Okay, Mike. Look, just wait a mo'. We're supposed to have digital authorisation on these things.'

'Do I look as if I'm about to cause you trouble? You know I've got the old man's confidence,' said Mike, now feigning slight irritation, 'and you know what he's like when he gets a buzzer in his helmet.'

He really was annoyed that Demrie was proving more difficult than anticipated but, inwardly, he warned himself not to overdo it.

'Oh, well, ... I suppose,' said his colleague, 'so I guess it's okay since it's you. Step in, Mike but please stay just here for a second. I'd better okay it first with Jerri.' Demrie stepped back further into the chamber, opened the door a little more, and, looking to his right he shouted to a figure just out of sight. Mike inched forward a little and as he did so he could see Jerrison, a middle-aged man, bull necked and powerfully built, advancing down the hall toward them. The whole floor area in the chamber was covered with positive grip layer; the material which made normal, or near normal, walking possible in the micro-gravity. Jerrison moved very naturally on that surface, almost striding toward them, though he was still around 30 metres away.

'What the hell's he doing here?' shouted Jerrison, only just audible above the electro-mechanical noise. Demrie shouted back that Mike was there to do something requested by Tenak, but Jerrison frowned and turned his head slightly, the way people do when they can't quite hear something said. Demrie stepped even further back into the chamber and shouted again, 'I said it's Mike and he's got permission from Tenak to ...'

'I don't care,' shouted Jerrison, his face suddenly aflame with irritation, 'cos he's not to be let in here, you gimbo. Can't you see the screens up there? We're on high alert. The missiles are ... Watch out! He's getting past you.'

Mike had had enough. It was now or never. He dodged lightly past Demrie and ran, or at least tried to run, as best he could, on the positive grip stuff, straight toward the main access aisle of the chamber, leading off to the right. He gave silent thanks that the route he needed was oriented in the direction opposite to the one being used by Jerrison, who was coming onward at astonishing speed.

Mike raced into the wide access corridor. The noise of machinery was louder here and there was a confusing array of large pumps and pipes. This really was the *electro-mechanical* heart of the ship – looking old fashioned to some perhaps, but a vital part of a vessel like The Monsoon. Heart pounding, Mike glanced back and saw that Jerrison had reached half-way across the hall behind him, running along the positive layer in a strange but efficient loping motion. He was, in turn, being followed by Demrie, lamely wheezing along as best he could and looking painfully embarrassed.

Mike knew he had to find, 'Emergency Access Panel Q 11'. He remembered seeing it on a formal tour he'd taken about two years previously, but he'd only discovered its real function when he'd taken the time, more recently, to study the ship's advanced technical manuals. He hadn't dreamed he would have ever need or want to use this access way – until now.

Lining the walls of the corridor was a whole series of access panels; Q 1 to Q14, which punctuated the walls at 6 or 8 metre intervals, but Mike knew that they were all sealed and could only be opened by authorised personnel. Only Q 11, Q 12 and Q13 allowed unimpeded access. As ship's secretary Mike already had authorised access to nearly every part of the ship but not the main firing chamber, *or this section*. Somehow, he had managed to cheat his way in here, more by luck than design. Most security personnel were engaged upstairs, and circumstances were unusual right now, to say the least. After this, if there was an *afterwards*, he knew no-one like him would ever be able to do this again.

As he sped along he kept a sharp lookout for the lettering on the panels. They were all placed at floor level and consisted of rectangular hatches only a metre and a half long, and about 60 centimetres high. He passed Q 8 and 9 and then, strangely, C 3 and 56. He didn't remember seeing anything about these. Where were Q11 and 12? He was sweating profusely as he hurried.

He could not hear Jerrison's footfalls behind him because the machine noise masked the slight tearing sound made when stepping onto the positive grip layer, so he was obliged to glance backwards. He got a shock. The engineer was now only about 10 metres behind him. In his mind Mike suddenly had an unwanted flashback, taking him back to the time, not long ago, when he'd been pursued by a madman with a huge knife.

Mike forced himself to focus on finding the right access panel. Finally, almost unexpectedly, he reached Q 11. There it was! He was panting, partly with the exertion but mostly with emotional stress. There was a wheel above the panel, to enable it to be opened. A wheel? The thought struck him as odd now, just as much as it had when he'd seen the plans. Even so, mechanical wheels were still used in many parts of the ship, mostly as back-up methods, but all panels could be locked by electro-mechanical actuators. Mike was relying on that.

Behind him, Jerrison had stopped loping and now he physically launched himself into the air, propelling himself, in the microgravity, like a bullet, straight toward Mike. As Mike began to turn the wheel, he felt its stiffness, and his heart jumped again. He could almost *feel* his pursuer closing on him. The panel started to inch open slowly. His heart continued to pound. He didn't want to have to fend off Jerrison. That was too risky, and he might have had to use his 'special' wristcom.

He was relieved when Jerrison, who had obviously set himself travelling through the air too fast, went sailing straight past Mike, missed a grab at his quarry, who shrank away from him, and then was forced to grab desperately at one of the padded grab-rails spaced out along the walls. But he failed to catch it properly, swung awkwardly and hit the wall with his right shoulder, ricocheting away from his quarry. As he bounced along the wall, several metres from Mike, he spat curses as he desperately grabbed at another rail. Demrie was following on, by foot but was still far away at this stage.

Mike's panel was now open, and he had the precious moments he needed to dive into the access tunnel. Another bit of good fortune, he realised, was that although another wheel was located on the inside of the hatch, Mike believed it could also be bypassed electronically from the inside. Frustratingly, in the darkness, it took him desperate moments of fumbling to locate the control surface, but he eventually found it set into the tunnel wall next to the door hinge plate. Slamming a sweat soaked hand onto the control surface causing it to light up brightly, his fingers danced over the icons. Within a mere second, he saw the access door close, much more quickly than it had opened, and Mike's view of the outside world was cut off, immersing the tunnel in darkness but for the control panel. He knew Jerrison and Demrie could use the wheel to open the hatch again, so he looked for the locking control. *There wasn't one*. His heart lurched. Understanding suddenly dawned on him like a hammer blow. Of course, he realised, why would there be one? This was an emergency access.

Cursing his oversight, he made another flash decision; his wristcom. Of course. He had not been keen to use it on Jerrison, but now he might be able to use it to seal himself in. From his knowledge of physics and his study of the plans he knew that the discharge would fry the circuitry and lock the hatch door. The interior of the hatchway was very cramped for someone of Mike's height, the only lighting coming from the control surface but this had now dulled to a low amber glow. Glancing behind him he could see a vestibule extending backwards for some metres, its far end an utterly black maw.

He became aware of a sort of squeaking sound coming from outside the hatch. They were turning the wheel. Mike backed some way down the vestibule, took off his wristcom and, aiming it well away from himself, prepared to give it the command to discharge. He had a moment of panic when he worried about the person turning the wheel outside, but all he could do was hope they didn't get electrocuted. Injury didn't seem likely, he thought and there should be a layer of insulation in the hatch door. There was no way he could warn those outside anyway.

Too late to let that distract him; he shouted at the device, ordering it to aim its discharge at the control surface. Holding it out in his left hand, with the tips of his fingers, the device fired a fraction of a second later, making the space around him light up like a flashbulb. A bright blue electric discharge forked from his wristcom, hitting the panel. The discharge seemed to spread back on itself in a microsecond and immediately burned a part of the skin on his left forearm, causing Mike to yelp loudly with the pain. He hadn't anticipated that, but it was not surprising, given the cramped space.

Mike clutched at his arm. It was stinging badly but he didn't think it was a bad injury. Then he saw that the control panel up ahead of him had been blackened. A noxious rubbery smell filled the air, drowning out the smell of his own singed body hair and skin. The stench of the burnt circuitry and cables caused him to gag and, reflexively, he backed away further down the tunnel, now in complete darkness.

But the job had been done.

He could hear the wheel outside squeaking again, but the hatch didn't open. Good. Sounded like they were okay, but turning the wheel would no longer be effective. Mike continued to cough with the fumes and withdrew even deeper into the space behind him. His heart was pounding so much he thought his chest would burst, so when he felt he was far enough from the worst of the fumes he just lay still, trying to relax. And he wondered what the hell he'd just done.

******

Gallius Statton stood at his console on the bridge, looking troubled, but resolute. Sub-lieutenant Brandon said, rather unenthusiastically,

'Guidance systems ready now, sir.'

Before he could take launch prep' any further a bright red light began to flash on the control panel below the 3D graphics hanging in the air before him. An emergency of some sort, with a com stream attached to it. A voice, heavy with anxiety, issued from the console. There was, for some reason, no video.

'Lieutenant Jerrison here, sir. I'm sorry Admiral, but I have to advise you to abort protonic launch. Abort!'

'This is Statton. I'm in command here. What're you talking about?'

'Commander Statton? Okay, well, sir, I'm sorry to report that the launch process has been compromised,' came the breathless reply.

'What?' said Statton, 'but the Admiral's been apprehended. And the Captain. I don't know how they …as he's … Explain quickly, Lieutenant.'

There were several moments of hesitation at the launch chamber end, then Jerrison replied, 'Sorry sir, I didn't know anyone would do this, but Mike Tanniss has got inside the blast-back antechamber. We think he's making for the exhaust chamber itself, but we can't get in after him. He's managed to seal himself into the outer vestibule.'

'Tanniss! How the hell? Never mind. We can get to that later. Can you get in any other way?'

'Yes sir. We're trying to open up an inspection panel but it's kind of small and it's going to take some time to enlarge. Sir, if Mike goes through to the inner exhaust hatch he can seal it completely from the inside. The comp can't open it for us immediately. It's time locked. We won't be able to get him out for about 12 hours. The point is, if you launch now, sir, the vibration from the exhaust nozzles will kill him. And if he gets right inside the exhaust vessel itself, he'll be burned to cinders by the rocket exhaust. And he, well, his remains, will get sucked out into space. Just … thought you ought to know that sir.'

'Yes, I managed to work that out all on my own, Jerrison. What the feg is he trying to do? Why wasn't he watched? I'll have someone's bananas for this.'

'And I'll have yours, if you don't comply with my orders quickly, *Mister*,' came an all too familiar female voice from the screen above the main consoles.

*****

Mike was extremely relieved that his wristcom was still functional, despite the electrical discharge, so he was now able to use it to provide some light, pushing away the inky blackness that threatened to engulf him inside the vestibule of the blast back chamber system. He still needed to get into the inner chamber, the actual exhaust tank, before they opened another access panel to try to get to him.

His mind momentarily drifted back to the 'Hall of the Native', back on New Cambria. This blast-back chamber complex was practically the scariest place he'd been since then, but the circumstances couldn't be more different. Up to this point, he'd only seen *this* chamber depicted on small scale computer illustrations. It wasn't the place but his reason for coming here that now distressed him and gave the word 'scary' a new meaning for him.

He reflected on the fact that he intended to do nothing less than stop his shipmates launching the nuclear torpedoes – if his plan worked. His guess, arrived at on the spur of the moment, back up on the command deck, was that, by doing this, they would be discouraged from launching. But the thought now occurred to him, like an electric bolt from his own wristcom, that he hadn't really worked all this out properly. He couldn't believe what he'd just done. It was as well that he hadn't had time to think it all through, for if he had he knew he would have decided against it.

The intensity of the emotional currents running through his brain now made him welcome the ragged stinging of the burn on his left forearm, if only as a distraction from his crazily meandering thoughts. He decided to move on quickly and to try not to think too much about the consequences. Continuing to squeeze through the vestibule he found, as expected, that it soon widened out into a larger chamber which allowed him to unfold to his full height, even though he was, of course unable to 'stand', anyway, in the micro-g environment. He could merely float.

Further progress was eventually blocked by a massive circular door, with a radius at least twice his own height. There was a strange sense of 'echoing' noise down here. He was suddenly aware of the largeness of the vessel he was now inside. Trying to ignore it he asked his wristcom to give him advice on how to proceed further, hoping there had been no damage to its memory banks since he had downloaded the details of this area. Back then, it had simply been a desire to learn more about how the ship worked. Even so, he had had to get Tenak to authorize him to have access to sensitive information, which he was obliged to lock into the unit, with instructions that it be fully deleted if any unauthorized person tried to use the device.

Unfortunately, it turned out there was no secret code to unlock the hatch. But it could be done by following the correct digital procedures. His wristcom spoke to him softly and he touched various panels on another console, next to the giant hatch, punching in a long, detailed, sequence. Eventually, the huge door rolled noisily back into a recess. It revealed the vast black void of another large chamber beyond, looking, in his wan beam, like some sort of gigantic metal cavern.

Peering into the emptiness before him, his anxiety rose. He could feel his agoraphobia returning, almost like the tides of the huge oceans which covered so much of that world far outside the ship. He found himself grateful that there was so much darkness, so he wasn't actually able to see the full enormity of the space, as he might otherwise have become so disorientated he would be unable to go further. Even so, trembling, he looked at his wristcom, and ordered it to show him where he needed to go next, but then asked it to restrict itself to a narrow-focus light beam from now on. Holding out the wristcom his heart continued to pound as the light beam revealed a wall ahead of him, about 12 metres away, its shiny metal skin reflecting the pale light.

The beam seemed almost like a bridge made out of light, stretching effortlessly across a gap, yawning like a crevasse in front of him, extending 'up' and 'down' and to all sides. There was another huge hatch set in the wall opposite. Mike didn't relish what he had to do next, and felt suddenly sick to the stomach, hesitating to move anywhere for several minutes, before he took a deep breath and launching himself into the void, pushing off very gently, very slowly and with huge trepidation. Holding his wristcom between his teeth, so its beam shone forward he aimed himself toward the opposite wall, his heart hammering like a panel beating machine. But crossing the void took only a few seconds before he was able to alight on the wall next to the hatch. He was surprised by how gently he 'landed' on the wall, but then he did have plenty of experience of micro-g. On alighting he was easily able to grasp one of the many handrails which protruded from the hatch perimeter. Within another minute he had operated the controls and, as the huge door rumbled open, he went through into the chamber beyond, the exhaust chamber proper.

Trying not to think about what he was doing, or why, and guided in the correct procedure by his wristcom, he made what he was sure was a final, fateful decision. It was to close the hatch door and command its control panel to operate the timer seal. He heard a strange whining noise as the control panel mechanisms went into action and once the noise stopped, he knew, with lurching heart and stomach that he was completely isolated and sealed in down here. It would be the last place he'd ever see – if the Captain ordered a launch. If not, it would be at least 12 hours before it could be opened from the outside. What the command decision would be was not something he wanted to dwell on, but he knew he wouldn't really be able to help it.

CHAPTER THIRTEEN

SURVIVAL PLANS

'Don't do it, sir,' breathed Sub-Lieutenant Brandon, a short but lithe member of the bridge crew aboard The Monsoon. She almost whispered, 'You'll kill Mike if you do this.'

'Yes, I'm aware of that, Brandon,' said Statton, as if forcing his words through gritted teeth.

The voice from the screen again, 'Commander, I'm starting to lose patience. Those missiles should have been launched by now.' Madraser's image still loomed on her AV link.

'Yes, I know, Ma'am. I know,' said Statton, the impatience and strain revealed in his voice, 'but, as you know, Fleet Admiral, there's a slight problem. I'm not too keen on *murdering* a fellow crewmember. I'm sorry about this but it …'

'*Mister* Statton. Are you, of all people, going to let a ship's secretary stand in the way of doing the right thing?' said Madraser, but then seemed to check herself before continuing in softer tones, 'Listen to me, Lieutenant Commander, I'm aware of your predicament, and your loyalties. And I know that Michaelsonn is your colleague, but you have to think carefully. You have to do the right thing – for everyone. By launching now you'll be saving three million lives on Oceanus and billions back home. You want them to live, don't you? I'm sorry to have to put it like this but you must ask yourself, what's the life of one man, even if he is a colleague, compared to all those others?'

Statton just stood there, as if paralysed.

'I know, Fleet Admiral,' he said after long moments, 'but at least give me the chance to talk to the mascla concerned.'

Madraser sighed and nodded, then Statton asked Brandon to open a channel to Mike's wristcom. 'Let's hope he's got his wristcom on him,' he said, almost under his breath.

**

Mike had floated into the exhaust vessel interior, then used his uniform waist belt to tether himself to a grab rail. The illumination given by his com device had dropped significantly. He realised, with heavy heart, that the hyper-battery must have been depleted by the discharge. The poorer illumination had nevertheless revealed much of the new chamber; another massive space, many metres across, and facing him now, exactly opposite his entry point, were the rearmost ends of four colossal missiles. These were the proton missiles powered by powerful but conventional rocket motors (fusion powered missiles would have had to be launched from the outside of the vessel and would be more vulnerable to attack). He could see that the base of each one was held in a massive cradle-like armature and its rocket engine opened out into a giant bell-like structure, with deeply shadowed interiors. Wisps of steam were now starting to issue from them. He was transfixed with awe and anxiety at the sight of them.

Set into the wall behind him, near the hatch through which he'd entered, were the openings of four enormous pipes, set in a diamond pattern, each pipe three times the diameter of a tall adult human. He also knew that not far inside each pipe there was a bend, each one forming an angle of about 45°, the pipe then radiating straight outwards for about 150 metres, through the bulk of the ship's hull in this section, far from the habitation part of the module. Each one emerged in an exit vent in the outer hull all, normally, sealed by blast doors – as they were at the moment. Before launch those would open fully, venting the rocket exhausts.

His wristcom bleeped suddenly and made him start. It was from the Bridge. Having set it to audio only, to conserve power he said answered it, tentatively, saying, 'Hello,' so quietly it was almost inaudible, even to himself.

'Hello, Mike?' said Statton's voice, quite faintly, as though he were speaking through a metal tube from a kilometre away.

Mike recognised Statton's voice. What had happened to Ebazza, he wondered?

'How's the Admiral?' said Mike, his anxiety about his friend and mentor rushing to the surface again. And don't josh me, Gallius,' he added, loudly and assertively now, 'I want the truth.' He was in no mood for messing.

'I think he's ... yes, I'm certain, he's okay, Mike. He's resting in the med bay. He'll be fine. Listen, Mike, I have been put in charge now. I think I know what you're trying to do but ...'

'No just wait, Lieutenant Commander,' said Mike, his voice rising in anger despite himself, 'I'm not going to come out. This idiocy has got to stop and ...' He felt his words petering out and his nerves starting to overcome him.

'You'll just get yourself killed if you stay in there, Mike. Do you understand what I'm saying?'

'I know,' said Mike, trying to stop his voice from trembling like the rest of him. 'But that's why I'm here,' he continued, 'cos I had to make you guys think again. Please don't do this, Commander. That mad woman, Madraser's, sick or something. You heard what the Admiral said about all this. Weren't you listening?'

A long pause, then Statton came back, 'Yes, I was listening, Mike. But he's not always right. I think he might be "out in the boondocks," on this one. It's a knife edge decision, Mike, but there's arguments both ways. Those aliens might be the biggest threat we've ever faced. You know that don't you? There doesn't seem to be an organic intelligence, does there? Maybe they're just machines, bent on destroying this star. And we now know the star itself is deteriorating. Don't we? You haven't seen the latest predictions, Mike. It's going to blow its surface off. And sooner than anyone thought.'

'You're beginning to sound like Madraser,' said Mike, anger starting to creep back into his voice, 'so you listen to me. The point is, we can't use nuclears against that planet thing. It's probably not even a planet like we understand one, Commander. Ask Jennison. We worked out it's almost certainly the alien "mothership". Their mothership, Statton! If you use the proton weapons on that thing, what sort of signal will that give them? Jennison and I picked up a signal but it's going to take time to decrypt it – but we can. Jennison and the AI can. Just some time. That's all we need.'

'We haven't got time, Mike. You know that.' Sharp tones this time.

'We have to make time, Commander,' said Mike, starting to lose his temper. 'If you use proton torps on that mothership you'll be starting a war that humanity just cannot win. *Cannot win*. Think of the billions who could be killed – or maybe … maybe enslaved or something. Isn't this just *the classic* scenario, Statton? You know, the one where aliens turn up on the Earth and humanity attacks them. Then, said aliens just wipe us all out. Except this time it isn't science fiction. This time it's for real.'

'And so is the danger you're in,' said Statton, 'so listen to me, Mike. The guidance AI has worked out how to open the seal remotely, but it needs your co-operation. We can get you out of there in about 20 minutes, if you help us. I'm willing to delay that long. Please help us, Mike. I don't want to have to … hurt you. You're a … colleague.'

'Well gee thanks, Statty,' said Mike with blinding sarcasm. 'You're starting to make me feel all warm and gooey. I'm your colleague, yes. But I know I'm not your friend. I know you hold the Secretariat in disdain. Think it's unnecessary. But you're wrong. All this … all of it makes it doubly necessary. *Doubly necessary*. If anything, it should be strengthened.'

'Okay, if you say so, Mike. Fine. And, if you co-operate with us we can talk about it.'

'I think you're just saying that. I'm sorry, Gallius. I don't think I can do that.'

'No, no, Mike. I do mean it. Please don't do this, Mike. No-one wants to see you get killed like this.'

Mike's eyes started to glisten, and tears started to stream from his eyes, evaporating quickly from his cheeks in the warm stillness and micro-g of the chamber. And it *was* getting warm in here, he thought. He nearly switched off the wristcom at that point but changed his mind and held it closer to his mouth. His words came out sounding like a frog's croak,

'I'm sorry Gallius, but I can't comply. Eleri …she is … She would understand what I'm doing. I've never been very religious Gallius, but … maybe, well, maybe I just might see her again. Soon. Who knows? Who knows?' He broke communications quickly, to avoid Statton and the others hearing his voice crack completely.

Back on the bridge, Statton heard the click signalling transmission cut-off and the sigh he issued turned into more of a guttural groan.

'Lieutenant Commander, Statton,' started Madraser, but Statton looked up with anger in his eyes.

'I can't be done with listening to you right now, *Ma'am*. I have to think about this, without *you* harassing me.' He signalled to a nearby comms rating to cut Madraser's transmission. She disappeared from the screen. There was a sudden cheer from the assembled crew. Statton looked surprised.

'Thank you for doing that, sir,' said Brandon. 'I'm sorry if you think I'm out of order but … Mike's right. Please don't give the order. The Admiral was right too. We don't stand a chance if we start some sort of war.'

Another officer piped up from behind him. Junior Engineer Plindon, a thin, round-faced crewman, who hailed from Mars, spoke now,

'The sub-lieutenant's right, sir. I know the arguments. We all know there's arguments – both ways. Right and wrong – both sides. But I guess we can't let our humanity desert us. Specially at a time like this. We don't know what sense of morality these … alien things have, if any. But we need to remember *who we are*. *What we are* – when we're at our best. What we can aspire to be, I guess.' Those last words seemed to disappear into a black hole as he looked at Statton, sheepishly.

'Wow, Plindon,' said Brandon, eyes wide with admiration.

'I know what you're saying, Mister,' said Statton, 'but I'm the one who has to balance everything, and I wish Madraser hadn't given me this job. But she did. And I have to live with it.'

Statton continued to stare into space. The tension on the bridge, already almost unbearable, grew palpably worse.

**

In the gathering darkness of the exhaust chamber Mike prepared for the worst. Statton was going to launch. He knew it. The XO was renowned for being a stickler for the echelons of command and had never really got to know Mike, precisely because he didn't believe in the need for the Secretariat. Mike knew it wasn't that he simply disliked Statton. He just had never made a connection with him because of his views about the job. Besides, even if he was disinclined to carry out the order, Madraser would force him – and it would be his own end. And probably the end for humanity.

He realised with shock, that this was not like him. Not at all. He was not used to being – negative. He remembered that the last time was when he thought Eleri hated him, and for a while she might have, in a way. Then, her love had returned, manyfold and then she had died – just like that. Like a light going out. The light of worlds. And now his whole outlook seemed to have changed. But he had to be realistic, here and now. He had placed himself in this dreadful position, so what else could he expect? And the consequences for the whole of humanity, if he died, were inconceivably greater than his own tiny, unimportant life. It seemed so strange to be thinking like that about himself, but it was true, nonetheless.

The place he was in had stopped giving him the creeps. There was no point in feeling like that anymore, but he wished he could be a bit more comfortable down here. His left arm still ached like it was aflame but that would probably end soon enough, too. Should have brought an inflatable chair, with its sticky bottom, he mused. He could have stuck it to the chamber wall. There were plenty of the chairs dotted around the ship. He almost chuckled. They were useful for evacuees, after all. How remiss of him to forget to bring one. He tried to let go of things then, chuckling out loud, almost uncontrollably, but it was a largely mirthless sound, swallowed up in the dark vastness of the chamber. His head began to ache, and his stomach churned.

He stared at the gloomy recesses of the massive engine bells and the wisps of steam still issuing from them. He wished it was all over. He didn't know how much longer he could deal with this. *Just get on with it, Statton*, he thought.

**

'Get her back on screen,' said Statton. A second later Madraser's glowering image flashed onto the giant screen on the bridge. Everyone on the deck simply glowered back at her.

'Well, Lieutenant Commander,' said Madraser, 'have you finally made a decision – after cutting me off, in that …'

'Yes, I have Ma'am, and I'm sorry but I have to cut you off again,' said Statton, 'because I've thought about this a lot. Your order is … just … wrong. Wrong in these circumstances. And I'm not prepared to kill a fellow crewmember. His position has nothing to do with this. As far as I'm concerned, he's a member of this crew. He's not the enemy. I'm just not prepared to carry out an order I don't believe in. Sometimes, not often, but sometimes, this has to be done. I'm sorry, Ma'am.' There was a thin smattering of applause on the command deck but it petered out rapidly as people gazed expectantly at Madraser's image.

Madraser sighed deeply and said, more with disappointment than anger, 'I see, Commander. So … you're finished too. Stand down, Statton. Now, who else do I turn to, on that bridge?'

Everyone looked around at each-other. Scanning the faces surrounding him, Statton said, with confidence, 'No-one here will carry out your orders, Ma'am.'

'No, I didn't think so,' she said, 'so all of you are *mutineers*, are you? You will have to pay for the consequences, presuming the Home System survives at all.' She turned to someone off-screen and after a few seconds turned back and said, her voice full of contempt, '*Mister* Statton, we are breaking orbit shortly and leaving. The Crossbow is too small to have carried more data pods, so I can't send word of the situation back home. There are four heavy cruisers behind me, which should have come through the conduit by the time I get to the outer system, but celestial mechanics means we won't be easily able to dock with them.

'So, I have decided to return to the Home System, to report in person, advise of the alien menace and get more vessels to return with. On the way out I'll debrief Admiral Robertson, commanding the lead cruiser. Please note that I intend giving her overall command here. I'll order the fleet to use their nuclear weapons on that alien thing and then to board The Monsoon. You'll be arrested, Statton, plus all the other officers currently aboard, and your ship will be escorted back to the Solar System. And, to head off any criticism from your resident Secretary – while he remains so, I will ensure compliance with the law and accept that my ships can't use their missiles until they're 40 million klicks past the orbit of Oceanus. It's a close call but be assured they *will* use their missiles. By the time the fleet gets to launch position I should be back here, to reinforce them and take any further necessary action. Do you understand me, *Mister*?'

'Yes, I do,' said Statton, an air of resignation in his voice.

The Fleet Admiral's image disappeared.

'She's running out on us,' breathed Brandon, with fiery anger in her face.

'No,' said Statton quietly, 'I don't believe that. She's misconceived about the answer to the aliens,' he continued, 'but just put yourself in her position for a second. She's been humiliated here. She can't board us and even if she could she knows we wouldn't let her. As she said, she'd have huge difficulties rendezvousing with the fleet, and she hasn't got room for any migrants, so she won't wait around. Might as well go home and advise the government, like she said.'

'With her tail between her legs,' said Plindon, almost under his breath.

'Okay, enough now,' said Statton, allowing himself a sly smile, 'because we've got work to do.'

'Yes sir,' said the assembled bridge officers.

**

In the bowels of the huge ship Mike still floated on his belt tether, trying not to think of his impending doom. In his increasingly sombre mood, his mind had begun to run over various parts of his still rather short life. He was thinking particularly of the first moment he'd met Eleri. How fresh faced and wonderful she was. Truly, a breath of fresh air. His heart ached like he'd just lost her again. But at least it would all be over soon and maybe he'd know whether he could meet her again, though he wasn't at all sure that he could. He would simply cease to exist, like she had done. His heart yearned for her lost life, all her lost opportunities. Things she'd never have a chance to do.

His trance like state was instantly disrupted when his wristcom bleeped once again, a tinny, pathetic sound, but it was enough to shake him alert.

'Mike? Are you okay, Mike?' came a tiny little voice. The device's battery was nearly gone.

'Statton? That you? What you want now? How many times do I have to explain …?'

'It's okay Mike. It's okay. We're not going to launch. I said we are not launching. But we are going to …'

'What? You're not …? Why? What's happened now?'

'I'll explain later. Madraser's gone. She's leaving the system. I've released Captain Ebazza from the brig and taken the guards from Tenak's med room. The Admiral's well enough to be giving orders already, Mike. And we're mighty pleased too. He wants us to return directly to Oceanus. We're going to pick up as many passengers as we can and stuff them into this can. The star is still deteriorating, Mike, so we haven't got much time. Now, we want you to help us to get you out. Have you got all that?'

Mike knew better than to think Statton was trying to dupe him but the whole thing seemed hardly credible. Despite the gulf between the two men, emotionally and philosophically, the guy was always as straight as a laser beam. This wasn't a trick.

'Yeah, I've got that,' said Mike. A feeling of relief suddenly overwhelmed him and, for a moment, he worried he might lose control of his bowels but he recovered, with gratitude. That would have turned out to be a huge embarrassment when his colleagues got him out.

****

Far from the ship and the concerns of its inhabitants three electric ground cars stopped outside a dome-roofed astronomical observatory, high on the lonely Gargamazha plateau in the southwestern part of the continent of Bhumi Devi, on Oceanus. A group of lithe men and women in immaculate dark uniforms stepped out of the vehicles and walked briskly to the main door of the building.

Deep inside the observatory a female astronomer, called Pabraskina, heard a distant door chime and a little blue bulb lit on her ancient computer console. Her high forehead wrinkled in puzzlement as she threw a white lab coat lazily over her broad shoulders and wandered over to the door. The lead uniform, a male, in the doorway spoke to her in deep, gruff tones.

'Be forgiving us Mes, but we must ask for admittance straight now. I am intel-securi chief Robsan. We have a warrant to enter and secure this facility, including prevention and ceasing of all such ongoing work here.' Robsan held out a gold-coloured badge and a warrant card.

When her jaw finally snapped to a closed position Pabraskina opened the door further and, with widening eyes, watched Robsan's guards march in.

A tall, white coated man, in his 50s, with a goatee beard and shock of black and grey hair approached them as they fanned out into the observatory's atrium. 'What is the meaning of such, now?' he said.

'Professier Trebiana?' said the Chief, 'I am warranted to cause all activity at this observtry to cease. Now. Please be ordering all your people to stand down from their computers and desist all further work. If you have a staff room or caffy area I suggest you all adjourn there for next few hours until tis decided what should be done.'

'What? Yet why are you …?'

'We have reason to believe that the existence of the new planet in our star system has been leaked to the Bhumi Devi press and that said info was so leaked from this facility. Tis contrary to Emergency Order 901, as issued so by the Government in Janitra, on the twelfth of this month.'

Trebiana's eyes narrowed and his face grew raw with anger as he turned to his small contingent of staff, all now gathered behind him. He glared at one person in particular, a rotund, fresh-faced woman of middle years.

Agalina looked hurt and fearful, but then her face took on a defiant look, as she said, 'I am sorry yet, Professier, but I did feel that the people should know what was happening. This is a time of the strangest of happenings, as you well know, and this apparition may cause great damage to this world. Our measurements showed that our sun is starting to behave ever more oddly and now, this new planet does appear. The popularia should know.'

'You prandler, Mes Agalina,' said Trebiana, 'as you do not know what you have done. We all are aware of the strangeness – and the dangers, yet you will have set in motion something which will end in panic and chaos. The government made that order for a reason.'

'But what of the amateur astronomica people across Oceanus?' said the woman, 'for I so believe many have large enough home-scopes to be able to spot the new planet themselves. Facto, I do know this, as do you. Many have been contacting this observtry, by phone, wanting info. I have not given anything away to them.'

'I know,' said Trebiana, a look of resignation and sadness on his face, 'but as long as we could withhold the correct info, they would not know what to make of this. The new planet shows just a tiny crescent and tis very close to Ra in the sky. Most amateur scopers would not have sufficient instruments to measure the mass and all the rest. Twas just a case of keeping a cover on the story till all this was over. Now, the glass-flies are out of the pot, well and true.'

Agalina looked sheepish.

'Thanking you, Professier,' said Robsan, 'for your words are true, but I must ask all of you to do as already requested. No criminal charges are being brought as of now, but you will be informed soon, if these are made. Your work here is at an end for time being.'

****

Admiral Tenak looked up with a smile when Captain Ebazza buzzed his door, then entered on his invitation. It was five standard weeks after the fiasco with Madraser and the huge ship was now parked in a high orbit above Oceanus.

'You asked for me?' she said. He nodded and drew her attention to a large screen on one of his desks. The sound level was muted but the images on-screen showed disturbing television transmissions from the planet below. There had been riots in most of the major cities, with many injuries and shockingly, even some deaths, but the securi-pol were finally gaining control. Tenak waved a hand at the screen and it switched to a scene in the centre of Janitra. A long column of people, carrying placards, marched along a heavily guarded main street. The camera zoomed in on one of the banners. It said, 'Navy must help us.' Another said, 'We demand rescue!'

'That's rich stuff coming from that lot,' huffed Ebazza. 'Last year they were calling for us to be expelled from the whole system. Some of them were attacking us.'

'I reckon that's human nature,' said Tenak.

'Okay, I suppose I don't blame them in this case,' she admitted with a sigh, 'and I genuinely wish we could get them away now. All of them.'

'So do I, Ssanyu. By the way, that newscast was from yesterday. The government has imposed martial law since that demonstration. All demos are banned. Have you been able to speak to Lew?'

She nodded sombrely.

'Yes Admiral,' she said. 'The OA government has sent crack units of securi-pol troops to guard the area around the landing boats. I was going to order Lew to put up auto-fences on a three hundred metre perimeter, just to be sure – but he's already done it.'

'Good man that he is,' said Tenak, smiling, 'but they'll need to extend that perimeter once we land the rest of the LBs.'

She nodded again and said, 'Was there something else you needed, Admiral?'

'Yes. I've been told to expect a personal transmission from the President, any moment now. Soon as they have alignment. I thought you should be here as well.'

'Thank you. By the way, are you sure you're okay now? And please give me an honest answer.' Ebazza's face betrayed sincere concern but just the hint of a smile as well.

'Yes, thanks, I'm fine. I've taken more than a few stunner blasts in my time. Well, maybe not from such a short range.' He actually smiled as he spoke.

'Yes, this one just broke six ribs, your sternum and did some nerve damage, eh?' she said. 'Bad enough in my view, but yes, I know, it could've been a lot worse. I'm just glad the idiot had it on ship's standard, not lethal setting. Otherwise, you wouldn't be sitting here now.'

'Something for which I'm even more grateful, believe me. Best forgotten now. I just wish I could do more for those people down there, Ssanyu. Here it comes.'

A bank of panels lit on Tenak's console and the screen flashed back to standard 'démóde' transmission method, meaning it was an 'out of date' method to which the ship's comp was having to adapt.

President Deramostra's elfin face appeared on screen, which flickered badly for a few seconds before settling. Deramostra's expression was an attempt at a warm smile but tempered by a degree of understandable anxiety. After the usual greetings had been exchanged, she began,

'Admiral, I need be telling you that the triage work is complete, and the chosen citizens are being transported to the site of the landing boats. I am ashamed to be saying that their vehicles had to be a-carrying armed guards. And their route was lined with anger-protesters. Many were hyper-aggressive, and bricks thrown. We do not know how they found out about the route, as twas kept so secret, or such we thought.'

'Yes, I'm very sorry you've had to impose martial law, Madama President. I guess that in any democracy there's no way to stop this sort of news getting out. Just like the news about the appearance of the rogue planet.'

'Deed, you are right, Admiral. Yet, our astronomica people now say they cannot see the new planet anymore. Has gone!'

'They are correct, Madama President. It disappeared. Just vanished – before we broke orbit around Ra. We have no idea where it went, or how it could vanish like that.'

'Our scientists are baffled, as are our AIs,' Ebazza piped up, 'but, with respect, I think that mystery will have to wait, Madama President. Our concern on this ship, right now, is to secure the evacuees and get them out of this system. And come back for more.'

'Absolute-so Capitain,' said Deramostra, 'but I have to say that we are unaware of so much of what has happened around Ra. Your ship has been out of touch for so long.'

'I know and I apologise, Madama President, but we had a few problems of our own to deal with,' said Tenak, glancing sideways at Ebazza.

'I must also tell you,' said the President, 'that we have instated an emergency shelter-building program, right across the inhabited zone. The program does involve many tens of thousands of the popularia – all helping to build many small shelters – in many different loci, for we have not the materials, or time, to build large ones. Builder citizenry are excused the curfew, so long as they keep working on the program. And so many are doing that yet, Admiral. Despite the actions of the aberrant few, in looting or rioting, most citizens are engaging in their community shelters, putting all differences aside. Tis wonderment, Admiral. But too little, too late, I am fearing.'

'It's never too late to try to do something constructive,' said Tenak, 'and if it helps more survive and gives people purpose, then it's a good thing.'

'What proportion of people do you think the shelters might protect?' asked Ebazza, catching a somewhat disapproving glance from Tenak.

Deramostra hesitated, then said, 'Yet too few, Capitain. Still, we may be able to improve it if time alloweth. I am worried so. Our own scientists have detected more instability in the star, so I am of great gladness of your return to help us – even if but for a few. Have your scientists discovered more deterioration?'

'Yes, I'm afraid so, Madama President,' said Ebazza, 'much more.'

'We'll take as many of your citizenry as we can, Madama Deramostra,' said Tenak quickly. 'We should be able to get as many as one thousand, two hundred, on board, this time, but we've got to move quickly. After we've taken the first tranche back to the Solar System, I'm confident the ship will return for more – but I'm afraid I will not be allowed to command it at that point.'

A shocked look from Deramostra at that, 'I am deedly sorry to hear that, Admiral. I cannot think why, yet I believe that that Fleet Admiral is behind it. Still, we hope always that your ship will return soon. Otherwise, Admiral, we are quite alone out here.'

'I know,' said Tenak, 'I assure you the ship will return. I would also mention that although the Fleet Admiral has left, she brought most of the Home System fleet with her, or rather, behind her. They're more than 6 weeks distant at the moment. I'm very sorry to report that they're going to try to attack the aliens again. I thought you should know this. They obviously cannot attack the alien planet, if that's what it was, but they might try to hit some of the machines orbiting Ra. I just don't know.'

'Tis exceeding foolry,' said Deramostra, with a flash of anger.

'I agree. They will not listen to me either, I'm afraid,' replied Tenak, 'but the fleet is led by Admiral Robertson. She's an old friend of ours but more importantly, she's a reasonable femna. We're fairly confident we can persuade her to spend less time *attacking* and more time *rescuing*. Unfortunately, no single ship has our capacity, but the whole fleet could probably pick up, maybe, 4000 people. And we will send down to you any equipment we think might help your people to prepare shelters. But we have to concentrate on the evacuation, limited though it is.'

'Thanking you again, Admiral,' said Deramostra and she continued, her face a mask of worry now, 'but yet tell me Admiral, Capitain, when do you think the star will blow? How much time do we really have?'

Tenak and Ebazza looked at each-other. Ebazza took a visual cue from Tenak. She spoke slowly, evidently reticent,

'Well, we, that is, our scientists, and those aboard the Antarctica, now think that the *surface of the star* will blow … in about 11 or 12 of your months. I'm sorry, but we can't be more precise than that.'

President Deramostra's expression looked like a balloon that had suddenly deflated.

'Tis really going to happen, ist not? And so soon. So very soon,' was all she could utter.

Tenak straightened and said, 'Yes, I'm very sorry to say so, Madama President. I know the Home System will work as hard as it can to get as many off the planet as is humanly possible within that time period, but I can't pretend it's going to be enough. I should also mention that those of your citizens who hide in the shelters will not be able to emerge onto the surface immediately after the event. But again, I will assure you that the Navy will send specialised teams down and get all survivors out as soon as possible after the event. However, I cannot pretend it's a pretty picture. I am truly sorry, Madama President.'

At that moment Deramostra looked down, her eyes closed, but she quickly raised her head again and with composure, said, 'Thanking you for your reassurance, Admiral. I should be advising you also that we – the government that is – and all the opposition parties *will all be staying* on Oceanus. We did not take part in the nation-wide ballot. Our immediate, "nuclearo", families will remain here too. If it be necessari, we will die here, on our home world.'

Tenak and Ebazza gave each-other shocked looks but gazed back at Deramostra full of admiration, before Tenak said, 'I did not expect, that is … I don't have the right words, Madama. It's so courageous. A terrible, painful, sacrifice … and one which will make all civilised people, everywhere, proud of your example. I'm sorry that there is nothing I can say which will make things any easier for you and your people.'

'I know,' said the President, 'and your words are kind-such. I know you and the Capitain have been loyal friends – to us all. We will never forget that. Meanwhile, I can but hope as many of my people as poss can get away from here, in the time this planet has left. That is most important thing now.'

PART TWO

FINAL REVELATION

CHAPTER FOURTEEN

DECLINE AND FALL

As Tenak and Ebazza conferred with the President, two of The Monsoon's remaining four LBs were already on their way down to the surface of Oceanus, ready to join Lieutenant Commander Lew Pingwei at the assembly camp outside Janitra. One of the vessels was a standard size boat, capable of taking up to 36 passengers. The other was one of the larger versions, normally used as troop carriers, able to hold up to 70 passengers and crew.

Mike had volunteered to assist with administration tasks on the surface. In view of his knowledge and experience of the planet, Tenak said he couldn't think of anyone better suited. Back on the ship Tenak had begun to thank Mike for what he'd done in the blast-back chamber but, unusually for him, had become tongue-tied. Mike had saved them both embarrassment by making a joke about how he'd nearly shat himself down there and that he probably wouldn't have done any of it if he'd had time to think about it properly. He'd also said he wanted to prepare to go down to the surface as soon as possible and excused himself from Tenak's presence.

He was flown down by none other than Sanders Dagghampton II, who'd finally been released from confinement to cabin. Mike had a joyous reunion with the pilot as he boarded the boat and he felt relieved that Tenak and Ebazza were satisfied that the agent had had nothing to do with the quislings. He was also a great pilot – and his skills were badly needed now.

On the way down Mike reflected on his first planet-fall here, and on the many things which had changed since then, for him, for Tenak, and the rest of the crew of The Monsoon. But things had changed even more for the people of Oceanus and now, for the Home System, and *for all of humanity*. He fretted too about the fate of

Eleri's family. On the ship he had accessed the roster of evacuees for the last couple of LB trips and her family weren't on them. They certainly hadn't been on the first run. What had happened to them? He couldn't even tell if they were *likely* to be chosen for rescue. Tenak had, with good reason, ordered that the OA government's procedure for the triage should be withheld from Navy personnel. Sombrely, Mike reasoned that he was almost certainly not the only one from the ship who had formed relationships on this planet.

Mike had tried using his wristcom to connect to the Nefer-Ambrell's ancient telephone device and as he had never actually phoned her, at her home, the ship's AI had been obliged to dig it out from the mass of data relating to the planet. Given the lack of info culled from this planet until now, it was not at all certain the hypercomp would find it. But it did, and he'd rung the number many times – and each time there had been no reply. Their voicemail system was full too. It was the same story when he tried to contact Professier Muggredge. He couldn't trace any number at all for his good friend, Hermington.

As the eastern side of Bhumi Devi came into view, on his seat screen, showing a patchwork of orange and blue-green way below a stratum of high, wispy cloud, he reflected gloomily on what would happen to Eleri's grave, and all the places the where the two of them had spent time. These were places like Fire Island, the Purple Forest, Simurgh and New Cambria. In the coming conflagrations, the land itself would remain intact of course but much of the plant cover would burn or wither. Uncontrollable fires would break out, on a vast scale. Debris would choke the sea margins. The fires would create so much smoke that, after the fires, there would be a planet-wide 'superwinter'. That would prevent renewed growth and destroy much of anything which survived the burning. On land, it was likely that some, possibly most, insectoid species would survive, together with some of the hardiest, smaller, animal species but not the larger animal species (the hog like borals, the large lizard things and the reptilian 'birdlings'). Even life in the oceans would be affected, mostly by a change in global temperatures but also by toxic runoff from the land.

Possibly *even worse*, however, would be the massive onslaught of damaging radiation, mostly from the curtains of proton plasma ejected by Ra. That would destroy much of the life from the outset but would probably lead to various sorts of gene mutations, as it had undoubtedly done in the past. Whole genera or classes of animal would probably decline and die out as a result. Of course, there might, he supposed, be new and as yet unimagined forms of life, new species, arising from all this. There would be survivors. Life would continue, as it evidently had many times on this world.

And the humans here? All he could think of was the dreadful reality that he, Tenak, and the HS scientists had been right about the need to evacuate all along, but there was no victory in that. Just sorrow. And now shock – that it was all happening so much faster than anyone had anticipated. It generated within him a dark exacerbation of his current sense of loss and grief. Worse still was that it now seemed clear that the aliens or alien machines, or whatever they were, had precipitated these latest deteriorations in Ra, hastening the demise of most of the planet's biosphere.

A similar catastrophe, for very different reasons, had happened on the Earth, of course, in the late 21st century, when the super-volcano had blown, poisoning water and generating a 'superwinter' that was years long, causing vegetation all across the world to die, crops everywhere to fail, and wars to break out over the scant resources available. But the fires that would rage all across the land on Oceanus and the radiation effects amounted to a much bigger, much worse, scenario, than what had happened even on Earth. The one fortunate thing was that the population of Oceanus did not figure in the billions, as had been the case on Earth. Even so, this disaster was big enough for Mike knew that it was going to prove impossible to evacuate more than a proportion of the population in time.

Mike ruminated about what 'history' might say about the actions of the Allied Home System Government in relation to this crisis, or about the crew of The Monsoon, and particularly those of Tenak, during the last few weeks. In comparison with the social disaster probably taking place below, right now, and the horror soon to unfold, any concern for himself or his colleagues seemed utterly trivial. The question nagging him still was, could he and the others have prevented all this, or at least delayed it? It threatened to turn him mad, so he tried to pluck his mind away from such concerns and concentrate on the job in hand, if he could.

And now he looked forward to seeing Lew Pingwei's friendly face again. A small thing perhaps, but the many small things are usually what matter most in a person's life, he surmised. On finally reaching the surface Lew greeted him and Dagghampton with relief, but the Commander's visage was grim indeed. That, in itself, spoke volumes about the situation down here.

The area swarmed with Oceanus citizens, hurrying about, most clutching hold-all bags, each of which had to be scanned thoroughly. Lew told his ship mates that, so far, there had been little of the panic they might have expected. He felt the people were remarkably collected; all things considered.

'Those hold-alls are the largest bags we're allowing as luggage,' said Lew, 'cos we just don't have more room. Some of these people ain't too happy about that but at least we haven't had anyone trying to take goats aboard this time.'

Mike allowed himself the briefest of smiles. Even now there was a moment for humour.

This area was far north of the city, a higher and drier location than the previous ones Mike had visited. He couldn't help thinking of it being like a tinder box going up in flames. He hoped he would be spared that sight.

'Maker,' Mike said, 'I reckon this planet seems even hotter now than when we first came here. Or maybe I'm not used to it anymore.'

The ship's Secretary had abandoned his customary white and black uniform for a dark blue and grey utility one. Despite its colour it was normally good at reflecting ambient heat because of a fine, almost invisible alloy film on the outside, yet it didn't seem to be making any difference down here right now. Mike sighed inwardly.

'It is hot,' said Lew, 'and it's not you. Our sensors suggest an overall increase of about 0.45 degrees, average, across planetary temperatures – over the *last three weeks*. Probably something to do with what's going on up there.' He pointed toward Ra.

'Listen up guys,' Lew said, signalling to his colleagues, 'I need to explain something – but not out here in the open.' He ushered Mike and Dagghampton toward one of the heavy-duty marquees, one of which was emblazoned with a sign which said, 'Navy Personnel Only'. Inside, it was several degrees cooler. Lew turned and faced his newly arrived colleagues.

'I need to tell you guys that we've set up to do medical screening only. We've got around four hundred people here. They've already won their right to get off the planet, far as I'm concerned. The thing is this, the Oceanus government asked us to do last minute security checks as well. They don't want serious felons getting off world before law abiding folks.'

'Strange. Didn't they carry out their own checks – when these people picked up their tickets?' asked Daghampton.

'Seems not,' said Lew. 'No time. Lack of resources. Whatever. The point is the government does have a number of separate databases but they're not linked up. They asked us to use our hypercomp facilities to do that for 'em. Their system is rubbish. We had to scramble it and start again – but don't tell 'em that. They'll find out eventually. Now we're able to screen each evacuee and check out their bona-fides. It's a "mirago's fart" but it's what they wanted us to do. The Admiral's given us the go-ahead but I guess it's slowed things down a bit.'

Lew asked Mike and Daghampton to go up to the main marquee, to help process the queue. On the way over, one of Lew's security guards called Mike over and asked him to look at something that concerned him.

The guard stood next to a low metal fence erected by Lew's people, beyond which stood a long line of Oceanus citizens, waiting to enter the main marquee. Mike's understanding was that the fence was simply to manage this group of evacuees before processing. Beyond them Mike could see the top of the high auto-fence which Lew's people had erected, marking out the perimeter of the Navy compound. A second, lower fence stood some metres inside that one, just as a precaution.

A few metres above the queue of migrants, the Navy had erected large, makeshift awnings to shade them from the heat of Ra. And they'd installed fans, set on tall poles, which sprayed them with a fine mist of water. Mike was in awe at how they had set up all this so quickly, but without it there would have been irritability and possibly illness. Mike remembered, though, that these people were inured to the local conditions. They were pretty tough, after all. His experiences on this world had proved that. Even so, it all helped.

'Sir, I've been asked to check over the tickets,' said the guard, 'and the ID papers of these people, to save time in the tent. I had a look at these two,' he continued, rifling uncertainly through a pack of paper cards in his hands. Mike guessed that, like he, the mascla was unused to handling info-data on such things as paper card. The guard continued, 'I don't like the look of these two.' He handed the bundle to Mike. The papers had been provided by a man and a woman who stood just a few metres away, on the other side of the fence. In the bright light from Ra Mike squinted at the papers, whilst the guard pointed out some suspicious looking marks on what purported to be birth certificates and proof of residence.

'They're just a bit smudgy, aren't they?' asked Mike.

'I don't know, sir. Maybe. I just thought …' began the guard, but Mike had left him to move closer to the fence and take a closer look at the couple. He'd noticed something familiar. Yes, they did look familiar – but he couldn't say why. Had he really seen them before, or was the heat starting to get to him?

'I'm sorry,' he said, to the two citizens, who were now shifting restlessly, evidently uneasy at the attention, and they were trying to avoid looking at him directly. Was that fear, he wondered?

'I'm sorry but could you two please move closer?' he said.

The two suspect evacuees started to back away then, and everyone else began to stare at them. Mike moved closer to the fence, preparing to climb over it.

'No, don't back away,' he said. 'Please wait. It's okay. I don't mean any harm.' The Navy guard had now moved up close behind. His hand touched the butt of his sonic weapon, then he removed it again.

The two uneasy characters found themselves pressed up against the rest of the crowd who stood, uncomprehending, behind them like a human wall. There seemed to be some minor scuffling. Then it dawned on Mike, like a bolt of lightning. He suddenly realised who they were.

'Didn't I meet you two at the ... yes, at the Meta-teleo temple?' he said loudly. 'Yeah,' he continued, 'say, you guys have got terrible disguises but it's you, ain't it? Yeah, you were the ones who gave the Admiral and me a real hard time. Pendocri and Ramo, or something like that? Wait!'

Before he could draw nearer the two had turned and slammed their way through those around them, pushing and shoving indiscriminately. They got through and disappeared behind the crowd. The guard drew his stun gun, but Mike put a hand on it, saying, 'You could hit someone innocent.' The guard nodded and pulled an old fashioned comm device out of his tunic jacket. A curious looking thing, Mike realised it must be an Oceanus device.

The guard grinned as he spoke into the device, 'This is the Navy. Inner compound. We have two suspects trying to escape toward the north gate. Please apprehend.' He turned to Mike. 'The Oceanus securi-pol are stationed around the perimeter in case they're needed. Just as well, cos the gate is open right now.' At the questioning look he got from Mike he explained that there was a new group of evacuees about to enter. Good job they're well behaved, thought Mike. He caught himself. Well, most of them, anyway.

**

Mike later heard that the two suspects had been caught and arrested. They were indeed none other than Arva Pendocris and Patchalk Remiro. They had been trying to get off world under false identities. Both were wanted for questioning on offences of corruption, conspiracy to cause public disorder and many other things.

They'll get what they deserve, thought Mike, with satisfaction. Their names would probably be taken off the roster for immediate evac'. They'd have to wait till later.

****

On board The Monsoon, Captain Providius, in holographic form, was updating Admiral Tenak.

'I've got some bad news for you, Admiral.' Her holo image flickered badly.

'Basically,' she continued, 'the alien micro devices have separated into even more bands. They really have formed *a cage* around Ra. Indications are that they're doing something else to the star. Something new. They seem to be drawing more energy off, somehow. The latest thing is that the Karabrandon waves have finally collapsed – and that's not the good news it might seem. The deep field magnetic field lines are doing something we've never seen before, and the "Chelley waves", from the deep core, have contorted violently. It adds up to something very nasty, Admiral. We think the star's going to go micro-nova. Most of the outer five to ten percent is likely to blow. That's several mega-quintillion tons of plasma.'

That really made Tenak sit up and take notice. He waited for her to continue but couldn't help giving voice to the obvious question, 'How long, Jennifer? How long have we got?'

Before she had time to reply he saw Providius become even more sombre. She pre-empted his question, saying, 'Stand by for this Admiral. The AI and most of our team are agreed we've got no more than *eighteen standard days* before the eruption. *I repeat, eighteen standard days!* Admiral, I'm sure you don't need me to tell you that when you leave for home, you'll need to factor in sufficient time to accelerate hard. Get out of the system far enough to be safe. We calculate that even with The Monsoon's electrodynamic protection envelope, you'll need to get at least eighty million klicks from Oceanus if your ship is to survive.'

'Lord above,' said Tenak, gasping, a look of sheer horror on his face.

'I can see we're getting the data cascade from you, now,' he said, recovering, 'but we'll need some time to pick up that sort of speed – to escape the wave-front. That means we've got about … *seven standard days*, at tops, to get the evacuees aboard. Looks as if Madraser might have been right after all. Those alien things really are destroying the star.'

'That may be true Admiral, but you're still doing the right thing. Please believe that. You couldn't have stopped this thing – this – force.'

'Probably. What about you? You'll need to get underway even sooner, won't you?'

He saw her face harden into iron like resolve, as she said, 'We're not going Admiral.'

When he heard this Tenak's face dropped, and his expression became even grimmer. He looked downward momentarily, evidently despondent.

'I know, and I'm sorry, Admiral,' she said, again pre-empting any comments from him, 'but the science team and my officers have all agreed we need to stay in close orbit and gather as much data as possible from close range. We'll keep transmitting it to you for as long as we can.'

'Captain. There's no need. Please. Leave some auto-probes. Just get out of there, Jennifer.'

There was a delay and then finally, he heard her response, spoken gently, her visage softer now, 'I'm sorry Admiral, but the data is needed. Auto-probes just won't cut the muster and you know it. And please don't try to stop us. We're not Navy, I'm afraid. The point is, Arkas, there's a desperate need to find out everything we possibly can about what these aliens are doing. I am correct, aren't I?'

'Yes, yes, you are correct,' said Tenak, eyes downcast again briefly.

'Thank you, Admiral, for everything – and I mean that.'

Tenak straightened up and said, 'Captain Providius, it's been an honour and a privilege to have served alongside you.'

'Thank you, my friend,' she said softly, 'but the honour's all mine, Arkas.'

'Maker take care of you, Jennifer,' he said, softly. He saw her eyes glisten when she heard his words.

'May fortune speed you and your passengers, home safely,' she said and saluted. He returned the salute sharply. The last thing he heard her say, as the AV cut off, was, 'Providius out.'

As her image disappeared a tear formed in the corner of each of Tenak's eyes. He closed them tightly then, and stooped, his fingers gripping the desk unit in front of him so hard his knuckles went white.

****

Lew approached Mike as he scanned the paperwork handed to him by an Oceanus citizen and her family.

'A quick word,' he said and motioned for Mike to step away from his desk. The Commander leaned forward so his mouth was right next to Mike's left ear.

'The Admiral's just contacted me again,' whispered Lew. Despite his closeness Mike almost struggled to hear him above the hubbub in the marquee.

Lew continued, 'And it looks like we've got a lot *less time* than we thought. He wants us all through here and leaving orbit *within six standard days*. You heard me right, that's six standard days. I'm sorry Mike but we've no choice. And listen, the government is not telling the nation how little time is left, but it's no more than 16 Oceanus days, at tops. They don't want all hell breaking out and we need to avoid the landing boats getting stormed by people trying to get away. Got it, my friend?'

Mike just nodded, his face blanching.

'So, the order from Tenak,' continued Lew, 'is to dispense with all but the most basic med checks. And I mean basic. We can't risk 'em passing something unknown on to the Home System, but everything else is to be dropped. The security checks are to be reduced to bare basics too. The Admiral also said we just ignore the checks the OA Government wanted. But, at the same time, we have to make it look like we're processing 'em, or one of those bright sparks will suspect something.' Lew patted Mike on the back and strode off.

Mike felt almost physically sick at the news. He could see Lew was affected too but you'd have to know him to realise it. He returned to his work and put on his best false smile for the benefit of the slightly built, local, femna, who sat in front of him with her husband and two small, freckly, children. They were the lucky ones. He tried to keep the thought of all those other people – dying from radiation burns as the huge plasma storms hit. Any civil disorder that had already happened would worsen as people tried, desperately, to get to safety from the plasma and the fires and – each other. He even felt sorry for Pendocris and Remiro. He paused for a moment and leaned on the desk, trying to steady himself.

He tried to work out the number of trips back and fore to The Monsoon that could still be achieved. At tops each boat trip would take several hours, including landing and embarkation, then pre-flight checks – always necessary, then the flight to orbit itself, catching up with the mother ship in orbit, debarking, then safety checks plus any necessary maintenance, and, of course, refuelling. Each boat needed to be full. Each had to count and they were currently 'crossing' with each-other; on going up and one coming down. This meant, however, that The Monsoon would pretty soon be full up, and the stark, terrible, truth known that there was no longer any time to return, or even for more evacuees to be picked up by the approaching Navy fleet. His face grew grimmer by the second and he felt shaky again.

The woman in front of him said, 'Mayst I help? You seem unwell, young manry.'

'No, I'm fine … thanking you,' he said, subconsciously using her own brogue and now touched by, of all things, *her genuine concern for him, of all people.*

'You can go straight through now, he said, 'please.'

'Real thing?' she said, 'but you have only now taken our papers to look at?'

'Please, just … go through. It's okay. Just go over to where you see the Navy guard, over there,' he said pointing the way with shaky hand. 'He'll take you to the departure tent and give you further instructions.'

The woman looked at him with huge, luminous eyes and smiled but gathered her family together and moved off. If only she knew, he thought, but was very glad she didn't.

Clearing his throat and trying to choke back the tears trying to form in his eyes Mike motioned the next family to come forward – quickly. They had to be quick. His mind and his insides were in turmoil once more.

And the nightmare was just going to get worse.

***

A large shuttle, full to capacity, was ready to lift off for The Monsoon and a replacement boat had already landed but, unfortunately, it was another 'standard size' one. It couldn't be helped. It was the only vessel available at that point. Mike and the team had just spent four hours continuously 'processing' evacuees and now, through the window he watched the larger boat, transporting a host of evacuees, piloted by his good friend, Dagghampton, take off in a swirl of hot, choking dust. He was suddenly and bitterly reminded of the alien holos he'd seen, albeit in 'safe' 2D mode, in his case; some of the scenes of chaos on the planet, suffered by the original natives, now made gut wrenchingly real again. History, on this planet, was repeating itself, with scary accuracy. And then a tremendously loud crashing sound intruded into his mind, causing momentary disorientation. Was it real, or his memory of the vids of the ancient natives? No, this was real; in the here and now. His heart leaped.

Mike saw Lew race outside, carrying his heavy-duty sonic pistol. Mike followed him in a flash. He'd decided it was a sensible thing to stay as close to Lew as he practically could, whenever potential danger presented itself. Behind him four or five Navy security guards followed on and soon overtook him. There was a problem at the nearby compound fence and as Lew raced toward it he called out over his shoulder for two of his guards to stay with the evacuees in the marquee. Many of the evacuees were alarmed too but some leaped up and began to follow the Navy team to the door. A couple of guards tried to usher them back to their seats, but several burst past them and raced out, adding to the commotion outside.

Blinking as he emerged into the blinding light, Mike saw a cloud of dust rising far beyond the low, inner, fence of the compound, out at the high, meshwork, auto-fence. A large group of Oceanus's own securi-pol officers were already past the inner fence, rushing toward a crowd beyond them, each of them holding some sort of long shield in front of their bodies and wielding long, whip-like, truncheons.

'Outer fence is breached!' shouted Lew. 'Stay here, Mike,' he cried out and, as he and the other Navy guards ran forward, Mike saw the securi-pol were already starting to gain control of an influx of local people. The crowd was large but perhaps not as large as at first appeared, and though various rocks and missiles had been thrown at the approaching guards, the securi-pol were evidently beginning to get the upper hand. The crowd clearly did not relish those whip truncheons. Lew and his group had already vaulted over the low inner fence and now walked warily toward the melee, probably choosing, wisely, he felt, to let the Oceanus police do their job. Mike knew that Lew would not have wanted to start using sonic pistols.

Several intruders had been apprehended and were being bundled into a large police wagon within the compound. The rest of the intruders stood on the brink of the compound where it looked as though the mob had uprooted a small but significant section of the Navy auto-fence. The fence was composed of a heavy wire mesh, made of an alloy not known on Oceanus, and practically uncuttable. But by sheer force of numbers the mob had managed to uproot the whole section and simply push it over, leaving it lying flat on the sandy ground. Then, appearing uncertain of what to do next they had halted a few metres behind the fallen fence, especially when they'd seen the securi-pol.

Ignoring Lew's warning, but still with some trepidation, Mike moved slowly up behind the Commander and his group. He wasn't feeling particularly brave. He just felt more secure close by his armed colleagues, and he'd learned to trust Lew's tactical judgements implicitly. It didn't stop his heart from thumping like a panel beater.

While the securi-pol were busy thrusting detainees into their wagon many of the other rioters halted near the broken-down fence but when some of the leading men and women in the group saw the pistols being held by the Navy people they actually began to back slowly away. The chief of the securi-pol turned and shot a warning glance at Lew's group, as if to say *we'll deal with this,* then proceeded, with his crew, toward the intruders, shouting at them to go home.

Gradually, the rioters began to disperse, sullen and angry. Mike wondered what they'd hoped to achieve. They weren't going to get off the planet by storming the evac' station. He caught himself. These people were scared, angry and desperate. Desperate people do desperate things. And they had scared the shit out of him for a moment, but he could see why they felt as they did – *and they didn't even know the whole truth – yet.* He noticed that most of the registered evacuees who had left the marquee had wandered back inside, but they looked shaken. Mike empathised with them too. Best thing was to get them off-world as soon as possible.

The chief of the securi-pol, a large, chunky man with a grey 'handlebar' moustache, had left his men and women and approached Lew. His normally dark blue uniform wore a skin of sand coloured dust.

Mike moved closer to Lew so he could hear what was being said but he was happy for Lew to handle this – and he didn't think the Commander would appreciate any interference at this point. Even if from a friend.

The securi-pol chief had paused, and placed a large, block like, hand-held device to his ear, and was speaking into it. A mobile phone, thought Mike? Or a radio thing? Another museum piece on Earth. The man put his device away and resumed his approach.

'Supposing I should be thanking you, Navy, for such intervening, but we had it covered. You must have seen as such?' he said, with a voice like gravel.

'Simply keeping watch,' said Lew, 'just in case. Don't take offence.'

'Well, you can yet do the work yoursels now-on,' said the chief, 'for I just heard from my bosso. You will not like this, Navy, and nor do we, that is for sure, but he said there have been out and out rioting in *all* the main cities. Seems now there is news, from somewheres, of Oceanus having mere weeks or few months before the sun bursts. Bad looting in Ramnissos, and attacks yet on popularia suspected of being members of the Meta-teleos. Many of them have been sorely injured, some even killed. The whole centre of Demnissos is burning.'

'I'm really sorry to hear that,' said Lew, his brow furrowing.

'You will be sorrier still,' said the chief, 'for the government has ordered that most of us are yet to be withdrawn from here – so to protect the government buildings in Janitra. There is more control over rioting in that there city, but trouble is gathering apace. We are needed there. I am sorry, but we have been told to remove fifty of us from here, leaving only ten. Seems you shall have to call to your ship for more of your crew in arms.'

Lew shook his head, 'No can do, man. We've got twenty Navy guards down here already. The remainder are needed on the big ship so there's no more to spare. That's why you guys were asked to help.'

'So, you will have to manage, sirra, because – listen now. *I am not intending e'en leaving ten here.* I am taking all my womana-manry with me. Tis not safe to leave so few here – if you cannot get more guards down from your ship, then I am yet sorry.' The man started to turn but Lew shouted,

'Listen, you can't do this, chief-man. What about these citizens? The ones here? Don't they deserve protection? Or is a building in Janitra more important?' There was more than a touch of venom in Lew's voice.

'No. Tis not that, manry. Most of the government people are still in that building. Tis also the seat of our independence. Tis a true symbol and must be protected.'

'That building won't be around much longer anyway,' returned Lew, evenly. 'The citizens here have been chosen by *your* representatives, to have the chance to leave this place. To get to safety. They should be helped to do that, man.' Mike noticed Lew stopped short of giving away the latest news about Ra. No need to spark even more panic.

The securi-pol chief just shrugged and said, 'Carnt be helped, Navy. The still peaceful populari in central Janitra do also need protection, be remembering. But, before we leave, we will first help you reset up your section of fence, downed by the yobbin-crowd. But then we do go, Navy.' His jaw had set firmly and Mike could tell Lew felt there was no point in further argument – and no time.

As the securi-pol started out toward the damaged section of fence, followed by some of Lew's guards, the pilot turned and said to Mike, 'Damnatious. I knew we should have pushed for that fence to be electrified.'

'I was wondering about that,' said Mike.

'*Their government* wouldn't let us,' said Lew.

'That was before the rioting, I guess?'

'Too late to worry about that. Fixing the thing is more important. Please go back to the evacs, Mike.' Lew started back toward the downed fence.

The mob outside had withdrawn far away as Mike strode back to the main reception marquee while Lew showed the local police how to operate the main stanchions, setting them upright once again, so that the auto-fence could dig itself back into the ground. But parts of the fence drive mechanisms had been damaged, and Lew told them, quietly, that it might not stand another large onslaught. Most of them seemed only mildly concerned and after helping Lew they piled into their wagon, a vehicle which was, by Oceanus standards, an unusually large, jalopy-like, electric truck. Although ancient in appearance it was heavily armoured, covered with grey steel grilles. Lew's guards opened the large security gate just long enough for the truck to speed through and off, then closed and electronically locked it.

After securing the gate area Lew returned to the main compound where he was joined by a security specialist named Jenner, a tall, large limbed woman. One or two other personnel also joined them. Mike had been looking out for more trouble and had seen it coming. They were never going to get the evacuees sorted, he thought. He joined Lew and the others.

He drew attention to a new menace. Gazing over at the far side of the compound, opposite the section previously breached, Mike shouted, 'Looks like we've got company, Lew.'

Another crowd had started to gather beyond the far fence on that side. They looked angry and Mike began to feel very unsettled again.

'Someone should talk to 'em, I guess,' said Lew, 'and see if they'll disperse – before things get out of hand.'

'You're not going outside the fence, are you?' said Mike, aghast.

'Even I'm not that stupid,' said Lew, frowning. 'I'll use a "digi-loud" and talk to them from this side. Who's coming with me? I want volunteers.' A nearby female crewmember stuck her hand up. A Lieutenant in rank, she was a short but stocky woman, with a firm yet kind face. A trainee engineer and tek specialist, she'd had some training in security, so had authority to carry a sonic rifle. Mike knew her as, Meridene and technically, she was Lew's second in command down here. Lew asked where the digi-loud was. Meridene said she knew and set off to fetch it. Lew started off for the fence at a cracking pace.

The digi-loud, or digi-L was a very small box capable of amplifying the voice much more efficiently than a loud hailer and much easier to handle. Meridene shortly caught up with him and handed him a little grey cube about 4 centimetres on a side.

Jenner too had followed Lew and was right behind him. Mike trotted along behind these three, feeling very reluctant about all this but prepared to back up his crewmates.

'Do you really think there's a point to this?' said Mike.

'We'll soon find out,' was all Lew would say, and half a minute later they stood before the far fence of the compound, facing an angry mob pressed against the other side. The gauge of the wire mesh was quite small but sufficiently large to enable the mob to be able to see what was going on inside the compound, and for Lew and Mike to be able to see *their* faces, as they squashed themselves up against it. As far as Mike could tell that they all looked very unhappy, which was not surprising, but many of them carried sticks, bats, and glass bottles. Some held large stones and bricks. They pushed against their side of the barrier and stared at the four Navy people and became noisy as they got closer. With broad Oceanus accents their mouths seethed with obscenities probably only known to locals. Mike was familiar with some of them. They were not particularly pleasant.

Lew held the box near his chest and as he spoke, the device, already attuned to his voice, amplified his words so that they boomed, reverberatingly, around the whole area.

'What do you want? Please tell us. We will help if we can, but I can't promise anything,' said Lew, with what Mike thought was a remarkable sense of tact and patience in his voice.

There was a sudden, almost deafening, cacophony of calls from the mob. Mike huffed. They obviously haven't got a 'leader', as such, he thought. But then he found he was wrong.

It went quiet when one man near the front raised an arm.

'We want justicio', he shouted. 'The government lied to us. The metas' lied to us. You, Navy lied and so, so. We know you can take us all away, up to that big ship o' yours. Send yet more o' those carriage ships down to us. We got as much of rights as those in there with you. Let us in, or yet we break in.'

'You're wrong, man,' replied Lew, 'we can't take all of you. Not yet. All of our boats are occupied … in orbit, trying to rendezvous with the mother ship. And we haven't got the room on the one down here. A way of deciding who should come with us was taken by your democratically elected government. It might not be perfect but there must be some sort of system. Otherwise, chaos will result.'

'Lies. More of lies,' shouted a woman near the first speaker. 'We did not yet agree to that "system" you speak of. Let us in now, Navy.'

Uproar again from the crowd.

'Listen … please,' said Lew. 'You need to speak to your own elected representatives, if you want to get that system changed. But, for now, please let us get on with the job of helping … at least helping the people who are here. Your behaviour is frightening them. Let them leave in peace. The sooner you do, the sooner we can come back for more people … more populari.'

More cacophony from the crowd, then a missile came flying over the fence, lobbed by someone deep in the mob. Mike and Lew saw it coming and dodged but it landed close to the feet of Meridene. It was only a paper bag, but it appeared to be full of something which had the appearance of faeces, and it stank. Human faeces, by the looks of it. The thing splattered as it hit the hard ground and some of it splashed onto the Lieutenant's uniform trousers.

'Real charmers, ain't they?' she said, as the four of them began to back up, and the crowd laughed and jeered.

'Watch it,' shouted Lew, as a couple of large stones flew over the top of the fence toward them, but, fortunately, they were wide of the mark. They kicked up dust where they thumped on the ground and bounced. Mike reckoned that since the fence was nearly five metres high they were good lobs. Just not good enough, fortunately.

'Okay, we need to withdraw,' said Lew and the three of them hurried back toward the inner part of the compound, to the sound of raucous jeering from the crowd.

'So, what now?' said Mike, almost breathless from the stress, his heart continuing to hammer in his breast.

"There's one other option that might help ease things,' said Lew, touching his wristcom, 'and meantime, we carry on with the mission.'

****

On board The Monsoon, Arkas Tenak paced along an increasingly crowded network of corridors, full of evacuees, toward the ship's bridge number two. He felt his wristcom buzz. It was Gallius Statton, on audio only. Tenak's earbud, for private comms, activated itself. It was Statton.

'Admiral, I've just had a call from Commander Pingwei,' said Statton, 'says he didn't want to disturb you. They're having some minor trouble down there. He wants us to send him a "Trojan Module" from the Mark 3 series. No more details but I wanted to get your approval first.'

'A Trojan 3?' said Tenak, 'well, that's interesting.'

'Seems fine, sir but, strictly speaking, it's against the Oceanus government's rules, isn't it?'

'Yeah, but if he wants one, he must have good reasons. Send it.'

'Yes sir. Glad to.'

****

Inside the marquee Lew pulled Mike aside and told him that he'd decided to dispense with any further checks at all

on the evacs. He knew the senior officers would understand.

'The main thing,' he said, 'is to get these people off world soon asap. Besides, my friend, we're not going to send anyone in this compound home at this point. Not with that baying mob outside'

'Guess you're right,' said Mike, 'but it means the boat taking off sooner. It won't coincide with the one coming down.'

'I know, but, well, I doubt we can't speed the process up in orbit any faster than it's going. We'll just have to wait. Anyways, I'll comm the big ship and explain the whole thing to them. Ask them if they can accept a boat early. Otherwise, it'll have to stand off.'

And so it was that after Lew got through to the ship again, Ebazza approved his plan, telling him they had hangar space for the boat earlier than expected. The boat on the ground was filled and took off. A little under two hours later Lew and Mike spotted the automated Trojan vehicle as a glowing red hot dot, high in the deeply azure eastern, sky. A full minute passed as they watched it approach; the vehicle's altitude and speed dropping quickly. They could see it clearly now.

To someone unfamiliar with Navy 'ballistic equipment,' it looked like a large, stubby barrel with a bullet shaped nose cone on top. It sank toward the ground, blunt end downward; four classic looking retro thrusters throwing out long orange jets of flame below it. As it quickly lost altitude and slowed further, an observer would have seen that it was, in reality, a hefty piece of equipment, about 8 metres wide and 9 long. A set of air breathing ramjets were attached to its blunt underside, interleaved with fins which formed a set of six, radiating symmetrically from the vehicle's base. The rockets cut out at about 300 metres and the ramjets took over, powering the vehicle to its final descent, down to a gentle landing. They blew up a miniature storm of dust from the dry soil of the compound.

Some of the remaining evacuees, whose numbers were still significant, emerged, once again, from the tent and gazed up at the module for the last part of its descent, slack jawed. They continued to stare after it had landed, bewilderment registering on their faces. Some approached Navy guards who tried to reassure them. It was meant to help provide safety for them, they were told, but they were not, unfortunately, able to take more evacuees off world. Some wandered back toward the tent, shaking their heads while others remained transfixed by the new machines. They would shortly be even more surprised.

Mike, Lew, and the others, were forced to shield their eyes from the billowing dust as the vehicle settled onto the ground, not far from where they stood. The thing just seemed to sit there for long moments; a bulbous, yet sleek bullet shape, all shiny black and grey metal. It looked ominous and Mike knew that, potentially, it was. This was one of the fully robotic modules, normally used only in large military operations. The Monsoon had 24 similar units, which came in three types. The Mark Two series carried within them units which had heavy duty machine guns, hyper-grenade launchers and battle-ready lasers. The Mark Ones had units with multiple rocket launchers and enough conventional, automated, ordnance, to make the toughest military aggressor quail. Mike didn't know much about the Mark Threes.

He wasn't sure, but this one didn't appear to be a Mark One or Two, though he knew Lew had called it down for a particular reason. And, he knew that these things were the 'thinnest end of the wedge'. The ship had hundreds of automated weapon carrying platforms at its disposal, bristling over its outer hull, for use on planet surfaces. Some swam, some flew and others trundled on wheels or tracks. All had conventional weaponry, but in theory, their combined fire power could destroy the entire human population of Oceanus within days, without any help whatsoever, from Ra. The mob outside were not New Rebel or Ultima operatives, so he was sure Lew would use the Trojan judiciously. He couldn't imagine it being otherwise, could he?

In any case, Mike very much welcomed the vessel's arrival. Not being combat trained or experienced in that work he had been feeling vulnerable up to this point. It was not a good situation to be in, down here, and he'd begun to regret volunteering for this and Tenak's ready agreement. Back then no-one knew the situation weas going to get so acute, *so fraught, so quickly*. He'd thought the debacle back on The Monsoon had been the end of the trouble to be had with people – as opposed to the aliens, anyway. How wrong could he have been? He hadn't exactly relished the thought of being completely incinerated, back on the ship. But at least it would have been ultra-quick. And, he had done all that on the spur of the moment; no time to think about it properly first. Besides, there would have been a point to his death, in that case.

This was different. The mob outside looked capable of almost anything and 'the end' might not be very pleasant, if that lot got in. Also, he didn't feel there was the same sense of purpose, somehow. Help the evacuees, sure. But you couldn't reason with unruly mobs. Besides, that had been tried, by the Oceanus guards first, and now by Lew. Lynching or being beaten to death by the mob was a terrifying prospect, and seemed extraordinarily pointless, especially when he was not responsible for the plight of these people. He found himself wishing he'd gone for the electroprobe therapy he'd been offered after the attack by Brundleton, on the ship, to try to settle his state of mind. But the emotional effect of that vicious incident kept imposing itself on his mind right now. It had made him generally more nervous.

And then he'd begun to feel guilty over his feelings of wishing he was anywhere but here. After all, Lew, Meridene, and the others were here too, weren't they? So why didn't that ease how he felt? Emotionally, he was torn and wanted to scream with the frustration.

However, the Trojan Three might change things around. He hoped it would bring the reassurance they all needed.

The engines of the thing were winding down now.

'That descent was noisy,' he said to Lew.

'Yeah, and the Oceanus authorities wouldn't approve of it – on a number of different levels. But who gives a shit about that now?' said Lew.

They could both see that the mob of locals behind a part of the fence over two hundred metres away, had also been watching the arrival of the module and virtually all of them had gone quiet. Remarkable, thought Mike. While he gazed, still on edge, at the sight of the crowd, which seemed to have grown since Lew's encounter with them, now spreading out further along the length of the fence, he heard the Trojan module start to disgorge its contents.

Turning to watch, the module, still steaming from its hot descent, opened from its apex, like the leaves of a flower, lowering to form four ramps, equally spaced around the vessel. For a moment Mike was reminded bizarrely of the man-eating plants in the Purple Forest. Maker, that seemed such a long time ago now.

Then, a number of bulbous, dark grey, spherical metal units emerged from the main module, almost by a sort of tumbling motion. Each three-metre-wide unit now unfolded, much like a flower bud again, and disgorged a set of tracks as it hit the ground, and each instantly raced out toward various points along the perimeter of the compound. Lew said he had already pre-programmed the Trojan remotely, from the Navy marquee. The disgorged units now moved out to their prearranged positions – and opened to their full sizes.

Although Mike had an idea what they were he had never seen one in action. The units were mobile weapon-bots and now each of them extended its heavy, metal body upwards, by means of a flexible ram, until it stood more than six metres high, secured on one pillar-like leg a metre wide. From each body, standing erect, a pair of two-metre-long sonic guns, known as 'turbo-sonics', quickly emerged and were held in readiness.

Small but heavy, tank like, tracks, inside the widened base of each unit's 'leg' or foot, allowed each to quickly station itself strategically along the boundary fence, about three metres away from it. The fence perimeter was long, so each bot was stationed many metres away from its neighbour. Even so, each bot pointed its weapons, in a decidedly menacingly manner, at the base of the section of fence nearest it. The message was clear: *nobody from outside sets foot inside this compound.*

An unfortunate development, especially for this planet, thought Mike, but sadly, a necessary one. He was sure Lew had arranged all this simply for its deterrent value. He didn't want to hurt these people; just scare them. Even if the bots were used, he guessed that the cannon would be set on mild stun only. In any event, the protection was fully justified. Most of the evacuees inside the compound were families, many with small children. Mike also felt his spirits buoyed. The hammering of his heart began, finally, to subside.

'Wouldn't it have been easier to just electrify the fence?' he said, walking over to Lew.

'That wouldn't help us now. Look over there,' said Lew, pointing to the opposite part of the compound, far behind the tents, where another large group of riotous civilians were rapidly preparing what looked like a massive battering ram, made from the remains of a huge larp tree. Others were huddled around what appeared to be a mass of glass bottles, which they were filling with some sort of glutinous liquid. Such fools, thought Mike. Where was all this going to end?

****

The Monsoon had lowered its orbit, to speed up transfers, but, as Lew had anticipated, the debarking and maintenance work could not be speeded up. Accidents in orbit, even in the 25th Century, were still too common and happened too easily to allow that. Space doesn't give anyone a second chance. As a result, it took around four hours, working at the fastest rate, to turn the boats around. And that was when The Monsoon was in the best possible orbital position for rendezvous. When the giant ship was on the other side of the planet it took nearly an hour longer.

And the crew were now beginning to experience spurious, and serious, electrical problems on board The Monsoon, as well as on the shuttle craft. Engineers thought they were due to the increasingly severe proton and electron flux coming off the Ra, despite the apparent redirection made by the alien bands. Some crew thought that maybe the flux was something to do with the alien things, themselves.

Everyone, including Tenak and Ebazza had been working around the clock to get evacuees aboard, settled in (as far as possible) and turn around the ships, but after the request for the Trojan unit Tenak became acutely aware of problems on the surface. Lew had not been very specific in his report asking for the Trojan, and Tenak had suggested to Ebazza that it had just been because he had his hands full.

Later, when Lew had contacted Ebazza, to ask permission to send the boat up from the surface early, he also gave her some additional, disturbing, news. Three more coachloads of evacuees had been expected at the compound. They were hours overdue and no word had been received about them, it being very difficult for the Navy people to establish contact with the OA government. Apart from security for those already in the compound another reason Lew had asked for the autobot cannoneers was that they might be needed to clear a way to get the new evacs into the compound. But no-one knew where they were.

They never showed up.

****

Statton contacted Tenak, with just a hint of relief in his voice.

'We have an incoming hyper-message from the "HSN Proclamation", sir, the lead cruiser from the Home System. Admiral Robertson thanks you for the warning about Ra. Her own ship has detected a problem too, but they also got new info from Cap'n Providius. They understand they'll get here too late to pick up evacuees. So, the fleet are altering course to take them into an ultra-wide parabolic orbit around Ra. They're going out beyond the zone of probable maximum plasma irradiation. She'll come back after the "event", pick up survivors from the planet and start immediate rehabilitation of parts of the cities. Assuming it's even possible at that early stage.'

'Good. That's sensible – and honourable. No point in risking themselves. They'll have to pick up the pieces later.'

'There's more, sir. Admiral Robertson said nothing about Fleet Admiral Madraser, but she did say she wishes you every good luck and says, "Admiral Tenak's heroism must be put on record for ever".'

'Not sure I deserve that accolade, Commander. None of us knows how history will judge us, but if she's right, the plaudits belong to the crew, not me.'

*****

The crowd of rioters had begun to spread out around the wide compound perimeter until they saw how the Navy's weapon-bots automatically followed their movements, their viewing ranges evidently overlapping with each-other so that they did not seem to miss anything significant. And, as they were able to move bodily along with speed, they were able to cluster near any one possible trouble spot or string out along the fence as necessary. The length of the perimeter fence was such that even the crowd was not able to cluster everywhere along it, so they gathered at various points, then moved on, in a group, to others. The bots always kept up with them. They may have realized that the bots were largely able to anticipate their moves. Perhaps the mobs didn't fully realise it, but the bots' cannons had a huge range, meaning that the whole of the perimeter was effectively 'neutralized' by the coverage of their stun weapons. The again, thought Mike, these people weren't stupid and, for the most part, the crowds kept their distance – but they didn't disappear.

Mike and Lew kept watch occasionally from a tent near the outer compound, Mike allowing himself the slightest of smiles at the antics of the crowd at one point which was virtually opposite him, at the fence, but his smile froze when he spotted one person in the crowd separate from the others and run straight at the fence. The man hefted a large bottle, full of liquid which had a piece of burning material trailing out of its neck. Lew approached and gave Mike a reassuring glance as the missile flew over the fence toward the nearest tent. It was, thought Mike, an extremely long shot at the best, though it was clearly a powerful throw.

The bot nearest to it moved extremely fast, evidently having anticipated the rioter's move, and it placed itself directly in the missile's path. It crashed against the thing's 'leg', shattering into thousands of shards and splattering its liquid all over the lower part of the machine. The fluid flared into bright orange flames which, themselves, seemed to trickle and drip down the bot's stanchion support base and tracks, all the way to the dusty ground.

The stuff burned for a about a minute, then sputtered out, leaving absolutely no mark or trace on the bot's metal outer skin, whence the machine promptly advanced a metre and crushed the remains of the bottle under its tracks. It then swivelled and rotated one of its stun cannons, so it pointed directly down at the missile thrower. With a look of sheer horror, the man immediately backed away, turned and raced off.

Having watched these events, most of the remaining rioters started to back slowly away. Shouting defiance and making a variety of obscene signs at those within the compound, they finally began to disperse. Mike saw that one man remained near the fence for a long while. Mike recognised that this was the one who had spoken directly to them before. He raised his arms high and even though he was some distance away they heard him when he shouted, at the top of his voice,

'We shall be a' returnin, Navy!'

Then he loped off into the scrubby woods beyond the fence, melting away, like his friends.

Lew's wristcom buzzed three times and he said to Mike, 'It looks like the next boat is on re-entry right about now. And it looks like Ebazza agreed to my request for a few more guards down here. Just in case. Now, we need to get the next bunch of evacs ready to embark, take off within the couple of hours or so. And our mates, inside, are, no doubt, still babysitting a couple of hundred civilians.'

'Right,' said Mike and set off with Lew toward the inner group of tents, which formed a ring around the LB landing apron. So, what the hell's going to be the next thing, he wondered? He felt sick as a dog about all this but what choice did anyone have in this matter? At least he and his mates would eventually be able to get off this doomed world. What fate faced the millions who had to remain did not bear thinking about.

****

The star that humans called Ra, had grown visibly larger, appearing as a bloated, puffed-up ball, while the rings of alien artefacts rushed spaceward away from it, speeding out at thousands of kilometres per second. Despite Ra being known as a yellow-orange star, most observers would now have said the light from its brilliant photosphere, the part of it which was its visible 'surface', was more like a very bright white. Its photosphere continued to brighten and took on a decidedly bluish tone; something which would normally happen over a period of many tens, or hundreds, of millions of years, but now a change which could be measured directly by humans, in mere hours.

****

The late afternoon heat of Oceanus weighed down those in the main marquee of the Navy compound, far outside Janitra. As he sweated from every pore of his skin

Mike reflected on the fact that, apart from the grotachalik attack, the last hours may have been the worst he'd ever actually spent on this planet. The loss of Eleri far outweighed the grotachalik attack, he felt, but he'd not even been on Oceanus when she had died. Right now, he had an inescapable feeling that things were just going to get worse on this planet. Again, that was not like his usual self, he realised with some shock.

The next landing boat, again a standard one, had already landed but Lew told Mike that Ebazza had warned him they would not be able to physically deal with any more evacuees for a while, for reasons of safety. So, there was little point in loading the boat yet. It seemed things were pretty hectic on the main ship and, worse still, Lew was having unexpected comm problems when trying to contact The Monsoon, making co-ordination difficult. Lew's teks were working hard to resolve it – but time wasn't taking any notice.

The restlessness of the evacuees themselves, clustered into large groups inside the marquee, had not yet manifested itself in open aggression; something which Mike had feared. They had simply been sitting, looking morose and uncommunicative, but he now saw that things had changed. Lots of heated, sometimes angry, discussion had produced a small band of chosen 'leaders' for the evacs, representatives who called themselves or 'spokeners'. Several approached Lew and the security guards, asking to discuss various issues. He suggested that for now they might prefer to confer together away from the rest of the groups, and he led them over to the furthest corner of the marquee, partly separated from the rest of the tent, and presently unoccupied.

Mike knew that, technically, he could contribute to this process but he felt that Lew wanted to keep the situation for the evacs as clear as possible, so that they all felt they had one particular person to go to, at least for now. Mike was more than happy about this but he watched from the back wall of the marquee corner section as the spokeners for two of the largest groups of evacs, put their points to his colleague. There was much whinging going on, about general conditions, which was to be expected, but the main thrust of their complaints was that they were fed up of waiting – again, as expected. Lew explained the situation as best he could.

One middle aged woman said that her group, the largest one, had decided they'd had enough and that they wanted, or rather, demanded, to be able to leave the encampment. They were all young, able-bodied adults, she said. They would make their way back to Janitra, where they'd heard large shelters were being dug.

The leader of the other group said his people also wanted to leave but, as the group consisted of adults and teenage children, they wanted to walk to 'Florentia', a small town, about 8 kilometres up the road, in the opposite direction to Janitra. They didn't trust conditions in the capitol city, but many had friends or family in Florentia.

Lew tried to dissuade the groups from leaving, pointing out the possible dangers outside the compound, which many evacuees had already witnessed themselves. He could not do anything for their safety if they left. His warnings seemed to go mostly unheeded.

So now Lew, looking deeply unhappy, let them out through the heavy-duty security gate in the outer compound but only after he'd used long range, infra-red, digital, view scanners to check that the mob had left the immediate area. The Oceanus afternoon was wearing on and an unusually bright Ra was starting to slip toward the horizon, wreathing itself in glistening layers of brilliant oranges and golds; a lovely sunset, to be savoured, if circumstances had been different.

That was when a disturbing sight was beheld by all. Far in the distance, to the south, a huge, sooty black, column of smoke was climbing high into the sky, silhouetted against the still bright horizon. Janitra was in that direction. Something very bad was going on there, thought Mike, and the hair on his scalp prickled as he thought about it. Things like this were virtually unheard of on Oceanus, but these times were strange indeed and about as unusual as you could get on this world.

The sight of the smoke alarmed many people in both the groups who had elected to leave. Some turned around, walking straight back in after venturing out no more than a few steps. Others left but returned an hour or two later, shouting, pleading, yelling, outside the compound until Lew or a security guard let them in. To their evident chagrin they were held up as Lew's crewmembers quickly checked their identities before letting them back in. They were shocked and frightened and related tales of seeing isolated buildings and farms which had been set alight. And they reported sightings of strange people carrying sticks and staves, stalking through the brush-woods.

The group which made off for Florentia never returned. Everyone hoped they had made it safely – but it meant that the total number of evacuees had now dropped significantly, though still exceeded 170. And that number greatly exceeded the capacity of the recently landed boat, of course. Mike's anxiety for the evacuees continued. And this time he had a prickly feeling that things were going to get tough *for him and his colleagues as well*. Would even they be able to make it off the planet before something terrible happened?

****

The Monsoon's crew continued toiling to overcome their electrical and other technical problems and get the eight hundred and forty-one souls who had already arrived, settled safely on board. This had almost been achieved when the next 'bombshell' hit. Tenak and Ebazza were on the bridge when they received an alert from Statton.

'Incoming auto-message from the Antarctica, Admiral. No holo. Too much interference. Just data. Feeding it to your stations now. It's tagged "Emergency level Alpha One."'

Ebazza asked the AI to translate and verbalize the data for everyone, and the artificial voice began, in an electronic, neutral tone, a sound which, somehow just made the emotional impact worse.

'This message is late because of difficulties being experienced due to plasma interference which cannot be offset. There has been another deterioration in the star. Repeat, another deterioration. Disturbances in the surface layers are now growing at a rate of "e" raised to power three, raised, itself, to power two. A summary of the data is being cascaded with this message.'

A millisecond later both Tenak's and Ebazza's desk units showed streams of figures and luridly coloured graphics. Sometimes the graphics seemed to waver and flicker but they kept going.

'The data for exponentiation shows a curve that's almost asymptotic,' said Ebazza, nearly breathless, 'so ... the line of growth is nearly vertical.'

'As the auto-message said it would be,' came from Tenak.

An instant later came an actual audio message, this time in Captain Providius's own voice, and evidently recorded a short while ago, which said, through heavy static noise,

'Our AI is predicting the star's surface layers will explode *within the* ... 11.7 hours. I say again, next 11.7 hours. Recommend you leave orbit *immediately*. If your engines ... at optimum, ... not delay. We will continue ... feed data to you as long ... we are able. Good luck to all. End message.'

The atmosphere on the bridge plunged into a dark and palpable despair. Everyone had horror etched on their faces but then all of them snapped into focus when Captain Ebazza spoke loudly to the AI.

'Alright ...,' she said, coughing briefly, and continuing, 'by using the latest data from the Antarctica, calculate the maximum time we have until we can reach the star's escape velocity and outrun the radiation wave-front.'

Tenak added loudly, 'Also, calculate the ability of the hyper-EM shields to provide protection for human life aboard the ship – if the wavefront should overtake us.'

They didn't have a long wait. The AI said, in its reasonably human sounding but inimitably dispassionate articulation, 'Assuming the data is within 90th percentile accuracy, orbit must be broken within forty-five minutes at latest. The Monsoon will then have a maximum of 28 standard hours to outrun the shock front, assuming maximum thrust is achieved within two thirds of that time duration. If the ship remains in orbit or leaves orbit after the 45 minutes specified, there is a probability of 0.87, that the wavefront will reach the ship within 16 standard hours. On an expectation of a median radiation dosage of 4.6 kilohofts per square metre, the ship's shields will provide no more than 28% protection for organic tissue, should the vessel be overtaken by the wave. Higher yields of radiation will reduce that margin in proportion to its decreasing natural logarithm.'

'We can't do it, sir,' said Ebazza, eyes widening, 'we won't be ready to leave orbit in less than 45 minutes.'

'We've got to,' said Tenak. 'There's no choice, Ssanyu.'

'But, sir,' she said, her face sagging, 'we won't have time to get the last boat up from the surface. And Mike and Lew and the others are still down there.'

Tenak rubbed a hand over his haggard looking face and said, slowly, 'I know. I know. What else can we do, Ssanyu? We have to think of those we've got on board. I'm sorry … but we have to act now. Prepare to break orbit as soon as all passengers are secured. And make sure that's double quick.' His voice dropped almost to a hoarse whisper, as he added, 'I'll talk to Mike and Lew now. I'll do it from my office, provided the comms problems let me.'

'Yes Admiral,' said Ebazza, with evident distress, for even as she tried to hide it, her eyes glistened with moisture, barely contained, as they followed Tenak's suddenly weary form, his shoulders hunched like a man thirty years older, as he strode toward his private office.

CHAPTER FIFTEEN

ABANDONED

On the bridge of the Antarctica, First Officer Florian spoke to Captain Jennifer Providius, in tones thick with apprehension, though he was evidently trying to disguise it.

'The long-range sensors report *even more* activity in the outermost bands of alien artefacts, Captain.'

'On screen, Lieutenant,'

A second later the vid feed came through, showing Ra, in a magnified image, right in the centre of a field of background stars. Ra was now taking on a distinctly ruddy appearance, and instrumentation showed it was swollen in diameter. To assist the crew, the AI overlay the image with graphics showing the location and shapes of the bands of miniature alien machines. The bands appeared to be moving outwards, away from the star.

'How can anything ... artificial ... have this effect on a whole star?' said Florian.

'Something very advanced compared to us, that's for sure,' said the Captain.

'I guess so. By millions of years, I would think,' said the First Officer.

The vid before them immediately changed to show Ra alone, showing as its actual visual size, the way it could be seen by human eye on the ship, so that it now appeared as a small disc. On that image AI graphics overlaid the otherwise invisible bulk of the alien artefacts, which the ship alone could detect, 'painting' them as a network of sharp, brilliant, purple lines. They were starting to form a pattern which looked like a meshwork sphere surrounding the entire star.

'So what the hell just happened?' said Providius, gaping at the screen.

Before anyone could respond the feminine toned AI said, in low, unhurried, tones, 'New information. This spherical grid shows the location of the outermost bands of alien machines which surround the star. The grid represents the bulk of the artefacts where they form a series of orbits 25 million kilometres from the surface of the star. The aggregate of artefacts is estimated to comprise 16 quintillion spherical units, each unit having a median diameter of approximately 5 centimetres. Our measurement error band is 38.4%. Sensors indicate that the network encloses a force field, the precise nature and purpose of which is unknown at this time.'

'When did they move out to that orbit?' asked Providius. 'There's been no indication of anything that far out.'

The AI replied, 'The machine artefacts did not begin to radiate in any part of the spectrum prior to 3 minutes ago, ship's time. It is assumed that they have been orbiting at their present location for an unspecified time. They are too small to be detected without irradiating energy.'

'Speculate as to their function.'

'Preliminary analysis suggests the units have created a quantum field of unprecedented proportions. Speculation is wasteful. More time will be needed to follow through this analysis, only if taken together with continued observation.'

'How much time?' asked the First Officer.

'Unknown, but at least three standard days,' said the AI.

'My God,' said Providius.

'Captain,' said Florian, his voice rising, but only very slightly, in pitch, 'there's something else going on now. He pointed at the left portion of the screen which was displaying a new graphic. The innermost bands of alien micro machines were suddenly accelerating outwards, past or rather, through the outermost bands. It was an expanding shell which would, if it continued enlarging at its current rate, eventually collide with the Antarctica itself. Providius barked at the AI to explain.

'The innermost bands,' it said, almost as if it was an everyday occurrence, 'are expanding away from the star at approximately 0.04 light speed, or 12,000 kilometres per second but the purpose of this development is unknown. Further data is needed. However, I should warn you that the bands will reach this vessel's position in orbit within approximately 2 standard hours. Please note that hull damage is highly likely to occur at that time. Furthermore, this vessel does not have the capability to outrun the shell.'

'It just gets better, doesn't it?' said Florian, 'except ... well, they might ... diverge around us again? Like the cloud did when it entered this system?'

'I hope you're right, Lieutenant,' said the Captain, 'or we won't get to see the end game here, after all.'

A hologram of Doctrow Manlington, a senior member of the Antarctica's science team, suddenly popped up in front of the Captain's bridge screen.

'I'm sorry but there's more bad news, Captain,' he said. 'The data we have shows the star's own surface layers, above the normal Karabrandon circulation, have already started upwelling. We think the process has gone too far this time to allow for any natural settling back. I'm afraid, we have virtually no time left – *and neither has Oceanus.*'

****

Tenak hurried from the number Two Bridge toward his private office but by the time he got only half-way, Ebazza buzzed his wristcom,

'We've had another message, Admiral,' said the Captain, transmitting on audio only. Ebazza's voice had a slight tremble in it, small, but it was there. She continued, 'We only got some of the message, due to interference, but our hypercomp filled in the blanks. The Captain said the Antarctica's hypercomp shows the star's surface layer, down to a full ten percent into the body of the star, has already started its final eruption.'

Tenak could hear her swallowing hard, and then she continued, 'and they calculate the million-degree plasma shock wave will reach them within 5.2 standard hours. And this message took more than ten minutes to get to us. I'm sorry, Admiral.'

'Not good,' said Tenak, struggling to keep his voice steady, his hands clenching into fists, 'so, *we've still got* ... about 11 hours. Damnatious! I wanted to save at least *some* of these people, Ssanyu. Divert all available resources to powering up the EM shields. Get the crew to round up the passengers and move them into the centre of the hub. The further they are from the outer parts of the hull, the safer they'll be. It also means they'll have minimum protection from the acceleration we'll have to apply but again, no choice.'

'We can try to get as many into the hub as possible, Admiral, but we've got nearly nine hundred people on board.'

'Even if we don't succeed,' said Tenak, 'at least it keeps everyone busy doing something. Less time for them to think about other things.'

'And there is a chance we might save some, isn't there, sir?' said Ebazza, regaining full composure in her voice, yet still sounding plaintive.

'Dammy, Ssanyu, but we will. We will save 'em,' said Tenak. His voiced dropped almost to a whisper as he continued, 'and I still have to advise Lew but I can't spend the time talking to them as I'd wished. It's going to be the bare bones.' The sound of sorrow ran through his voice, like acid drizzle.

'I know, Admiral. Maybe they can find some way to survive. I have every confidence in Lew. And Mike's a good back up for him. Really, he is. I was wrong about him. Between them they might ... well, find a way. We can only hope.' There was a momentary pause and then she resumed, her voice sounding sombre but level-headed, 'And Commander Statton advises he has cascaded the new info-data to Lew's hypercomp anyway. They will be aware of the situation now. May the Maker have mercy on them – and us all.'

****

In his more rational, calmer, moments Mike Tanniss could think of nowhere better to die than in the place which he acknowledged had become his favourite planet. Had he finally come of age here, he wondered? He had learned to love, really love, with all his heart and soul. That heart had been broken by loss, of course, but then, he surmised, with heavy heart, and a wisdom which surprised even him, isn't loss the inevitable consequence of love – for everyone – at some stage?

He found himself aching for 'her' company right now, but maybe it was better this way. His heart missed a beat as he thought about what had happened to her. But her end had been quick and – hopefully, painless. The demise of this planet and the people on it was not going to be so painless and probably not very quick. She would have hated to the core being a witness to the land and the wildlife she loved so much, burned to a cinder, and the seas and oceans become toxic, all happening in front of her eyes. Once, a very long time ago, long before even the supervolcano, he mused, some people had thought the whole Earth was catching fire because of carbon dioxide. Those people had been wrong. No such thing had happened for that reason. Not even the supervolcano explosion had quite done that. Here, on Oceanus, the imminent explosion of Ra's surface promised to cause something very much closer to the once vaunted fate of the Earth.

Mike knew, in his heart of hearts, that Eleri would either have elected to stay on Oceanus until the last possible minute, and would have wanted to be with him, here, now. And then she would have shared his likely fate anyway and seen her beloved world die around her.

When The Monsoon had downloaded the latest data from the Antarctica Lew, Mike and the other Navy crew had been utterly shocked at how incredibly fast the star was changing; much faster than anyone could have imagined. But maybe that was better too. There was nothing worse than waiting for the inevitable, thought Mike. Now it would be over much sooner and perhaps some would live to see the aftermath, though that wouldn't be pretty.

The real clincher for Mike, Lew and the others had happened a little earlier, when, after an evident struggle with the ship's comm system, Tenak had contacted Lew personally. He had given him the first indication of the coming destruction from Ra, even though they had thought, till then, that they had at least *some* more time. Speaking on audio Tenak had explained he had no time to do more, and that he had confidence Lew would be able to break the dreadful news to the other crew in as 'Navy way', as possible. Mike was told that Tenak had found it difficult to keep his own voice from breaking and there was a deeper sorrow as to the fate of the whole population, too.

Lew had, in fact recorded the message from Tenak and soon afterward he had shared it with Mike, Meridene and a couple of security guards, in the privacy of the comms tent, with personnel who had happened to be present at that time. There'd been no time to gather the others together. Those present had listened to the message, heavily distorted by interference, in utter silence. Mike recognised that Tenak was having some difficulty in keeping his voice from breaking, but to his credit he had succeeded. Apart from not being the 'Navy Way', lapsing into emotional outbursts wouldn't help anybody, least of all those under his command. It was the curse and necessity of all military commanders, since time immemorial.

At the end of his missive, Tenak had said, as far as his audience could tell, given the continuing audio interference, 'Lieutenant Commander Pingwei – Lew, I have every confidence that you and all your team, including my great friend and confidante, Mike, will do your utmost to ease the burden for the civilians in your charge – in your care – and help them to deal with whatever comes at you during this event. Never give up hope and try not to let those who rely on you, give up. The only thing left to say is that it has been my honour, my good luck, my pleasure and my greatest pride to have served with you all. But make no mistake, I fully expect to see you all and meet you again, soon. Make sure you don't disappoint me in this. Until then, all of us on The Monsoon, salute you. May good fortune favour us all. Tenak out.'

Lew never once questioned the Admiral's order, and, Mike felt, he seemed to take the news of their being stranded on the planet with a fortitude equal to Tenak's own, though Mike thought he detected that his friend was, as expected, deeply perturbed, just as they all were. Was that a hint of moisture in Lew's eyes? If there was any doubt about that it was only because Mike, himself, found it hard to restrain tears, at that point, and found he couldn't quite see properly. He blinked them back as best he could. It was important to back up Lew's obvious need to keep everything from falling apart. Inside himself, he quaked, and it was only the desire not to break down in front of Lew and the others, as well as the fortitude he knew 'she' would have shown, that stopped him doing so.

Mike had felt all the hairs, over his entire body, stand on end during the course of hearing the message. There could be no doubt that Tenak's message was deeply inspiring and despite the military bearing of the missive, he had also found it hugely personal. Meridene and the few others standing by, were totally speechless, looks of shock on their faces but there was steely determination too, as with Lew. Mike knew they also understood and accepted their fate– though not one of them really had a choice, of course.

Afterward, Lew had called in the rest of the crew, in twos or threes; all 19 of them, into the more enclosed area at the far end, of the marquee, informally dubbed, the 'mess' area. He told them the dread news, all of it, as quietly as possible, so as not to alarm any nearby civilians. Although remarkably sensitive in his handling of such a difficult situation, thought Mike, Lew was simultaneously firm about the fact that everyone was still part of the Navy and had a job to do. That job, he'd said, was now to protect all the civilians gathered in the camp; people who were under their protection. Mike had felt eternally grateful that it had not fallen to *him* to do all this. His admiration for Lew grew yet greater.

Most, but certainly not all the Navy crew who'd not heard the message itself, had taken the news with a fortitude similar to Lew's, and now they sat or stood around, mostly not speaking to anyone, with faraway looks on their faces, or expressions of anxiety. The vast majority did what they could to suppress the most outward expressions of what could be expected of any human in the circumstances. They knew they still had a job to do. That was true until Mike, also sitting alone with his thoughts, noticed that just a handful of crewmembers seemed to become agitated, rather than accepting the situation. But then, such things could only be expected. Not everyone was going to take it equally well, despite their supposed military training. After all, some of them had relatively little experience of service, so far. And military or not, they were still human. This situation may even have been more desperate than many a deadly combat scenario, but Mike thought wryly, he couldn't really judge that; knew nothing of such thing and was glad of it. Tenak, however, had been through it all and who could say what would now become of him and the others aboard the ship? For, although not dwelt upon by the Admiral in his message, The Monsoon was also in very deep trouble.

They would all now have to play their parts in helping the civilians – and themselves. The landing boat, the '*Venturer*', had arrived only a couple of hours ago.

Mike believed the pilot was called Daviesberger, a person he knew little about, except that he remembered Lew saying he didn't rate him much as a Lieutenant. Apparently, the Commander didn't doubt his abilities as a pilot but had some reservations about his general attitude. Even so, Mike felt desperately sorry for the guy and the few guards he'd brought down with him. He'd landed straight into the middle of a briar patch, or, on Oceanus, a giant thorncrush plant. Just like the rest of them down here, the latest crewmember to arrive had 'drawn the shortest fusion tube in the pack'. Now he noticed that Daviesberger appeared to be one of the people who looked most disgruntled. That was understandable.

As for Lew, himself, Mike noticed the Commander was busy studying the behaviour of his crew. He seemed deep in thought and Mike began to wonder how various members of the group would hold up during the coming hours. Most of all, he wondered how *he* was going to hold up. He got up and walked to the window set into the marquee wall and stared out at the dusty compound. The tent itself, and the various bits of Navy infrastructure, cast long shadows in the early evening illumination. He became acutely aware that his hands, back and armpits, were wet with perspiration and it wasn't all because of the heat. It became increasingly difficult to concentrate. He felt as though he would burst, emotionally. With a sinking feeling he realised he had the same sense of suffocating descent toward oblivion as when he'd been attacked by the grotachalik, but he said nothing about that to anyone.

Anxiety about his own fate, annoyingly, he felt, seemed to want to overtake consideration of the evacuees. A classic case of self-interested emotion overtaking his intellect, he wondered, with horror? And it gnawed at his insides. Not long ago he'd assumed he and the rest of the crew would be able to get back to the ship. How wrong could he have been? He berated himself for these feelings, yet he knew he could do nothing to eradicate them. But perhaps he could at least restrain them; rein them in, stop them becoming all- consuming. And, setting his jaw, he was determined not to let Lew down. He hoped, more than anything, that he'd succeed in that.

Within a few minutes of Lew giving everyone the news, he could see that his friend had decided to get everyone involved in *doing something*. First, he ordered that no-one should inform the evacuees of the real situation, just yet. He said he had to think, to work out a plan of action and no-one wanted the alarm and panic which could ensue once those people knew the full truth. For the moment Lew wanted most crewmembers to circulate amongst the evacs and talk to them in what, he hoped, would be a reassuring way. He encouraged everyone to concentrate on chatting about the evacuees' families and about life on Oceanus, before all the troubles.

Before they could set about this work, however, Lew asked everyone to rack their brains as to how the crew were going to 'protect' the evacuees from the coming cataclysm. He divided up the crewmembers into small groups for this purpose.

Mike kept asking himself: what Tenak would do? There was no way out, so they had to improvise. The recently arrived landing boat was parked up outside the marquee. And it was one of the small ones – there'd been no other choice for The Monsoon. Too bad, he thought, but that was academic now. There was no purpose in trying to escape the planet because The Monsoon had broken orbit and was leaving Oceanus behind. The mother ship's speed and altitude would already be far too great for the boat to catch up with it, and any attempt to do so would result in being stranded in space. Up there, the ship's occupants would be even more exposed to the coming plasma storm, as well as hard acceleration effects.

Mike had joined one of the groups, most of whom simply looked at each-other despondently. He could see they'd all considered various options already and had probably come to conclusions similar to his own. One or two ratings mentioned that one idea would be to start dismantling the marquees and erect a type of shelter, a smaller structure, with the metal tubing, tables and 'furniture' that was available. There was not universal enthusiasm for this. There were murmurings amongst the mass of the crew for a few minutes but then the commander, standing with his back against a table, facing the front row of seats, looking increasingly at ill ease with himself, suddenly launched off.

'Okay,' said Lew. 'We have to tell them. We have to tell all those people out there right now. Forget what I said earlier. It's not right to keep this from them any longer. Just going to cause problems later on and, frankly, they deserve better. I'll talk to 'em, and I know I can count on your support and your help.' Some crewmembers looked puzzled at this change of heart but, thought Mike, Lew had obviously been thinking deeply about it. His reasoning was sound.

A few civilians had wandered up to the small opening into the mess area and approached Mike, who was closest to them, to ask what was happening. All he could do at that moment was to politely ask them to sit at the front, in the main marquee. Equally politely, they obliged him, though there were definite signs of impatience on their faces.

A few crewmembers objected to the Commander's idea, speaking about the panic it would induce, so Lew spoke again, as quietly as possible, the crew helpfully forming a small, tight knot around him. 'I know there's going to be problems,' he said, 'but we have to deal with it. We're the ones stuck with this task. No-one else. What I want from you guys now, is ideas on how we can protect the maximum number of people out there. The odds are very much against most of them surviving.'

A voice from the back of the group spoke up, 'We get them to take cover – in here – under anything we can rig up, sir.'

'Yep. But we need more than that,' said Lew.

Daviesberger, the most recently arrived pilot, the only other pilot present piped up, '*We* might not survive this, *sir.* We have a right to life too, don't we? How do you plan to do that?'

The man looked around him as though expecting to get cheers but there were only some mutterings amongst the larger group. A very small contingent of crewmembers, who seemed to surround Daviesberger himself, were the only ones who appeared to agree with him. From his vantage point Mike mused about the agitated demeanour of Daviesberger; a large man, as tall as Mike, maybe taller, but chunkily built and with surprisingly good, 'square cut' looks. None of us are taking this well, he thought, but that mascla looks about to bust. Hardly surprising, he thought but he was uneasy about his attitude toward Lew.

'Well, if you've got any brilliant ideas, Daviesberger,' Lew was saying, 'I'd be glad to hear 'em. Of course, *we'll* try to survive, but our priority is to help those people out there. You know that. We have over 170 evacuees looking to us, and 46 of them are children!'

Meridene spoke up, 'Sir, regardless of any structures we might build, I reckon we should collect all available material, like blankets, towels and the like. Anything that's definitely non-flammable. Then we instruct each evac' to wrap themselves in them.'

Mike doubted that there was enough material to go around but he could tell that Lew didn't want to scotch any ideas at the moment, no matter how unlikely they might at first seem.

'Good thinking,' said Lew, 'but we could also soak the blankets in as much water as the facilities here can still provide. And we've still got some supplies of flame retardant. We could even cut up pieces of the outer marquees and use them for protection.'

'But where's the best place to put 'em? The evacs, I mean, especially the children,' said a male security guard near the front.

'I'm working on that,' said Lew, 'but I think we might be able to use the boat.'

Mike decided to speak. 'We can't take them off-world, Commander,' he said, from his position, standing at the back. He was being deliberately formal, he felt.

'I know, Mike,' said Lew, 'and I didn't mean that.'

'Then you could use the boat itself, for protection, I guess,' returned Mike.

'Good. That's along the lines I was thinking,' came Lew's enthusiastic reply.

Mike, watching his fellow crewmembers, noticed that Daviesberger, and a female guard standing next to him, a crewmember he thought was called La'Brady, both seemed to have become agitated. La'Brady, was a well-built security femna, with a large, round face, and flame coloured, close cropped, hair. She seemed as perturbed as Daviesberger. Mike was aware that the two of them seemed very closely 'linked' to each-other since arriving on the surface. Maybe they were even lovers, but he wasn't sure. The two of them whispered together persistently and there was a lot animated chattering involving several other crewmembers standing around them. What were that lot up to, wondered Mike?

'Okay,' said Lew to those assembled, 'get 'em organised out there – as much as poss. I need to speak to them now. Need to get it out of the way.'

Meridene spoke up, 'Sir, I know they're aching for someone to let them know what's happening, but they're not going to like this. And what do we do about the children, sir? Do they, … I mean, should they hear it – like this? How are they going to understand?'

'I know. I'm really sorry about it too, but I think the children will have to hear all this as well,' said Lew, with evident anxiety, or at least as much of it as he could dare to show, thought Mike.

'Can't we take the children, at least the little ones, down into the back section of the marquee? Let their own parents tell them … in their own way, later on?' said Jenner, the security specialist.

'So how are you going to separate the parents from their kids without telling the parents why?' said Lew, with a nonplussed look on his face.

Another female crewmember said, 'We could try to persuade the parents to come with us and explain it to them, separate from the kids, but I kinda get it that something like that could end up causing more problems in the end.'

'Exactly, Rating Kirshner,' said Lew, 'so I guess, no, I don't think there's a workable alternative. I'm sorry. I'll try to be as easy going as possible, but the options are limited, aren't they? So let's get to it. The sooner the better, now.'

The crew started to file out, faces full of misery, but Lew called them back momentarily.

'There's something else,' he called. 'Some of the evacs have expressed … concern about the sonic weapons we're wearing.'

There were puzzled looks all around. Lew continued, '*Some of the family groups have said the weapons are making them – or at least their children – nervous – or whatever. Kind of ironic cos none of us has ever used the things around them. But don't forget – these are peace loving people.*'

'Is that why Janitra's burning right now, sir?' a crewman commented.

Lew nodded and said, 'Yeah, I know, but I'm guessing that's it's not family groups doing that, and, well, the situation out there is extreme, ain't it.' There were muted sounds of disapproval as crewmembers realised what Lew was going to say next, thought Mike, as the Commander continued, 'I know, I know, but let's show willingness to accommodate. If this situation is not easy for us, think what it's like for them. I want everyone to store their arms in storage locker number two, over at the back of the marquee, there. That way we can retrieve them if and when we need to. And I'm guessing we may need to - eventually. I'm going to put my pistol in there right now. The rest of you follow suit. The we go and talk to 'em all.'

****

On the bridge of the research vessel, Antarctica, the Captain and her first officer stared at the approaching wavefront of alien micro machines. The '3D screen-form holo,' showed them as a rapidly enlarging sphere of filmy white. It was a near-translucent curtain, almost as though composed of a gigantic swarm of tiny insects.

No-one said a thing as the graphics and images to one side of the holo counted down the moments to impact. It was as though time was standing still, and virtually no-one seemed to draw a breath. Many had closed their eyes, waiting for inevitable disaster, and the febrile atmosphere hung like a dark, dread, pall throughout the ship. They had been through something like this before but this time disaster seemed more certain, more concrete.

The time of impact came – and went. Nothing happened. Or so it seemed. Before they'd had time to draw breath again and realize that they were still alive the next surprise came. Their screens were still showing the bloated red image of Ra, slightly dulled, as though being viewed through a coloured, damask, veil, when, without warning from the instruments, or the AI, the brilliant, ruddy, surface of the star began to expand outwards in all directions. Streams of data feeds now indicated that the outermost surface layer of the star had blown off and was heading toward them, pouring out into interplanetary space, as though it would fill the gap between planets, ready to engulf everything, whole worlds, people, civilisations.

'Well, that's it,' said Providius, exhaling, as if rising from a fathomless free dive in a sunless sea, but then simply ascending to an even darker place above.

'It's finally gone nova,' she breathed. 'Looks like it's just a few hours till Ra vaporises us. I only hope all this data is going out to The Monsoon, so it helps the people back home at least.'

'The info' looks like it might be going out but there is some interruption to the data stream,' said the First Officer, with a croaking voice, 'and, in any case, it won't do them much good. Observation data we got before the cloud thing reached us suggested The Monsoon hasn't reached the velocity needed to escape Ra's gravity. Or at least, they hadn't, as of 9 minutes ago, when the light would have left their ship.'

Providius hung her head and closed her eyes. A holo-image of Doctrow Manlington's head suddenly popped up from a large bridge screen, suffused with static noise.

'Cap'n. Something else is happening,' he said, as though speaking through layers of gravel. 'The hypercomp indicates that part of the cloud of micro machines broke off as the wavefront reached us. But it's not like before. You know, when they simply by-passed us? This time a relatively small cloud of those things has formed a separate sphere, totally *enveloping the ship*. And this time scans show that the wall of that sphere is becoming denser. The particles, machines, or whatever, seem to have, well, ... almost joined together, like a solid mass. We're at the centre of that sphere. Readings also show it's ... contracting around us – and getting denser as it does so.'

A new glance at the screens on the bridge showed Providius that the image of Ra was no longer properly visible, except as a vague, slightly glowing patch in an all-enclosing region of rapidly growing darkness; a darkness which was starting to *block out all vision* of the ship's environment.

'Looks like they're reserving some special fate for us. Are they going to crush us now?' said Providius, more to herself than anyone else.

****

At the front end of the evacuee tent, Mike stood nervously, as Commander Pingwei positioned himself before a nervous and noisy crowd who sat before him. Navy crewmembers stood around at the ready, should aggressive turmoil erupt. If it did their orders were to try to protect the children, first and foremost. Lew began to speak, and several crewmembers, including Mike, tried to quieten the crowd, but to no avail. Lew persisted in trying to gain everyone's attention. The guy commanded immediate respect and attention amongst his own crew and aboard The Monsoon, mused Mike, but it was different down here. And Lew's relatively thin voice simply wasn't the kind of loud, penetrating, or piercing voice that could demand attention instantly, not when everyone else was talking at him, or at each-other.

Then he saw Lew touch a tiny grey box he'd placed on the desk in front of him; the digi-loud. Now, his voice rang out loud and clear and most people looked up, but there was still a hubbub of noise.

'Please, good popularia,' said the Commander, 'please let me have your attention. I have something very important to tell you all. It is vital you listen.'

Now for it, thought Mike. He didn't envy Lew this job. The Commander began to explain the latest news about Ra, and the terrible, dreadful, fact that there were now only a few hours to go before the plasma wavefront from the star would reach Oceanus. And he related that there could not be any more lift-offs because The Monsoon had been forced to leave orbit. Mainly for the sake of the children he tried to tone down the most alarming aspects of his news but there was only so much he could do. He avoided, mostly, talk of the burning of the environment that was likely to result and of the deaths that would very probably occur. The evacuees may have been a largely non-technical audience, but they were certainly not stupid. The place, as expected, erupted into noise and agitation. Many stood and there were angry mutterings, with many withering comments thrown at him, often directed straight at the Navy. But Mike knew it was mostly just anger and frustration. Most of the evacuees were now standing and shouting. Lew again tried to calm them. Mike and the crew couldn't do much to help but mainly look on with an anxiety they were themselves trying to hide.

Alarmingly, Mike heard intimations, loud ones, from some, that the Navy had known about this for a long time and hadn't wanted to tell them.

'Please, please,' said Lew, 'I promise you we did not know about this development until a few minutes ago and – please – and remember – we're in this with you. *We can't leave here, either.* But we're determined to do all we can to try to help you, to protect you. We ... believe we can survive this but only ... only if we all work together.'

There were hoots of derision from many but also, to Mike's surprise, admonitions from others, to be quiet and listen. Small children started crying. There were some shrieks from others as anxious parents tried to console them. The anxiety of the smaller children, and there were a lot of them, was a feeling mostly transferred from their parents, he thought.

'What canst you do, Navy! You have as much said we are yet finished,' shouted a man standing at the front, his voice shriller than most. He was pointing at Lew with a shaking right arm. His female partner then stood and said, 'We wish to leave, Navy. You must not yet keep us here no more.'

Lew once again gestured for all to be calm. He said firmly, 'Anyone can leave, if they wish. You are not prisoners. And it's been tried, remember? Besides, where? Where will you go?'

'We shall yet return whence we came,' said the woman.

'Or seek shelter in the forests,' shouted another man. Several others nodded in vigorous agreement.

Mike felt he had to say something. This was madness. He shouted at the top of his voice, to be heard above the noise, 'But the forests will probably burn. Listen to me. *The forests will burn!*' There, he'd said it. No getting away from it. He hoped Lew wouldn't hold it against him. A glance at the Commander seemed to confirm that.

'Then shall we seek shelter elsewhere,' shouted a woman near him.

There were sudden moments of calm as some evacuees sat down again, many hanging their heads in despair. An older woman rose and said, in a meek voice, 'But we, my family and I, have yet come from three hundred lints and more. We cannot return there.' Her eyes were downcast as she sat again. The family around her tried to console her. Many in the crowd were sobbing. There were more angry shouts but miraculously, after some minutes, a more sustained period of relative quietness descended, and Mike saw Lew take advantage of it.

'Please people, populari,' he said, more quietly than before, 'I really believe we will stand the best chance of surviving if we work together. Help each-other to survive. We've come up with a plan.'

Mike wondered how this idea was going to go down. Many evacs were paying attention now.

Lew began again, 'We feel the best chance we have – all of us – is to gather together all the clothing you have brought with you, all the stuff in your bags. And collect as much material as you can find in these marquees. You'll find bedding in tent number two and there's tarpaulins all over the place. We can also start to cut large pieces out of some of the marquees and fuse them together. My crew will help you. We'll need to soak the material as much as possible, but nearer the time of … when … the plasma storm gets here. We've got a few hours to go. Also, please gather together any medical equipment, such as drugs and bandages. We might need them. And collect all food containers in one place. We're going to have to sit this out for some time.'

Good, thought Mike. Get everyone working, preferably toward a single goal. But he doubted any of this would avail them.

****

'It's proving to be a bit of a struggle with the evacs, as you predicted, Admiral,' said Ebazza, aboard The Monsoon, using her wristcom. The Monsoon was now under constant acceleration from a continuing burn of her giant engine. The ship was under two gee forces at the moment and it would get worse. Ebazza continued, 'but, as we expected, we've got a lot of evacs starting to get ill with the gee forces, specially the kids. The forces are going to get worse so we're trying to get as many evacs into pressure suits as possible, but there's limited numbers of them. And very few are suited to children.'

'Can we get them into the pressure bubbles we can use for emergency isolation measures?' said Tenak, from his position on the hub Bridge. He was referring to the large beach ball type, blow-up, insulated spheres that could be used to protect crew in the event of an emergency, when full suits weren't accessible.

'Yes, we're trying that but there aren't nearly enough of them, and they give a sense of claustrophobia too.'

'There's nothing much we can do about that, Captain,' said a grim faced Tenak, 'cos they either go in 'em or suffer the gee forces. Make sure any bubbles used are secured too. The ride's going to get choppy. Are there many in the med bay, Ssanyu?'

'Yes sir. The medics have their hands full. Lieutenant Karalia's even set up makeshift sick bays along the core bleed tank corridors. It's not ideal but …'

'Can the sick bay in the hub withstand the radiation wave, Ssanyu?'

'We're not sure yet, Admiral. The AI says probably not. I think we've got to start moving all major med equipment into the core bleed tanks, just to make sure.'

'Agreed. And Ssanyu – we know the acceleration's going to get worse – probably to around 5 gees. I won't ask the ship to go higher as we could start to lose a lot of the evacs, especially the kids, so we'll have to hope it's enough.'

'Yes, sir. We're caught between the devil and the deep blue.'

****

After Lew's address the crowded main marquee dissolved again into a sort of animated chaos, though now it was more of an 'organised' chaos, thought Mike. To be fair, many, if not most, of the evacuees seemed to have thrown themselves into the tasks which Lew had suggested, and they were now being split into groups by those Navy personnel who were putting their Commander's orders into practice. But that was not everyone – and Mike, in the odd moment when he had time to check, sought out a view of Lieutenant Daviesberger, and his group of 'supporters', over on the far side of the room. They seemed to disdain involvement. In fact, Mike saw several civilians approach Daviesberger's group, asking for help, only to be met with icy stares and perfunctory 'help'. Mike was dismayed to see that Jenner was one of that group.

Mike, himself, was overrun with civilians wanting to know what they should do and how to do it, as well as the inevitable and understandable, but awkward, interrogations which some evacuees seemed determined to subject him to. Lew had asked Mike to give general information about the location of items in storage, but a group of evacs and their spokener, commandeered him to themselves. The 'leader', a bulky, middle-aged man, told him, curtly, that they had all decided to leave.

'Okay, but where will you go?' Mike asked.

'When we left, our grand-neighbourers were building a set of bunker-hollows, under the ground, lined with big rubble mix and cementy walls. We think they are yet big enough so we mayst join them, if we leave now. Please to let us out.'

'I can't let you out without Lew … the Commander's, permission – and he has the e-key to the gate, not me. Let me find him.' But Mike couldn't see Lew anywhere. Probably mixed up with all the crowds he thought. He stalled for time, 'So, how deep are these … these bunkers, sirra?'

'They are all of 3 metres so deep,' said the man earnestly, then, with increasing impatience, 'but list now, we need to leave soon. The place is over 10 lints distant.'

'I don't think it's enough – deep enough, I mean,' said Mike. He didn't have the heart to tell him that the minimum would probably be about 8 metres and even then, there would likely be significant problems with air recirculation, without the sort of equipment that these people simply didn't have – and neither did Lew.

'Still so, please be letting us out,' the man insisted but Mike had to admit he didn't know where the Commander was and he implored the spokener and his group to stand by for just a few minutes, while he went to look for him. Mike glanced at his wristcom, pressed it a couple of times but nothing happened. That was odd, he thought, as he made his way through the crowd and found himself approached by yet another group. But this time it was Daviesberger and his adherents.

'Where's the Commander, *mister* Secretary?' said Daviesberger, with a sort of a growl. He continued, 'I can't get through to his wristcom.'

'Neither can I, *mister*,' said Mike, looking at him sideways, 'I'll tell him you want him, *when I find him.*'

The pilot huffed, began to walk away and as he did so, said loudly, 'shipload of use you are.'

Almost immediately, Mike was waylaid by another group of civilians but these, mercifully, did not want Lew, nor did they want to leave. The female spokener asked Mike about where they could find the medical equipment. Mike took them into an anteroom, showed them several, locked, refrigerated chests, one of which contained medical drugs, bandages, hypo-syringes and the like. He encouraged them to work together to carry them into the main marquee and went back to the main tent and – and *there he was*. Lew had reappeared and was heading into a room hived well off from the main tent; a small space which had been unofficially taken over for use as his 'office.' The space, not a large one, had been incorporated into the marquee by its Navy designers, specifically for use by a commanding officer. Mike remembered that Lew had been at first reluctant to use it, preferring a more 'open' approach to command, but the exigencies of the current situation had impressed on him the need to start using it. And Mike had encouraged him in this.

The so-called office was separated from the rest of the marquee by a full-length fabric flap and Mike now followed the Commander through that and the five-metre-long corridor beyond, the through another flap entrance, into which his office. Mike ruminated on the fact that these flaps didn't make it much of a 'private' space. He knew Lew's reluctant acceptance of the need to use it was simply that it would give him at least a chance to speak to crewmembers privately, away from the hubbub of the civilians. And it was place where he could draw up plans and logistics, and *just think.*

Mike didn't yet know the significance that this aspect of 'privacy' would bring with it.

*

Lew smiled at Mike as he entered.

'Lots of people asking for you,' said the Navy Secretary.

Lew nodded, standing behind the fairly large desk near the back of the room, and said, 'Been busy, man. I went out to the boat. I was working on *your* suggestion, and I think it'll be possible to use it as a refuge for a lot of these civilians. Well, as many as we can fit in – mainly the children. All the children, I think. I know the hull is reinforced with hemillar insulation but you were right when you said it needs more than that – a lot more. So, I've diverted all the power from the main energizers, over to the two induction coils, fore and aft. That should stave off most of the proton and ion flux, at least for a while. It's as much as we can do.'

'That's extreme. Doesn't that mean we can't ever use it again in flight?'

'Correct. The energizers will be burned out afterwards. And the coils will probably get fried by the magnetospheric shockwave that's coming. But we have no choice, man. It's either that or die out in the open, or inside these tents.'

Mike nodded dourly. He was starting to shake inside but desperately didn't want that to show. It was not just some sense of, perhaps misplaced, shame, that he had about showing his feelings. Lew probably would have understood. But he wanted, at least, to appear to be strong – for these civilians, trapped as he was with them, and, he now realised, with some surprise, it was for Lew too. This man was in charge down here; a very unenviable position, but Mike felt that their best chances of success probably rested with the Commander. He would do his best to support Lew. Besides, what else could he or anyone else do?

'And, I reckon,' said Mike, 'the rest of us should be able to shelter underneath the wings and fuselage. The EM field should help us as well. We'll just have to hope that's enough.' He tried to keep the shake out of his voice.

'Exactly,' said Lew, 'and we need to put as much furniture from the tents out under the fuselage as poss. Use it as a kind of barricade against the air pressure systems that'll come with the burning. And we'll need to use as much reflective foil as we can find in here and fit it over all the furniture. We can spray it with retardant too. I don't think there's a lot of spray stuff left but, we should be able to raid the extinguisher pods in the boat. Run lines out.'

'Okay,' said Mike, 'and I've done a recky on the food and water situation. I think we can get by for a few weeks here.'

'Good. That's why I'm putting you in charge of commodities. You don't have to do it. You know I can't order you like the Navy crew, my friend.'

'That's okay, Lew. We're all in this, as one.'

'Thank you. So where are we with main supplies?'

'Well, the food's depleted to about half. Not great, but we should be okay for reasonably longer with water – which'll be more important. Piped water from Janitra stopped yesterday, so I'm kind of glad the Navy anticipated a possible problem with a pure supply. The automated bowser they brought down before they left is just outside the tent here. About ten percent gone. But if we have to stay here a long time we'll need more. So, the ship can help again, can't it?'

'Yeah, I guess, as long as the main batteries last they can synthesise water for some time but after that …?'

Mike brightened and said, 'And, … I reckon we should be able to rig up some solar cells from materials in the ship – or even find some in local towns. The locals are good at that. It all depends on how long we have to stay here, in this dammy place.'

'Where else do we go, Mike? At the very least we'll need to make this our base. Safest bet around, unless we can find somewhere more suitable. You do realise we're going to need those people out there, don't you? The civilians. They've got basic skills … skills we've forgotten in the Home System. Tek will help us in the short term but not far beyond that. Not without back-up – and the fleet won't get here for months.'

'Understood,' was all Mike could think of to say. It was a bleak prospect at best.

'Keep your prow up, matey,' said Lew, with a wan smile, 'we have to believe things are going to work out.'

'I know,' said Mike, trying to sound positive, his throat starting to get very dry, 'and, by the way, there's another group of locals who want out of here. And – Daviesberger's been trying to talk to you.'

'I'll bet he is,' said Lew, 'that man is definitely not happy. And I think I know what's eating him.'

'We're all unhappy. I don't see what's up with him in particular,' said Mike.

Lew gave an ironic half smile then summoned Meridene on his wristcom. When she arrived he asked her to take the e-card and let out the group who wanted to leave.

As she left a shaft of late afternoon sunshine poured in through the transparent aluminium based window on one side of the room. The beam penetrated almost horizontally, a shaft of gold and orange. It reminded Mike of the first dusk he'd witnessed on this planet. He and Tenak had just made planet-fall. He felt another pang of regret, a sort of anticipated mourning for this beautiful place. It was so intense he felt it as a sharp stab in his guts and chest, and his scalp prickled. The heat the light brought in contrasted curiously with the chill he felt inside himself.

'Be dark soon,' said Lew. 'Not a good time for anyone to be leaving here, but it's their choice.'

Mike heard the flap door of the office being rustled. Lew's brow creased as both he and Mike heard mumbled voices approaching and within a few seconds Lieutenant Daviesberger appeared in the main office, accompanied by the rating, La'Brady and seven other crewmembers, including Jenner. They were a mix of security guards and tek people. There was just enough room to comfortably accommodate them all, plus Lew and Mike, though there was sufficient space for them to stand the other side of the broad desk from Lew, as protocol, regarding respect, for senior officers required.

The pilot pushed rudely past Mike and spoke gruffly to Lew, and yet his voice held the detectable tones of a plea of sorts.

'Sir, I ... that is, we, want to put something to you.'

Mike started to leave. This sounded like something which didn't really concern him, but Lew called him back, saying, 'Stick around, Mike?'

Daviesberger looked peeved but resumed, 'We've been talking about this and we think we should ... well, we should use the boat to escape.'

Lew looked puzzled and said, 'Well, that's interesting. Please explain.'

Mike had reckoned Lew's reaction would be a vigorous rebuff but here he was, being the perfectly diplomatic commander.

'What Davey means,' said La'Brady, with impatient tones, 'is *we think* it serves no purpose to stay here. We can take the boat and fly it over to a remote island, out in the Eastern Ocean. We've looked at the shipNet and reckon there's one or two good candidates. They've got limestone substrata. And that usually means caves. Caves, *sir*. Don't you get it? That means somewhere we could take shelter. Properly.'

'Yeah, sir,' Jenner piped up, 'cos we believe we stand a better chance of survival somewhere like that, rather than staying here, sir. A remote island, uninhabited, would be safer, wouldn't it? It makes sense, Commander. You can see that, can't you?'

'I'm sorry but I think it's a bit of a gimbo's idea,' said Lew.

Mike sighed inwardly. So much for diplomacy, he thought. But his friend was right. Their plan was a non-starter, for lots of reasons.

'Okay, look,' said Lew, with a more conciliatory tone, 'I can see where you're coming from. But I've got a plan for our survival, which means staying right here, helping those civilians out there.'

Mike was completely baffled by the position these crewmembers were taking. He found himself saying, almost involuntarily, 'By the way, what makes you think there'll be caves out there you can use? Didn't you know, Lieutenant? The native population left most of the islands in isolation. That means, *not surveyed*. And if they haven't investigated there won't be anything reliable on our shipNet.'

Daviesberger suddenly looked angry about Mike's intervention but Jenner jumped in with, 'It stands to reason, Mike. Limestone strata always has caves.'

'Say you're right. Do you know how deep or, say, accessible, those caves are?' said Mike, 'And what about about how safe they'll be for civilians, like this lot, to climb into? What about the children?'

'Where is your nearest … island, anyway?' Lew intervened, his voice betraying impatience. Watch out, thought Mike.

'The nearest ... safe one's about four thousand klicks off the east coast,' said La'Brady

'So, if we were to take all of this lot out to these ... caves, you think exist,' returned Lew, 'we'd need to make at least three return journeys. There's no time. Even with sub-orbital lobs.'

'We know that ... sir,' said Daviesberger, hesitating for a moment, before blurting out, 'and that's why we do *one* journey. We take all the crew – and as many locals as want to come and can fit in.'

Lew looked aghast. Mike's mouth dropped open.

'We're not leaving anyone behind, *mister!*' said Lew. 'There's more than 140 people out there, 46 of them children. How're you going to decide who goes and who stays?'

'We'd take ... we'd have to take the strongest and most able to survive,' said Daviesberger. 'It's a pity but it's the best bet. I'm sorry, sir.'

'So am I, Daviesberger,' said Lew, 'cos the answer's, no. I already said. Mike and I have worked out how we can use the boat for protecting up to 50 people, including all the children, right here on the ground. I've already programmed the boat to divert all energiser power to the coils. The rest of us can shelter under the ship. We take our chances.'

'What? Why did you do that?' spluttered Daviesberger, now more agitated. 'You're throwing away our chances of survival. We won't be able to use the boat afterwards. And you know full well, there's minimal chance of surviving the fire storms on the continent. Our way – at least some of us will survive.'

'Listen, Davey,' blurted Jenner, standing behind Daviesberger, 'the Commander might be right on this.'

'Just shut up,' said La'Brady, contempt spreading all over her face.

'Listen, all of you,' said Lew, 'just do your jobs. Remember the oath you gave when you joined up? "Protect and serve." Remember that? We can't leave these people to face ... whatever's coming, on their own. What does it say about us if we just take ourselves off? Abandon them?'

'It doesn't matter anymore … sir,' said La'Brady. 'There won't be many left alive on the continent to tell the tale. It's everyone for themselves now.' There were guttural murmurings of approval from behind her.

'*It matters now more than ever,*' returned Lew, sounding incredulous. 'Even if most people die on this planet. We'll know what we did – even if, eventually, all of us die. Yours is not the legacy I want to leave behind and not the legacy the Navy wants, either. And to that end, I need to tell you, I've been recording all events here and putting 'em in the duralamium box in this desk – so posterity *will* see what we did here. Got it? So, no, Lieutenant. I'm not putting my name to this, and neither are you. Get used to it. The decision's been made. Return to your posts. Do what you were trained to do.' Lew paused for a moment, then added, in more conciliatory tones, 'Listen, guys. I know this is difficult – for all of us, including me, but it's what we all knew could happen when we signed up. Let's make the best use of our time here. Even if only for posterity.'

Daviesberger hissed something under his breath as he and his group turned, morosely, and slowly left.

Mike was totally shocked. He had to admit, to himself, that he'd almost been tempted by the group's suggestion. But only for a second or two. Daviesberger's plan was horrible, and it wasn't practical. And he hated the thought that he'd had sympathy with it, even for a fleeting moment, despite his shock at the group's impudence. The 'deputation' he'd just seen were people cracking under the strain. And he thought *he'd* be the one of the first to crack – but not like them. Never like them.

Mike turned to go, and Lew caught his eye with an expression which might have said, *I hope I've made the right decision,* but he didn't say anything. Mike smiled reassuringly and nodded as he turned and said, 'I'll get back to organising the stores.'

As he left, he glanced back and saw Lew thumbing his wristcom, a grim look on his face. After leaving Lew's 'office' he wondered how much worse things were going to get. The strain was building. And there was probably not much time left – for any of them.

****

Already several million kilometres from Oceanus, The Monsoon's giant fusion engine continued to blast it along the widest parabolic orbit permitted by its own limitations of fuel and the ever-present laws of astrophysics. Inside the main command deck, within the hub, weighed down by gravity at a strength of more than three Earth equivalents, Captain Ssanyu Ebazza and the main bridge crew, like everyone else, sweated under the strain.

She spoke into her wristcom, wheezing slightly as she did so, 'Admiral, I thought I should tell you that the ship's long-range sensors have indicated that ... the Antarctica has disappeared – completely.'

Arkas Tenak, in a pressure suit, was in the med bay. He'd been assisting Senior Med Surgeon Atrowska and Padrigg Lomanz, tending, under supervision, to various injuries sustained by evacuees. Some of them weren't holding up well under the intense acceleration. Everyone in the med bay was in pressure suits but outside it the situation was different. No-one had anticipated the need to carry this number of people under such intense acceleration. They had all thought they had months.

Tenak had told the medics he'd wanted to be fully occupied, *doing something* practical, and to leave the routine running of the ship to the Captain. For their part they were glad of his help, particularly his ability to inspire calm amongst people who were completely out of their element.

'What do you mean? Are you saying the Antarctica's exploded?' he said with horror. He screwed his eyes up as he awaited Ebazza's reply. The gee forces were affecting everyone, including the crew.

'No, thank the Lord,' came the Captain's voice. 'Well, at least we've picked up no signs of radiation or debris from an explosion. No, the ship just ... disappeared off the sensors. But there's even worse news, Admiral. The long range has also picked up a massive rise in the surface temperature of Seth, the planet nearest to Ra. The surface of the planet is melting, Admiral. And star obs report that the flares and prominences coming off Ra are extending up to 9 million klicks from its surface before falling back. Thankfully, none have broken free of Ra's gravity, as yet. But there are billions of tiny prominence - like gas tendrils rising off Ra's surface. It's looking really bad for the whole of Oceanus.'

Glancing around to check if anyone was in a position to listen, Tenak breathed back, 'Sounds like we're nearly there, Ssanyu. This could be the final phase. The endgame of the aliens.'

****

In gathering darkness, unseen by most people, hands belonging to some Navy personnel, greasy with sweat, surreptitiously and carefully removed, one by one, the cache of sonic weapons out of storage locker number two, in the shadows of the crew's makeshift mess, at the back end of the Navy marquee, outside Janitra. Not a word was spoken as the arms were handed out and the crewmembers made their silent way past the back wall of the main tent. In the darkness, borne of the need of conserve power, the other crewmembers hadn't noticed them, surrounded as they were by large groups of evacuees who they were helping to prepare food, water supplies, medical supplies and shelter.

The thieves of the armaments had been careful to hide the weapons under swathes of retardant clothing and material they had previously gathered, for protection from the coming fire storms. With relative ease they moved quietly but confidently, not creeping or acting in any obviously suspicious way, gathering little attention to themselves. Most of them paused occasionally, to talk to isolated evacuees, smiling and exchanging pleasantries, and sometimes stopping to make 'useful' advice.

*

Mike Tanniss paused by a group of evacuees being assisted by Lieutenant Meridene. She squatted by a group of Oceanus women, helping them to sort through a basketful of medical supplies, before placing the most suitable items into several sturdy duralamium boxes, for removal to the Venturer, the landing boat.

'Lieutenant, have you seen Lew?' asked Mike, 'cos I can't raise him on his com – again.'

'No sir. Sorry,' she said.

'I wonder if he's out at the ship again,' said Mike, then moved on, but before he could get far a female evacuee, a couple of metres away, evidently sharp eared, despite the background hubbub, stood and said to him,

'Were you yet looking for the commanderman, sirra?'

Mike nodded and she said, 'He did go back toward his office-place some minutes ago. Back there.' She pointed toward the far side of the tent.

'Yeah, I know where you mean. Thank you, Mes,' said Mike.

*

Lew stood, on his own, behind his desk. It was nearly dark outside; Ra was sinking rapidly to the west of the main marquee. He glanced out at the Venturer, deep in shadow now, standing no more than a hundred metres away, appearing as though crouching in anticipation of being brought back to life; to take off once more and shoot up into the stratosphere, and beyond. It would never do that again.

Some minimal artificial lighting was starting to come on inside the marquee, the natural waveband fluorescent stripes, woven into the marquee fabric, bringing some illumination to the interior of his 'office'. They flickered numerous times for over two minutes, and Lew's brow furrowed, then relaxed.

At that point he heard the unmistakeable sounds of people entering through the flaps in the corridor. Looking up, his eyes widened as he saw Daviesberger's group of nine storm in, a heavy, humid, waft of air from their hurried entry, stirring up his jet black hair.

The group looked wild, but worse, they carried sonic weapons, downward pointing at this stage but evidently ready for action. They halted the other side of Lew's wide desk, standing right up against it, and for long moments there was silence, sizzling with tension, as the group and Lew stared at each-other across the gap.

'Well?' he said, calmly, breaking the spell.

'Well? Well, did you say? What shit sort of question is that?' said Daviesberger, then continued, '*Well, sir,* we're here to find out what the feg you've done to the ship?'

The others in Davieberger's group nodded and muttered angrily.

'We tried to get inside,' said La'Brady, 'but it won't open, and it won't obey any commands we give it via our com units.'

'That's because I've disabled the minor AI, and all its main functionaries,' said Lew again calmly, 'except for routine subfunctions, which it will only carry out when it's unlocked – by me.'

Amid gasps of incredulity, Daviesberger raised his voice a notch and said, 'But why? Why would you disable the AI and main functionaries?'

'They draw too much power and we won't need them for our purposes. Least, not yet. If we survive tonight, we might be able to resurrect the AI, if we need it.'

'You – you're an idiot,' spluttered Daviesberger. 'Of course, it's needed. *We* need it!'

'I told you, *mister,* we're staying here, to look after these people. Weren't you paying attention, Lieutenant?'

'I was paying attention. But what I heard was just bollocks!'

La Brady said, 'You're wasting time. Cut to the chase, Davey,' and she swung her weapon up to point it directly at Lew. Even Daviesberger looked shocked at that, as did several others in the group. They hesitated for a moment but then followed suit. Lew's calm but very focussed expression didn't change one jot.

'You must have used a key code. Give us that code – sir. Now,' said Daviesberger.

'I can't,' said Lew, 'you know I can't.'

There was silence for long moments, as though no-one knew what to do next, the opposed parties continuing to face each-other across the desk.

**

Mike wondered why Lew still wasn't answering his wristcom. He knew the commander wasn't out at the ship as he'd just popped out for a few seconds to peer at the brooding hulk of the Venturer. No lights on in there. No sign of activity. Returning indoors, on an impulse he decided to check his wristcom for the manifest on food and water supplies, just before he reached the corridor to Lew's office. He commed Digby, a tek rating, who was seeing to the supplies for the moment.

'We'll have to take purifier plunge-sticks with us, sir,' said Digby, on audio, 'just in case we can't get back into the tent after the storms.'

'Good idea,' said Mike, 'the tents might get burned up completely, or blown away. So, we'll need to neutralise the natural water supplies. At some point we'll almost certainly have to switch to them. Good work.'

Signing off he walked nonchalantly into the corridor and through into Lew's space, and ... what the feggery was going on? It was Daviesberger's group, facing Lew – again. But they were – what, carrying guns? The group had obviously heard his approach, and some of them had swung to face him, at which point he was presented with at least four sonic pistols pointing straight at his chest. His heart rate shot into orbit. Then, he glimpsed Lew beyond the group and saw that at least he seemed okay. Mike breathed a sigh of relief inwardly and he saw Lew's eyes roll. Guess he picked the wrong time to come and to see him.

'Mikey!' said Daviesberger, 'so nice of you to turn up. Come and join our little party.' The guns waved him around toward Lew.

'Jenner,' said Daviesberger, 'I want you take a position near the corridor. We don't want any more "unannounced visitors".'

Standing to the left side of Lew's desk, and becoming rooted to the spot, Mike swallowed hard and tried not to sound panicked. Then he said, his mouth dry as a bone, 'Guys. What're you doing? Are you all … mad or something?'

'Just keep out of it, *mister secretary,* and you might not get hurt,' said Daviesberger.

Mike's heart leapt again when he peered more closely at the pistols the group were toting.

He couldn't help blurting out his thoughts, 'Are those things on lethal setting? Cos if they are, could you please turn them down? There's no need for this.'

'He doesn't listen, does he?' said Davisberger. 'I said, keep out of it, secretary man or I'll shoot you now.'

'Yeah, just shut your mouth, you feg-wit,' said La'Brady, a leering smirk on her face.

'Just when did you guys lose all your self-respect?' said Lew.

'I don't need any lectures from you ….' began Daviesberger, but La'Brady interrupted.

'Let's just cut out the shit, shall we?' she said. 'Just give us the code, *mister* Pingwei. Now!'

'No,' he said.

Shock registered on the faces opposite him. Lew continued, 'so what're you going to do now? Kill me? You'll never get the code then.'

Daviesberger and La'Brady looked at each-other for a second and then turned to Mike, both swinging their guns in his direction.

'No, maybe we'll just kill *him* instead,' said La'Brady. 'Maybe that'll encourage you to change your mind, *sir.*'

Mike's heart rate leapt yet again. He began to sweat profusely. He wanted to run for help but he knew he couldn't. What was the point of all this? He knew they wanted to get away in the boat, but he couldn't understand how things could have got this bad. He wanted to say something, but his throat had gone so dry his voice croaked and nothing would come out. He just stared at Lew, bug eyed.

Lew continued to try to stare down his wild-eyed aggressors. Mike suddenly realised what Lew was doing. He was relying on the Navy training these guys had had and the fact that, despite everything, they might have some remaining vestiges, some torn shreds, of respect for Lew, and for their duty. A very dangerous game, thought Mike, but what else could be done? He just prayed it would work.

Daviesberger and La'Brady started to tighten their grips on the buts of their pistols but there were sudden mutterings of disapproval amongst others in their group. From the back of the pack Jenner piped up, 'Davey, don't do this. I want to get away as well, but I didn't sign up for murder. You said Lew would cave …'

'Alright, Jenner,' said Daviesberger loudly. 'We know how you feel. It's a bit late for second thoughts, isn't it?'

'Yeah,' said a male group member behind Davisberger, 'so just shut up Jenner. We all agreed we'd do whatever was needed to get away from here.'

Mike's hopes were alternatively raised, then dashed, all in a few seconds. But then, more reason to hope.

A male guard at the back spoke loudly, 'Jenner's right, sir. We didn't agree we'd do murder.'

Others in the group muttered their unease but fell silent when Daviesberger spoke again,

'No,' he said, 'we don't have to kill anyone. Not really.'

There were some sighs of relief, thought Mike. Barely audible, but they were there. Then La'Brady said, 'No. Not kill. We'll just stun the commander here. Then we'll use a laser cutter to slice bits off him, till he gives us what we want.'

Even Daviesberger seemed shocked. He looked at his mate with evident surprise. But then he smiled and nodded.

This just gets better and better, thought Mike, with total disbelief. It was like some damnatious dream. No, a nightmare. The worst sort, because it was real.

'You'd really go that far?' said Lew.

Mike was amazed by how the Commander was fronting this out. He just hoped he wouldn't resort to winding them up even more. Maybe he should give them what they wanted, if they felt they needed it so fegging badly. But no, that wasn't right, and it wouldn't do them any good anyway. They probably wouldn't find the kind of shelter they were looking for, even if they still had enough time to reverse Lew's induction coil changes and get where they wanted. Maybe they'd see that and relent. But it would be too late for the people out there. What about them? He couldn't understand why he didn't feel as brave, in this situation, compared with when he'd been on the ship. Then he remembered Eleri. She would tell him to keep going.

It was then that he noticed Jenner, whose face registered a strange mix of anger, and confusion, was gradually walking *backwards*, one slow step at a time, getting ever closer to the 'corridor'. She didn't have far to go, after all. No-one had apparently seen her. In a split second the 'fusion wrench' dropped for him, and he realised what she was intending to do. He forced himself to pull his gaze away from her, to prevent giving the game away. The next second La'Brady was peering at him, quizzically. Did she notice he'd seen something? He stared back at her, not daring to even glance, for a millisecond, in Jenners' direction. He wore a look of brazen defiance on his face. She sneered and looked back at Lew. Mike also stared at Lew. He had to make a concentrated effort to ignore what was going on at the back of the room.

Lew spoke up again, 'Are you so degenerate you'd resort to torture? That's something you'd hear from an Ultima operative say, or the New Rebels. Is that who you are? More quislings?'

At this most of the group broke into a mass of lame protestations.

'Listen guys, listen to me. He's just stalling for time,' said La'Brady, 'but …'

Lew interrupted her, 'And by the way, I told you, didn't I, that I was recording events here? In fact, my wristcom is recording everything that's happening in this room, right now, but it's not transmitting to any box in here. It's transmitting to a micro-block I've buried in the grounds out there, just in case no-one survives the storms. It'll be a record of what we did – just for posterity. Remember that?'

'Lies, just lies,' screamed La'Brady, 'don't listen to him.'

This was not going well, thought Mike and he dared to glance toward the back of the room, through just peripheral vision. No Jenner. Good. He wasn't sure exactly when she'd actually got out, but no-one else had noticed. He prayed she'd do the right thing out there.

'No,' said Lew, 'no lies …'

'Okay,' said Daviesberger, 'get that com off your wrist now. Put it on the table. I'll make sure it's finished – just like you.' There was a chorus of approval, but Lew cut through it.

'It's too late,' he said. 'You're already condemned. Even if none of us survives, the beacon the box will send out, and the recording, will alert the fleet, even before they get here. Admiral Roberts's teams will hunt you down, like Prithvian bloodworms.'

'Nonsense. This is shit. Just wackerbag,' said Daviesberger, clearly losing control of his group as various members started arguing amongst themselves.

'Even if you find your *island*,' continued Lew, 'just imagine what'll happen when they catch up with you. If you don't get shot on sight, you'll be lucky to get life imprisonment on Mars. And think about the shame the SolarNet will heap on you and your memories – and your families.'

The group were becoming very agitated now and several began protesting loudly to Daviesberger.

'Nothing's changed, you idiots,' shouted La'Brady, raising her pistol again and making a show of taking deliberate aim at Lew's head. Lew's eyes widened, then narrowed with defiance. Mike's jaw dropped again.

'I say he's got to give us the code *and* the position of the micro-block,' she shouted.

'Wait,' said her partner, sudden indecision racking his features. She stared up at him, a puzzled look spreading across her face.

At that moment another member of the group, near the back shouted out, 'Where's Jenner? She's gone!'

They all turned around as the crewmember who had spoken edged nearer the corridor and said, 'That's strange.'

'What the feg is it? Just tell us, Achmah,' shouted La'Brady.

'It's … well, nothing,' said the crewman, 'cos it's totally quiet out there. The locals are always chattering. It's what they do best, ain't it. Just weird '

'Damnatious. She's alerted them,' growled Daviesberger, and as he spoke some of the members of his group made a break for the office flap. One shouted back at Daviesberger, 'We need to get out before the others come for us.'

Another said, 'If they're out there we'll have to shoot our way out.'

'No,' said Daviesberger, 'don't be stupid. We can use these two as hostages and …'

But it was too late. He was interrupted by the distinctive sound of sonic weapons fire from back in the main marquee. Ironically, sonic beams themselves made no audible noise to humans, the only sound being made by the inner workings of the devices, particularly their electrical recharging action, especially the sonic rifles. Totally unlike the noise made by projectile weapons, it consisted of a sort of singular 'pinging' noise, followed by a low, throaty rumbling; almost innocuous unless you knew what it was. These people knew that sound well, thought Mike. And there was a lot of that noise, now mixed with the sound of shouting. Part of Daviesberger's group must already be involved in a firefight. Mike knew that of the remaining crew, around 14, including Jenner, only about 11 were guards, who had weapons. It sounded as though that group, after alerting by Jenner, had gathered their weapons from the mess area and were battling the mutineers.

Mike was suddenly aware that only Daviesberger and La'Brady were left in the office, the rest of his group having disappeared through the flap and out of sight. La'Brady turned to her lover and stared into his face with glistening eyes. Touching his face gently she said softly, 'Sorry baby. Guess it's all over,' Then she uttered a strange, guttural cry and ran toward the corridor, brandishing her gun.

'No! Come back,' cried Daviesberger, 'I said …' He turned and glanced at Mike, who was surprised to see a completely disconsolate expression on his face.

'All we wanted was to live our lives together, man,' said Daviesberger, 'just to survive together. Just …' Without completing his sentence, he stopped, held still for a second and, his face taking on an expression of utter despair, he raced off after La'Brady.

Mike's shoulders slumped and he breathed as if for the first time since he'd walked in on in it all. He stood unmoving, totally numbed.

'Not over yet,' barked Lew, 'take cover in here, matey.' He raced around his office and Mike realised he was looking for something to use as a weapon. Within seconds Lew had pulled a toolbox from his desk drawer and was prising it open. The peculiar tones of sonic weapon recharging continued to intrude from outside. The shouting continued too, much of it desperate, emotionally torn, heart wrenching. Mike thought that they seemed to reach a sort of crescendo.

Then everything seemed to go silent, but not quite. Lew had yanked a large wrench out of his box and was saying, 'Here's one for you,' he said as he threw the wrench across the desk, for Mike to pick up

'Lew, I think it's all over. Gone quiet,' said Mike, but his sense of relief was suddenly tempered by the fact that he didn't know what the outcome of the battle had been. He prayed Daviesberger's group had been defeated. Had all the others joined to resist them – or had some joined *with* them? Mike couldn't believe that people like Meridene and the others would fall in with them. But maybe they'd been overcome? What then?

'I can't stand it, Lew. Not knowing what's happened. I can't wait here,' he said and began to make for the corridor.

'No, wait Mike. We're outgunned. You go out there and you're a sitting duck. Better to see what comes through and deal with it on our own terms. And … watch out cos …'

Mike didn't hear the rest of what Lew said when he heard a rush of sound nearby and instinctively stopped his forward momentum, as Daviesberger crashed in under full steam. The man was not about to slow down and thrust out his broad right arm in a sweeping motion, his forearm connecting loudly with Mike's upper chest and neck. Mike hardly saw the strike coming and just felt an explosion of force, a jolting of his whole upper body, sending him flying backwards. He landed heavily on the floor and quickly realised he couldn't breathe properly. His vision swam and he gripped at his throat. Then the pain hit him; a feeling he'd been bashed with what felt like a massive bar of iron. He could still hear normally though, and he realised Daviesberger was screaming at Lew.

'You feggin bastard,' shouted the man, almost in tears, as he faced Lew, shaking his pistol at him. 'It's all your fault. They shot my baby out there. She's hurt bad because of you. I'll make you pay.' He took aim at Lew's upper chest but suddenly the Commander shouted wildly and threw his arms up, almost as though he'd already been shot. Daviesberger seemed to hesitate for a split second and in that moment, Lew launched himself downwards and to his left. The move saved his life but Daviesberger had fired and it caught Lew in the upper right arm. Lew grimaced but mostly ignoring the injury he rolled across the floor, making for cover under the wide desk. Daviesberger snorted loudly, fired another shot which hit the desk, punching a dent in it, tiny pieces of wood spraying up. Then he stood stock still and followed Lew's frantically evasive movements.

Daviesberger ducked low and squeezed off another shot below the desk but Lew had anticipated that and scrambled out from behind it. The commander took only a second to grab the wrench he'd found earlier, then he had hefted it at his attacker with his uninjured left arm. It missed.

Mike's head had started to clear but more importantly, he found he could breathe again. He sucked in deeply and as he did so he suddenly remembered – his special wristcom; his newly *refurbished* wristcom. As he squinted upwards, he saw Lew scramble up from behind the desk but Daviesberger fired again, this time hitting his left leg. Through a mist of his own pain, Mike saw Lew go down amid shouts of agony.

'Good,' said Daviesberger, 'I'm starting to enjoy this. I'll carry on like this. It's better than just killing you outright. Blow bits out off you.'

But the man had evidently forgotten about Mike, down on the floor, who had dragged himself nearer the desk, still wheezing with pain and trying to suck air into his lungs. He was now within half a metre of Daviesberger, who continued to stand in front of Lew's desk. The man was almost leering, voyeuristically, at his target who writhed about on the floor the other side of the piece of furniture. The sounds of a renewed fire fight drifted in from outside and Mike gave up hope of some sort of immediate rescue from that direction. He was finding it a massive struggle to push aside his pain, yet he knew he had to help his friend. He'd have given anything not to be there, in that situation, at that moment, were it not for the fact that this guy was killing his friend! The scumbag would just carry on shooting bits off Lew, one piece at a time.

Daviesberger was lifting his gun again. Mike clawed at his wrist, trying to find his device, located it, and in a series of movements as smooth as though they had been rehearsed hundreds of times, he turned it toward Daviesberger and tapped it appropriately to aim and arm it. He brought it swiftly up next to Daviesbergers's right leg, planted near him. The man was so close to Mike he could smell the sourness of his sweat.

A fraction of a second, a final tap on the side of the device and a crackling blue arc, like a burst of mini lightning, connected fork-like with Daviesberger's leg. The man seemed to leap three feet in the air. Screaming with shock he lurched sideways and, as he lost consciousness, he fell heavily – right on top of Mike. It hurt.

CHAPTER SIXTEEN

LAST DAYS TO EXTINCTION

First Officer Statton made an urgent call to Ebazza and Tenak, who were on the med deck aboard The Monsoon. The ship had shut off the engine and the hard acceleration had, with relief, ended. In reality they needed more speed to escape the ion storm but that would have used up the ship's fuel too quickly and propelled the vessel out of the Ra system so fast they would have *taken years* to return to the system. And they'd have been beyond any way of getting back to the Solar System. They would be, literally, 'lost in space'.

'This is the kick-off, I think,' said the officer. 'Our sensors show Ra's photosphere has blown up like a balloon. The star's almost 30% bigger than just a few hours ago when those massive coronal things exploded from it. I'm sorry Admiral, Captain, but the initial radiation-front is now predicted to hit us within 58 minutes.'

'Have you shut down all non-essential processes, ops?' asked Ebazza, horror on her face.

'Yes, ma'am. The engine core's been damped to its lowest level and all crew and ship's hypercomps are primed for emergency protocols. All unnecessary energy use has been stopped and couplings redirected to the coils. The torus is locked down and all bulkheads secured, ma'am. Professor Jennison and his team have closed down the obs station on the torus. They're on their way down to the alpha two science deck, below your position. He's rerouted the minor functionary AIs to the science deck nexus. I'm sending the feeds from our instruments over to them. Lieutenant Jennison wants to know whether you would intend to "monitor events" on this bridge or on the science deck.'

Tenak asked Atrowska if she could manage without his further help.

'We'll manage for now, Admiral,' she said softly, 'but thanks for your help.' All the med bay staff and Tenak had, in any case, had to cease their work when the gee forces of the acceleration became overwhelming. Many evacs had been badly affected, especially the children. Now a new danger threatened.

'We'll try to help you as much as we can when we get the radiation burns coming in,' said Tenak. Atrowska just nodded, a dread but resolute look on her face.

Tenak turning to Ebazza, said, 'Ssanyu, will you accompany me to the science deck? Statton's doing a good job on the bridge.'

She gazed into his eyes, her own glistening, and said, in a voice evidently thick with emotion – felt, but not spoken, 'I'm sorry Admiral, but I think my place is on bridge One at this time.'

'I understand Ssanyu. I'm going to the science deck. I want to … try to understand what's going on, as much as poss.'

'I will be alert for any orders you give.'

'Thank you. I'll let you know if I have anything useful to contribute, Ssanyu, but I want to make sure we gather as much info as we can which'll be of use to others. And maybe try to work out why … all this, in my own head.'

There was a pregnant silence, which he broke when he said, with a bittersweet smile, 'All being well, I'll join you on the bridge afterwards. Good luck, Captain. I have every confidence in you.'

She saluted him and said, 'Good luck, Admiral.' And with that she was gone. Tenak watched her go and made his way toward the sci-deck.

****

Lieutenant Meridene crouched protectively over Lew, as the Commander lay, half sitting on the floor behind his desk, propped up against it. Blood was running from two severe wounds. Meridene was deftly applying a tourniquet to his upper right arm, staunching the flow from there. Mike sat on a chair, the other side of the room, still having difficulty respiring, his breaths short and rasping. He fretted about Lew. Again, the fate of a friend and esteemed colleague made him feel ill. Meridene had had some med training but she wasn't a full field medic. A male tek called Davies was the official medic but he was apparently fully occupied, tending to the wounded in the main marquee.

Lew was only semi-conscious, gasping with pain, as Meridene began to work next on his left leg, trying to stem the blood flow which oozed out over the floor and, seemingly, onto everything else. She was soaked with it as she strapped the wound with Navy issue battle dressings. Standing after a while and moving a few metres from Lew she touched her wristcom and said quietly, 'Ask Davies to *get in here now*, if he possibly can. I'm worried Lew has nicked his brachial artery and I think he's got a comminated fracture of the femur. He keeps passing out periodically, but I don't want to give him any meds till Davies has seen him.'

She returned to Lew, who was starting to regain consciousness and, valiantly, trying to sit more upright. As she got closer he reached out and touched her shoulder, weakly pulling her closer to him.

'Listen … Meri … I want you to take command now.' His voice was very faint.

'Sir, no,' she began, but he continued,

I'm out of it, for now anyway. Make Mike your second. You can work … with Mike, can't you?' he said, gritting his teeth through the pain. She nodded vigorously.

'Good … good,' he said, 'And make sure you listen to him about the science stuff. He's good with that … and … logistics. It's over to you, now, so …' He never finished his sentence as he passed out again. Meridene got on her com device again but Davies was suddenly there, hefting a large med kit.

'Let's get him onto a table out there … and … Evans, help us over here please,' he said to another crewman who had just walked in.

Mike sat still as a statue, trying to breathe properly. As though through a slight mist, he could see Meridene, Davies and Evans start to lift Lew and he tried to join them to help but found he couldn't do much lifting without extreme pain in his chest, so he just followed them, falteringly, out of the 'office', where they set Lew on a table in the main tent. Davies got to work. Meridene came over to Mike and after a quick examination of his chest said she reckoned he had severe bruising of the neck and chest, and possibly a cracked rib, but no long-term damage. She asked him if he was otherwise okay, and he nodded. He felt anything but okay, in fact, though the way he *felt* emotionally was not something she could do anything about. He realised how deeply shocked he was by the whole business but then resolved to put it to one side if he could. There was too much to be done here. Suddenly, however, he began to shake uncontrollably and there seemed to be nothing he could do to stop it. He didn't feel cold after all.

Around him the main marquee was an utter mess. There was debris everywhere as well as blood spatter in various places. Crewmembers were milling around. Several of the 'mutineers' and some of the loyal Navy crew had been wounded and were lying or sitting around. Mike was sickened by it, emotionally and physically. And he was starting to feel *angry* with the futility of it all. Very angry. He noticed that this seemed to help, somehow, with the shakes.

Apart from Lew, the crewmember closest to him was a man called Shapps, lying prone on a bench, with heavy bandaging on his head and an arm. They looked like bad wounds. Meridene told Mike that she and the 'loyal' crewmembers had used their sonics on heavy stun, at first. It was when Shapps had his hand blown off that they realized the mutineers were using their rifles on full, lethal, so most of them had switched to lethal setting too. She pointed toward the far end of the room where Mike could see the completely inert, completely prone body of a crewmember. A large piece of cloth had been draped over the head and upper body, the legs left exposed. Meridene said it was, La'Brady.

Mike gasped, feeling physically sick. That it should come to this, he wondered. And yet, somehow, he found it difficult to feel sorry for La'Brady. She had wanted him and Lew dead and would definitely have killed them if things had worked out differently. Even so, he couldn't bring himself to feel joy in her fate. It had all been such a waste.

He asked Meri what had happened to Daviesberger, and the others, and was told they'd been trussed up with 'glue-stape' and placed in the freshment area. Daviesberger had apparently been inconsolable and raving.

Meridene then walked to the centre of the area of devastation. Standing amidst the surrounding ruination she began to make an announcement, as loudly as she could, the other crewmembers looking up from their tasks.

'Okay, listen up guys. The Commander has asked me to take over here, with Mike as my second.'

Mike felt surprised.

She continued, 'What happened here is awful, but it's over. We can grieve later but right now we've got to start moving – and quickly – cos we've got way under two hours left before the main plasma blast – according to my wristcom. We've got to go fetch all those evacuees. You know, the ones we parked, for their own safety, over in the crew's mess, and get 'em out to the ship – soon as. All the gear we've organised, the retardant material and blast protection needs to go out there too. There's not enough of us to do it all – cos we're kind of depleted now – so get as many of them organised as you can. Now I know there're real scared by what just happened, even though they were kind of sheltered from most of it, but we need to make them understand that their survival depends on being organised and helping us – to help them. Okay? Any questions?'

All the crew still on their feet looked exhausted and among them there were several who'd been lightly wounded but, like she said, they had to get the OA people organised. Mike would play his full part. He just wished he didn't feel so much like shit but he felt lucky not to have been seriously injured.

**

He was extremely glad to get outside the marquee, though It was much darker now. There was still some light in the western sky. A raging westerly wind blew across the compound, howling as it rasped around them, roaring over the large marquees, making their tops quiver just a little. And it drove clouds of stinging grit and dust before it, making it difficult for the evacs and crew to gather and put the tarps, sacking material and survival gear under the Venturer. The ship itself had now been 'anchored' into the ground as deeply as was possible, given the hardness of the ground. Meri thought it would hold through high winds, but no-one could be sure.

Mike and Meridene had split the evacs into teams, each with a crewmember as its leader. Each team was assigned a set of tasks and team leaders co-ordinated with each-other by wristcom. There wasn't time to draw up more complex plans, but, Mike thought, things were actually going fairly smoothly now, despite of all that had happened before.

They would probably be sheltering under the ship for a long time, so, they moved the food and water supplies behind a protective 'barrier' being erected under the ship. The ship itself would also, they hoped, provide solid protection above them, though the area covered was, unfortunately, limited to the outline of the ship's fuselage and swept back wings. It was still substantial, and it was all they had.

They would also have to take care of toilet needs, unless they wanted to endure a long wait surrounded by human excrement and urine. A team of evacs had managed to uninstall several of the Navy's portable, ion driven, toilets, from the freshment tent and had placed them under the ship's tail. With the help of the tekkies, large pieces of marquee material had been affixed to the ship's underside, to provide some privacy but, if this wind persisted, Mike thought, there'd be precious little of that. And if the wind eventually dropped there'd be the smell, but nothing could be done about that.

Mike had tried to help as much as possible with the emplacement of food and water supplies, but his chest and throat injuries were dragging him down. He was offered analgesics but refused. No-one knew how long their limited drug supply would have to last, nor what they might yet be needed for.

As the evening darkened still further the ship was partly illuminated by setting up of small floodlights, simply to allow them to see what they were doing. They would be recharged by super-efficient solar panels by day, or so they hoped. The evacuee children were already making their way up the steps and into the ship. Considering most of them were very young, they were all very subdued, but then, it was hardly surprising. Many were still frightened by recent events. The poor things must be very confused about it all. And, he thought, grimly, who could say how many for them would survive the night, even inside the relative protection of the ship? And that was a terrible thought indeed. He dragged his mind away from it quickly.

Mike had helped to get Lew into a wheelchair from the med tent. There was no possibility of a magneto-chair down here, there being no metal substrate in the ground, just compacted soil. But the med bay chair was a typical navy affair. It had multiple wheels, was motor driven, and could be raised up and down on its undercarriage, so it could negotiate almost any terrain smoothly. Lew was slumped in it and very silent. He'd been given heavy sedation. As Mike glumly guided the chair toward the ship he heard a strange, loud, screeching sound from high above and realised he'd heard this before. It was a long time ago but he knew what it was. Even he was surprised at what he saw when he gazed upwards.

The sky was almost entirely filled with a flock of 'Raptoria-birds', as they were known. He and Tenak had seen some when they'd first arrived on Oceanus. With a three-metre-wide wingspan these things were half bird, half ancient lizard creature, which flew at high altitude, usually seen in groups of only two or three. But now he saw, with utter astonishment, that there must have been thousands of them up there. And they were all going in the same direction, heading out toward the sea, to the east. They were like a high, grey-black cloud. And despite their altitude, their calls were unmistakeable, almost like a mixture of screech and bark, but dimmed by their distance. It was decidedly unsettling, he thought and once again, the hair on his neck and back stood erect. It seemed clear to him that the animals, somehow, knew what was coming, even if most humans out there, in the cities and towns, didn't quite know – yet.

****

Tenak, Jennison, and several other science deck officers gazed up at the giant image generator dominating the room. It looked like an ordinary thick gel screen but there were data streams and graphics rolling down large cuboidal shaped holographic columns at the two vertical edges. These represented the masses of data coming from the minor AI functionaries, via the observation sensors. Then the hypercomp threw out a holo of the innermost zones of the Ra planetary system, showing hypercomp extrapolations – all based on all data so far received, including information from the Antarctica before it disappeared. Tenak looked grim, yet his face betrayed a sense of wonder and awe at the strange, powerful, never before witnessed, events, unfolding in the vast sweep of this stellar system.

A view of Ra appeared, an image blown up to about 3 metres across, floating in front of the screen. The brightness of the star had been toned down by the micro-AIs, and Ra's normally smooth sphere now looked decidedly bloated and spiky. The true colour of the star had changed from its recent blue-white, back to the original orange, but was now changing yet again, turning a deep red. And, rising far above the bristling surface were gigantic orange and yellow flares, erupting from multiple parts of its surface, mostly around groups of massive star spots that now littered its surface. They looked like gigantic, dark, pits and crevasses. The super flares from its surface were writhing up inside a brilliant white halo of superheated atmosphere which hung above the star's surface. The computer suddenly superimposed another pattern over the image.

As the crew continued to watch, the images began to change even more rapidly. A thin but bright blue latticework materialised out of black space far beyond the fiery perimeter of the star, beyond even the prominences. It looked like some sort of net of unimaginable size.

'Computer, remove the graphic, please,' said Jennison, in gruff tones.

'The image is not a graphic. It is a natural view of what is being observed,' said the hypercomp voice, a subsidiary of the main AI.

Jennison and Tenak looked at each-other with deep frowns, as the scientist said, 'What do you mean? Are you saying that the network, that thing is … actually out there? But what is it? What are we looking at?'

'I am unable to advise,' said the AI's voice, 'and that is because the ship's instruments cannot adequately analyse it. I have no infodata against which to compare the phenomenon.'

'What? Well then, speculate, for feg's sake. Speculate,' said Jennison, clearly rattled.

'Very well. The lattice is perfectly geometric in morphology …'

'Yes, yes, we can see that.'

'Now observations suggest it is extremely tenuous but highly luminescent. There are approximately seven thousand lattice edges. Each "edge" is approximately one and a half metres in diameter but three million kilometres in length. What sustains the "structure", if that is the correct term, is unknown. It is not certain how there are nodes at the vertices of the lattice but I would suggest that at their centres of the nodes are groups of the larger alien artefacts, numbering therefore approximately six million.'

'Alright, we can see it's … huge but for feg's sake …'

'Professor?' said Tenak, 'if I may? Computer, please give us your best estimate of what energy makes up the lattice?'

'The image you see is the fluorescing parts of a field; a field, similar but not the same as that of the electromagnetic or gravitational ones. The nature of this particular field is, however, unknown at this time. My best speculation is that it is most like the strong nuclear force.'

'Nonsense, fields don't form nets like that,' spat Jennison, 'and we all know that the strong force only operates at the nucleon level of atoms. It binds protons and neutrons together in atomic nuclei. There's never been any indication that it can cover a volume as large as a star! How could it?'

'You did ask me to speculate, sir,' was all the hypercomp could say, in response.

'Professor,' said Tenak, 'it only said it was *most like* the strong nuclear force. Not that it was the same. We have to consider the possibility. I wish Mike were here now. I miss his special insights. No disrespect to you, Lieutenant.' Tenak sighed heavily and Jennison, although he appeared as though he was going to say something, clearly thought better of it and remained silent. After a moment, he said, 'I'm sorry Admiral. I really am. But we're on our own. And neither Mike nor anyone else who has ever existed, can save us now.'

Tenak looked at him sideways. 'It's not over yet,' he said, with heavy emphasis.

****

In the evac' compound preparations for the coming proton storm, plasma bombardment, infrared flux and the likely fire tempests which would follow, continued feverishly. Before being sedated Lew had revealed that he'd already modified the air system inside the Venturer, so that it could be piped into the ship's cargo hold in its underbelly. He'd also cleared unneeded equipment out of there, earlier, so that more evacuees could be accommodated inside the hold, for protection. Anyone going in there would have to sit on the metal floor and it would be cramped and pitch black. Even so, it could provide useful shelter. Mike was in constant awe of what that guy had earlier achieved, in such a short time.

Equipment, cloth sacking, and other protective material had now been banked up on the ground all the way around the ship, and Meridene was calling for crew and (former) evacuees to gather inside the protective confines of the 'barricade'. It hadn't been possible to line up the Trojan Mark Three bots because their original programming could only be altered by way of Lew's command pad – and, unfortunately, that had been destroyed by sonic blasts from Daviesberger. The bots now stood, sentinel like, around the perimeter of the compound. They could still perform their protective function, all along the perimeter fence, but nothing else. Noone knew if they would be able to withstand the ion storm but unlikely they would not be affected to some degree.

Mike suddenly realised that there was a job he needed to do, so he commed Meridene, then trotted off toward a part of the compound beyond the main tent, at the same time as she and other crewmembers fetched the final group to be brought under the ship's protection. The last group to be brought out were none other than the surviving mutineers, their forearms stuck together by glue-stape; their legs having been freed, for now. Jenner had been brought out much earlier. She had been treated more leniently by being spared the restraints, because she had alerted the rest of the crew to the attack on Lew. But she was still under watch.

Meridene had decided to leave La'Brady's body in the crew's 'mess'. There had been no time to bury her and the Lieutenant had explained that there was too little space to afford it storage under the ship. She was also concerned the body would start to deteriorate and become a health hazard. Everyone knew it was a distasteful situation but unavoidable.

Even so, she had ordered that La'Brady be discretely and sensitively wrapped with tarpaulins, and she had personally pinned a label to the wrappings, stating she was, 'An unfortunate casualty – misconceived but a once valued crewmember of HSN, The Monsoon.' Daviesberger, however, remained incensed. He shouted protestations wildly, as he was led from the tent to the ship. He screamed that her body must be taken with them, and that she should be treated with more respect – because her remains might be blown away by the winds. Meridene, and the other crew ordered him to calm down and shut up, lest he upset the evacuees. If not, they would simply have him gagged.

Meanwhile, Mike was on his way to the Navy science station which Lew's crew had erected on first landing. The other side of the main marquee from the Venturer, the station consisted of large cabinet within which was a suitcase sized control box, surmounted by a set of small screens. From the cabinet sprouted a tall, heavy, stanchion supporting a robust 3-metre-wide, parasol like antenna. The antenna was a deep space sensor and fed data on Ra into the system's micro-computer. Such was the power of the device; it could monitor the position of The Monsoon and any other ships in the star system. The antenna swayed slightly in the strong winds but stayed mostly stable.

Mike quickly checked the data screens inside the cabinet and touched a couple of illuminated panels next to it, before asking it to link itself with his wristcom. That way, he'd be able to monitor the data from the sensor apparatus from a position of safety under the ship. With bated breath he read the data already gathered before returning to the protective shield of the ship. He didn't feel confident about the ability of the antenna to withstand the winds they were likely to experience later on. They'd have virtually no further updates if it collapsed.

When he got back to the ship, he thought he'd better check in with Meridene. 'I checked for info updates too,' he said, 'and it looks like The Monsoon is well on its way out of the system, but I'm still not sure it's far enough out to be safe from the plasma wave. Just too hard to say.'

'Nothing we can do about that now, 'sept hope,' she said.

There were loud grumblings from Daviesberger, who was sitting against a barrel shaped container a few metres away. He was surrounded by former evacuees, all sitting on the ground or standing just behind Meridene.

'What's he doing here?' asked Mike. 'Wouldn't the ship's cargo hold be the best place for him?'

'Didn't think of that,' said Meridene, 'but I'll keep it in mind.'

'He's just going to cause disruption,' retorted Mike, but continued with his report, wearing a sardonic half smile on his face, 'And the other fabulous news update from the station, is, and you'll like this one, we've got just 51 minutes' left before the initial radiation storm. After that, the main plasma storm, and the infra-red and the ultraviolet blast comes at around the three-hour mark. Lovely to know, ain't it?' He grimaced and Meridene just nodded, glumly.

'Nothing to do except wait,' she said after a few moments.

Suddenly Daviesberger seemed to be on top of them, shouting wildly. His forearms were still stuck securely together, and they were glued to the middle of his body, so he would be unable to use his combined arms as a kind of weapon. It didn't stop him trying to thrash about crazily, now, gesticulating with the fingers of his bound hands.

'Just let me go, you gimbos, you whippersnapes,' he shouted.

'Get back where you were, Daviesberger,' said Meridene, snarling.

'You should have buried my darling,' he continued, 'you know she'll be blown around when the marquees are hit. You been disrespectful to my baby. Those bird things'll feed on her body …'

'You're imagining things,' said Mike, with sour disdain.

'Just calm yourself, *mister*,' said Meridene, 'and remember your training. You're supposed to be a Navy officer. Start acting like one, even if you are a traitor.'

At that, Daviesberger glared but seemed to exert some self-control and sidled back to where he'd been sitting. Mike and Meridene gave each-other quizzical looks.

'I told you,' Mike said. Secretly, he wished they'd left the mascla next to his "darling". But then, he rebuked himself inwardly. That wouldn't be right either. Although, …

After a while he said to Meridene, 'I keep thinking about some of the people I got to know kind of well, when I was here before.'

'Where are they now?' she asked.

'That's the point. I don't know. Haven't been able to find out. Could be in real terrible danger, could be safe. I just don't know.' He felt himself slipping into a kind of despair as he spoke.

'Never thought a beautiful place like this could end like this, so quickly,' he continued. 'I've learned to love this planet – more than Earth, really. Place used to scare me. Now, I just … kind of miss it, already. Do you know what I mean?'

'Yep, think I do,' she said. 'We all knew this was coming but … this fast? No-one could have ….'

She couldn't continue. It was Daviesberger, again. He'd stood and was moving toward them, moaning and shouting.

'I heard what you fegs were saying,' he moaned, 'and I say this damn planet is like a hump-jammer's arse. And its people too.' He pushed his way between some of the locals, all dwarfed by him, but as he got closer, Mike, who had been standing with his back to him, his face a picture of anger and distaste, turned suddenly and swung his right forearm, with full force, across Daviesberger's chest and neck. Mike was surprised at himself for the vehemence and force he used, as Daviesberger went down like a nine-pin. Mike leered at the man who sat heavily on the ground. Then the pain in his arm hit Mike but he desperately tried to cover it up. Daviesberger wheezed, trying to claw at his throat and chest.

There were cheers from some of those nearby, but at that moment Mike just wanted to dispose of this hateful man. And it was not like him to hate anybody. He suddenly found himself striding toward Daviesberger, who was sucking in air. He growled at him, 'How would you like some more of this,' he said, pointing to his wristcom and holding his arm out toward Daviesberger, 'cos I can give you more if you want it.' The pilot just sat mutely, staring up at Mike with bulging, fearful, eyes.

'No, didn't think you did,' Mike said, 'but maybe we should just see what happens if I set it off again.'

There were sudden looks of anxiety in the faces of several migrants who stood nearby.

'Mike! Enough!' said Meridene. 'You're starting to frighten people. This isn't helping.'

Mike suddenly seemed to come to. He looked around at gawping faces and back at Meridene and said, 'Okay, Meri, it's okay, I'm ... sorry.' He hadn't meant to go that far but he'd had enough of this man's nonsense and what he'd done to the person who he, next to Tenak, held in the greatest regard. He'd already been told it was possible Lew would never recover properly if several months passed before the fleet arrived. In the meantime, they'd all have to scrabble around like Prithvian worm rats, just to survive on this world. How could Lew get through that? So, yes, he realised, he had meant to go that far.

He looked sorrowfully at the evacuees around him and felt he had to get away from this place. But where could he go?

Meridene called to him as he began to sidle away to the other side of the ship's underbelly. She looked distressed and, turning her attention back to Daviesberger, she saw that he had recovered his wind, for there he sat, swearing again with a gravel raw voice, spitting vehemence at her and Mike and everyone else.

'Okay, my friend,' she said, in Daviesberger's direction, 'cos you can't say I didn't warn you.'

And with that she marched over to a storage barrel, fetched out a reel of heavy insulation tape, tore off a wide strip and returned to Daviesberger. Enlisting a couple of crewmates to hold the man down and, despite his efforts to avoid his fate, she roughly covered his mouth with the tape. 'Should have done that before,' she said, with satisfaction, to more cheers from those around her. They also taped his legs together – very tightly. 'We'll set you loose when you have proved to me you can really be trusted. I'm guessing that might be a long time. Think about it. Kind of hard,' she said.

*

Things had now gone quiet under the ship's belly. The floodlighting had been switched off and though some of the vessel's navigation lights remained on below the ship, for slight illumination. They provided a dim blue glow only, toned down to save energy. A sort of hushed, almost ethereal, cloak of darkness had descended on all those sheltering under the Venturer.

Mike sat on the other side of the ship from Daviesberger, near the barricade. Most of the large group of evacuees around him were dozing fitfully, lying on pieces of tarpaulin; families lying almost on top of each-other, mainly for a sense of security and warmth of human contact, for it was not particularly cold. They had been though a lot, Mike thought. One or two crewmembers sat nearby, propped up by the ship's undercarriage struts and wheels, just a few metres away. Few people spoke. Suddenly he sensed someone approaching in the darkness. Meridene sat next to him.

'You okay, Mike?' she said quietly. He struggled to make out her features in the dark.

'Yeah,' he said. 'Look, I'm sorry … about what happened back there. I don't know what came over me.'

'No need,' she said. 'You just … Well, you just snapped. It's not surprising in the circumstances. Don't think about it anymore.'

'I really wanted to kill him you know.'

'Yeah, I understand. Good job you didn't, cos I'd have had to arrest you for murder.' She chuckled very lightly and continued, 'but there'd be no point in me doing that, would there? No-one back home would know about what happened – not anymore. What would it matter now?'

'I guess it would, though,' said Mike, 'cos that's what Lew was saying. *We'd* know. The point is – what we do here, now, is important – even if no-one ever finds a trace of us.'

'Aren't we the philosopher king tonight?' she said, smiling benignly at him, though he couldn't see it. They were silent for a while, then she broke it by saying, 'Sorry, Mike, I don't mean to take the wicky-wip. Besides, you're right. Way on right. So was Lew. Do you reckon he really did plant a micro-recording block somewhere out here?'

Mike shook his head. 'Nah, I think he was playing for their weak spot. Found it too. He had the measure of Daviesberger, that's for sure. How is our pleasant friend, by the way?'

'Oh, I taped his foul mouth over.'

Mike managed a half-smile and said, 'That'll have to come off eventually, too.'

'Yeah,' she sighed, 'I know. But let him stew a while. By the way, I'm glad to have got to know you, Mike. At least, I think I'm getting to know you.'

'Likewise,' was all he said.

'I'm sorry to tell you this,' she replied, 'but I didn't much like you on board ship.'

He sighed and said, 'A common enough feeling, I guess.'

'Oh, not with most people. Most seem to like you well enough, especially *female* crew.'

Silence from Mike.

'But things change, don't they?' she said wistfully, 'and people can change.'

Mike wasn't sure which way this conversation was going.

'I'm sorry to mention this too, Mike,' she continued, 'but I heard about what happened on this planet, … back last year, and all that. Real archismo, yeah?'

Archismo, he thought; an old-fashioned word, probably in vogue when Meridene was quite a lot younger. It meant 'extremely sad; traumatic, very unfortunate'.

'Yeah,' he said, 'real archismo. Like this whole thing, I guess.'

She nodded and was silent for a while.

At least she respects my wish not to talk about *her*, he mused. Eleri, that was her name. He knew he mustn't be afraid to name her. He mustn't try to blot out the recent past. It wouldn't do any good. He liked Meri but he just didn't feel he wanted to, 'open out' to this older femna, or anyone else, about these things. Not right now. Though he was sure she was trying to get him to do that. He mused that some would definitely not have appreciated her even referring to the tragedy of Eleri, but he had grown beyond that, he felt. Yet, further than that he knew he would not play ball. Maybe, he might, if they survived this night. And as for anything else, he didn't feel attracted to Meridene in *that way*. It was also much too soon after … Eleri. He speculated that it might always have been so, if the current crisis did not threaten to blot out all their lives. After all, when you've had the best, he thought, then nothing else will do. And no point in being concerned about it now. It might all be over soon enough. If so, would he be joining Eleri, then? Nah, he couldn't honestly say he believed that. Wouldn't it be good, though? Too good for words to convey. Such concepts could never be expressed in terms of mere words, he thought.

Eventually, Meridene spoke again, 'Listen, Mike …if you thought I was prying just now, I'm sorry. I wasn't. It's just that this … well, this situation makes you think about things … all the things that matter, doesn't it?'

'Yeah. Don't worry about it.'

He suddenly realised that he especially liked this femna, purely as a friend, now. And, in the situation they found themselves in, he felt pleased that he had found another genuine friend amongst the crew.

'What … what about you, Meri? Who, … do you leave behind?'

'Oh, I've got three husbands back home. I'm in the process of unbonding with one of 'em but the other two are good enough. I think about them and about my sister. She's on Mars. Haven't seen any of them for some while. No children though, thank the Maker.'

'I guess the realities of the job make it kind of difficult?'

'Yep. Besides, they'd be totally bereft of a mother soon, wouldn't they?'

'You don't know that.'

'Really? But you don't believe we're going to get through this in one piece, do you?'

'I … yeah, I'll say it … *I hope* you're wrong. But the odds are stacked against, that's for sure.'

'But then, I guess, you're right. We should dare to hope.' She continued after a while, 'so, do you have family back home?'

'My mother and my brother, on Earth. Saw them just before we came back out here. My mother isn't going to be helped when … if my pay transfers stop. And I promised my brother I'd try to … help him, when I got back. It's funny, isn't it? Neither of them wanted me to come back out here.'

A silence again; a poignant space, into which she inserted, 'By the way, I heard what you did up there – on the ship. If it means anything to you, I think you were absolutely right – like Admiral Tenak and Ebazza, and the others too. But it was you. You initiated it.'

'Actually, it was Tenak. But, yes, that means something to me, and I appreciate you saying it. Not that it really achieved anything in the end. Guess we were just wrong about those alien things. They're not benign.'

'Of course it achieved something, Mike. If the ship had fired on that alien world, or whatever it was, The Monsoon probably would've been blasted or vaporised, or made to disappear, or whatever those things do. The fact that it wasn't means the Admiral was at least able to get some of the people off this world in time.'

'If they get the ship far enough away from the star.'

'If anyone can do it, the Admiral can. You know that. And we can hope for that too, can't we? There's that word again. I like the Admiral, Mike. And I know you do.'

Mike couldn't see her face properly, but Meridene's eyes had begun to dribble silent tears.

Mike stared up into the blackness of space, his gaze trying to peer far beyond the confines of the atmosphere. He tried not to think too hard about the evenings he'd spent doing precisely that – with Eleri.

Eventually, he said, very quietly, 'I guess we're just flotsam, floating in a vast, uncaring, universe. How about that for being profound?' He chuckled mirthlessly. The cloaking night seemed to swallow up the sound.

Recovering herself, she looked up too and said, breathily, 'More like puppets, Mike. The puppet masters are out there – and they don't give a damn about us.'

****

Admiral Tenak fussed with the controls of an old-fashioned instrument; a strangely out of place device which was a sort of left-over, mostly redundant, part of the science deck equipment. The device was a large box-like visor which jutted from a control panel. Tenak gazed into the instrument, his face almost completely concealed by the deep view-box.

'I'm not sure why you think you'll get anything useful in that thing, Admiral,' said Jennison.

'I believe I told you, Lieutenant. I'm trying to detect some sign of the Antarctica's optical – or radio signal. I'm trying small sections of sky at a time. Yes, I'm aware this scope is outmoded but with the power ratings subdued I didn't want to ask the minor AI to divide its energies from its main tasks. Besides, I wanted something to do. This waiting is deadly.'

'I'm sorry sir. I know. And you're right. The waiting is getting me down too. It's the *not knowing*, that's worst. Have you … actually found anything?'

Tenak turned from the instrument and shook his head grimly.

The minor AI suddenly spoke, and what it said made Jennison blanche. Tenak's eyebrows rose too, as he listened.

'Please take note. The sensors have detected a sudden, more radical, change,' it said, 'which involves the iridescent field lines. The visual data is being fed through to you now. You should know that my sensors have been blocked from further analysis, by what I assume is the lattice field.'

As they watched the lattice-like pattern, shown earlier to be surrounding the star, seemed to move outwards, expanding – but fading in brilliance as it did so.

'It's becoming more rarefied,' said Jennison, 'and its speed of expansion must be … incredible.'

As the field virtually disappeared the surface of the star itself seemed to boil upwards, the AI toning down the whole screen in the face of the brilliant upwelling.

'It looks like something *is* happening now, or it did some minutes ago. I wish I hadn't said anything,' announced Tenak.

Jennison sat on one of the 'casual' seats fixed to the deck behind him and buried his head in his hands. Tenak looked at him, his brow furrowed with concern, as the minor AI said, 'It is not possible to determine precisely what is happening, but the star's surface appears to have *stratified.* That is to say, the upper 143,000 kilometres, plus or minus 600 kilometres, has blown away from the rest of the surface. I would advise that the field blocked my ability to detect the precise time the upwelling of the surface began. Now the field has dissipated I estimate that it began approximately 247 minutes ago.'

'You mean we haven't been looking at a *real time* view of the upwelling?' asked Tenak.

'Correct,' said the minor AI, and continued, 'And I am now able to warn you that the calculations reveal that the initial shock wave will hit this ship … in approximately 6.3 minutes. The main plasma field will reach it approximately 46 minutes later.'

'Well, I guess this really is the aliens' end game,' said Tenak, facing Jennison, who appeared not to be listening. He was bent over on his chair; his face still buried in his hands.

'I don't want to know,' said Jennison, his voice sounding muffled.

'Hold fast there, Professor? Orben? Are you alright?' said Tenak, but then turned and said to the hypercomp, 'Please launch our last datapod, after recording to its memory all available data on the star. Ensure the pod leaves the ship within 6 minutes and that it initiates maximum fusion power as soon as practically possible.'

'Acknowledged,' said the AI.

'At least we can do that,' Tenak said to Jennison, 'and its velocity will be added to our own, so it stands a better chance of making it back to the Solar System. I know the data isn't as fine-tuned as the Antarctica's would have been, but it'll give them something to go on back home. Lieutenant? Did you hear me?' Tenak spoke softly, framing the question in as gentle a tone as he could.

There was no response from Jennison. Tenak glanced behind him. The two other science deck operatives present had taken to their so-called 'shock seats'; two of the special chairs which were fitted on all decks, especially the two bridges. The seats were reinforced and fitted with padded, grip strip harnesses, designed for 'rough flight situations.' Tenak directed Jennison to another shock seat and he moved to take the one on its left. After sitting again, the Professor immediately bent forward once more, as far as the seat's webbing would allow him, and started to make a kind of moaning sound.

Tenak fastened Jennison's wrists onto the shock seat's arm rests then sat on his own seat and secured his own left wrist. He hesitated for a few moments, but then gently placed his right hand on the back of the Professor's shoulders and smoothed it as though stroking a baby suffering with colic. Nothing was said. Silence filled the deck.

****

Most people were now asleep below the Venturer. Mike was surprised at how cool it had become, the prevailing, warm winds having dropped some while ago. He'd thrown on his dust and dirt covered uniform, a warmer Navy topcoat, equally soiled, and tried to get some rest. It would not come. He felt uncomfortable throughout his body. It was unpleasantly reminiscent of some of the attacks he'd had after the grotachalik incident. Fortunately, this was not as bad. Not by a 'ten-metre stick'. He thought the microscopic particles which had caused his malaise back then, had been expunged, but he also knew the medics had not been able to guarantee this. Nothing was ever that simple.

Many of the people around him, only recently known as, 'evacuees' lay, sat, or were slumped, in close knots, and he could hear various coughs, grumblings, mutterings and other noises coming from them. Odour drifted over from some sort of stew that some of them had been cooking, a few metres away. At first, they had used battery operated cooking cans from the Navy's stores but then changed to a sort of cauldron they'd cobbled together, under which they'd lit a small, real, fire, all under the cover of the Venturer. The smell reminded him of something from the past, but he wasn't sure what it was. In any case, he wasn't hungry. The aroma, mixed with other, much less savoury smells, emanating from the toilets, way back toward the stern of the ship, drifted over to him, despite the presence of the curtain-screen back there. Nice, he thought, with irony.

It was sometime later, when he had finally started to drift off to sleep, that Meridene turned up again. He was not pleased but had to remember that Lew had given him some responsibility here. He'd shirked responsibility some time ago, on this planet and it had not gone well afterward.

'You okay, Mike?' she asked, as he raised his head, turtle like, from beneath the overcoat.

'What's that? Yeah, I suppose,' he said. 'What's the prob?'

'Just done the rounds. The lone crewman we've got on the ship says the children are very restive. Getting difficult to control, even with the ten or twelve parents we've got in there with 'em. Says the washment rooms can't be kept clean either.'

'Not surprising,' said Mike. 'What time is it?'

'Nearly two hundred hours. Say, you don't look too good.'

Now, how could she know that, he wondered?

'What … what can we do about it?' he asked, struggling to see her through the darkness and his sore eyes.

'Suppose not. Have you eaten anything?' she said.

'No. Don't feel hungry. What? Did you say, two hundred hours?' Mike felt his mind spark into life and his heart started thumping. This was definitely not right. He dragged his arm from below the coat and gazed at his wristcom, illuminated with a short tap.

'I don't get this,' he said, 'cos the updates from the sci-station show no change. Nothing big. Just a slight increase in background radiation levels. What the feg is going on?'

'Shit, you're right!' she exclaimed. 'The proton storm should've hit by now.'

'Either my com' isn't working properly … or…'

'Or the science station isn't.'

'No, damnatious!' he said, as he realised what must have happened. He wondered how he could have let this pass by.

'I forgot to recharge my wristcom at the science station,' he said, like it was an admission of religious heresy. 'Dammy. It would only have taken about 4 minutes. When I discharged it the hyper-battery must have run down. Feg me. It did that before.'

'It's okay, it's okay,' she said, with a consoling tone. 'If I place my wristcom on top of yours we can drain some of my power into yours, like normal.'

'No. No. It won't work with this type of wristcom, Meri. There's only one thing I can do. I'll have to go over to the station and check the reading directly. I can recharge my device as well.'

She sounded fearful as she said, 'Mike, if you leave the cover of the ship you won't have the protection of its field. And I'm sorry if you don't like me saying it, but I don't think you're really up to going over there right now. I reckon you're stressed or something.'

'What else do you suggest?'

'I could go instead.'

'Are you qualified?'

'Yeah, I'm qualified.'

'To Level 12, astrophysics?'

'Of course not. My background's in acoustic applications.'

'There you are. I'm sorry, but I have to go.' Mike began to rise but almost fell back. He suddenly felt dizzy.

'Just look at you. You won't make it on your own. Let me go with you, at least.'

'What's the point in that?' he said, tiring of the conversation, 'cos then you'll be exposed too.'

'We can help each-other. I don't reckon you can get over there and back quickly enough if the proton storm hits.'

'You'd be surprised. Didn't you know I was given "theta strips" in both legs – after the attack on the ship? Remember?'

'No, I didn't know. Your medical procedures aren't exactly general knowledge. Besides it's not your legs in trouble right now. Seems it's your whole system, or whatever. So, I'm coming with you. Besides, there's something you're forgetting.'

'What's that?'

'I'm in charge.'

'Oh yeah.'

Mike finally demurred and after he had shaken himself fully awake and made a gritted teeth effort to press his general ill feelings aside the two of them launched themselves out from below the wing of the Venturer. Clambering over the protective barricade of sacking, storage barrels, furniture, and odd and ends, they ran out into the depths of the purple darkness. Mike had some difficulty negotiating the barricade but picked up speed after that, shooting off ahead of Meridene. Take it easy, he thought. It's not a race. But she was right about his condition. He still felt disorientated and dizzy, but he also felt his legs remained strong – at the moment.

'You weren't kidding about your legs,' she shouted after him, but the next second Mike fell forward, heavily. She caught up with him and as she helped him up, he said, 'You weren't kidding either, were you.' She smiled amenably and the two of them continued, Mike shambling along, nursing a limp after hitting his right knee on a stony patch of ground. She asked her wristcom to provide illumination and held it in front of them, for as they went further from the ship the darkness deepened. There were no more working lights out here.

They reached the science station, about 300 metres from the ship, Mike opened the cabinet and tapped the control interface, bringing its curved screens into action. As he worked the machine several sets of figures and graphs leapt into existence, seemingly hanging in the air, just a few centimetres above the screens. Mike couldn't believe what he saw in the data stream.

'This ...,' he said, 'this shows the same as my wristcom. The same. How the feg ...?'

'Either the station's malfunctioning or ... or what?' said Meridene.

'Or the original data predicted the wrong timings. I'll ask it to do a self-diagnostic.'

After a few seconds he said, 'No, nothing wrong. Just shows a slightly elevated level of background radiation way up in the ionosphere. Real high.'

Meridene glanced around nervously, as though she half expected to see something awful looming out of the gloom which enveloped their tiny pool of light.

'If the data's wrong,' she said, 'it means the storm could break over us at any second.'

'No,' said Mike, almost absently, as he continued to scrutinise the data displays, 'there'd be ... there'd be some warning. The sky would fluoresce. It's the cascades of fundamental particles that'd be dangerous. You know, as the protons hit the air molecules?'

Mike shut down the screen and was about to move off when Meridene reminded him about his wristcom. He quickly slotted the device into a notch on the station and it hummed. It was then that he felt extremely dizzy and almost slumped against the station. His companion looked worried.

'It's a bit like … the old problem I had from the grotachalik … but …,' he said.

She looked puzzled.

'But it's not the same,' he added. 'Don't know about that either? No. Why would you?'

She shook her head.

'Doesn't matter. Not one bit,' he said – and the next moment, without warning, all around, the visible horizon of Oceanus lit up brilliantly. Soon, the whole sky started to glow with an electric blue light, spreading up from the horizon toward the zenith.

Meridene grabbed Mike's wristcom and his coat and started to yank him backwards, saying, 'If that's the sign you were talking about, we'd better get going – now!'

'No, I don't think it is. It's not what I would expect.'

'Well, *mister level 12 astrophysics*, I say we get going. Come on.'

The two of them hi-tailed it back toward the ship, Mike's legs struggling to keep the rest of him going, even as his internal dizziness tried to sabotage the effort. Meridene kept one hand on his shoulder and pulled him along until they made it back below the wings. Climbing again over the barricade, Mike slumped breathlessly. As he gradually recovered he showed Meri the readout on his device. The device stuck to its story that no significant change in radiation levels had come, yet there was something else being detected by the science station. It had found something new, far out in space, nowhere near the planet.

Mike felt confused but, as he, Meri, and everyone near the Venturer's wing edges and fuselage, peered out at thin sliver of sky they could see, they had another surprise. The sky gradually turned from its electric blue to a deep and increasingly angry looking orange-red, like cosmic flame. It was very reminiscent of a Ra sunset, except that it was the middle of the night. The whole compound around them became bright with the ruddy glow and the various structures in the area began to cast deep shadows.

Mike had a terrible sinking feeling in his chest and his gut, which had nothing to do with his malady. With a gnawing ache of sadness, he reasoned that this was the first sign of a massive firestorm starting on the opposite side of the planet – the daytime side. It must be spreading around this world, he thought, with dread. The whole planet could soon be engulfed. He wondered if he should say something to Meri, but, by the looks of things, she'd already worked it out for herself. Her face took on a grim and almost haggard appearance. Mike's blood seemed to turn to ice.

'Guess this is it,' said Meri.

CHAPTER SEVENTEEN

DESPERATE MEASURES

The heavy, gloomy, atmosphere on The Monsoon's science deck was suddenly punctuated by an unwelcome audio warning from the minor AI, saying, quite unemotionally, 'Two standard minutes to contact with initial wave front.'

Tenak, bleak faced, looked up. Jennison groaned and started to raise his head but as he did so the giant gel screen at the front of the deck seemed to explode into brilliance. Previously, the 'real view' image of Ra had been sitting there, reduced to a tiny, angry red ball in the centre of the screen; the rest of the image filled with the velvet blackness of space. Now, the whole screen lit with an electric blue phosphorescence, and mixed with it were dancing filaments of purple-white light, like writhing, living tendrils emanating from the glaring star, seemingly reaching out toward them.

'Professor,' said Tenak loudly, 'so now what's …?'

'That … shouldn't be happening,' grunted Jennison, his face a ragged mask of horror.

Ebazza's voice came crackling over the intercom,

'Admiral? Professor? I'm assuming you're seeing the same as us? What's going on now?'

'Not certain yet,' said Tenak briskly, 'and the AI doesn't seem sure either. It's not said anything.' Then he said loudly, 'AI? What are we …?'

Before he could finish the screen began to change again. The blue radiance still suffused the outer edges of the view, but the image of Ra, at the centre, had changed again. The orange-white orb now seemed to be throwing off a massive, diffuse, halo of ruby red brilliance.

'That's more like what we expected, isn't it?' said Tenak, 'The atmosphere of the thing is exploding – as we knew it would.'

The AI finally spoke, 'I wish to point out that Ra's atmosphere is not exploding.'

'What? So what are we seeing?' shouted an exasperated Jennison.

'Unable to explain at this time,' was the machine's only response.

'It's lost it,' said Jennison, 'it's lost its logic modules. AI madness. I knew it could happen at some point.' He buried his head in his hands again.

'No,' said Tenak, in awed tones. 'I'm not really surprised at the AI's response. I don't think this is anything any human has seen before – or has theorized about. Look again. Look, Professor. The red wave is spreading from the star too fast. Faster than a proton wave. That's obvious just from this optical image. And ... the data feed is starting to roll in. Look.'

As volumes of data, in brilliant yellow-white symbols, began to run down the screen's left and right edges the minor AI spoke again,' The expected protonic wave has not hit the ship – or Oceanus. The light wave you are seeing would have been issued 18.4 standard minutes ago. This is the time it is now taking light from Ra to reach us ...'

'Yes, yes,' said an impatient Jennison, 'we know about the speed of light – but what is your analysis of it?'

The machine continued, 'You are observing simply the standard optical wavelength of light in the orange-red end of the spectrum. But the radiation also contains an exceptionally large component of ultraviolet ...'

As the machine spoke the screen view changed to show the ultraviolet element of the emanations, with graphics indicating the intensity of the emissions.

'That's a prodigious amount of UV,' said Tenak.

The AI continued its peroration, 'And there is an excessive neutrino flux, on the order of ten to the one hundredth power per cubic millitrem.'

To accompany this comment the screen changed to illustrate the otherwise invisible neutrino flux, 'drawn' in by the computer, showing it as a brilliant yellow-white wash of colour, which swept across the screen, completely filling it for several moments. Data, now glowing in bright red, continued to provide an info-commentary along the borders of the image.

There was an ominous silence on the science deck. None of the four crewmembers present seemed to know what to say.

Eventually, the Professor said, 'Is that it? Is that all? Just optical light, ultra-V blast and a fegging big flux of neutrinos? What … what happened to the proton storm? The plasma flux? The shock waves? What …?'

'None of those phenomena have been detected yet,' said the AI, 'but I will advise if any are found.'

'What the shit …' said Jennison, incandescent, but Tenak called out,

'Blue Two, what probability do you assign to the chance of us – or Oceanus – being hit by a proton or plasma wave, within the next, say, 48 standard hours?'

'I cannot make reliable predictions, due to the uniqueness of the current situation – but I suspect the probability is less than … one in ten point four to the minus ninth power, with an error of less than four point eight to the second power, or possibly four point …'

'Alright,' said Tenak, 'I think we get the picture.'

'But what is the basis of your calculation?' said Jennison, finally appearing to recover his composure.

'The calculation is based on the stabilising pattern of Ra's photosphere and my detection … wait … please note results currently being received at this time … show relative stability of the Karabrandon waves – at least to a depth of 245,000 kilometres inside the star.'

'Stabilisation?' exclaimed Jennison.

Tenak's jaw dropped.

'My suite of sensors is beginning to detect stabilisation in all the major components which constituted the extreme variability initially detected by humans in this star, approximately 4.7 standard years ago, in the Home System time frame. I would remind you that these required many thousands of observations of Ra and of approximately sixteen hundred other, similar, stars, in various stages of their development, over the intervening time period, again, in Home System time frames. This implies that ...'

'Yes, I know what you're implying,' said Jennison.

'What exactly does this all mean, Professor?' asked Tenak, then added after a moment, 'but wait. Surely, it's not what I think you're thinking, is it?'

'I haven't a clue what you're thinking, Admiral, said Jennison, 'but to my mind it means that the natural variability that Ra must have exhibited for – what, probably over three billion years has been ... well, what, ... expunged? The instability is no more, sir – if we can really believe all this.'

As if to underline the outrageousness of Jennison's conclusion, the AI then announced, 'I have now been able to carry out further analysis of the blue, semi-regular polyhedron shaped force wave which was detected more than 3 standard hours ago. My finding is based on the fact that within the force was a weak but significant gravity wave anomaly. The gravity wave pattern shows it emanated from the nodes of the field. This pattern mirrors the type which was observed when the "foreign object", you have called, "alien", entered its distant and wide orbit of Ra, shortly after this ship arrived in this system.'

The giant screen then showed two separate images. On its left side was the pattern of gravity waves detected when the object, now believed to be the alien ship, first appeared, many months previously. The right half showed the gravity wave pattern of the luminous blue lattice which had surrounded Ra, the AI superimposing the pattern as a set of red concentric rings centred at the multiple nodes. The left side was then moved over the image on the right side. It was an impressive sight, even if it was created by the computer, designed to illustrate what was otherwise invisible to human eyes. The patterns were an almost exact match!

'But we can surely conclude now, can't we,' said Tenak, 'that the aliens must have – *done* something to the star to change the upwelling Karabrandon waves? So, where do the gravity waves fit into the picture?'

Jennison was quiet.

The AI said, 'Although posed as an enquiry my estimation is that your implicit conclusion is correct, that the significance of these patterns may be that their appearance is linked in some way to the means the *aliens*, as you have called them, employ to travel through space.'

'So, that suggests,' said Jennison finally, 'that the aliens have somehow projected the Karabrandon waves into … what? Into what, for feg's sake?'

The AI rejoined with, 'I am unsure as to who "feg" is, so I cannot comment on their sake. In any case, I am unable to make any plausible suggestions as to what has happened to the waves or where they have gone. I am merely making comparisons and drawing – largely speculative conclusions.'

'So, the waves have disappeared,' said Tenak, with huge relief evident in his voice, 'but do we conclude that the radiation from the star was also similarly "conveyed" away – somewhere?'

'That conclusion would also seem valid,' said the AI.

Tenak's wristcom buzzed against his skin and he recognised it as a signal from Captain Ebazza. He said to the unit, 'Patch it through to the screen here.'

Ebazza's face then graced the screen, appearing gigantic in the shadowed spaces of the science deck. She was wearing a smile – cautious to be sure – but a smile, nonetheless.

'Admiral, Professor. Praise be. It seems we may be out of the "horror zone" and we have been fed the hypercomp's conclusions. It seems God was kind to us this time, Admiral.'

'You may be right, Captain,' replied Tenak, 'but we might not be free of all the troubles yet. AI, please tell us whether you are able to detect any of the alien artefacts, orbiting Ra, or anywhere else in the observable Ra system?'

About thirty seconds later the AI spoke once more, 'I can detect no signs of any alien artefacts – at least as they were seen before. All artefacts previously observed have vanished. I repeat, all artefacts, as previously observed, have vanished.'

'That doesn't mean there are no alien *things* in this system at all, Admiral,' said Ebazza, verbalising some of the scepticism evident in her demeanour, 'so I agree with you that we must exercise caution.'

'Yes,' said Tenak, 'but I have a feeling we're … well, I think we're going to be okay now. If we were going to be wiped out it would have happened by now. By the way, Captain, how are the evacuees coping?'

'Not sure,' said Ebazza, 'as we've been a bit busy. I know a number are still in the med bay but I will call in reports from all stations now. I have not heard any negative messages.'

'Good. Please let me know of any serious new problems. There's something else. Have you tried contacting Lew and Mike on Oceanus?'

'We have, Admiral, but the particle fluxes or whatever they are, *out there,* seem to have prevented comms with the surface. We'll try again now, sir.'

'Very well,' said the Admiral, 'carry on. I would like to speak to them as soon as possible.'

'Of course, sir,' said Ebazza.

'By the way – congratulations, Captain.'

'Congratulations to you, Admiral,' said Ebazza's now smiling image as it faded out.

Tenak turned and looked at Jennison. The scientist was standing open mouthed, utterly dumbfounded but also apparently, annoyed. He stared at Tenak and said, 'So that's it? Congratulations – sir?'

'What is it?' said a puzzled looking Tenak, his eyes narrowing. 'Just speak your mind, Lieutenant.'

'It's not you, sir…sorry about my …. It's just that I don't get it. We went through all that … hassle. The people on the planet went through all that suffering and the problem just … vanishes? The threat just goes away?'

Tenak pondered for a moment, then replied,

'Yes, that's my ardent hope, Jennison, and we have good reasons to believe it, don't we? I know everyone has been through a lot of aggravation. Suffering, just as you say. Do you think I don't know that?' Tenak' sounded brusque but he had the hint of a smile on his face, a continuing smile of relief. He resumed, 'Listen, Orben. You talk almost as though you're disappointed – that we weren't all *extinguished* by that – phenomenon out there. Almost disappointment that we're all safe; that the horror we all believed was coming, seems to be over. Try being thankful, Orben. Truly, fantastically, thankful. If it really is all over, then we and the Oceanus people have so much to be grateful for. The same goes for all of humanity. Everyone. And that *really is* a big deal – isn't it?'

'Yes … of course I'm not disappointed. You're right, Admiral. But … is this really the end, or just the beginning?'

****

Mike Tanniss continued to study his wristcom's readouts, re-transmitted from the sci-station. He still couldn't understand what was going on, despite the fact that dawn was finally arriving – and still nothing disastrous had happened. Nothing! The utterly weird electric orange- red sky had given way to washes of mauves and purples which had flooded the heavens from horizon to horizon. That had been over three hours earlier, since when a brilliant but steady, dusky, violet haze had settled over the sky. It was only now being pushed slowly away by the phosphorescent oranges and golds of the Oceanus dawn – a fairly normal dawn on this world, albeit brighter, and more intensely hued than usual.

After everyone had spent an uncomfortable night under the confines of the Venturer neither Mike nor Meridene had been able to stop the would-be evacuees from wandering out from the protection of the ship, stretching their legs and drawing deep breaths of fresh air. They had first gone out in ones and twos, then in larger groups. Neither Mike nor any Navy personnel had been able to persuade them that the danger had not necessarily passed. But then, thought Mike, neither could they explain why the expected disaster had sort of just – gone away; vanished in the night just passed, with nothing more serious than the strong winds of the previous evening and the later, brightly coloured, skies.

Attempts to persuade the evacuees of the possibility that either the original data from The Monsoon was faulty, or that the science station was somehow not giving a true picture, fell on deaf ears. And, thought Mike, who could blame them? The whole thrust of the Navy group's messages over the last few days had been to the effect that catastrophe was imminent. It was true, of course, that there had been a disaster of sorts, one which had, unfortunately, claimed one life and resulted in many injuries. And that conflict too had all been in aid of the belief that planet-wide destruction was coming. At least the fatality and injuries had not been amongst the evac's themselves, although Mike thought that some of them had probably been traumatised. Not that they showed any sign of it this morning. These Oceanus people just continued to impress him. Their resilience was enviable. Few in the Home System could hope to match them.

And neither did the evacuees show any sign of resentment, or anger, that they might have, somehow, been given 'false' information about the threat from Ra, or the aliens, or that they might have been the victims of incompetence; or worse, that they might have been deceived, for some unknown purpose. They just walked joyfully in the sharp early morning sunshine now, chatting amiably, laughing occasionally – probably about something that had happened during the nerve- wracking night just gone. Many were busy brushing off the tiny weevil like insectoids, things they'd called 'barbinects', some of which had started to get into people's clothing whist they all stuck were under the ship, hunkered down on the sandy soil. The critters had begun to crawl onto the skin of some and caused irritation, though, fortunately, nothing worse. Medic Davies was already deploying micro-UV projectors; Navy devices, which, happily, seemed to have the effect of stunning and then enabling the removal of these minuscule irritants.

In short, it was abundantly clear that the civilians who Mike and most of the Navy team had spent days struggling to protect were blissfully relieved to be free of their restriction – and so was everyone else. These 'citizenries', observed Mike, were simply deliriously happy, happy to be alive – and so was he – beyond measure.

But how could he and the crew of The Monsoon have been so wrong? He was pretty certain of the science, or as certain as it was possible to be in the science; assured that the predictions had been accurate. If not, then what had the last couple of years been about? He mused, ironically, that it showed, yet again, that there is no such thing as 'settled science', though it had been the intervention of the aliens which had 'thrown a spanner in the fusion link'. The alien presence was, in itself though, a slap in the face for accepted scientific thinking. These things kept occurring to him over and over, until he came to the conclusion at last, that the alien artefacts, or beings, or whatever they were, had given all of them some sort of reprieve. But how? Why?

Mike had emerged from underneath the Venturer, after helping several locals to gather up their sparse belongings. He'd then decided to check out Lew and the other injured crewman. Davies had stayed near Schapps all night, tending to the Commander and the patient was apparently rallying this morning. On the other hand, Lew was still only half awake. Mike guessed that Meridene had administered further analgesic therapy, so he left him alone and walked out into the still, bright, air, dusting himself down. Then he spotted Meri' striding purposefully toward him.

'Ho there, Mike,' she said cheerfully, 'I wondered if you're still getting updates from the sci-station? I've had a look at the station again but maybe you could interpret the latest data? Doesn't seem much changed to me.'

'Yeah, I've looked at the updates, Meri,' said Mike, 'and you're right. Not much change, except maybe a slight increase in the ordinary solar flux reaching the planet's surface, but it's minimal. The ionosphere is successfully blocking everything else. There's slightly more ultra-v as well but again, that shouldn't be a problem. But I think maybe we shouldn't stay out in the sunlight too long, without protection. I wonder …'

At that point Mike's wristcom buzzed against his skin. After glancing at it he said to her, 'The sci-station is picking up a signal but it's weak. Bad interference, so I guess that's why it hasn't come directly into my wristcom.'

Mike told his device to project the signal, weak as it was, on open audio, so Meri could hear it too.

The wristcom announced that an incoming message was being received, on audio only, as a one-way transmission. It was faint, but was from none-other than Lieutenant Commander Statton of The Monsoon. *From the ship!* Mike's eyes lit up and he couldn't help a wide grin cracking his face. They were okay. He would have loved to talk to him but his device advised that it would not be possible to respond.

In sound which crackled badly, Statton's voice could just about be heard by Mike, and Meridene, who pulled closer to her shipmate.

'Hello, Commander Lew, Mike, and all crewmembers at Janitra Alpha Two station,' said Statton. 'I hope you receive this message in full. It is ... broadcast on continuous cycle, at 10- minute intervals. We are encountering ... interference due to the residual strength of the alien force fields, which still permeate ... Ra system. The nature of the .... is unknown ... present, but they appear to be dissipating quickly so better comms are expected ... 30 to 36 hours, standard time. We all hope everything is well with you. All is well on board The Monsoon. I repeat all ... well on board. ... The evacs have been through a lot but .... think they're .... to be okay. We are guessing you will also have realised by now that the expected explosion of the surface layers of Ra did not happen. All plasma layers in the star appear, as far as we ... tell, to have settled completely but we have carried out continuous monitoring since that time.

'Admiral Tenak, Captain Ebazza and Professor Jennison have authorised me to say that they are reasonably satisfied that ... danger is over. The aliens appear to have generated the force fields I mentioned ... and these – somehow – drew energy off the star. At least, that is what we *think* happened. The AI – and Professor Jennison, believe that the field somehow projected or dissipated the energy into the vacuum. Needless to ... , it is something which they are still working on and will be, I'd say, for a ... long time.

'The Admiral also advises that he will be in contact with the government authorities in Janitra, as soon as … , meaning when their comms tek can mesh with The Monsoon's, which is likely to be … the interference diminishes sufficiently. He will advise them of our latest scientific findings and will take responsibility for advising them that we believe the emergency is, effectively over. Whether they accept that advice and act on it … entirely up to them.

'I also need to tell you that, unfortunately, the ship will not be able to insert back into orbit around Oceanus for at least eight standard weeks due to the velocity we had to build to … escape the expected conflagration. But we have already begun a braking burn.

'We hope you will be able to manage on the surface for that … as you will not have support from The Monsoon for some time. We understand that the fleet will arrive at Oceanus approximately four weeks after the Monsoon's own projected arrival. Admiral Tenak gives his apologies … not sending this message in person but he and the Captain are busy attending to issues raised by the evacuees in our care. Both of them send their very best wishes and look forward to speaking to you in person. As do we all. Message ends.'

Mike stood in silence for several moments as he felt his inner emotions threaten to burst. He was sure in his own mind that Statton was right; there seemed little likelihood that the star's surface layers would start to cause problems again – not after all that had happened. Whatever the motivations of the alien things, none of this would make sense if the situation were suddenly to be, somehow, 'rewound', back to the start of the problems again. But since when did any of it make sense? With relief he blew hard through pursed lips, which came out as an awestruck whistle and tears began to form in each eye. Meri was smiling as though all her birthdays had come at the same time. She looked as ecstatic as *he felt*. Her eyes glistened too.

Quite obviously, thought Mike, the realisation that they were safe, that the whole planet was safe, was only now beginning to dawn on them. For the first time in what seemed like forever, he felt a radiance begin to spread inside him, as though the summertime of his spirit had been unleashed; freed from the burden he now understood had been weighing down on him, and all his colleagues, and so many others, for so long. The sense of relief was becoming overwhelming and intoxicating.

He sank to his knees and the tears ran freely then. Meridene threw her head back, started to laugh, with wild abandon, but then she put her head in her hands began to sob too. Spontaneously, the two of them grasped each-other tightly in joy, and hugged and hugged till it hurt.

After a while Mike nudged her and said, 'Don't you think we should tell the others?' Their behaviour was, after all beginning to attract a lot of attention. Crewmates were standing and staring. Mike suddenly became self-conscious and didn't want them to get the wrong idea – but then, he'd see what *they did* when they heard the news.

****

And so it was, that after wild and joyous celebrations the remainder of the Navy team on the surface of Oceanus, picked themselves up and got on with trying to restore the camp to something approaching the condition it had had before the retreat to the Venturer. In particular, an attempt was made to resurrect the medical tent and those who'd been injured in recent days were able to receive a slightly better degree of medical care. In restoring prior conditions, they were helped by many of the erstwhile evacuees, although others began to drift away, very slowly, clearly intending to return to their places of origin. Mike was pleased that most of them, over the days, thanked the Navy people. They didn't seem to hold the fact that nothing terrible had, in the end, happened, as though it was some trick or massive mistake by the HS Navy. They had all seen the strange, if relatively innocuous events of the past night and knew *something* big – but mysterious – had happened.

But smoke still rose from the horizon. Both Meridene and Mike tried to persuade the restless evacuees to wait until they had established communications with the Janitran authorities, the pair attempting to do this by using their wristcoms; trying to tap into the planet's old telephone systems. Mike was impressed when a link was established, surprisingly quickly, with some minor officials in the Janitran government, then later with the 'Minister for the Interior.'

Before Mike was able to relay the good news from the instruments at their disposal, he was told that they had indeed, themselves, been contacted by Admiral Tenak, but no comment was made as to what they felt about his message. Given the history of the OA authorities, thought Mike, he couldn't see their attitudes changing very quickly.

They told Mike that the government were relaxing some emergency measures but not all. Nevertheless, they felt that sufficient order had been restored so that Janitra was now, mostly, safe. To his surprise, Mike was told that the OA governments' *own* observatories had determined there was a very good chance that the anomalies of the last few days and weeks were dissipating. But they were not at all sure how accurate that was. They were expecting more comms from The Monsoon shortly.

They also told Mike and Meridene that the civil authorities had broadcast the good news to the populace in all they ways they knew how and had begun to re-establish control in most areas of the continent. The rioting had been bad, at least in Bhumi-Devi terms and would, unfortunately, have historical significance. Mike blessed the fact that the people of this planet were not, after all, particularly prone to extended bouts of full-blown anarchy. Most people just wanted to carry on with their lives. And their lives were simple indeed, when compared to those led by most in the Home System. Perhaps a better term was, *more straightforward*.

In the days and weeks which followed Lew began to make a better recovery, once medical facilities had been restored. Heavy equipment which they had been simply unable to get to 'safety' under the ship, was retrieved and renewed solar power supplies energised them and restored them to operating efficiency. Lew eventually felt well enough to resume command, though he remained, for now, confined to a wheelchair. Mike was overjoyed to have his friend 'back' again. Lew's semi-comatose state had frightened and disturbed Mike profoundly.

The Venturer could no longer be used for transport, so they were mostly stuck at the compound. And yet, after a few days Mike was contacted by the government and was extremely happy to hear that, as soon as circumstances allowed, they would send out a small fleet of electric cars to pick up both the (former) 'evacuees' and the navy crew and take them to a 'place of safety'. Everyone, including Mike and Lew, had expressed a desire to leave the encampment as soon as practically possible.

The compound had stocks of food and water to last at least a couple of weeks, but everyone was fed up with the place. But still Lew ordered that the location be secured before he and the crew left and he, in particular, would need to have some med equipment taken with him. The government, expressing its 'undying gratudinry' for everything they had done, or at least, had tried to do, generously offering to allow the Navy contingent to be accommodated in the government buildings in Janitra, at no cost. They would also have meals provided if they wished – but there were strings attached: they were to engage fully with efforts to help rebuild, following the troubles.

There were damaged and looted building to be reconstructed and fire damage to deal with, as well as 'lectric' work to be done. Virtually none of the crewmembers objected and all became engaged in one way or another. Even Daviesberger and his rebel group had, begrudgingly, become involved. In fact, they had had little choice, as they would not otherwise have been fed, and Lew made it abundantly clear to them that, this way, it would go down better with the Admiralty and the Home System Authorities. Mike knew the mutineers were only too aware the fleet would arrive eventually, and there was really nowhere to hide. Lew had also reminded them what had happened to Heracleonn when she had absconded.

Most of The Monsoon crew had engaged especially with the recovery of electrical power and infrastructure work in Janitra, while Mike had got involved with helping in the clearance of damaged buildings. He found the work physically hard, and dirty, but it was better than waiting around at the old encampment. Although the rioting had not been too bad, by Earth standards, it had still been very destructive. There was a lot of fire damage to many of the larger, older buildings, in the central districts, but they could be recovered. Mike was told that some of the newer 'living houses' on the outskirts had been burnt down completely. It would take longer to recover from that, because they had to be 'grown' again over a long period. It made him think of the gro-stat he had stayed in whilst on his trip into the Purple Forest. A shame for the people of Janitra. He was sure the facility out in the Purple Forest was still serviceable. But he had no intention of trying to get out there to check it. Noone else was going to go live out there anyway.

Mike's accommodation this whole time was an extremely small and bare room in the basement of the Janitran government building, and the meals served in the 'refrectra' were basic; often cold and sometimes inedible. But neither he nor his comrades had any credits with which to purchase anything better, since to work properly on Oceanus required a permit, which none of them had, or could get. Even so, neither he nor many of the others complained, although he heard that, predictably, Daviesberger had been ruffling feathers. He also heard that the Oceanus authorities had managed him with aplomb.

Despite putting up with the conditions with, what he hoped, was fortitude, Mike eventually came to ache for the arrival of The Monsoon. Sometimes, though rarely, he felt almost as though he was part of a forced labour system. At other times he had to admit that, for the most part, it was just very different and really wasn't too bad. After all, though the work was usually very tiring, no-one seemed to expect him to do any seriously dangerous tasks, and he had some leisure time. He developed a few friendships amongst the recovery teams and emergency workers, and everyone was keen to know more about life on board starships. Still, he found he eagerly awaited 'rescue', as the reasons to leave this world started to slowly build.

Much of this had been exacerbated because of some personal, emotional, shocks he received whilst he awaited. Things which made him unerringly sad. The first had come soon after he'd left the Navy encampment. Mike had established coms links with the University of Janitra, to look up his old friend, and was told that he would not be able to get in touch with Professier Muggredge because, sadly – he was dead. He had died about two weeks before the fateful day when everyone in the evacuee compound had believed Ra's surface was about to explode.

Mike was numbed as he was told the news by a colleague of Muggredge's, that the Professier had suffered a heart attack. There'd been no hint of any problem previously, but rumours were that the strain of the perceived impending disaster on Oceanus had proved too much for him. But others said he died of grief, being unable to get over the death of his beloved Eleri. This was more in line with Mike's thoughts, and, sadly, once again, he had missed the great man's funeral wake, apparently a very muted affair, given the unfolding crisis at the time.

The demise of Muggredge devastated Mike once again and he began to spiral down in mood. He had to fight hard to stop the slide. He had been very fond of the Professier and even he had begun to think of him as 'Unkling' Muggredge. The awful news also reminded him starkly, once again, of the loss of his beloved Eleri, and the aching had begun to feel acute once again, becoming almost overwhelming at times. He felt he couldn't really talk to anyone about it, not Lew, nor even Meridene. She was usually the other side of the city anyway, heavily involved in trying to get OA electrical, water and sewage systems back online. He hardly ever saw her, or Lew, for that matter. The Commander was accommodated in some sort of 'sanatorium' the other side of the city and the work Mike had to do didn't allow quite enough time to carry out any lengthy visits.

Another disappointment came when he had asked his wristcom to look up Danile Hermington's number. He desperately wanted to talk with his old friend, but his device explained that it had been blocked from gaining access to Danile's private telephone number. When Mike asked about it at the University, he was told that Danile had been assigned to a geological expedition, a 'geolry find-trip' they called it, forging a path into the mysterious and remote central regions of the continent. He would be gone for several months.

Then, some eight weeks after being 'secreted' or stored away in the government building, as he felt his stay to be, Mike heard his first bit of positive news since the end of the crisis: a holographic communication from *none other than Captain Jennifer Providius*, of the Antarctica. He had already heard from The Monsoon, that she and her crew had survived the crisis.

At Mike's joyful reception of her message she said, 'I am also very glad to see you, Mike.' Her beaming 3D image seemed to be standing right next to him. He wished he'd been standing on board her ship. *If only*, he thought. *Away from here.* The audio message was reasonably clear but her holo- image, though bright, had ripples of static interference running through it, too often for comfort; once again, either the effect of the residual interference in the Ra system, Mike thought, or something to do with her ship's speed relative to Oceanus. It didn't really matter because Mike was simply pleased to hear from her.

'I can tell, you're really living it up down here,' she continued, through the static interference. He could see a slight smile playing on her lips, as she resumed, 'and I bet you can't wait for The Monsoon to get there?'

Mike chuckled and waved off the comment – unconvincingly, he thought, then said,

'Oh, I guess it's not too bad here, Captain, but, yeah, I could do with a change. It's the lack of credits and the inability of any of us to get full time work to get enough of 'em. Anyway, I heard from Admiral Tenak that you were okay. Relieved doesn't begin to cover it. He gave me an outline of what happened out there. Seems just – astounding. What else can I say? It could take generations to try to understand what really happened.'

He noticed that there was only about a six second delay between their responses to each-other; easily manageable. That meant that her ship was only about two million klicks away from Oceanus.

'Yeah, it was "astounding", indeed,' she said, her face taking on a deeply serious look for a moment, leavened then by an obvious sense of relief, as she continued,

'Unfortunately, our data was cut short at the critical moment, just after the remnant of the cloud surrounded us, tight as a drum. *We all passed out, Mike.* All of us. Went out like lights. No idea why. The AIs went offline at the same time. *We were all out for about two minutes.* Just two minutes, Mike. It's so weird, but everyone just woke up – slumped in their seats. Some found themselves on the floor. Luckily, most of the crew were strapped in, so there were no serious injuries from falls, just a few minor bruises. The AIs couldn't shed any light on what happened to us, *or to them*, but it seems the little cloud of alien machines protected the ship from Ra's plasma surge. System-wide interference stopped us from being able to contact The Monsoon for a long time and we were kind of busy checking the ship's systems.'

'So, you got away, free as the proverbial penkie-dog? Wonderful,' said Mike, whistling through his teeth.

Providius paused and her face turned deadly serious, almost mournful, before she replied, 'It was wonderful, yes. But it wasn't quite "free as a penkie", Mike. For a few days we lost most of the major AI functions and some minor ones. It was … well, kind of difficult for a while. We thought we were "dead in the water." But seems, we were lucky – again.'

The momentarily vanished look of relief she'd had spread quickly across her face once more, as she continued, 'and I'm pleased to say navigation and propulsion suddenly came back online – just like that. But a lot of the peripheral electro-systems were burned out. And the trash recycling system has stayed offline. The ship is a mess, even now. We had some trouble with the air recyclers. Had to jury-rig a system, which held, just about, till most of the minor functionaries came back online. You know, it's curious, but our wristcoms don't work anymore. But I'm sure I'm boring you now. The main thing is that we were all essentially unharmed, and it's really fortunate we were able to start a burn to get us out of that inner orbit of Ra. As you'll have gathered, we're in an orbit round Ra that brings us close to Oceanus right now. Still carrying out repairs. And, well, still trying to piece the whole story together. I think it'll take some time.'

Her story sounded horrendous to Mike. He also guessed that Jennifer was vastly understating the problems she and her crew had faced. It must have been appalling – being without power, drifting in orbit – and unable to call for help, which, even if there'd been any, would have been many weeks away.

'I'm really sorry to hear about your troubles, Captain,' said Mike softly, 'and I can assure you, I'm not bored. But, as you said, the main thing is that you're okay. It's, sort of, well, it's virtually a miracle.'

'It is at that, Mike, and it might be one we can get to understand one day – but not yet. By the way, please call me Jennifer.'

'Well, thank you – Cap – sorry, Jennifer. I hope you're right. The whole thing, your survival, the planet's survival – unaffected – and The Monsoon's – just seems so … so "gondo-weird". Though I have a theory, but now *I might be boring you …*'

'No, no, please, spell it out.'

'Well, you might think this crazy, but I reckon the aliens *never wanted* to damage the star in the first place. For me, everything we saw, everything we analysed, says so. None of it seems to point to any kind of malice, or intention to destroy, either the star, or us. Of course, we didn't know that till it was all over. But now … we can see that, well, that I don't think they meant any harm at all, did they? They *might* have reacted badly if Madraser had been able to attack with nuclears – but they didn't retaliate when conventional weapons were used. Our AI on The Monsoon was eventually able to tell us that the energy from the conventional missiles was – simply absorbed by the alien artefacts. And, I reckon, they look like they actually protected your ship. The other thing is – where are they now? The aliens machine things or whatever they were? The Admiral tells me there's no sign of them whatever – and that planet sized thing that we kind of identified as, maybe, their *mothership,* has disappeared too.'

'Yes, and the star is, essentially, back to normal,' she added, 'or rather,' she continued with special emphasis, '*better* than normal. Our own analysis, as far as our partially damaged sub-systems have allowed, suggest that the current composition of Ra, *as far as we can tell,* is what would have been expected if the star had never had any history of Karabrandon wave disturbances. In effect, Mike, it shows every sign of following an ordinary, reasonably peaceful evolution toward old age – pretty much like our own Sun. Too early to be sure of course. I guess we, and other ships like ours, will have to keep station on this one for a long time. Anyway, I like your theory but, as you say, we can only speculate until we have more infodata. And no disrespect to you, Mike, but I think this mystery is going to keep a lot of people and their hypercomps, busy for a long time.'

Mike nodded and they stood in silence for long moments before Providius spoke again,

'And what about you, now? What will you do?'

'Not sure, Jennifer. The Monsoon should be in orbit in a few days. Admiral Tenak tells me the fleet will arrive in about 3 weeks, but apparently, Admiral Robertson's assured him she'll allow him and the crew to take the ship back home, without the need to board her. Another shot over Madraser's bows!'

'That's great. Good for Robertson. I know things won't be easy for my good friend, Arkas. And I'm sorry Mike, but I hope you don't mind me being blunt, but they don't look so great for you, either.'

'No, no. You're right, of course.' Mike was untroubled by what she'd said. He'd had far worse news in recent days. Providius then told him something he'd remember and be grateful for, till his last day.

'Listen, Mike, I can't say too much right now. I've got to talk to some people back home first, but I might have a sort of long-term proposition for you when you get back home. Might make things – maybe choices – a lot easier for you. But, as I say, I can't go into details, yet.'

'I'm intrigued, Jennifer.'

'Okay, Mike, I have to go now. Duty calls. In a few days we're expecting to dock with a robot supply ship from the Home System. Much needed food supplies and fuel. Otherwise, we wouldn't be able to get home.'

'Ah yes, I know about that,' said Mike. 'cos they've sent a large, automated barge, piloted by AIs, haven't they? Apparently, it's going to supply The Monsoon with fuel as well.'

'I hope it's got enough food for them as well. I'm sure the Admiral must be low on supplies, especially after caring for all those evacuees. Recycling and virgin manufacture only goes so far.'

'Yeah, right, but he can't last till the barge gets here. Said he's going to purchase bulk supplies from the OA government when he puts into orbit. No choice really. I believe a lot of barges are coming out to supply the rest of the fleet too.'

'Yeah, it seems that now the need for evacuation seems to be over, the Home System government is prepared to be more generous with its spending. Only joking, of course. Okay, Mike, it's been great to talk with you, as always. Really great. I'll see you back in the Solar System. All the best till then. Good sailing and keep your spirits up. Remember what I said. Providius out.'

He smiled broadly at her as her holo disappeared.

Intriguing, he thought. He was certain that he would be booted out of the Secretariat when he got back to the Solar System, but, in fact, he thought he could guess what Jennifer's offer amounted to. So, despite recent events he felt he had reason to remain positive about his future.

Even so, yet another upset came knocking just a couple of days later, when he tried, for what must have been the twentyeth time, to get in touch with Eleri's family, using his wristcom to patch him through to the number it obtained. This time, the ringing phone was, for the first time, actually picked up by someone. Unfortunately for Mike, it was Marcus of Tharnton. He was pleased that at least Marcus didn't put the phone down straight away.

Trying to be as diplomatic as possible, Mike said he'd tried to get in touch many times but there'd never been a reply; that he had been extremely worried. He was surprised to find that Marcus gave an explanation – of sorts. The mascla gave little detail but said, gruffly, that he and Elen-Nefer, with their daughter, Meriataten, had travelled, with a few other local families, out to the foothills at the margins of the Purple Forest. They had sheltered in a kind of bunker dug into a hillside by a friend's family. This friend had radio contact with people in Janitra and, after a few days, they'd been advised that the expected conflagration wasn't going to happen. They could return to their homes, which, thankfully, they found intact when they arrived.

Mike was overjoyed to hear that they were all okay, but before he could finish speaking, Marcus interrupted, saying pejoratively, that he had explained what had happened out of common 'Oceanus courtesy' – but now he wanted the conversation to end. And then – leaving no doubt in Mike's mind that he did not want him to contact him, or his wife, ever again, he had slammed the phone down.

Mike was numbed. But not surprised. How could he ever talk to the family again, in the circumstances? It was just another marker which said his time on Oceanus was coming to a close. He felt that he still loved this world, for he could not do otherwise, but with another flash of insight, he now realised, he was quite simply *restless*.

FINAL INTERLUDE

GARDINERS

They did not move the star, nor destroy it, for even they could not have done those things had they wanted to. Nor did they change the very type of star it was, for neither were they capable of this. But they had been able to change its character, from a volatile, disruptive star or, as they would have it, a diseased thing, to a more docile and amenable sun. And then, their labours completed, they rested and counted the cost, for there was, as always, a cost to be borne. Then they prepared to move on.

**

The full adjoining of all the beings on the massive parent ship had begun to dissolve at last, the mission having been completed, so that most would now sink into a deep, induced slumber, ready for the journey to the next destination. And yet, there was a sense of disquiet flowing throughout the harmony-meld.

Sensing the disturbance, Percepticon's thoughts flowed into her kin, Hermoptica and, more distantly, Demetia, by way of her cyber-brains, which flashed,

We must modify the meld, should we encounter sentience otherwhere. This sojourn has been an informative yet disturbing experience for the harmony-meld.

Hermoptica's thoughts flowed back to her, almost in unison with them, but he added,

We should not have projected the ship's hyper-simulacrum, known to the Others as a hologram, into the innermost planetary space around the star, our Qardestriana. Our intention was to stimulate a desire in the Others to remove themselves from close orbit, but it caused more confusion and fear than we anticipated. We were right to assume their concept of holography is nascent only. But we meddled and we must never do so again. They may have tried to use fusion weapons against the simulacrum and when that proved fruitless become even more frightened and aggressive. Their actions may have resulted in harm to themselves. They are indeed a fractious and precipitous species. We also erred in trying to send a signal, which we thought simple enough for them to interpret. But we were wrong. It caused more confusion. Their appreciation of mathematics is not sufficiently mature, and we overestimated their level of sophistication.*

Percepticon flowed with empathy, *The super-adjunct has ruled similarly and clarified that its signals were nearly a billion times too dense and too fast for their own adjuncts to interpret. They will eventually decipher our signal, but full and correct interpretation is improbable - to a degree raised to the tenth power of the binary.*

Demetia also adjoined with his thoughts, opining that,

The organic others have singular brains, unattached, without full diversification, and their adjuncts are not equal to the task of advising them appropriately. With the Others, each organic unit lives entirely on its own and each is isolated in the hyperverse. This is what leads them to precipitous actions and interference and thence, into peril. They are confined by their physiology and psychogenic horizon. They cannot be held responsible for their errors in this instance.

Yes, we feel their pain. We feel their loneliness …, flowed Percepticon, the warmth of her kin-companions' thought flows coinciding with hers, *…for their lives are indeed isolated and their cultures full of anguish, as once was ours. Despite this, they may still survive – as did we.*

Hermoptica flowed profusely,

The super-adjunct reminds us that in our encounter with the Others we were obliged to sacrifice a hundred million robotinoids, in order to protect the organics in the vessel which remained close to Qardestriana, for otherwise the stellar outflow purge we initiated would have destroyed its simple systems – and the organics within.

Percepticon returned with,

And so must we leave now the gravity well of Qardestriana chonis-eta which was the birthingplace of our own Dependriaticam; our species. Our tasks here are finished.

Yes, we leave Dependriaticam, flowed Hermoptica, *but without having sensed it in full, close, proximity.*

As the ancient disease of the star has been extinguished and nullified, now and forever, flowed Percepticon reassuringly, *we can hope the Others will, henceforth, make Dependriaticam their ancestral home too, and nurture it always, making it their wellspring, for now there can be none better. It will forever remain that sacred place from which we originally came, so many millions of cycles past.*

We can but hope the Others are capable, warned Demetia, with a hint of foreboding. *Nevertheless, The Super-adjunct bids us now set forth for "Arbetrarchium-cjema" and her worlds; our new destination, eleven hundred cycles distant in standard R-Space. This involves us in long deep-torpor, even in C-Space.*

Yes, adjoined Percepticon, *And we know that there we will be unhindered by the considerations we faced here. We also know that the organics whom we have encountered in this zone, cannot yet reach it.*

Hermoptica flowed once more, though his energy was waning now, *The Super-Adjunct warns that our world vessel's energy has been severely drained by our activities in this system. Thus, it shall pause on our new journey at the high-density micro-star Zasterxane Arrin, but 8.232 light cycles distant in Real Space; there to recharge our depleted world-vessel by means of its hyper- magnetic field. Then we may continue. The transit to the micro-star shall take merely 1.0224 cycles in C-Space, and we are reassured that the temporary orbital insertion and energy recharge will not require that our organic parts be awakened from repair-slumber. Thus, all is well.*

The super-fast thought streams of the beings began to settle toward the slumber soon to come, though they were still joined together in their collective happiness and sense of joy. But their vast chamber was slowly darkening, a reflex action by the Super-adjunct, quickening now, as the colossal ship began to accelerate thither.

Percepticon and Hermoptica felt their presence in the realm of Real Space start to slip away, their cyber adjuncts gently stroking their thought streams, reminding them of the need for deep slumber and repair. Suddenly, they felt Demetia being moved away, both physically and mentally, as the being was drawn away on its platform, very slowly, sliding gradually into the distant, deep shadowed regions of the vast hemisphere in which all lived. With a kind of neural tickle which engendered both deep sadness and yet sparks of intense pleasure, the nerve bundle ties between Percepticon and Hermoptica were delicately but fully separated. These beings also then slipped apart, drawn away from each-other on separate platforms; Percepticon high above, near the upper dome, and Hermoptica far below. Each being was still awake, but only barely. Deep shadows descended over the hundreds of organic platforms, the space illuminated intermittently by the vibrant streaming of multi-coloured energy ribbons flowing past, outside the vast transparent canopy above the hemisphere. The journey had begun.

Percepticon's last waking thoughts were of the power and meaningfulness of travel through Complex Space and yet, strangely, how relatively slow it was by comparison with the means evidently employed by the Others they had encountered in this system. But the disadvantage for the Others was that they were trapped inside a small sphere within Real Space – unless they could – perhaps in some far distant cycle, break free. It had been intensely interesting to discover the organic Others, she mused, and she felt a kind of kindred spirit with them, sensed now as though across a wide, bottomless, gulf.

She uncoiled her metal tentacles then, draping them into the honeycomb of chambers below her, where they would stay settled, happy and ready to maintain her throughout the journey. They hung motionlessly from her body, resting for the time being. Gentle electrical discharges from the distant Super-adjunct, caressed her organic minds and facilitated sleep but she was slow to respond. Then, she felt the gentle chiding of one of her cyber-brains, this one attached to her tenth tentacle, cajoling, imploring her to allow herself to become immersed in deep slumber. And so, the huge hemispheres of her eyes closed gently, and she drifted into sleep.

CHAPTER EIGHTEEN

SHOCKWAVES

<u>OCEANUS:</u>

<u>26 STANDARD EARTH MONTHS AFTER THE END OF THE 'ALIEN' EMERGENCY</u>

The little monument marking Eleri's grave outside the town of Chantris, had become decorously overgrown with bright green-blue tendrils of 'geminius' plants, rather like many vine species on Earth, which had emerged from the surrounding soil, weaving now a seemingly protective cage around the stonework. Early afternoon Ra-shine splashed orange-yellow light over the stone. Mike gazed at the miniature monument from a nearby wooden bench.

Some, on Earth, might have found the undergrowth off-putting, but Mike knew better. He was absolutely sure Eleri would have approved. Perhaps her parents would allow the whole of the small monument to be completely overwhelmed and obscured. Even then, Eleri would have approved – absolutely. Her remains were still there, after all, but she had emerged originally from this landscape and would become a part of it again; the world she loved so much in life.

A trickle of warm tears ran down each of Mike's cheeks. This place would always affect him like this, but he felt he was learning to live with his grief. And, anyway, he was always at ease here. He felt he'd like to spend all day in this place of peace, but remembered he was not on an extended leave and there were things he wanted to do. He'd been given just three standard days' shore leave by Jennifer Providius, who'd recently been promoted to 'Science Commodore' over all Home System

Research Vessels. The refitted vessel, Antarctica, was currently parked in a high orbit above Oceanus, visiting to study again, at close quarters, the current functioning of Ra; just to keep monitoring the status of the star, following its miraculous 'recovery' from the earlier troubles. Minor problems with operations on the Antarctica had prevented Mike from arriving on the surface until early afternoon, so he'd already lost part of a day's leave.

'Tis strange! That is not yet a Navy Secretary's uniform, I see,' said a familiar male voice, from behind him, pulling Mike out of his reverie.

'Danile!' Mike said and turned, a feeling of joy coursing through him. He rose immediately to greet his old friend, 'I didn't expect to see you here, fella-me-mate.'

Subconsciously, he wiped the tears from his face.

Hermington appeared wilder looking and even more willowy than Mike remembered. The two greeted each-other in the warm, crossed, two-handed handshake, characteristic of Oceanus people, then they hugged each-other briefly.

'It's so good to see you, Danile. Real good. How did you know I'd be here?' said Mike, beaming.

'Yes, the word came from your Commander, Provincios? She has been intermixing ideas with Professier Daxia, the new head of biolry, at Janitra. T'was she who told me you had been given some hol-leave to use up and had already come down to the surface. I am guessing you would be coming here fair-soon after landing down. I hope you are not minding. I do not wish to intrude.'

'No, no, of course not. I guess you probably come here every now and again, don't you?'

'But yes,' said his friend, 'Very much so. I too miss her sorely, Mike. You will know this.'

Mike nodded and the two fell silent for a moment. Then Mike remembered his manners and invited Danile to sit with him. He smiled and, ignoring Danile's misreading of his new commanding officer's name, said,

'And you're right about the "uniform". We all have to wear this sort of dull, grey, thing. It's fairly smart, I guess, but hardly matches up to Monsoon gear, does it?'

Danile chuckled lightly. 'No. I am supposing tis exceeding strange to you, to be back here – with a new commander and a new ship?'

'Didn't you hear what happened?' said Mike, with genuine astonishment. 'Boy, news really is slow in getting out here, ain't it?'

'I know most about what happened with Ra, coursry,' said Danile, a little defensively, 'and I know that your Admiral Tenak pitted himself against the superior Admiral officer, in words and in deeds. As did you, my friend, as did you. So I hear on good authority. I was just thinking, hopeful, that you all were given pardon. After all, rightness was on your side, wast not? And everything worked out for the good? Our star now behaves itself and no harm came from the aliens. All good.'

Mike gave an ironic smile. 'I'm sorry Dani, but that's not how it works. At least, not back home. But you're right, the star is "behaving itself", so far, but we still need to keep an eye on it. That's partly why I'm here. But I didn't just change my job, Dani. I had to "leap before I was thrown". I broke the rules. Badly. I was allowed to disagree with the Fleet Admiral's plan of action, and I could have reported back to the Secretariat – as if that would have changed anything. But I wasn't allowed to interfere with a military action once it had been ordered. I did, and I paid the price.'

Danile looked amazed. 'There is no justicia in your home system, Mike!'

'Maybe,' said Mike, 'but I broke my contract and a bond of trust with the Secretariat. They were going to boot me out, Dani. I knew that, so I didn't give them the chance. And strangely, I've actually received a belated commendation from the Navy itself, of all people, so it's not all bad. Besides, I like my new job. Better than the old one.'

'A commendio? But you were never employed by them. And you just said, you did break your contract.'

'That's true. I was employed by the government, Danile, but I worked on a Navy ship and they wanted to award me for, well, I guess, what happened *on Oceanus, not on the ship*. The final part of the crisis, if you want to put it like that – in the evacuee camp. They're allowed to give commendations to non-service personnel, even though they disapproved of what I'd done earlier. Strange – but I'm kind of proud. And it's one in the ocular for old Ebazza. Of course, I'll never be allowed to serve on another Navy ship. Don't want to, though.'

'Ah, I understand yet, but I am also proud *for* you. So how came you to work with the research people?'

'Guess it was my sunny personality. Didn't you guess? Nah, I was just lucky, Dani. Jennifer Providius had already put in a good word for me with the Home System Research Consortium. They own the research ships, Dani. The government just hires them, and the crews. The Commodore requested I be offered a job as a junior research scientist on her ship. I should say "science flagship" now. Her seniors agreed. So, here I am. It was really good of her.'

'Mes Providios must have some deep influence,' said Danile, 'and you are yet fortunate.'

'I am. Jennifer was the only one who came out of the whole debacle over here smelling of treminius flowers. Of course, she was never part of the military plan but her actions here earned her massive acclaim. Plaudits well deserved, I'd say. And it got her quick promotion to Chief Science Commander, then Commodore. She's famous now, back home, and with that has come influence. Strange to think, Dani, that those events were – what – more than two years ago – in the HS time frame, anyway. Changed a lot of things, though.'

'But Mike, Mes Providios is, I believe, celebrated by many here too. And I feel you have yet been changed by what happened, my friendling. I mean, as well as by ….' Dani glanced at Eleri's stone but fell silent.

'Yeah, I know what you want to say, Dani. It's a shame it took … *that* and the crisis here to make me realise what I really wanted to do in life. And to make me, well, sort of grow up, I guess. And now – now I've been given a second chance at a career in science. I should have done this a long time ago. Eleri told me that, you know. Bless her.'

'But friendling, had you stayed in science, first time, you might not e'en have met her.'

Mike nodded, sagely.

'By the way,' added Danile, 'I do like that you have that white streak in your hair. Ist yet deliberate?'

'What this?' said Mike, running a hand over his dark locks but now sporting a wide, natural, streak of pure white hair running over the left-hand side of the crown of his head. 'No matey, this isn't "deliberate",' he said. 'It's weird. Seems to have just … appeared, gradually, since I left the Ra system. Don't know what caused it. And, yeah, I guess it's true that my time in the Secretariat wasn't really wasted, was it? I don't begrudge all those years flying around the stars with Admiral Tenak. Saw some of the wonders of the Universe matey, at least in the locality of Earth. And as for Tenak… that man was a kind of father to me. I owe him a lot. More than I can ever say.'

'Then you have deedly changed, Mike Tanniss, because I am believing that you would not have admitted to that, so open-like, at any times before.'

'Perceptive as ever, my friend,' chuckled Mike, feeling a little embarrassed. 'I think I should apologise if I ever came over as less than grateful, or if my behaviour sometimes seemed selfish or obsessive or whatever. You know – back then?'

'Do not self-scold, Mike. No need of it. And come, let us have no more of this, friendling, for I am betting that you did not know about the plaque?'

Mike was genuinely puzzled.

'But,' said his friend, 'tis more than a plaque. Tis more an honorary *wall*. They have erected it outside Janitra, and there is another on New Cambria. You have been honoured, as has Eleri. In facto, all of us have.'

Mike's jaw slackened in surprise.

'Yes, I did think you would be surprised,' continued Danile. 'Now who is the one not abreast of the news? But tis only to the good, for I would like to show you the plaque, in person, if you will agree?' Dani's face was a picture of enthusiasm.

Mike was intrigued and a bit embarrassed, but he didn't want to upset Danile, so he agreed to go see it. His friend said he would take him to look at the plaque the next day and, in the meantime, Mike accepted his friend's invitation to go with him to his own home close-by, so they could reminisce, and get up to date, in a more relaxed way. Danile even made a generous offer to put him up at his own house for the night, which, Mike thought, might not be a bad idea, especially as he hadn't yet arranged accommodation.

***

Mike sat in the bijou back garden of Dani's house in Kelmrie – a hamlet a few klicks west of Chantris. It was the middle of the afternoon and Dani's small but pleasant larp tree provided welcome shade. Mike held a cool glass of 'barggleberry juice' in his hand. It would have been an ideal setting, but it was starting to remind Mike of similar times not so long ago; times he shared with someone else, someone he still missed like she was a part of his own body that was gone. He decided he must try to put these things to the back of his mind. He was enjoying Dani's company after all, and his dwindling 'shore-leave'.

He relaxed more as he settled into the coolness of the shade. A welcome breeze blew up, rustling the leaves of the tree. Danile was saying that further joint studies of the Dome on New Cambria had confirmed that it really was an important control centre for the co-ordination of mass evacuations of the natives, the original, highly advanced, sentient, species on Oceanus, during the ancient troubles with Ra. Other domes and infrastructure were thought to exist under the shallow shelf seas around Bhumi-Devi; areas flooded during continental plate movements, even though relatively minimal over the last eight million years.

The Oceanus government's expeditions had failed to reveal any domes in the central parts of the continent but then, they didn't have the use of facilities like landing boats. Even so, there were encouraging signs of new agreements between the OA and HS governments about the use of hi-tek, even about overflying the continent and the use of robots to survey the continental shelves.

'Coursry, I should now tell you about staggrinten things we didst find on my last expedition, Mike,' said Danile, looking a bit smug. At Mike's insistence he spit it out, he continued, 'Well, the team of twenty I was in, we went due westward, about four and half thousands of kilometres into the interior. Long ways. And there, hidden in a vast cleft, a very deep ravine, by accidento, we found a rock sequence, cut by an old river, over eons. Twas never seen before.'

'I'm not surprised on this world,' said Mike, 'and so ... what about it?'

'Well, the overflies of one or two shuttles didst not see either,' said Danile, defensively. He continued, 'as twas well-hidden but didst show a sequence of strata dating, far as we could tell, from about 342 millions years ago, at top, to about 460 millions, at bottom.'

Mike felt intrigued and willed his friend to continue. Danile was enjoying this. He said, coolly, 'There were yet *three bands of carbonised rocks,* Mike. Just like the one on Simurgh – but no reptiloid remains, coursry. Much older than that. But three, Mike! Separated at intervals of around 8 to 10 millions of years. The most recent layer was very near the top of sequence. Still we wait for tests to check for beryllium but I think we know what it shows, Mike?'

'Fascinating. Amazing,' said Mike, with enthusiasm. 'And the funny thing is, it confirms recent observations of Ra like stars we've done back in the HS. The latest studies suggest that other stars like Ra blow off their surfaces several times, over tens of millions of years, then there is stability for tens of millions of years, maybe even hundreds of millions, before another period of instability occurs. It varies a lot. Seems it's around the 300 million mark, in the case of Ra. And I'm guessing that the rocks around most of the margins of the continent are much younger than 342 million years. Am I right?'

'Yes. But in some cases only by a narrow margin yet. Some are much older, some outcroppings are a few billion years old but most of the coastal areas are made of younger sediments, special so in the settled areas. We still yet need to find other such sequences like we found, but seems you're right, Mike. And it explains something else, I have long wondered about.'

'What's that?'

'There had to be enough time for the evolution of complex animal life on this planet, to result in the reptiloids – the Natives. At least the time gaps we found in the wilderness.'

'Yeah, you're right. I'd wondered about that too. But until recently we had no other data to go on. But it seems clear that the Natives – and us humans – were around just at the wrong time in the cycle of this star's internal processes. Mike then looked glum and said, And if only we'd known about your ravine a long time ago, maybe a lot of trouble might have been saved.'

Then Danile said, 'Well, but we would not have had permits, back then, to go into the interior and if we had, still might not have found the ravine and we wouldst probably not have discovered the Hall of the Natives and all those wonders. Praps it all would have taken as long a time anyhow. And there was the situation with the aliens anyways, Mike.'

'Sure. That did cut things short a bit, didn't it? And don't forget, the strata you found inland was very old anyway. Almost certainly wouldn't have convinced the Oceanus government of an imminent danger – without the discoveries on New Cambria.'

After a while Danile asked Mike about the reaction to the aliens, back in the Home System, especially as there was, in general, a fairly positive attitude toward them on Oceanus.

'I just wish that were the case back home,' said Mike, 'but the truth is there are so many different views about *them,* Dani. One school of thought is that they feed off stars like old Ra, here, then moved on. Another is that they actually caused the problem with Ra, in the first place, then fed off it, but with the accidental side effect, *for us,* that the star's variability was wiped out. But I think it's fair – and reasonably safe – to say the star does seem to have been "cured", if that's the right way to put it.'

Deedly. Mayhap they did "cure" the star,' said Danile, 'but yet, what is *your* view on the aliens, Mike? I mean – about what they did.'

'I can't be sure, man. No-one can,' said Mike. 'I think they came here to effect some change in the star, for some unknown reason – then just left. But the whole thing is so weird, so hard to understand – *unless we can find them and make contact.*'

Danile nodded and said that there was something of a renaissance in the thinking of the OA government and the people generally. Perhaps they were becoming less isolationist, maybe more open, more 'interstellar' in outlook, even though remaining committed to the way of life they loved so much.

Mike said there were many changes afoot in the Home System too, particularly, he felt, a renewed faith in the Navy. Even some territorial disputes and trade embargoes between colonies in the Solar System might be put aside. Some of the City States, who had been about to secede, had re-joined the government alliance, especially in the face of what looked like a resurgence of the Rebel forces, and a possible threat from the aliens. Mike wondered whether the closer ties would last.

'And so, what happened yet to the crew of The Monsoon, Mike? You were going to tell me much about Admiral Tenak – but I should say, *the great* Admiral Tenak?'

Mike chuckled at that and said, 'I don't think he'd really like that appellation,' but then he explained about how the crew had all been reassigned to other vessels, the officers all being demoted too. Ebazza had not been charged with anything. Tenak had tried to convince the Board of Enquiry that he had coerced her into insubordination, though no-one really believed him. But she had accepted the embarrassment of 'retraining' and demotion to Second Officer, assigned to the armed skiff, Ulysses. Mike surprised Dani when he said that Ebazza had accrued a lot of shore leave and had come, now, at Providius's invitation, to Oceanus with them, on the Antarctica. Statton, also now a plain Lieutenant, had also come along.

Out of all the officers, Mike said that only Lew had come out 'smelling of roses.' Obviously, he'd had nothing to do with what happened aboard the ship, as he'd been on Oceanus at the time.

And his actions in the evacuee camp earned him, very deservedly, in everyone's opinion, multiple commendations, as well as a Navy 'Tritonite Cluster and Star'. *And he'd had promotion to Captain* – assigned to the new Flag vessel, the Kalahari II, effective once it was completed. Mike related the story of how Lew, in anger, had nearly turned it all down.

'I haven't seen much of him recently,' said Mike, 'but I know he wanted to protest about Tenak and the others. Said he would have done the same thing in their shoes. But I also know that Tenak spent a shed load of time persuading him not to say that to the Board of Enquiry – and to accept the promotion. Tenak made him swear to distance himself from the affair on The Monsoon. I think Ebazza worked on him too.

'But what about his injuries, Mike? Is he yet better?'

Yeah, don't worry. He made a pretty good recovery aboard The Monsoon on the way home. Turns out he didn't even need the cyber enhancements he was granted when we got back. I reckon he could have done with one or two, but he refused anyway. Walks with a bit of a limp now and again, like me, but said it was a constant reminder of the "need for vigilance", or something like that. That's rubbish. He couldn't have guessed what would happen.' Mike smiled knowingly.

'And what about that fleet admiral person?'

Mike told Danile that she had been disciplined – *not for what she did in the Ra system* but, so her Disciplinary Tribunal said, because she had allowed negligent practices to develop in the building of the Kalahari, leading directly to its catastrophic loss. They'd hardly been able to criticise her general actions in the Ra system, itself, given that she'd been granted a mandate from the Security Council. But the Admiralty were known to have disapproved of her *precise* actions and had distanced themselves from them. They had recommended demotion to Captain, in charge of the logistics of repatriation from Prithvi, but she had protested vigorously and had resigned her commission. She had disappeared from public view. Danile breathed a sigh of relief at that. Mike chuckled again.

Then, Mike related, with a degree of grim pleasure, how her standing and reputation as a Navy officer had been treated badly on the Solar SocioNet. He could tell Danile didn't really know what he was talking about.

Danile asked specifically what had happened to Tenak in the Home System.

'Well, what can I tell you, Dani? Tenak's a wily ol' guy. You wouldn't believe it, but his disciplinary tribunal was held *in camera*, so I wasn't allowed to attend. I got the whole story from the Senior Navy Secretary present. A mate of mine. He recorded the whole thing, in secret. So, Dani, you need to know that this info can never be disclosed to anyone, got it?' For, probably, the first time that evening Mike sounded deadly serious.

Danile nodded, soberly.

Mike related how Tenak had refused legal representation and defended himself. The charges had been gross insubordination and neglect of duty but counsel for the Navy, a Commodore, had not pressed them with any real vigour. Tenak had explained his actions and his reasoning, in typical, matter of fact, manner. The three judges had then said that they were cutting short the prosecution case and moving straight to verdict. They decided that he was guilty of insubordination, but not neglect of duty.

Astonishingly, in their judgement they said that Tenak had been placed in an extremely invidious position. He and the whole crew had faced a scenario which no other person in human history had ever had to face. They agreed that although the former Fleet Admiral had been in a similar position their view was that, in essence, the actions Tenak had proposed to the Fleet officer, at the time in question, were *correct*. In court, Tenak's jaw had, apparently, looked like it might hit the floor.

As Mike related this story, Danile looked joyous. But Mike explained that the court had gone on to say that Tenak's refusal to carry out the subsequent orders of a senior officer couldn't be forgiven easily. That, and his attempt to sabotage those orders, weren't acceptable behaviour for a serving Admiral of the fleet. There had to be punishment – in some form. They'd offered him a chance to say something in mitigation, before passing sentence but Tenak, typically, had refused, asking them to just to get it on with it.

The Tribunal had expressed the unanimous view that Tenak had given exemplary service over many years and that he was one of only two *decorated* Admirals remaining. Mike winked at Danile when he said that the panel had referred to Tenak's popularity on the SocioNet, so that he was now regarded as a 'cosmic folk hero'. The Solar System News Nexus seemed to be celebrating him too. The judges had referred to 'garish and exaggerated sentiments' in the media but nevertheless saluted the courage, integrity and dedication he'd shown in the Ra system, and over many decades in the Navy. They considered his decision to remain in orbit around Oceanus, to try to save as many people as possible, before events overtook him, as totally outstanding.

However, said Mike, they had also said they couldn't overlook his insubordination and so, couldn't allow him to remain as an Admiral on active service. But then, to Tenak's utter astonishment, they had offered him a new position, as a 'Specialist Consultant' to the 'Navy Development Committee'. They promised him exemplary pay, a considerable say in Navy Policy, and felt he could be of great help in the fight against the resurgent New Rebels, and in discussions about how to deal with the 'alien' issue.

Tenak, said Mike, had soured things slightly, by suggesting they were trying to keep him quiet by offering a 'sweetener' and, at the same time, benefitting from his experience. The lead judge had said she doubted, 'a whole fleet of Nova Class Cruisers could keep you quiet, Arkas Tenak, if you did not wish it. At that, mirth had broken out across the entire courtroom and even Tenak had seen the humour.

Tenak had then politely declined their offer and said he didn't think he could get enough satisfaction if he was not able to fly real missions. He was sure they had enough people who could help with the New Rebels and felt he had made his lasting contribution to that cause a very long time ago.

At this point in the story, Danile started to look glum. Mike said, 'But listen up, Dani. After wishing the Navy well in their efforts to deal with their problems, that's when he revealed that the other reason he had to decline was that he had *decided to emigrate to Oceanus.*' 'Yeah,' he continued, 'said he'd long since applied to the OA authorities and that very morning had heard from them, accepting his application.'

Dani was overjoyed to hear this.

'So he is to come here, Mike?'

'Already here, Dani. He was lucky, cos your people hardly allow any immigrants to come to such a pristine, fragile, world as this. Population has to be strictly controlled, and all that. But yeah, he arrived many months ago, so I believe. Got *married pretty quickly too*, to a local femna, so I understand.'

'That is staggrinton, Mike! I never did know.'

'Yeah, anyway, the tribunal concluded by expressing regret at his decision and saying that they had no alternative but to strip him of his rank of Admiral and of his service with the Navy.'

At Danile's glum look Mike just grinned and said, 'But listen, Tenak's real hardy. Doesn't let too many things get to him. I'm just glad I didn't have to press ahead with my campaign.

'Your what-such?'

'Some of my old Secretary friends, and others, got together on the Solar SocioNet to protest at Tenak's arrest and Court Martial. We enlisted some big names, from the net's "personality" streams, to support our petition not to have him imprisoned. Luckily, it wasn't necessary.'

Hermington took a long look at Mike and said, 'And what of the traitor-populia who had interweaved themselves into the Navy; the ones you call, "quislings"?' asked Danile.

'Them?' said Mike, 'Oh, well, there was an entirely separate Inquiry held by some sort of Board involving the government and the Navy. Poor old Tenak had to appear at that one too, as did Ebazza, and the other senior officers. And Commodore Providius was called. But I don't think there were any overall conclusions about how the quislings were able to do what they did. Oversight errors at departmental level is all they said, I think.'

'So that is finish of that?'

'Nah, far from it, my friend. There's been a huge crack-down on security. And I think the Navy has tightened up massively on recruitment, training, the lot. All expected stuff, I suppose, but with a vengeance, mate. The biggest thing, I think, is a Solar System wide investigatory panel has been set up. That top level guy in the government, Indrius Brocke, is in charge. No idea what's going to come of that. To be honest they've got their hands full, what with worry about the aliens, as well. It's to do with that concern, I suppose, that's Commodore Providius comes in. I guess that's why we must find the aliens, "out there" – somewhere – *before* they find us. Meet them on *our* terms … if that's even possible.'

'Then let us be hoping that peaceful contact is establish-ed. *Praps you will find them*, Mike. Imagine yet!'

'Not sure 'bout that,' said Mike, 'but I agree with the sentiment. It's a massive "if", ain't it? Anyway, to change the subject, Dani, tell me more about that plaque. Isn't that what you called it?'

'Ah, but yes and I hope we shall see it on morrow-morn. Tis in the "Darvenhay Gardens", some lints outside Janitra. Tis a primary, I shouldst say, *the* primary garden of remembrance or praps, garden of celebration, on Bhumi-Devi. There are many exhibitions in it, Mike, and now does include *a full-scale model of the "Native" from Newcam*, and best still, a wall. Tis a semi-circular shape wall and on there the plaque, praps 3 metres high. And on one side of it – is us! W*e are all there.*'

'*We are all there*?'

'Yes, as I said before. Well, nearly all. *All we who were at New Cambria* … are carved into the wall – in the old-fashioned way – in relief – you would say, and larger than life. Eleri is there, coursery – and you and I, and all the others who were such part of the great discoveries on Newcam. Even Professier Akrommo and his great protégé, the Strider robot.'

Mike couldn't help but grin at that, and he was glad Akrommo and Strider had been honoured too. 'Well, Dani, I do indeed feel honoured. Not sure I should really be there but I'm glad Eleri is. And what about poor Rubia?' Mike then remembered that she had never made it as far as New Cambria.

'No, tis sad,' said Dani, 'for, in truth, she should have been so honour-ed. And so too, Professier Muggredge – who started it all off.'

This made Mike feel a little bit downcast, as he remembered his friends, but Dani continued, 'Though yet there is a metal plaque to the great Professier in the University. And there is …'

Before Dani could say anymore Mike's wristcom seemed to burst into life, trilling and buzzing.

'Sorry,' said Mike, 'but this must be urgent. I asked not to be disturbed today,' and with that he lightly touched the skin below his right ear.

Mike now had a com-bud permanently embedded deep in the flesh under his right ear, so that confidential messages could be passed via his wristcom, straight to his inner ear. The device had a minor AI which allowed him to answer calls or give directions to his wristcom, by sub-vocalising, instead of giving fully verbal answers. The insertion had given him pause for thought at first, but he felt it was better than having something inserted into his skull, as did some.

'I'm sorry, Dani,' said Mike after a few moments. 'That was the ship. I have to leave. Right now, 'fraid. A lander's come down to pick me up. I've got about two hours.'

'In two hours still? And a lander, you said? Yet I did think the Antarctica had no such thing?'

'She does now, Dani. The ship's bigger. Almost been rebuilt. Got two landers – atmosphere capable, but they're small ones. How do you think I got down here yesterday? By beaming down?' Mike chuckled amiably.

'Coursry. I did not think. So used to "Navy operations", I didst not think anyone else had lander ships. I suppose.'

'Don't worry. Easy mistake to make.'

'But why so must you go now? I didst want to show you the gardens.'

'I know but … it'll have to be another time. Sorry. The ship told me it's picked up a burst of radiation with "alien characteristics". They reckon it's too similar to what we saw before, to be chance. You know what I mean, Dani - like the burst of radiation The Monsoon picked up, when the aliens entered the Ra system? Only this time it's coming from somewhere called the LJJ 4437 system.

'So, what ist?'

'A super-dense white dwarf star, Dani. Been known about for hundreds of years. It's about 130 light years from Earth but just 9.8 light years from here. Unfortunately, we can't just go there, from here – as you know.'

'So … how could they get … I mean the aliens … how could they get to that white dwarf in 20 Earth months, when it has yet taken the light they have given off, 9.8 years, to get here? Something wrong there.'

'Good point. I suppose they could have gone to that star – if it really is them – *before* they came here. Would it take them nearly 10 years to get here? Well, only if they travel at exactly the speed of light, or nearly, I suppose. Nah, a lot of things say that's wrong. But it doesn't look like they use conduits, after all. Sorry, Dani, I must be boring you.'

'No, no. I am just cofus-ed. Please to carry on.'

'Well, I'm not sure, either. No-one is. But I reckon that if they used a conduit to get here *directly,* cos, say they've conquered the "cage" problem, then we wouldn't see the radiation burst at LJJ 4437, for over 9 years after we discovered them in this system. So ...'

'Are you yet saying you think they have gone to this white star *after* leaving here?'

'Well, could be, Dani. But how could they do it? Unless ... unless they use something called "complex space". Some people back home have theorised the existence of complex space, and that a sufficiently advanced species might use it to get around. But we have no idea whether complex space actually exists.'

'You mean complex, as in complex numbers? Mixtures, yet of real and imaginary numbers?' asked Hermington, 'but how can that relate so to space itself?'

'Dead right about the maths, 'said Mike, 'but this idea is related to the concept of the substructure of space at its most fundamental level, at the so-called "Plank scale", millions of times smaller than an atomic nucleus. Scientists have been trying to investigate the Plank scale for centuries.'

'Alrighting. So, you think the aliens use this Plank scale?'

'Maybe, sort of. Perhaps they magnify or invert this aspect of space in some way. Thing is, the theory suggests that the complex numbers which might describe the "foam-like" architecture of space itself, means that space, at that level, forms a different kind of space-time dimension which is at, sort of, "right angles" to our four dimensions of space-time. You know, three of space and one of this. And remember, this is just a theory. But it could be that at larger scales complex space becomes "flattened" out into what you might call "normal space". Maybe the aliens fly through complex space itself. It's a real crazy idea, I know. I've had trouble getting my head into it, but I reckon there could be something to it.'

'I do believe 'twill remain a long-time mysterioso. And seems to me the origin of the aliens also is a mystery.'

'Yeah, understanding's a long way off. Otherwise, wouldn't we have seen some sign of them before now? There's something else too. I know I've got no evidence for this – but I sometimes wonder if they ... the *aliens*, are linked in some way with this planet – specifically this world.'

'How so?'

'I don't know, Dani. It just seems strange that they should come to this particular, tiny speck in space and – "cure" this particular star.' He went silent, contemplative.

'So, now what are you thinking?'

'As I mentioned earlier, in the last few months we've been able to identify even more stars – just like Ra, with the same problems it had. And we're keeping all of 'em under obs'.'

'Where are such stars?'

'Mostly way, way, off. Nearest one's about 1200 light years away. Maybe the aliens will go there, but we don't know *how fast* they can fly through space – complex or otherwise.'

'So, why would aliens – if they go such through complex space say, travel at some speed, t'ween stars, so to be different from what humans do?'

'No-one knows, but conduit travel is different, isn't it? We talk about conduits like they're tubes or filaments, but I like to think of them as almost like doorways. On a cosmic scale, they're like microscopic pores between the gigantic bubbles which represent different star systems. Think of it like this. Just as it takes a fraction of a second to walk from one room to another, through an open doorway, we can go from one star system to another ...'

'So, we take a tiny fraction of the time it would take to go the long way...such as would happen if there were no "door".'

'Exactly. The conduits are negative energy filaments, so it could be that they're taking us through another dimension, but I like to think of them as, sort of, *inverses* of the larger Universe in which all the star systems are embedded.'

Danile was looking a bit confused.

'Yeah, I know. I don't get it either. Anyway, point is, none of this infringes Einstein's rules about ...'

Mike's exposition, which he was enjoying immensely, was interrupted by a gentle bleeping sound in his right ear. A reminder. Insistent.

'Sorry Dani. That's the ship again. I should be on my way. The shuttle is at Janitra spaceport. Would you like to come see me off? Or have you got work to do? Please don't go to any trouble, Dani. You've been real kind already.'

'Coursry. I am pleased to yet say I have the rest of the day off. And I have not seen a shuttle take off for long times.'

*

And so, they left Danile's little house and started along a quiet path, a wide woodland track, toward the nearest autocar pick-up point. Mike was concerned about getting to Janitra in good time. It was still some kilometres distant and he knew Providius didn't like waiting around. She was remarkably like Tenak, in that sense. He felt a sense of loss about not having had the time to go see him during this all too brief shore leave.

'But if tis *them,*' Danile was saying, as they walked, 'why wouldst the aliens go to such a place as this white star? Ist not a sun with a dense core, that shines by thermal energy, because it has used up its fusion fuel?'

Mike was genuinely impressed. 'You really know your astro-stuff, don't you,' he said.

'I have so studied. And yet such stars, because they be very dense have very high magnetic fields. Not so?' added Dani, a little defensively.

'Yeah. The ship's database says this one's got a magnetic field four thousand times more powerful than the Sun's. So, we're sure there's no naturally occurring life there. I think there's only one probe been sent – a long time ago.'

'And you say *you are going there?*'

'Yeah, sure. The ship's got to go back to the Solar System first. Pick up fuel and supplies. And a couple of new passengers. Then, we're going back out – to the target star. The ship's database confirms that a conduit is available going from Sol to that star. But no human's been there. Remember, we've not properly explored all the systems we're linked to.'

'That high magnetic field does yet sound dangerous, friend-mine.'

'I know, but I'm happy to say the Antarctica's had massively upgraded radiation deflectors, similar to those on Navy ships. Seems a lot's been learned from the episode here. Anyway, I think the plan is to keep out of the star's inner zone, just to have a look around, that's all. We 're not sure if this a genuine sign of the aliens or if they'd still be in the system when we get out there.'

'Fascinatio! And exciting.'

'I guess so, but a bit daunting too. I'm glad we've got a load of experts aboard. Linguists, tek experts, "exobiology" people. I'm in the best possible company – sept for people like you, of course. The three people we're picking up back home are government politicians. Can you believe it?'

'Then you are sure to have problems,' said Dani, with a wink.

Mike laughed and said, 'Yeah, I know what you mean but it was inevitable really. Especially since we've got no way of communicating with the Solar System directly – or quickly. And it's a condition we're stuck with. Besides, I'm told the people concerned are also science experts in their own right. Maybe there's hope for politicos yet.'

'As you do say, it had to be so. I am hoping yet that a mess as nearly didst happen last time may be avoided.'

'So do I. And it's not just academic anymore. This could be epoch changing for humans.'

'Things have already chang-ed for all humanity, Mike. *Just by knowing about the aliens.*'

'Absolutely. Lots of changes I guess – and all because of *this* miraculous world. This amazing star system.'

Danile smiled broadly for a moment but suddenly his expression became more contemplative.

'Tis a miracle world, Mike. So please do be coming back here again – soonest?'

'Thank you, Dani. I have every intention of coming back here. But meanwhile, there's a lot to see out there.' Mike waved a hand toward the heavens.

'Yes, I do agree friendling,' said Dani, 'for, as someone famous once said, "we do live in interesting times," do we not?'

Mike chuckled and said, 'Right. Look we'd better pick up the pace.'

*

They caught an autocar surprisingly quickly and continued to chat on the way to the capital, though much of the journey was spent in contemplative silence. Mike didn't mind. He drank in the luxuriant sights and smells of the Oceanus countryside and again reflected on what he now considered a stroke of good fortune, in coming here again. At one point, when discussing the science missions of the research ship, Danile asked him why Ebazza and Statton had accompanied his ship back here.

'They decided to come out for an ordinary visit to Oceanus. Sort of holiday, I guess. But, you know, it was really a chance to visit Tenak. Jennifer had some capacity anyway and was more than happy to let them come. Wouldn't normally be allowed but the Commodore's got a lot of weight nowadays. And they've even been making useful contributions to the science discussions. Don't think they have much choice with Providius. Anyway, it seemed strange having them as crewmates again. But it was fine. Ebazza came down on the other shuttle, to go see Tenak, but she's been recalled now too. The alternative is to get stranded here and miss duties on her ship. I think her shuttle is due to take off before mine.'

'I know you would have liked to see Tenak, too, Mike. Pity yet about that.'

'Yeah, haven't seen him for ages. But "duty calls," I guess.'

Mike then remembered he wanted, *no, needed*, to talk to his friend about security before the vehicle got to Janitra. He realised he should have mentioned it earlier. Now was as good a time as any, he supposed, especially as they were on their own in their particular car in the 'car train', so he raised the issue. He knew he had to be tactful and not too alarmist, but the situation was potentially serious.

'Dani, I just wanted to mention personal security to you.' Danile looked puzzled. Mike continued, 'I'm sorry I left it till now but it's just that I've picked up some ... intel from some mates, including Captain Pingwei – about possible terrorism – new terrorism – and possibly on Oceanus.'

'What in the heavens are you saying, Mike? I just told you the metateleos on Oceanus have been "fried away".'

'No, Dani. I'm not really talking about *that lot*. I can't give you much detail right now and I might even be breaking some protocol or other in telling you, at this point. But, well, you *know me*. It's just that Home System security agencies seem to have picked up some data on the activities of a different group. It looks like Ultima have started being active again in the Solar System and I'm pretty sure I'm right when I say that they've inspired a new breed of "rebels", if you want to call them that, who might even be operating on Oceanus. If that's right, they would probably make the metateleo problem look like a pleasure park holo' ride. This new lot look a lot more dangerous – more violent than the metateleos ever were.'

'Surely not, Mike? But there has been no sign of problems like that here. Not for long times. Hardly ever-so.'

'Maybe not, but I know your government has been informed about this and, just in case it's a "damp squib", I'd be grateful if you keep this to yourself for now. After all, it's your government's job to alert people, not mine.'

'Oh, right so, Mike, and I do not want to get you into some sort of trouble, but if that is so, what do you expect me to do about it?'

'Nothing much, I suppose, but I think … well, I just think you need to keep on the alert. Watch out for strange occurrences and things – in respect of your own safety, I mean. And that of people you care about. In the Solar System there've been a couple of incidents involving the "new" version of Ultima and they were horrendous. Innocent people gunned down. A couple of assassinations. The perps evaded capture every time, but chances are it's *New Ultima,* as they now call themselves. You see, the word is out … and like I say, no-one seems too sure of exactly how serious this is, … but word is that the new Oceanus group, who apparently call themselves – "New Future", or something like that, are angry about the closer ties of Oceanus with the Home System. Seems they're pissed off about your government – and your people, becoming more involved with our lot. You know, less isolationist, like you were saying. Looks as if they particularly dislike people of prominence who they think have been "involved" in this.'

'Well now, I wouldn't say I am a person of "prominence" am I?'

'Probably not. I reckon they're thinking more of politicians. But you, and a lot of others, of course, were involved in the uncovering of the truth about Ra, with us, weren't you? Might consider people who cooperated with us as "traitors" to Oceanus – and all that gumpo.'

'Yes. Suppose. Didn't think of myself like that. And all that was yet surely to everyone's benefit, wasn't it?'

'Yeah, of course, Dani, but you know how deranged some of these political extremists get. Look, Dani, please don't get too steamed up 'bout this. I didn't want to scare you, but I thought you should know about all this. As you say there seems little solid evidence about any actual *activity on Oceanus*. Not much to go on right now. It's probably nothing. But all I'm asking is that you just take a bit more care in your … daily activities. Just keep your wits about you. That's all. I'm sorry, my friend.'

'Okay, Mike. Okay. If you say so.'

'Yeah, well, perhaps we should change the subject now, anyways.'

Dani smiled obligingly but he certainly began to look a little anxious. Mike wasn't surprised and regretted it, but he felt it was important his friend should be forewarned – and hopefully would never need to be genuinely alarmed. They had now arrived at a station outside Janitra.

Unfortunately, they faced a long wait before they could get a connection to the airport and Danile complained of feeling hungry. If Mike wasn't so late he'd have suggested they stop off for a bite somewhere and he encouraged Danile to do so, but his friend said he would like to see a landing boat take off again. Dani asked him about the two shuttles.

'Oh, they aren't quite up to the standard of the Navy boats, you know,' said Mike. 'They're adequate, is what I'd say. Only room of about ten passengers. Carry more equipment than people really, and not much of that, compared to the Navy.'

The late afternoon weather was turning dark and the road was slick with previous rain when they got to the 'airoport', and after alighting Mike led Danile along a wide driveway, around part of the perimeter of the airport, in the direction of the 'spaceport', such as it was; an area separated from the main airport used by large turbo-prop airliners. They reached another roadway into the spaceport zone, along which some crew, passengers and supplies would pass and normally enter through a security gate in a large fence which encircled the apron area.

Mike pointed over at the Antarctica's shuttle which sat, in full view, about 50 metres beyond the gate. It was silver coloured and fairly streamlined but short and squat compared to a Navy landing boat. It stood on three sets of triple wheels, carried on long triangular oleo legs and had large engines hanging below its stubby wings. Mike smiled and rolled his eyes at Hermington.

They stood for a moment, as the rain began to fall again. Then they hugged, very briefly, shook hands warmly and, gathering up his day bag, Mike walked over to the gate where two armed guards emerged from the adjoining gatehouse. One of them examined the pass documents Mike presented to him, while the other quickly ran a scanning gun over the scientist. A minute later Mike was quickly let through the gate and as he strode toward the waiting shuttle, he turned and waved to Danile.

As he approached the ship Mike again wondered whether he should have applied, like Tenak, to emigrate to Oceanus but he loved doing the science too much and knew he'd miss being on the cutting edge of things. And the wide-open vistas of Oceanus still bothered him, though he'd had good results from the new type of electrical implants he'd had placed under the skin just below the occipital part of his skull. And, although he was a junior member of Providius's team right now he hoped he'd be able to get promotion, within a year or so, to senior scientist. Jennifer had almost assured him of this anyway.

He was glad to get out of the rain now, up the short flight of steps and into the shuttle, a vessel called, 'The Faraday', but he glanced back to see if he could still spot Hermington. Yes, he was still there, just waiting. Mike knew the guy desperately wanted to get something to eat and he actually wished he'd just go off and do that. The sight of him looking on reminded him rather too much of the time he'd watched Eleri waving goodbye as he had lifted off for his fateful mission aboard the

Antarctica. He had never seen her again after that. Of course, he didn't have the same emotional investment in Dani, but it was waving goodbye like that which had done it.

As he sat in one of a comfortable pair of seats near the back end of the shuttle Mike suddenly realized he was hungry too, but he would be able to eat aboard the shuttle after lift-off. It would take about two hours to get up to a high enough orbit *and* catch up with the Antarctica in its own orbit. It wouldn't be long before night fell over Janitra, but the ship was flying *back* into the daylit hemisphere of Oceanus; 'chasing the light', as some said. There were a few scientists from the Antarctica already aboard and they greeted him as he sat down. The seats were in rows of two on each side of an aisleway and there was no-one next to him, so he shoved his day bag into the overhead locker and relaxed in his seat on the left hand side of the ship, then exchanged some words with the people behind and in front of him. Yes, he felt he'd settled in well into the science crew aboard the research ship.

****

Hermington watched the ship take off, rising vertically, levelling out high and disappearing into the obscurity of the heavy clouds. Then he turned and made his way toward an eatery and 'fembo bar', as they were called, located in the backstreets of the part of town nearest the airport. It was late, getting darker, with some lights coming on, as he set off along winding streets in the area which was the oldest part of town. Once or twice he came across the burnt out ruins of a building which had been attacked during the riots, only a couple of years ago. Not many people were around but at one point he noticed three young, sturdy, rough looking men walking along a few dozen metres behind him. He stopped a couple of times, to look in the windows of shops, closed now because of the late hour. Whenever he stopped he noticed the men behind also stopped and began looking in windows too. Yet they seemed to keep their eyes on him the whole time, set in hostile looking faces as far as he could tell. As he walked on, he noticed that they began to draw closer to him but didn't approach him directly. He began to pick up his pace.

After a further ten minutes he found what he was looking for: 'The Argaran Arms, Fembo Bar and Eatplace'. He entered the surprisingly large, warm and humid, space inside, walked to the bar and scanned a menu lying loose on the counter. The place had subdued lighting and it was rammed full. There were twenty or so small tables full of people eating but not so many standing at the bar, a counter stretching about six metres, around in a wide curve around a corner. Then he happened to spot the three young men, the ones who had followed him, walk in and take up a position way over on the other side of the bar from him. They seemed to be paying him no heed. As a crowd of other people walked in and approached the bar he called to a female bar tend, standing with her back to him, as she pressed an optic. She was of medium build and her long black hair fell in cascades down to her waist.

'Scusa,' he said. 'Mayst I …'

The barperson turned, walked toward him and his expression changed to one of recognition.

'Halloya. You are … Are you not … Merimata? Eleri's sister?' he said. 'Do you not remember me? I was a good friend to your sister. I didst visit your fam-home once, praps twice.'

'Halloya. Yes so,' she said with charm. 'You are right about me but not the name. Tis Meriataten.'

'Yes, coursry. I am sorry, Meriataten. I would not yet have expected to see you over here. Since whenso? I came to this place only just about 6 months ago and did not see you then.'

'No, I didst start but two months and a bit past. And you are … Dani? Yes? Danile Hermington? I might ask you too, what brings you to this part of town?'

'I just saw Mike Tanniss, off on a shuttle. You remember him, do you not?'

'Ah well, yes. I do so remember *him*,' she said, with a sombre face, her words dripping out of her sounding as though laced with acid. Recovering herself she said, 'I didst not know he was on the planet again. I … hope he is yet well.' She tried to smile but only partially succeeded.

Danile looked slightly puzzled and said, 'Yes, ist fine. He was not here for long. And what so about you? How are your family, Meria? How are your childers? They are called Jod and Neferi, were not?'

'Oh, they are fine. And my daughter is, Nefirikare. I didst leave them in the main care of my mother.'

'Elene-Nefer?' Do you not see them much then?'

'Why yes, Dani, coursry.' Meriataten was starting to sound a little irritated. She continued, 'And so, yes, I do get over to Chantris every weekend, well, most times.

'That is … good-great.'

Meriataten's manner changed again and her face went sour looking and sad.

"But, well, I will tell you,' she said, lowering her voice, almost conspiratorially, as she continued, 'that I didst sort of fall out yet with my family, as you might put it. I felt that it was best to become more independent of them and I did need the work, the money. Didst not do well enough with my books, 'fraid. This work I do brings me fair good pay, well enough, and so my childers are well provided for, back in Chantris, special so with *dear meather* looking out for them. It is not the best of lives here, but it will do.'

'I'm sorry to hear about the rift with your folks,' said Danile with conviction, 'but it carnt be so bad if Elene-Nefer will take care of the childers.' As he spoke so he glanced over at the characters who had been following him. They were laughing together and drinking, the other side of the long bar, completely ignoring him.

'Meria' – do you know those three masclas?'

After turning and glancing at them she said, 'No, but yet I have seen them before. They are in here sometimes only, and I have not spoken to them. Why do you ask?' She was smiling amiably now.

'Oh, nothing. Nothing at all.'

'Didst want something to eat Danile, or just a drink. I can recommend the thrimsin juice. Tis a new flavour, made with berries from way far out north west coast. No alco-ol but has a similar effect. Very good. Only do be ordering soon. You will make me look bad, Dani. Customers are waiting.' Her face was starting to turn sour again.

'Okay, let me look at the menu again.' Danile stared down at the menu and as he did so, out of the corner of his eye, he spotted Meriataten moving slightly. He glanced up surreptitiously, as she hadn't noticed him watching her. He saw that she was staring at the three characters at the far end of the bar. In fact, she was glaring, making some sort of face at them. They seemed to notice her expressions and immediately put down their drinks and started to move away from the bar. Danile quickly looked down again as Meriataten returned her gaze to him.

'Well, so, Danile, *friendling*?' she said, with evident sarcasm.

'Um, well, I do not feel so hungry now. Praps you could get me a dram of that thrimsin, please?' As he spoke, again through his peripheral vision, he noticed that the three men had totally disappeared.

Meriataten smiled drily and fetched his drink. Then she went off to attend to other customers. Danile drank the thrimsin, or as much of it as he could stand, put the glass down, turned and left the eatery.

'Goodbye yet, Danile,' cried Meriataten, after him, apparently chuckling, and he turned for a moment. She was no longer looking at him. He smiled wanly, to no-one in particular, and left.

Hurrying back along the streets, turning frequently to look over his shoulder, he saw no signs of the men, at first. Then a pair of furtive individuals, who, in the darkness, looked like two of the men, appeared far behind him. There were few other individuals around, the bars not having turned out yet. He began walking much faster and soon reached an autocar station, where he spent a full half hour waiting for a car-train to turn up. He kept scanning the surrounding area for signs of the men who had followed him but there was, so far, no sign of them. He suddenly realized he was shaking.

****

The Faraday had reached high orbit and was nearing its goal, the revamped Antarctica, virtually now a whole new ship. The vessel had not only been refitted internally with updated equipment but had been extended and enlarged. Mike wondered why they hadn't just built a completely new ship but evidently, this way was considered a faster, less expensive, option. Even so, the ship had needed new sections of hull to be added because of the requirement for landing craft; the shuttles, one of them being the Faraday, the other, a similar vessel, called the 'Rubin'.

As his shuttle approached to dock with the Antarctica, Mike could see through the window, and on the seatback screen in front of him, the main ship's extra sections, consisting of large extensions, like lobes; one on 'each side' of the vessel, if that was right way to describe it. They were almost like bulbous 'wings' for the main ship, though that, of course was not their function. The wing-like extensions began near the forward end of the ship, expanded outward to their greatest extent, then tapered back toward the aft end of the Antarctica. Aft of that was the ship's wide habitation centrifuge and a shield, and behind that, the engine modules.

Each shuttle was able to dock 'underneath' each lobe, attaching itself to the main ship by a docking port in the shuttle's upper fuselage, its 'ceiling'. And as the Farraday approached the starboard lobe from 'below' the main ship, Mike could see that the Rubin had already docked, over on the port side.

He reckoned that Ebazza and Statton had probably already debarked onto the main ship. He wanted to catch up with them soon, as he was itching to know what they had to say about Tenak, and how he was faring. He again had a pang of regret that he hadn't had time to look up the old guy himself. He was also surprised he was actually *looking forward* to meeting with Ebazza. He seemed to be getting along with her just fine these days, something he was pleased about. Although not too pleased, he thought, sardonically. Best not to get too far ahead of yourself, he mused. She still had what he thought of as her 'funny' moments. But then, he found her more amenable than Statton, who acted pleasantly enough but, as usual, still seemed stand-offish. Mike was still grateful that the Lieutenant had done 'the right thing' during the alien crisis – and saved his life, or rather, spared it, but, to be fair to him, Statton never talked about it.

As the Faraday reached the docking port, approaching very slowly, so as to dock with the underside of the Antarctica's 'right hand' lobe, most of the Rubin became hidden from him by the ventral section, the 'belly' of the main ship, mostly now obscuring the view of the other lobe. His shuttle had slowed to around half a metre per second, and as it closed to docking position Ra itself vanished from view, casting a deep shadow over the Faraday. Another full minute and the shuttle came to a stop relative to the Antarctica and he soon heard the sound of the 'thumping' of the vessel's docking collar connecting, then locking, with the collar on the underside of the lobe. From his seat Mike could now see only the aft end of the Rubin, over on the other side, where it projected past the swell of the Antarctica's ventral bulge.

As everyone aboard the Faraday waited for pressures to be equalized between the shuttle and main ship, and for the connecting port to be opened, Mike reflected on the fact that these types of docking systems were essentially the same as those used since the earliest spacecraft but replaced more recently by the hangar decks found on larger vessels like The Monsoon. Nothing like that here, though. The Antarctica was only a research vessel, relatively small, even when refurbished and partly rebuilt, compared to the large Navy ships, but with substantial finance having gone into the funding of its science equipment. There were few luxuries on board, but it was reasonably comfortable, and it certainly carried out its functions with flair.

Now, many of the passengers, for the most part scientists like himself, had unbuckled and left their seats, all chatting amiably. Microgravity, which was still often wrongly called 'zero gee', meant that everyone had to float, assisted by handholds, down toward the front of the cabin, to debark via the docking tunnel in the ceiling. A large, bulky man called Peterson floated gently past Mike's seat on the way forward and said, 'How're you doing' Mike? Have a good bit of downtime on the planet?'

'Yeah, thanks,' said Mike. I did. Your first time to Oceanus, isn't it?'

'It is, or should I say, "tis". Their dialect takes some getting used to, don't it? But it's a beautiful place sure enough. I can't wait to come back.' He laughed amiably.

Mike smiled broadly as Peterson floated on past. 'But I guess we got some work to do first, eh?' the man said and winked affectionately at Mike.

Mike watched several colleagues float up and through the docking tunnel near the forward end of the cabin and prepared to unbuckle himself.

◊◊◊◊

Then it happened! As he began to turn his head to the left, away from his view of the docking port down the aisleway, he was assailed by a blinding flash of light from the window to his left side. He closed his eyes reflexively but as he reopened them a second later, struggling against an afterimage, he instinctively looked toward the source of the flash – and received the biggest shock of his life. The other shuttle, the Rubin, was exploding – as he watched. The terrifying vision hit him like an electrical bolt. A huge ball of bright red, orange and yellow incandescence, was billowing outward from the place where the shuttle had been. Again, reflexively, Mike glanced away after a second. His heart leaped into his mouth and the hair all over his body immediately stood on end. He could feel the shockwaves from the explosion rattle the Faraday like a rag doll, because they were transmitted thought the hull of the main ship.

More disorientating was that, because of the so called, 'weightless' conditions of orbit, the whole of the Antarctica, with the Faraday attached to it, had been slammed into a dizzying spin, rotating around the main ship's axis *and simultaneously* pushing it, laterally, causing a shift in orbit, away from the source of the explosion. There were several loud, metallic, banging and 'pinging' sounds throughout the cabin, at the same time as the noise of terror broke out aboard the Faraday; people gasping, shouting, the sounds of mass incredulity.

Many of the people who had started to unbuckle were thrown around, colliding with each-other and with seating. It was sheer noise and chaos. Most who had been thrown around managed to grab hold of seating and bulkheads, even other passengers, but there were continuing cries of pain, and fear. Most seated people strained to see for themselves what had happened. Mike gave out an almost involuntary groan of alarm and sought to grab the flailing leg of a female passenger, from the seat in front of him, unseated while unbuckling. Her companion, still buckled, grabbed her and hauled her back down, as she cursed loudly.

Mike continued to gaze at the attempts of people to settle back into their seat belts. He felt disorientated but risked looking back out the window, only managing it for a few moments. Even so, he saw that debris from the Rubin's explosion had been flung in all directions. With utter disbelief he noticed that the whole of the aft end of the Rubin, previously the only part of it that had been visible from his seat – had just gone – completely. It was obvious that pieces of debris had bounced off the intervening ventral section of the main ship itself, because they had ripped off sections of the outer skin of the Antarctica's ventral hull. As his mind started to clear Mike realised, with *some relief,* that the intervening ventral section, the 'belly' of the Antarctica had probably saved the Faraday from being hit by most of that debris. The pinging sounds must have been small pieces of debris hitting the shuttle. He hoped there would be no rapid decompression but, again relief, as that didn't seem to be happening. But how could such a horror occur? A million things seemed to be careening around his mind. He felt himself start to physically shake.

Many other passengers still craned their necks to see outside. Mike got views of their wan, frightened faces, mouths twisted in disbelief, seemingly all around him. He was sure the same sort of look was on his face. He was, himself, disbelieving. There were still loud shouts of horror, swearing and curses. People were gasping and arguing about what exactly had happened, and whimpering sounds came from somewhere up front. The seat back screens had stopped working, so there was no information from them. Mike felt his shaking get worse. He couldn't control it.

Within seconds the main ship's computers had started to apply compensating force, by way of dozens of attitude control thrusters spread around the hull, but the spin was slow to abate. Mike closed his eyes and avoided looking out of the window again, trying desperately to keep from being sickened by the continuing rotational motion, made worse by the chaos within the cabin.

Mike was determined not to unbuckle for if he had he would only have added to the chaos and been another flailing body, likely to be injured and injure someone else. He watched with bated breath as most of the 'loose' passengers manged to get reseated and buckle up again. Many had minor injuries, and he saw droplets of blood floating in the air, because the 'weightlessness' prevented them from dripping onto the floor. He noticed that Peterson had a nasty cut above his right eye, but he was otherwise okay. Mike was very glad he, himself, had stayed buckled up, but he felt badly sick, and he thought his chest would explode simply from the hammering of his heart.

The spin of the main ship had now stopped. He asked nearby passengers if they were okay, not that he could have done much anyway. Someone had already accessed a large first aid kit up front and was administering help to a few fellow passengers. Cries and moans continued to emanate from those around him, but people's attention seemed to be returning to the scene outside.

Mike saw the woman in the seat in front look at him through the narrow gap between their seats. He remembered her name was 'Penny'. She rasped, 'Mike. Was it the fuel? Was it the fuel?'

Mike said, though it came out more as a squawk, 'Don' know. Don't think …' Before he could continue, her partner, a man Mike thought was called, 'Brin', barked out, 'Nah! Not that kind of fuel on these things. Feg it!'

As they were in space there had not, of course, been any sound from the explosion itself but vibrational energy was continuing to cause a loud rattling and groaning noise inside the Faraday, still transmitting itself through the hull of the main ship. The shuttle's docking tunnel aperture squealed peculiarly. Chaotic shouts and wails still reigned within the cabin. All the other passengers now seemed to be frozen in motion, or tried to stay immobile, as far as they were able, most of them trying to look out the windows. There seemed no rational explanation for this disaster. Mike knew such a catastrophe was unlikely, yet it had happened! Crazily, inexplicably, a real living nightmare. He kept praying that everyone had gotten off the Rubin before it blew.

The view outside was different now because the deep blue sphere of Oceanus seemed to be 'hanging' above them, instead of appearing 'below', but the new orientation didn't matter. What mattered was that the Rubin had simply vanished. Mike could now see that some debris was still sticking out, like spiky plates of metal, from the Antarctica's lower hull, but, worse, there were several gaping holes in the ventral hull furthest away from the Faraday, where hull plating had now come adrift. The view seemed to almost stop his heart and he hoped that the damage didn't extend through into the pressurised part of the main ship. There was no sign of that though. He started to breathe again, almost as if for the first time since the whole horror started.

There was still cacophony in the cabin and, now that the main ship's rotation had stopped, many people seemed to feel there was enough stability to start unbuckling again, and trying to move, but where could they go? Some seemed to want to get to the docking tunnel again. Mike didn't think there was any point at that stage, but he could understand it. The analytical part of his mind realized then how much danger the main ship was in. That held yet more dread. Vibration continued to make the Faraday tremble and there were more squealing sounds from the docking hatch itself. The shuttle explosion had evidently been a massive one. He was amazed to find that the logical part of his brain continued to dissect the situation. He realized, with yet more anguish, that it simply *couldn't have been an accident.* There was not enough flammable or explosive fuel, or material, onboard one of these things, to cause that big an explosion. And these shuttles carried no ordnance.

He also became even more convinced that it was a mistake to try to leave the shuttle, to get on board the main ship, and that point seemed to have now dawned on most of his colleagues too, but there were still some trying to get up into the docking port. No, he realised, they weren't. Above the shouting and cries of alarm he could hear that the people nearest the tunnel were shouting into it, *trying to get others to come back*; the ones who had already disembarked.

Mike shouted at the top of his voice, 'Everyone needs to get back in their seats! Buckle up. Close the hatch. The shuttle needs to disengage.' But no-one took any notice. A colleague, in the seat behind, shouted, 'Why don't you just shove it! I'm getting out of here.'

Up front, Mike's friend, Peterson, was halfway through the docking port and someone was tugging at his legs, trying to pull him down. This is just stupid, thought Mike. Just then, a figure appeared right at the front of the cabin, the door to the flight deck flung open behind him. Captain Ferris stood there and shouted, with a voice so loud it even penetrated the panicked hubbub, 'Get back in your seats, everyone! Please! We have to disengage immediately from the Antarctica.'

'Why?' said a passenger. 'The main ship isn't in that much danger, is it?'

Mike wondered how anyone could believe that.

'We're getting some bad telemetry from the ship and …' began the Captain, then looked over his shoulder for a couple of seconds before turning back to the passengers.

'My copilot just said our comps have received messages from the main ship's AIs. There's catastrophic damage in parts of the ship. It looks like most of the upper port section is breaking up. We need to disengage – now!'

'I can't,' said Peterson, 'my third wife's aboard the ship. I'm not leaving her. I've got to get her out.'

Another voice, a female one, said, 'Yeah, one of my bonders is in there. Let's get 'em out. Please! We can grab 'em and get to the ship's lifeboats if we need to.'

'I'm sorry,' shouted Ferris, 'but we have to leave now. There isn't time for us to get in the ship, pull out people, and get to the lifeboats. We'll stand off and if the ship can recover itself, we can go back. Otherwise, we land on the planet.'

Anyone could have seen that the guy was pissing in the wind and he returned to the flight deck. Mike had been trembling since the explosion and the shaking got worse. His friends were on board the Antarctica as well, he thought, bitterly, with a rising sense of dread. Providius had become a wonderful colleague and he respected her enormously. First Officer Florian and Doctrow Manlington were also good friends, let alone Ebazza and Statton – assuming they'd left the Rubin. What would happen to them now? Could they make it to the five lifeboats the ship carried. Maybe they already had. His prayers and hopes for the safety of all of them burned inside him so much it hurt.

Try as he might to suppress the feeling, he knew now, deep down, with horror in his guts, that the Antarctica was finished. The explosion would have ripped out much of the ship's electrical sub-relays and generators and caused serious fires. The vessel's automated fire management apparatus might not – probably wouldn't – be able to control the effects. Once the fires got to the large tanks inside the hub, the ones with supplies of liquid hydrogen and oxygen, used to generate the ship's own supplies of water and air, the game would be up. Even though the tanks were plated with armour, there was every chance they wouldn't withstand the conflagration.

He thought about the main ship's own external armour plating, with a rising sense of panic. Even though much thinner than that used on Navy ships, which needed it for combat situations, it should have withstood the shuttle explosion. But the damage was evident. The explosion could only have been caused by one thing! His thoughts were distracted by the sudden worsening of the vibrations coming through the main hull. Fortunately, common sense seemed to be returning to the passengers and most of them were 'swimming', in the microgravity, back to their seats as quickly as they could, their faces pallid with anxiety and distress.

Mike knew the shuttle had to stand off, awful though that was. Maybe the crew and the AIs could regain control of the damage onboard the main ship. Perhaps it could still be contained. Yes, he thought, it might be, it must be, contained. But what about …….

!!!!!

Just at that moment a small but incredibly powerful charge, hidden deep inside a package located in the equipment hold behind the Faraday's passenger cabin, detonated. It exploded with a brilliant flash, followed by a massive concussive blast which blew the hold and its contents forward into the passenger compartment and filled it instantly with expanding, superheated, gases. Less than two seconds later the fuselage of the Faraday burst open, flinging thousands of pieces of itself, large and small, out into space – but mostly into the starboard side of the Antarctica, causing seismic damage to the main ship's superstructure. The explosion threw the vessel into rotation again; the attitude thrusters automatically slowing it a little before they too failed, as the ship's systems buckled. Everyone aboard the shuttle perished, all the hopes and fears, all the trials and tribulations, their wishes for the future, their knowledge, their skills, their ambitions and their love for their families and friends, all gone.

Within a further two minutes the Antarctica itself started to break up. Its internal atmosphere rushed out into space, pulling debris with it – and bodies. Within a further thirty seconds the ship's huge internal capacitors and electro-magnets were burning and had ignited combustibles. When the heat sources reached the liquid oxygen and hydrogen tanks, including the tanks for the fusion engines, the Antarctica itself exploded – silently in space, like a brilliant, tiny version of a supernova. Large chunks of the ship, most of them glowing like incendiary bombs, were thrown outwards at tangents to the still rotating core of the vessel, whence they would enter lower orbits and eventually burn up on re-entry into the atmosphere of

Oceanus. Most of the other pieces were blasted away from the planet, where they would enter higher, elongated orbits, eventually also to fall back to the planet. Dozens of lives aboard the main ship tragically vanished, all in a matter of minutes.

The whole disaster had taken place high above the western seaboard of the continent, during the hours of daylight, so no-one on the ground would have seen much, even if they had been looking upwards. Some might have seen a bright flash in the brilliant blue- white sky, but no more, until various pieces of the ship re-entered. But much of that would be in time to come and what there was would fall mostly over the vast Western Ocean. Hardly any human eyes would be out there to witness them.

****

Very early in the morning of the very next day, on the planet, a young woman left a 'safe house', near the Argaran Arms, on the outskirts of Janitra. She carried a large hold-all bag and walked the half kilometre or so to the main passenger transport section of the airport at Janitra. She queued at the gate for security checks, such as they were, then surreptitiously, somewhat furtively, she acknowledged the presence of five 'colleagues', as they strolled along, separately, during their walk to the departure building. At one point they all joined up, very briefly, very nonchalantly, before they all checked in, again widely separated from each-other, before moving off to the departure lounge nearby. Her associates included another woman and man, who were from Oceanus, and three men from the Home System, one of whom was an engineer and the other two, explosives' experts.

All six checked in with their large bags and all remained seated separately inside the none too large departure lounge, waiting to board their aircraft. For this trip just about everyone else had checked in large bags; the journey was not one undertaken for short periods. After sitting quietly for about twenty minutes, apparently minding their own business, they were able to board a turboprop' aircraft, together with around fifty-three other passengers, bound for a distant location on the far side of the continent. All sat in separate, pre-booked seats, and none ever spoke to each-other during the flight. They would have preferred to have travelled in different aircraft but there was only one flight per day to the remote town where they were headed, in the north-western coastal region. And they needed to leave quickly. The flight took off on the first leg of what was, for Oceanus people, a very long journey.

****

It's likely that no one on Oceanus had noticed the demise of the Antarctica and they would not do so for some time. But two large 'hyper-monitor' satellites, belonging to the Home System, did observe. These were part of a fleet of eighty-four similar robotic craft left by the Home System Navy, with full Oceanus permission, in a wide orbit around Ra, about 5 million kilometres further out than the orbit of Oceanus itself. They were designed to keep a watch, as far as possible, for signs of any new 'alien' incursions (and a subsidiary lookout for other things the Home System preferred not to mention) and to give early warning to both Oceanus and the Home System. The two satellites closest to the planet picked up the light from the explosion and recognised its significance as soon as it hit their supersensitive receptors.

The nearest of the satellites was around forty-one million kilometres away from Oceanus and the next closest, fifty-three million klicks distant. That meant the light from the terrible demise of the Antarctica hit each one at a slightly different time, but the processors of the machines immediately began analysing it. The monitors did not have pre-existing data on the identity of the object but they quickly concluded that an explosion had occurred. The machines' micro-AIs immediately began to analyse the chemical signatures of the light. And, from its viewing angle, the satellite spotted the partial emergence of a large object: a ship, probably a lifeboat, rising out of hub of the Antarctica's torus. It also observed and recorded the destruction of that same vessel by the blast from the explosion of the main ship, long before it could get completely clear.

The monitors then sent a message to an automated platform floating in an orbit even further out than theirs. The platform carried four small data probes, each with its attached, disproportionately large, fusion engine. The signals from the monitors took a few minutes to reach the platform, but then its own AI had to make a decision as to whether or not the event justified launching a data probe back to the Home System. It did not have sufficient information as to the identity of the object which exploded, so it asked the two monitors for additional information, received their answers and decided to launch. The whole interrogation and decision process took around forty minutes, nearly all of that taken up by the time light took to travel between the various machines.

The two original monitors then signalled the nearest of four communications satellites which were orbiting Oceanus itself, to advise they alert the authorities on the ground. As part of an 'aid package', following the widespread rioting and pillaging on Oceanus, during the debacle two years earlier, the HS had financed these satellites. But they had only been allowed to install a small amount of the technology they actually required. The Oceanus authorities managed to get the last word on most of their functioning and design, which was primarily weather prediction and communications. Consequently, their technology was poor compared to the hyper-monitors and so there were coding complications and digital confusion between them and the monitors. This took a long time to resolve but eventually the monitors decided that the Oceanus devices had finally understood the importance of the information and could be trusted to impart it to the humans on Oceanus. The orbital satellites, themselves, later relayed the information to the ground computers, *such as they were*, in a control room in Janitra. Operatives on the ground were initially slow to pick up the data until an official finally realised its shocking importance.

All in all, this being Oceanus, it was nearly two weeks after the incident before the Oceanus media were given the tragic news by the Oceanus government and ran with the story. Meanwhile, people in various northern locations were perplexed to see nighttime 'firework' displays as, unknown to them, sizeable pieces of debris that had been lobbed into higher, but degenerating orbits over the planet, burned up on re-entering the atmosphere. Fortunately for them, as the vast majority of the planet was ocean, most of the largest chunks landed in the sea, with the exception of one or two spotted coming down in the direction of the Purple Forest. No-one was hurt but questions were asked, and rumour abounded, most of it nowhere near the truth. Until the story finally broke.

****

Two weeks after the disaster in orbit Danile Hermington sat in his kitchen in Kelmrie and picked up the newspaper which had been delivered by a boy on a bike. Danile had thrown the paper, the Bhumi-Devi Times, on the table, poured himself some kaffee, then sat down to read it. The headline made him turn pale. It ran:

DISASTER IN ORBIT AROUND OUR WORLD

It has been made known that on the 14th of the month, a full twelve days past, that a terrible disaster did befall the Home System Research ship, the Antarctica, in orbit then above Oceanus. An explosion did occur shortly after the second of two shuttles took off to return crew to the vessel, causing the loss of all lives aboard the ship. These did yet include the renowned personage of Commodore Jennifer Providius, and our great good friend, the explorer extraordinaro, Michaelson Delenius Tannis, and yet more of our friends, the former Captain Ebazza and Officer Statton of the Home System Navy. Many crew and other scientists were killed in the blast, making, it is believed, as many as total fifty-eight dead.

Home System satellites have yet determined that there is now no danger to any person on the planet, but this tragic event does yet explain why some citizens have of late reported seeing large meteorites, though these have stopped.

It is not clear still what the cause of the explosion was but ...

Hermington was unable to continue reading. His face was frozen in a grimace of horror and disbelief. He held his right hand over his face and leaned heavily on the table.

*

One hundred and twenty kilometres east of Kelmrie, in the northern part of the prime agricultural belt of the continent, a former Home System Navy Admiral left his hand-pushed rotovator, a soil turning machine, and walked through a gate into a smaller field adjoining a little stone cottage. His brow glistened with light sweat, in the early morning Ra light, as he picked up a hoe, ready to till the soil, momentarily resting on its handle.

A middle-aged woman approached him then, her long, dark, dress, sweeping unconcerned across the soil. She carried a newspaper, and she wore a deeply troubled look on her round, benign, face. Handing him the paper she looked him deeply in the eyes but said nothing. Her eyes were wide and her mouth downturned.

Arkas Tenak gently accepted the paper, looked at her and at the paper, wearing a puzzled frown. Then he read the story on the front page. His mouth fell open and he dropped the newspaper as he bent over and began to crumple to the ground, holding on to his hoe for support. A low, awful moan came out of his mouth and his wife sank to the ground beside him, one arm preventing him from sinking further, the other wrapping quickly around his shoulders.

EPILOGUE

There was shock and genuine sadness amongst many people in Oceanus society, following the news about the Antarctica. Elene-Nefer was devastated and, perhaps surprisingly, Marcus of Tharnton helped her erect a memorial stone to Mike in the same gardens as Eleri's interment stone. Later still, the Janitran authorities, prompted by the University, and Arkas Tenak, erected a stone statue of Mike very close to that of Eleri's own, in Chantris (a bronze bust of Professier Muggredge had long since been set up near that spot). Busts of Jennifer Providius and Ssanyu Ebazza were set up in the Darvenhay Garden of Remembrance and Celebration.

***

Immediately after the event the Oceanus authorities carried out an investigation, starting at Janitra airport, just in case there was any question of fault on their part. At that stage no-one suspected foul play, though it wasn't ruled out. The investigation revealed nothing of significance. Once news reached the Home System an investigation was launched by the HS government, with the eventual, if relatively slow to start, full cooperation of the Oceanus government. But lack of cooperation by some locals, and even elements of Oceanus border security, hampered the initial investigations of the HS team. They weren't going to let that stop them, however, especially when Arkas Tenak weighed in, after being invited to collaborate, and when there was massive pressure from the Research Companies in the Home System.

Apart from the shock and dismay concerning the loss of life it soon became widely known that the Antarctica was notable, not so much as the most expensive single piece of equipment ever launched into space, but mostly because of the huge expertise and experience of its science crew, which could never be replaced. This was to set back the search for the 'aliens,' significantly. Although other research vessels became marginally involved in the search efforts, the project was effectively stymied until more could be known about what had happened to the Antarctica. Could it have been some sort of failure of its advanced technology? After all, something similar had happened to the prototype of the Kalahari, years before.

*****

The monitor satellites continued to analyse their data after the disaster and when cross-checked with other quantum computers certain features of the light spectra they gathered didn't seem to precisely fit what should be expected in an accident; a huge leap given that no-one quite knew what, in ships as advanced as the Antarctica, could have set off such explosions. There was even a hint of evidence of foul play but little real evidence to go on. Then, several months later, some wreckage was recovered from remote parts of Bhumi-Devi, utilising information and data put together by Danile Hermington, and his exploratory teams. Much more wreckage was recovered from the shallow shelf seas along the northwestern margins of the continent, after the Bhumi-Devi authorities gave the Home System permission to send a limited number of submersibles down to the sea bottom.

Some of the debris bore unmistakeable signs of the use of explosives. This material was of a completely new kind though; an experimental and incompletely analysed substance, not sanctioned for use in the Home System or its affiliates. It was eventually announced that there had in fact been sabotage of the Antarctica, possibly a terrorist attack, and yet no-one had claimed responsibility.

When this news was divulged to the Oceanus authorities, they renewed their desire to investigate their own part in this. A sudden revolution in their security arrangements, assisted, as far as possible, by HS security teams, burst forth. Renewed questioning of staff at Janitra airport revealed anomalies the night before the Rubin and Faraday had taken off. All airport securi-pol staff came under intense scrutiny. Loopholes in procedure and extreme lapses of procedure by some personnel were found. Some staff were disciplined, then retrained, though many were fired. There were even arrests for gross negligence leading to the more serious lapses, but, in an absence of claims of responsibility, little further was discovered as to how the attack had been carried out, or who was behind it. But there was much speculation.

****

Three years later came a breakthrough, back in the Home System, when a trail led to the seizure of undeleted e-documents belonging to the heads of engineering corporations who had been under surveillance for some time. These contained details of the new explosive, and more interrogations showed connections to New Ultima.

Trails of evidence found in the investigation of the corporations led to the identification of three HS people, who had moved to Oceanus in an old, 'good faith' exchange procedure and had continued to live there, unobtrusively and under false identities, for some time. At the invitation of both the Oceanus authorities and the Home System, former Admiral Arkas Tenak, led an Oceanus team who eventually traced the HS perpetrators. They were indeed found to be New Ultima operatives and, in turn, they revealed the complicity of the Oceanus saboteurs, *including Meriataten*, Eleri's sister.

Meriataten, after refusing to cooperate for a long time, eventually admitted her complicity. In fact, she had been the 'leader' of the group and had instigated the attack. She said she had done it because she resented what she saw as the continued 'infernal interference' of the Home System, which she hated, in the affairs of Oceanus. Her Home System co-conspirators wanted less cooperation with Oceanus too and had also violently disagreed with the policy of trying to track down the aliens. Meriataten had gone along with this but psychological evaluations revealed, and she eventually admitted, that her actions had also been fired up by her hatred of Mike Tannis. She had hated him from the outset and had blamed him, vehemently, and all his HS colleagues, for the loss of her sister. She pleaded guilty at her trial, said she was proud of what she did, and seemed to openly encourage the nickname she gained among the people of Oceanus, as, 'the destroyer'.

The three HS saboteurs were sent to the Mars penal colony, where one was later shot dead when attempting to escape. The three Oceanus people went to separate prisons on Bhumi-Devi. Meriataten was sent to Darklengton Centre for fifty years.

Over subsequent months further investigations by Oceanus, also given technical assistance by the HS, uncovered connections leading to arrests of some of the Oceanus sect of New Ultima; the shadowy group called New Future.

*****

A year later Marcus of Tharnton died; some said it was because of a broken heart. Unfortunately for her mother, Meriataten showed no interest in her father's death, refused to see her mother and threatened to destroy Mike's statue and uproot his memorial stone if she ever got out. And she also abused and threatened her mother in letters to her. For all these things she was given another five years. And, eventually, Elene-Nefer took the rarely used step of invoking an old Oceanus legal procedure, allowing her to 'divorce' her daughter. By Oceanus law, children were usually allowed to inherit property on the death of both parents, even if not mentioned by will. The step taken by Elene-Nefer now meant that Meriataten would never inherit her mother's estate and would not benefit from it, even if she was eventually released. That was unlikely.

******

Four years later, Darik Yorvelt, the HS Secretary General, died and there was a battle amongst those who wanted to succeed him. Indrius Brocke, Deputy SG and HS Security Chief, looked as though about to take over. However, there were many who were suspicious of his activities outside his governmental roles and he became distracted from scrutiny of him by hubris and the minutiae of running for election for office. At this time the investigations into New Ultima bore fruit and full details of the terrorist crimes on Oceanus came to light but were withheld from public disclosure in the Home System. Set up by people loyal to his predecessor, the investigative team were able to link Brocke with the sabotage of the Antarctica. Weeks later, just as the election was due to take place, Brocke was finally linked with the attack on Mars, by the Pterodactylus, some years earlier. After arrest he was eventually shown to be the acting head of Ultima at the time of the attack, and of New Ultima, and subsequently charged with multiple, heinous crimes.

But no-one was naïve enough to think that the ideas and activities of New Ultima, or their various offshoots, had gone away.

***

Information about the Pterodactylus, gleaned from the 'Indrius Brocke files' resulted in an extra push for research into using a system of five 'Kewsers' on ships. Development of those technologies eventually led to an enhanced ability of the Home System to travel through conduits, not only from the Sun to stars 'directly' linked to it, but from one star system to other, entirely separate, star systems. This effectively 'broke' what Mike and others had described as 'the cage', and, potentially, enormously expanded the number of stars that could be reached by humans – for good or ill.

As for the aliens, long before the new system was adopted, small research vessels and robotic craft had begun again, in earnest, the search for the aliens first encountered in the Ra system, but no signs were found.

****

Fifteen years after the sabotage of the Antarctica and after hundreds of test flights had proved the effectiveness and (relative) safety of using the new 'five kewser' systems, Navy vessels and research ships began a more comprehensive and effective search for the aliens. The quest was headed by the entering into service of a new, improved, chief research vessel, appropriately named, 'New Antarctica'.

****

Then, amazingly, it happened! Eighteen years after the sabotage of the Antarctica, electromagnetic waves, with certain specific characteristics, emanating from a 'micro' gamma ray burster, were observed, coming directly from a red dwarf star system 'only' thirty-five light years away from Earth. It was believed to be the first new signs of the alien presence. This star system, which would have been unreachable just a few years before, was linked by a 'lateral conduit' to another system, that of a white dwarf star, which was, itself, directly linked to the Sun's solar system. It would still take a ship many weeks to get there but the distances led theorists to believe, or to hope, that the aliens might still be there, or that traces of them might be found. The New Antarctica, accompanied, by a second research vessel, were quickly despatched.

Would a new era of discovery, or perhaps even a new era for all humanity, soon dawn?

No-one could say, but what is certain is that Mike would have been very proud.

AUTHOR BIO

When not writing the author loves to follow developments in the world of science, and is a student of history, a subject which, he feels, has so much to teach us about ourselves. Gareth is also heartily engaged in creative arts and crafts, especially painting.

He is also currently trying (struggling!) to get to grips with learning the piano and is endeavouring to compose his own music.

The author lives in Cardiff with his lovely wife, Lindsay.

Cover art on this print version, and on the kindle version,

by the author © Gareth L. Williams 2024

Printed in Great Britain
by Amazon